Tangled Threads

A Family Saga based on real lives

Tangled Threads

A Family Saga based on real lives

By

RC Marlen

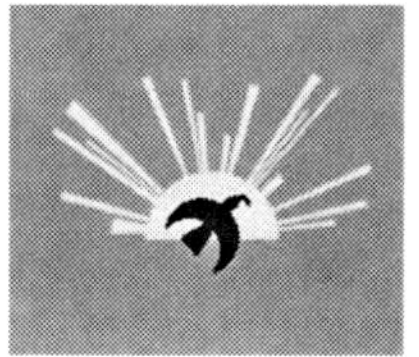

Sunbird Press
Salem, Oregon
State Registry # 346580-96

Sunbird Press books may be ordered through booksellers or directly from www.rcmarlen.com

Sunbird Press
1945 Saginaw Street S
Salem, OR 97302
503-581-4092
rcmarlen@hotmail.com

This is a novel, though based on the lives of the author's parents, names have been changed, dates moved, and some parts of the story are a figment of the author's imagination when the whole truth was not known or when some fantasy added to the story. But the personality and characteristics of Ellie and John Bartlett were patterned as accurately as possible after the author's mother and father, Norma and Thomas W. Marlen, Sr. as well as the author's grandparents, aunts, uncles, etc.

Most incidents in the story really happened or, when stretched into fantasy, have some aspect of truth. Actual historical events and information about St. Louis and United States were researched and written into the story to coincide with events in the lives of the characters.

ISBN: 978-0-9779752-1-1

Dedicated With Love to
My Mother

Born: 27 May
Died: 25 September

If you build castles in the air,
your work need not be lost;
that is where they should be.
Now put foundations under them.

Henry David Thoreau

Other Books by RC Marlen

Inside the Hatboxes (2005)

The Drugstore (2006)

Acknowledgements

Thanks to Kim and Carolyn for the baby talk they invented while learning to speak so many years ago (Chapter 13), to Andrea Whalen for sharing parts of her family life as when she told what her mother had done upon finding a Playboy Magazine stuck between the mattresses in her son's room (Chapter 17), to Cindy Bond Thompson for photo help, to Adele Heagney from St. Louis Public Library's Main Branch who helped gather and find information about St. Louis history, to Todd Silverstein for being the first to read and for relating his insight, to Dave Picray for endless editing, to Ellen Robinson for her perceptivity and devotion, and finally to Kristi Negri who made the story better through her evaluation.

Preface

One doesn't give much thought to threads; yet, threads are important to our lives. Humans have searched for centuries, discovering and valuing material from which to make thread.

> Twist and pull the soft, white, downy balls to make cotton threads.
> Twist and twirl the fine, curly fleece to create threads of wool.
> Twist and twine the coarse threads of hemp to produce rope.

Threads exist everywhere. Beyond comfortable cotton, warm wool, and strong rope, nature makes a plethora, as thread from worms spinning shimmering silk and gossamer threads for spider webs.

In whatever form, threads make a complicated path, weaving through and around, looping over and under, or winding back and forth to form rugs, nets, sweaters, and fabrics. Whether one has a piece of yarn, a strand of silk, wool, cotton, a filament of lamb intestine, a metal wire, or any thread-like material, the path can be lost as it twists and curves into a product with colors, textures, and sounds. Yes, sounds! Pull strands from gut of a lamb and one has threads—twisted, braided or wrapped— for strings of violins; pull hairs from the tail of a horse for the gliding violin bow. These special threads vibrate into notes, to blend into music, to fill the air and our minds. When the bow touches the strings, notes are connected, flowing out into a piece of music. Even when the sound vanishes, a thread of music can play in our heads.

> Weaving threads.
> Stitching threads.
> Crocheted threads.
> Musical threads.

Now take the idea of threads into another dimension. Threads can display stories. The obvious way is through tapestries; people have created tapestries for centuries to depict stories. The tapestry in Bijou near Normandy, whose threads were woven 900 years ago, depicts William the Conqueror's invasion of England. Scholars have looked deeply into this particular tapestry to follow the threads and learn the special stitch of linen and wool; to learn the secret of the art; to learn all they can know. But few of us want to follow threads. Few of us want to delve into the secrets of their intricacies.

Beyond the stories woven into tapestries, I find that lives are made of threads. Each life is a continuous thread of events; woven, stitched, and knitted into loops connecting the past to the present; made by some enigmatic weaver. Some call the weaver God, others destiny. Your weaver starts with one thread and, day by day, more threads are added and blended to create each person's story. Slowly and carefully the weaver works, adding colors, carefully connecting events, and developing your special tale. But, every now and then, problems occur in a life, like a dropped stitch in a sweater. How does one mend the error? With a sweater, one needs only to pull the yarn, return to the mistake and start again. But life can't be fixed like a sweater.

Once a mistake occurs, one can try to cover it with a patch, but it will never disappear, and to pull the thread of life to unravel a problem is impossible.

In this story, we will follow the threads of Ellie Bartlett's life as they weave and wind, blending with friends and relatives, creating times of humor and happiness, only to lead to an inexplicable mystery. Threads of her life will be difficult to see as they twist and curve often disappearing behind, in between, mixing with passing people and places. Knots form, nettles sting, Ellie's threads mangle and snarl into unwanted events. Can they be rewoven or mended? Her story is a complicated, elusive tapestry delicately stitched with love and kindness, acumen and brilliance, until a gash tears the fabric of her soul.

Have you ever turned a tapestry over to see the back? Have you ever turned a dress inside-out to see the stitches? Have you ever taken the effort to learn why a friend has lost her way? Behind the beautifully draped dress, hidden on the other side of the tapestry, and deep in the mind of your friend are tangled threads. Knotted in places, unevenly cut, ragged, and snarled into ugliness. Behind each life are messy secrets we may need a lifetime to find. And, once found, who can untangle the threads?

Characters

Note: Numbers represent the year of birth.

1877 James August James — Best Friend: 1878 Wallace (Wally) Duggan

Married to:

1878 Bertha Caroline Hofenfeldtin

Children

1893 Virginia (Ginny) James

Married to:

Jack

1896 Elizabeth (Ellie) Mary James

Married to:

1900 John Winfield Bartlett — Best Friends: 1896 Franny (Françoise) and 1883 David (Jerry) Jerome Cohen

Children

1929 David Jerome Bartlett
1931 Elizabeth Rose Bartlett+ Rose Cohen
1935 William (Billy) Bartlett
1937 John (Johnny) Bartlett
1939 James (Red) Bartlett
1943 Rebecca (Becky) Bartlett

Relatives of the druggist:

Sisters: Louise
Clara

On Missouri farm: Laura and Harry Williamson (Uncle Will)

Cousin in Illinois: Dale

John's second wife: Sara and her sons, Mike and Pat

Part 1

Ellie's Childhood
1896-1910

I shall set forth for somewhere,
I shall make the reckless choice
Some say when they are in voice
And tossing so as to scare
The white clouds over them on,
I shall have less to say,
But I shall be gone.

Robert Frost, 1874-1963
The Sound of the Trees

Chapter 1

27 May 1896
The Great Cyclone

Frantically their horse ran, causing the planks of the wagon to twist and strain. James held the reins, but no longer was in control. The mare was running scared, and James figured it barely mattered who was driving. As the rain stung his face, he muttered, "We're riding into hell anyways. May as well let this dad-blasted animal go where she wants. She just might git us to shelter."

"James, the sky is green!" Bertha's words were unheard as they blended into the whoosh of the wind. "James, I can't ..." and she stopped to scream in anguish.

They moved so fast it was difficult to look back to the bed of the wagon, but James turned and saw little Ginny's wide-eyes staring at her mother who squirmed in pain on the tattered, plaid blanket. James' body jumped from the bench as they hit a raised cobblestone; a wheel lurched, wrenching the old wooden cart—nails popped and boards loosened. With that bump the souls of his family were thrown to the wind, and their fear intensified. The rain stung like a sheet of glass breaking in his face. Bertha gave another shrill screech.

With his shirt billowing and hair flipping into his eyes—he had lost his hat a couple of blocks back—James reached behind the seat to push Ginny further into the space under his bench. While trying to keep his daughter safe, he knew he could do nothing to help his wife until they got to a doctor. Rising a bit to turn back around, he fell over the edge of the wagon, banging his shoulder but catching himself. His huge bony hands clutched the metal frame of the bench as he strained to pull his lanky six-foot four-inch frame back to the seat.

When he righted himself, he retrieved the lost reins.

James saw that the late afternoon sky was a dirty greenish color with clouds pouring from the west like mahogany-colored molasses—sticky and shiny with glints of green in the flash of the lightning.

Moments ago, when the wind had gone from nothing to a gale, people ran into their homes or any shop for safety, but James had not stopped because of Bertha. Trees had started doubling over, doing backbends until branches snapped like the three-inch limb that had fallen on them and spooked their mare.

He could hardly believe the neighborhood had been quiet minutes ago. James had noticed it was eerily calm with no birds chirping and no squirrels in view. He thought *squirrels always scamper about in the sycamores here on Arsenal Street, but I don't see none. Yep, I knew a storm was comin', but ain't never seen nothin' like this.*[1]

As they rode across Hampton Avenue, James shouted, "Bertha, we're almost there! I see the hospital!" In the distance, buildings loomed—the Missouri State Complex with the Women's Hospital, the City Poorhouse, the Old Folks Infirmary, and the St. Louis Insane Asylum.

Debris was flying across their path. James turned his head to the right into the wind and could barely keep his eyes open. Dust swirled into his face and stung his cheeks. An abandoned bike lifted from the edge of the road and crashed into their cart. Then, just as James started to turn from the battering wind, he saw it.

... the Devil's ahead!

It was a twister!

Only a few blocks away, the tornado was lifting things and dropping others, jerking and twisting. *It looks alive. Like it can think!* Unlike the gusting wind, the gray funnel meandered here and there, pointing its tip in jerky motions from one place to another, yet steadily creeping toward them like a fat sow rutting with her snout. Suddenly he saw the twister veer and rip the side from a three-story building. Bricks cascaded down with sofas and tables, candlesticks and dolls.

James looked away for a place to get out of its path; he pulled hard at the reins and shouted to his family, "We're gittin' close to the hospital!"

And so was the twister.

Up, up the funnel elongated with the top bending above James' right side and with the tip on the left, arching in front of the horse and wagon. *I gotta git out from under it!* Suddenly the funnel attacked their destination—the Women's Hospital. In seconds, the tornado went crazy, shaking its sucking tip, ripping the whole structure—like a mad dog attacking and biting in a frenzy, twisting its head from side to side—whirling beds and equipment, breaking walls and windows, creating rubble until all was flattened or flung to the wind. The din of destruction and the speed of demise left his mind humbled. *Damn, ain't possible. The hospital's gone!*

James raised the reins and beat the horse again and again. "Move! Move! Git the hell outta here! Oh, damn it, git!"

"Daddy, Daddy!" Ginny screamed beneath his seat. She turned to her mommy who didn't respond and then, crying hysterically, reached out under the bench to touch her daddy's legs. She grabbed his trousers and held on, clutching for security, but any comfort eluded her.

James turned the horse another direction only to watch, with the clap of thunder, the Poor House disappearing as every piece was sucked up and flung out like grain to chickens.

Now, with the wind at his back, he turned the straining, worn wagon again; this time toward the huge, brick and stone Insane Asylum, a structure girdled with metal bars across every window. He headed for the shortest route, flying across lawns and plowing through bushes. The air held unbelievable objects. Chairs flew by; rakes and what looked like bedspreads soared like magic carpets. A plate and cup landed in the wagon, clanging as they hit and broke. The wind at their back sped their progress, but James' hope for a safe haven was dashed when he looked for the closest entry to the asylum. *It's a block away!*

Glancing around, James shouted to the wind, "Where in tarnation has that twister gone now?" He didn't see it anywhere. On impulse he looked straight up and there she was.

"Hell and damnation!"

The wagon moved frantically toward the St. Louis Insane Asylum and the twister hovered above with the tip pausing … tapping its finger on the ground and deciding what to destroy next.

When they were fifty feet from the building, spokes started breaking in the back wheel. It collapsed, throwing James and Ginny out of the wagon. The old mare nearly fell, but steadied herself and started to yank at the wagon—plowing the ground with the downed side while Bertha, still on the wagon bed, slid with a jolt against the wooden frame.

James picked up his three-year-old and swung her to his back as he raced to the wagon. "Hold on, Ginny! Grab tight! Gotta hold on cuz I'm going to carry your ma!"

Bertha looked terrified and clutched her belly with another contraction. She screamed just as James reached inside, pulling the plaid blanket and dragging Bertha to the edge of the wagon. He wrapped her in the blanket, lifted her into his arms, and started to run with Ginny bobbing on his back nearly choking him to death. Glancing around, he cursed, "Damn it all! Now where's that twister?"

Everywhere he heard relentless noise from objects bashing into other objects, the wind howling, the rain battering, and sirens blaring in the distance.

But, beneath all other noises, James heard a distant roar and continuous rumble—the tornado. *It sounds like a train is comin' at me.*

Some boards came from nowhere and slammed into James' legs, hitting him in the calves. He fell to his knees and crumpled on his side, falling with a bruising force as he cradled his wife to cushion her. Terrified, Ginny flew from his back on impact; quickly she scrambled to him and slipped under his arm. Lying on the ground, he peered up to see the tornado pick up his wagon and mare. The horse and three-wheeled cart disappeared into the funnel.

His heart jumped in his chest. Aghast, he wasted no time and rolled over frantically gathering his family. Scrambling on his knees, he grabbed at Ginny's little arms and wrapped them around his neck; keeping her to his chest, he pressed her legs around his waist. He decided to scramble on his knees the rest of the way and drag his wife with the blanket. He reasoned, *maybe that damn sucking twister goes after things stickin' up! So, I'm gonna crawl.*

From this angle he could see a stairwell at the end of the Insane Asylum. *It's close!* A dim light was shining from windows at the bottom of the stairs.

Looks like those stairs go to a basement.

Two thick pillars were holding up the sturdy brick and concrete roof that jutted out from the height of the first floor, overhanging the stairwell.

Maybe it's a delivery entrance.

Pulling the edges of the plaid blanket, James brought Bertha across the grass in jerky movements as he groveled on his knees toward the world of the St. Louis insane.

James was bothered by howling and couldn't discern if it was the wind wailing or his wife bawling. *Or maybe it's those poor insane people, peering from windows and yowling.*

Suddenly, out of the corner of his eye, he saw a rectangular, dark object coming at them. *It's big and heading right fer us!* He let go of the blanket, wrapped an arm around Ginny, and rolled down the steps. Popping his head up about four steps down, he watched a bench swiftly tumble between his wife and him. *It looks like a seat off a Ferris wheel.* Amazed, while it sailed by, James watched it rock and bounce along the ground like some crazy new carnival ride.

He released little Ginny from his grasp, "Git into that corner down there!" He pointed as she looked to him with pleading eyes. "Now git, Ginny! Quick!"

He rushed back for his wife, slipping on the steps in his eagerness and bruising his shin. At the top, a boot flew at him. Yes, some unknown person's shoe. He tried to duck, but the wind gave that boot an extra kick and gashed James on his left eyebrow. The blood gushed and blocked the sight in the left eye. Reaching for his wife, James didn't stop though fears rang in his head. *It got my eye! I lost my eye!*

Not remembering descending the stairs, James began to beat his fists on the glass windows of the door. Inside he could see a wide corridor with many doors along both sides, but no people. He gently placed Bertha down against the door. *Gotta stop my bleedin'.* He pulled his handkerchief from his trousers and pressed it against his eye.

I can see! What luck, it's just a cut on my eyebrow.

Hammering his fists on the doorframe, he screamed, "Help us! Please, help us! Ain't nobody there?" He turned to look for a rock or something and then picked up the boot that had hit him to break the pane of glass closest to the doorknob.

Later, when James remembers this storm, he will find it strange that he had no idea about the passage of time. So, he didn't know how long they were in the storm or how long he had beat on that door. He didn't remember seeing someone at the far end of the corridor when he reached through the broken window to open the door and carry his wife inside. But what was even stranger was … he remembered no colors. In his memory, everything—trees, the Ferris wheel bench, the magic-carpet blanket—were black and gray.

An older man, carrying a candle, ambled up to them and exclaimed, "My, oh my! Where did you come from?"

James, grasping the edges of the blanket and, sliding Bertha down the dry corridor, answered, "Help us! We need a doctor."

Dumbfounded, the old man stood and gaped at them.

"Ginny, come on!" James called, but the child remained curled on a step outside the door. While walking backwards to Ginny, James pleaded to the gentleman, "Ain't there a doctor? Our baby's coming!" James gently cradled his little girl and smoothed the dripping hair from her face as he knelt down to place Ginny beside his wife. James opened the plaid blanket and placed his huge hands gently on the mound, hoping to feel life within.

Looking up in exasperation, "Tarnation! Ain't there a doctor here?" Not one to be shy, James lifted his wife's dress and saw the emerging crown of his child. Bertha cried out in pain again, and James screamed, "Damn it! Help us!"

It finally made sense to the old man. Turning to rush away, he repeated, "My, oh my! I'll go for the doctor!"

Within minutes, a doctor came to help with the birth of baby Ellie. As the doctor worked, the old man walked to the end of the hall to shut the still open door. At the click of the latch, Ellie popped out and replaced the sound of the storm with her bellows.

It was the twenty-seventh of May, and the family will refer to this day, not as Ellie's birthday, but as Ellie's Storm. Each year as her birthday approached, they will say, "Ellie's Storm is almost here." The family had no idea what they were saying by calling it Ellie's Storm; they didn't know the relationship the tornado formed with this child born under its rage. As bizarre as it seems, through the years, Ellie's life will touch down like the tornado at the same places in St. Louis. Inexplicably, the storm chose to mark a ten-mile path where misfortunes and disasters will darken Ellie's life.

While James and Bertha huddled on the floor of the Insane Asylum, holding this precious dark-haired child and, while Ginny smiled and cautiously touched her new little sister, the tornado continued fuming outside, showing—like a mirror where everything is seen in reverse—Ellie's future. The twister ended its ten-mile swath reaching the Mississippi River, wrecking sixteen steamboats, and knocking out the Eads Bridge on the Illinois side. The end of the tornado will be the beginning of blows against Ellie's life; in fourteen years and under the Eads Bridge, Ellie will fall into her first calamity. The storm had pointed its deadly tip at another street and marked the place in downtown St. Louis where Ellie will bump into a deadly killer who will haunt her through his life. The vortex of the storm had hit a high ridge along 12th Street, destroying all the tenements and killing fourteen people; this area will be rebuilt as Soulard Market and, in later years when Ellie and her family are watching the destruction of their drugstore, they'll walk with their troubles in that same place. Continuing back over the tornado's path to the City Hospital where Ellie will lose a grandchild to an illegal abortion, the storm floated bedridden patients out windows—killing only one—before it completely destroyed the entire hospital. It touched down in Compton Heights, where Ellie will make her home and raise her children, yet on and on the tornado raced to Shaw's Garden, Vandeventer Street and Lafayette Park; somewhere in this vicinity, those closest to Ellie will betray her.

Finally, many decades later, Ellie will leave puzzled friends and a devastated family, to return to her place of birth. About sixty years from now, and not by accident, Ellie will return to where the tornado started its destruction at the St. Louis Insane Asylum on Arsenal Street.

But she'll return as a patient.

Chapter 2

March 1900
Dogtown
(Located on the west side of St. Louis)

Ankles were coming into view as hemlines went up. To most, these fashions were an exciting topic of discussion. To older women, the new styles created only a feeling of chagrin. Without a doubt, men loved the new view, as did Mrs. Bertha James. She sewed fashionable clothes for a living and, with the changing styles, women had nothing in their closets to wear. Consequently, the business, known simply as *Mrs. James*, flourished. Bertha had a knack for designing and was an expert seamstress. The wealthy women of St. Louis were keeping her busy and vying to have the *Mrs. James* label in their clothes.

Interestingly, she didn't dress herself in the latest styles.

Frequently she'd say to her customers, "I still wear my corset because I look dowdy without it."

Or, on another day, she'd comment, "The new fashions just don't hang right on a woman like me." What she meant was that her ample bosom and protruding midriff prevented her from wearing these new fashions that cater to the svelte. But, in reality, she didn't have the time or money to dress like her customers. She sewed to put food on the table.

At the James home, Ellie sat on the floor among cutting-scraps of a hound's-tooth skirt that her mother was making. She listened to her mother confess, "The truth is I ruined my figure having babies."

Without understanding the words, dark-haired Ellie of three years looked up with her piercing blue eyes. Nevertheless, the tone of her mother's voice and the body language of her sister Ginny, who played in the corner, gave Ellie a clear message that she and her sister had done something horrible to their mother.

Ellie looked down and found a triangular swatch to place over her soft, well-loved cloth doll, trying to make a dress like her mommy. As the child raised the doll, the piece of material fell. Puzzled and approaching frustration, she looked up for help, but knew better than to interrupt the rhythm of the treadle of the sewing machine. With each rock of the foot, the Singer whined a one-note song.

Bertha usually sewed in the morning to have light to see that each stitch was perfectly placed. This day she was sewing with dark-colored fabric and the brightness reflecting off the new snow gave her more light. At the end of the seam, she stopped and reached to the floor, rummaging through the various shapes and sizes of hound's-tooth scraps. Choosing a large one, she cut a hole into the center before slipping it over the head of the little rag doll.

Ellie smiled. The mother smiled back, only with her eyes.

The two were working in the dining room behind lace-curtained windows that looked out onto a porch on the south side of the house. The clock on the mantel began to chime in pleasant harmony with a singsong chant coming from outside.

"Scissors, Knives, All your blades …"

Snatching a couple of her scissors, Bertha rushed out the door without her coat to catch the weathered, wooden cart with *Scissor Sharpening* in once-red letters scrolled along the side. To stop the two huge wheels, the vendor dug in his heels and leaned back from the wooden handle—worn smooth and thinner where his hands had slipped and grasped from pulling and pushing this cart up and down the streets of St. Louis.

Elle went to the open door and watched as, down on the street, the man and her mother exchanged greetings. The vendor made a polite bow as he lifted his hat and commented about the sunny winter morning. With only a silent nod, Bertha answered.

He opened a small drawer and grabbed an oily cloth with the tips of his fingers that poked out from tattered woolen gloves, looking much like the handful of crocuses peeking out from the dirty snow along the walk. After wiping the scissors' blades, his toe pumped a pedal and the sandstone wheel whirred. In a couple of minutes, he was done. Mrs. James dropped pennies into a cup wired to the cart, and he leaned into the load to push off with a "thank you ma'm."

Hastily, she returned to her home, put a log into the pot-bellied stove, and returned to her sewing.

Ginny wandered over, “Mama, why …?”

Bertha interrupted and, in a huff, recited one of her many rhymes, “A stitch in time saves nine.”

Quietly Ginny turned with her head drooping and walked back to her corner in the living room. Ellie wondered how her sister could have forgotten not to interrupt.

At the sound of the living room door opening, Ellie watched as her mother bristled even before Ellie’s father, James August James, came into view.

“Why don’t you use the back door? You’re ruining the carpet!”

Without noticing Ginny in the living room, he started to walk by Bertha in the dining room, but saw his littlest daughter and stopped, “What’re ya making, Ellie?” He placed the metal milk tin and small package wrapped in newspaper on the dining room table before squatting down. Two rabbits hung over his shoulder where he had tied them at the feet. He leaned his shotgun against the doorframe.

“A dress for dolly.”

Picking up his daughter, he pulled from his jacket pocket a butterscotch candy wrapped in waxed paper. “Mr. Harris sent one for each of my little girls. Where’s Ginny?”

Ginny peeked around the wall, but stopped as her mother ranted some more without missing a stitch.

“What were you doin’ at the tobacco shop all the way over on Manchester Road? You weren’t spending the rent money on pipe tobacco I hope.” She stated that, knowing he’d never do it, but she liked to say it. “What’d you buy in the package?”

Ginny slipped back into the living room.

“I earned fifteen cents watching the tobacco shop, so’s Mr. Harris could get to the bank. I bought some beans and milk. Gotta take the milk tin back. I hadn’t planned on earning any money, so I didn’t take our milk tin and …”

Bertha berated, “That’s your problem. You have no idea how to make money.”

James put his littlest girl back among the wool scraps, "Ellie, I'll help ya with the candy paper, but let me take off my jacket and put the milk in the ice box."

"Don't talk to her when I'm addressin' you."

He grabbed the shotgun with a furrowed brow, but bit his tongue; they'd had this argument so many times.

Bertha persisted, "They're hiring at the brick factories again."

"How many times do I have to tell ya? I ain't goin' to work at the brick works like my pa." The lanky frame drooped more than usual as he ambled into the kitchen pantry with the beans, ducked to avoid the six-foot-high doorway, and placed his shotgun onto a high shelf. Ellie followed him, pulling at the paper around the butterscotch. He opened the back door and hung the rabbits on a nail out in the cold on the screened-in porch.

After he poured the milk into their tin and put it into the icebox, he pulled out a kitchen chair to sit and lifted Ellie onto his lap, "See, just hold both ends," he put her pudgy little fingers around the twisted paper, "and pull." The candy twirled, and he put it into his open palm for her to wiggle the treat out of the wrapper.

Above the whine of the sewing machine, Bertha called out, "You're spoiling her lunch!"

James clenched his teeth.

Standing and going toward the kitchen, Bertha turned the skirt right side out and gave it a quick shake. "I don't appreciate you making the child see me as the mean one."

Opening a slim door near the stove, the ironing board dropped down, and she placed the skirt on it, arranging it just so. She took a pressing cloth from a hook inside the ironing board closet and picked up the sprinkling bottle. With the cloth over the skirt, she shook out droplets of water. Grabbing the wooden-handled iron off the stove, she touched her finger to her tongue and then the iron bottom. It sizzled.

"I want to go deliver this skirt and jacket to my client. I'll be gone an hour or two. You can stay with Virginia and Elizabeth."

"No, I can't. I done told Wally I'd go by his shop to work."

"Without pay, of course."

James grabbed his jacket and the borrowed milk tin, "Wally helped me with our shed last month, using his own wood scraps. I'm payin' him back." He headed out the front door with a bang. Outside he placed the tin on the porch bench so he could put on his jacket again. While pulling his wool cap over thick brown waves, he saw Ginny and Ellie at the dining room window, looking with sad-eyes.

He leaned in the front door, "Girls, git yer coats and come wit' me. Bertha, I'll skin those rabbits later, and I'll be gettin' supper for the girls in town."

Ambling down Tamm Avenue in Dogtown with Ellie on his shoulders and Ginny on his back, they could be seen for blocks. With his right hand he held tight to Ellie's feet and with his left arm bent behind his back, he made a seat for Ginny to sit. Ginny clutched her daddy's arms with the butterscotch in her fist.

The girls were wearing warm winter coats Bertha had sewn. She spared no effort for her daughters and had made matching yellow and pink winter coats from some leftover brocade. The matching hats fanned out with wide brims around their faces.

"Mr. James, your little one looks like the sun shining," a neighbor commented as she proceeded toward them across the cobblestone street, dodging a bicycle. Ginny peered around her father's shoulder, "Oh, and I see a bright, full moon peeking out from behind your back." The lady turned on a pathway into a small vacant lot and her voice, along with her footsteps, trailed away among the trees and bushes, "With you so tall, Mr. James, they's way up in the sky just like the sun and moon."

Dogtown was a neighborhood of St. Louis in the gentle, rolling hills on the western edge—more country than city. People started calling the place Dogtown about twenty-five years earlier when the Irish, Welsh, and some Germans came to settle near the clay factories. There was the Laclede Brick Factory and the Missouri Brick and the Mitchell Brick Factory, to name some of them, all located out Manchester Road.

Historically, nobody was completely sure how the name Dogtown came to be. James had a couple of renditions he liked to tell to new neighbors or visitors. One version he'd tell when there were a few dogs in view on the streets, "Every house in Dogtown's got a couple of dogs. You know, everybody needs watchdogs or good huntin' hounds. Well, our dogs love to nip at the heels of horses when the farmers and tradesmen are heading down to market or to the steamboats with their loads. With so many dogs runnin' after them, they started callin' us Dogtown "

On the days when James saw no dogs, he would go to his second version, "Squatters were run-off from that area where the city was makin' Forest Park. Poor guys headed into our part of town and put up some shacks. They had no jobs and no money and no nothing. They went around for handouts to eat and nearly froze to death in the winter. You might'n say that they led a dog's life, so we started calling the place Dogtown."

As he and the girls approached Wade Street where the Catholic Church, St. James Parish, was hosting a fundraising dinner, many greeted them with a smile or hello. Women, carrying baked bread, roasted hams, and chocolate cookies, nodded at them.

"Don't youse worry, girls. We goin' come back and git some of those fine vitals tonight."

When they passed in front of the rectory, they glanced at an elderly gentleman with a pipe holding the door for the parade of food going in.

"Oh, now don't that smell good?" escaped from James as he took a deep breath.

Ginny giggled, "Oh Daddy. Momma says you so skinny cuz you love tobacco more'n food."

Sitting on her daddy's shoulders, Ellie was too young to get the gist of the comment; besides, she was concentrating on her daddy's eyebrow hairs. She liked to finger his bushy brows. She pressed the coarse hairs down, liking how they sprang back against her touch. She would like to feel the moustache, but knew he wouldn't allow that. Her nose was turning red from the cold and starting to drip.

Crossing another street, Ellie flinched at the crack of a whip. Wooden wheels clattered on the cobblestones. When almost at Manchester Road, James said his usual, "Now, don't tell your Ma we stopped here," as he poked his head into Dolan's Saloon and Hotel.

"I won't," they chimed together. But, in a few days, Ginny will let it slip.

Only a couple of customers sat at the bar; it was too early for business. "Hey, Mike, hold a pint for me 'n Wally. After supper we're plannin' to play some tunes. Did Mr. Dolan let you know? I asked him yesterday."

"He sure did. See you tonight."

Back out on the wooden sidewalk, James walked around a sleeping mutt and picked up speed again. As they approached the grocery store, they listened to the rise of a woman's voice arguing about the price of apples. James didn't slow his gait. Inadvertently, Ginny slipped down his back a little as they turned a corner onto a dirt street where the snow had mixed with mud and had frozen. Now James slowed to maneuver among the ruts and furrows. Ginny grabbed tighter to his shoulder, preparing for the release. They were almost there.

They turned up an alleyway, waited while a horse clippity-clopped past them before Ginny slid down to push open an unlocked gate. Wally's unnamed dog heard them coming and greeted the three with lots of wiggles and wags before following them inside.

Each time the girls entered the shop, they noticed pleasing rich scents of wood wafting in the air. Every visit they heard music and laughter from the two friends. They passed many happy hours in Wally's shop among their father's unfinished inventions, the clutter of wood scraps, fiddle music, broken lamps, and other paraphernalia in need of repair. During these times, they developed a love for Irish music and, even as adults, a subconscious desire to pick up a piece of wood and smell it because they learned to associate the scent of wood with happiness.

"A good day to you, James and your wee ones," Wally said.

"Good day to ye, Wally." James went to the back and reached for the old fiddle Wally had given him years ago.

Ellie and Ginny learned indirectly about their own family in Wally's shop. They knew their dad and Wally had known each other since childhood, growing up and playing tunes in Dogtown. And they understood why James stored the fiddle at Wally's shop.

Ginny helped unbutton her sister's coat. Quietly counting with a rhyme as she pushed each button from a hole. Soon Ellie whispered the rhyme as well, "Rich man, Poor man, Beggar man, Thief. Doctor, …"

"Oh, you're going to marry a doctor, Ellie." Now Ginny unbuttoned her own coat and they repeated, "Rich man, Poor man,

Beggar man, Thief. Doctor, Lawyer … Oh look! Mama gave me one more button and I'll marry a lawyer."

After opening his battered case, James wedged his fiddle under his chin so his hands were free to pluck the strings and turn the tuning pegs, "Oh, I stopped at the tavern and they know we gonna play tunes tonight. Oh, by the way, I wrote a new one. Here, tell me what ya think. I call it *Tomcat Reel*."

"In a town called Dogtown, you make music about cats?"

The men laughed and Ellie smiled as James pulled out the bow and started to play.

The catchy tune of the reel filled the shop as Ginny bobbed into a dance with her arms at her side. Her legs went up and down at the knee trying to do an Irish dance. Every once in a while she twirled and looked up to her daddy's broad, toothy smile.

James finished and gave her hair a tousle, and then he let out a hee-haw laugh, slapped his knee as he explained, "Last night a cat made a mistake of wandering into our street. Like ya know, we don't have a dog, but everyone else does. The fight woke me and kept me awake. Even our chickens started to squawk. So, I wrote this reel in my head."

"Aye, I like it, James. Let me give it a try," Wally said, reaching for his fiddle. After hearing the melody just once, Wally could play along with James.

They played for a few minutes and Ginny never stopped moving to beat. Ellie tried to dance, but just bobbed at the knees, not moving her feet.

They finished and Wally said, "They're gonna like this one at the tavern."

Ellie told her Daddy, "Mama sews with threads and you make music with them."

Then without another word, the two men put down their fiddles; Wally returned to his work with some wood he was sanding. James walked over to his corner, pulled his watch from the pocket in his vest and hung it from a nail in a stud.

James looked to his girls, "We don't want time to get away from me. We gonna eat at the church 'bout six."

"How you gonna pay for it, Daddy?" Ginny wanted to know.

"I saved a few coins from the last time I played at the tavern. Now go enjoy yourself."

Strange looking contraptions were sprawled here and there on James' workbench. Pipe rods jutted up and out on things that look like a kid put them together; metal plates and bolts formed unknown creations that only James understood. On the floor was an old remade bicycle frame with pulley ropes attached to a small wheel where normally the tire was. James picked up a glass bottle with a narrow metal tube attached to the top by a rubber stopper with a cog screw. He sat down on a high stool and began to make adjustments.

Ginny took Ellie's hand and went to their usual place. Months ago, Wally had shown them a three-foot-high chest with a multitude of small drawers containing wooden knobs, bolts, rubber washers, nuts, screws, scrapes of wood, and other paraphernalia for the odd jobs he did. The girls could play for hours, arranging patterns on the floor or building "inventions" like their daddy. In the summer, they went outside and played with Wally's dog.

The shop was filled with rasping sounds, pings and taps. Ginny talked in whispers to some invisible playmate, Ellie carried objects over to a little table James had made for her. And the men worked in silence. All were lost in their own worlds. Concentration and the immense satisfaction of their endeavors bonded them in camaraderie while time ticked from James' pocket watch.

Suddenly there was an explosion and a flash of light.

"Eeeeooo," James wailed.

"Mother Mochroi!" Wally turned and grabbed an old towel as he rushed to James and began to wind the cloth around James' head. The shop had filled with acrid smells of burning hair. Ellie rushed with wide eyes to her daddy and wrapped her arms around his legs.

Carefully Wally uncoiled the towel, "What's you doin' over here, James?" Wally took a hard look at James and started roaring in laughter. He slapped his friend on the back. "So, I see you invented a way to trim your eyebrows and moustache without going to the barber."

James leaned to his right to gaze into an old broken fragment of mirrored glass that sat on his workbench. He busted out in his horselaugh with his toothy grin, and Ginny joined in laughing. Ellie didn't understand quite what was going on, but feigned laughter.

James had singed his brows away and his moustache has lost the ends. Most humorous was the fringe of kinked hair around his face.

James commented, "How will I explain this to Bertha?"

That created more laughter.

"Tell me now, the idea of tellin' Bertha puts more fear in you than the explosion. Don't it?" Wally asked and took out his handkerchief to wipe his tearing eyes. "I haven't laughed so much in a long while. James, just what were you doin'?"

"I've been workin' on makin' a better striker. I'd like to have one for my pipe like the ones they have for cigarettes. Have you seen them? This morning when I was at the tobacco shop, I saw one of the latest strikers for cigarettes. You wouldn't believe the size. Why, it fits in your pocket! It's called a Wonderliter and made by a company called Ronson. Darn it all, I been workin' on mine for a couple of months and they come out with something 'bout like I was makin'. So, I thought to change mine for pipes." James walked over to his workbench and picked up the small bottle. "It has gasoline in it and here is what makes the spark. I just can't get it to burn with a small flame."

Wally started laughing again and said in Irish, "*Ababuna*—good heavens! You sure can't. I think you should sell it to the barber shop for trimming whiskers."

"Well, you know it was a good idea if a big company made just what I was thinkin'. Trouble is I have too many ideas and don't concentrate on one. To be successful, I gotta be the first ta git it out."

James stopped, "Oh, I plumb forgot to tell ya. Down in the city I stopped at the buggy shop and started shootin' the breeze wit the owner, a man called Russell E. Gardner. We're both interested in learnin' about gasoline-powered buggies. You know, those automobiles. I said I'd love to work on automobiles. So, he showed me one of his. It's called a Duryea and he had it shipped last year from Massachusetts. He even opened the engine and tol' me how it works. When he opened the doors, he moved a wheel fer steerin' it right and left. I ne'r saw anything like it. Finally, he talked about the windows goin' up and down and, just like that," James snapped his fingers, "I seed I could invent somethin' to make those windows work better."

Wally started laughing, "James, just listen to you go on. It's for sure you're an inventor. I know you gonna make it someday. Just keep workin' at whatever you think."

"Well, you didn't let me finish. Gardner gave me a job. He wants me to learn about repairin' and makin' automobiles. I couldn't refuse. It's not only a job … it's one that suits me!"

Chapter 3

1904
Dogtown Grows

After four years working for Russell E. Gardner, James became adept at working on automobiles. He dreamed about selling his window opener design to Ford, but he never got it working quite right.

Coming home from work one day and before he opened the door, James heard Bertha screaming at Ellie.

"You know the rule! Do not play with my sewing things. Ellie, why can't you learn to do what you should, like Ginny? Look at all the thread you've wasted."

James found Bertha down on her hands and knees gathering spools. Incredible as it seemed, it appeared that Ellie was so tangled with dozens of spools that she couldn't move. The scene was almost comical to James as his wife crawled around on the floor, breaking threads to free the spools.

Bertha looked at James, "Well, you could help!"

"Sure, I'll help," he said.

Now Bertha directed her wrath at James, "I was in the kitchen makin' chestnut glaze and syrup. I was so busy. You know that all the chestnut trees are a dyin' and they say that this blight can't e'er be fixed. I's tryin' to make enough to last us. Why, I seed some of the trees with cankers on the trunks. All the trees on the east coast are gone and now all the trees in our woods are goin'!"

She turned back to Ellie who was completely tied-up in threads, "Elizabeth, I'm so mad at you for wasting my time and all this thread."

Little Ellie sat unable to move and slowly her lower lip protruded and trembled. She started to sniffle in little spasms. Her whole body jerked with each snivel, and it looked like she would start bawling at any moment. But she held back.

James explained, "Ellie, you know better. You ain't 'posed to touch your Ma's things."

"Don't call me her *Ma*! I hate that word! I'm her Mother."

James just clenched his teeth.

Looking at his daughter, it was obvious Ellie must have been playing for a long time to be so entwined in all those threads. Threads were wound around her arms and legs and even circled her head. He glanced at Ginny and she made a sheepish look.

He leaned over, swept Ellie into his arms, and reached for a small scissors. Immediately he started clipping long threads attached to her. With each cut one spool stopped following her across the floor although a dozen others continued to clatter along as he moved with his daughter into the living room. He collapsed on the couch, putting Ellie on his lap, and continued to snip her free.

"You look like Jeb the spider."

With that one statement, Ellie was still upset, but she made a puzzled face; he had whetted her curiosity.

He continued, "You know about Jeb?" James raised his bushy brows and squinted, "Ain't I told you the story?"

Ellie was still weeping silent tears.

Hearing her daddy's storytelling voice, Ginny emerged from behind the bedroom door where she had been hiding. She scurried in, sat on the carpet, and leaned on her daddy's legs.

James began his tale, "Well Jeb—you know that's short for Jebediah—he was a young spider who couldn't learn how to spin a web. His mama tried to teach him; his daddy tried. Jeb always ended up in a tangle with spider web threads around his feet and head, even threads squeezin' his big fat belly with tangles and clumps of leaves mixed in. Often, when tryin' his best, he would fall from the tree, cuz he was so tangled. He'd spiral down, down, down, on a long thread of webbing, stoppin' just inches from …" James sucked in his breath, dramatically stopping midsentence.

Ellie had sad, large eyes above her dripping nose, but her lower lip was no longer trembling. The skirt of her dotted-swiss pinafore was caught among the threads and gathered up under one arm, exposing her bloomers. With dimpled hands she pulled at the pinafore to cover herself.

James clipped a couple of threads to release the skirt and put on a look of surprise to finish the sentence, "Jeb fell, stoppin' inches from a cowpie."

Ellie smiled, "Oh, Daddy," she drawled.

"Now Jeb's daddy crept slowly down to help his son outta this mess. Well, it's kind of like the mess I'm workin' on wit' you," and James snipped a few more threads here and there.

"I'm not in any old cowpie," Ellie insisted.

James hugged her and carefully clipped a thread near her ear before continuing, "Jeb sat wonderin' if he'd ever learn how ta make a proper spider web ta catch some food. At those times after he'd failed and was in a tangled mess, Jeb sat and looked at the stars. He loved the stars—how they'd sparkle and move slow across the sky. He could name the Big Dipper, the Bear, and lots of others.

"So, in spider time, the years went by and Jeb is 'bout three when he finally makes a good web. Now, t'wasn't a normal kind of spider web. He worked all day on it 'til he had it just right. That evening at just the right moment when the stars were just where he knew they'd be, he called his parents, his aunts and uncles, his cousins and friends. He tol' 'em where to sit on the limb of the tree.

"'Look up,' he said. And there above 'em was the most marvelous web anyone had ever seen. Every place where one strand crossed the other t'was a star shining through. In this amazing display it looked like Jeb had connected all the stars in the sky and caught them in his web. No one had e'er seen anything like this and every spider gasped at the wonder of it all. As the stars twinkled, every corner in Jeb's web was blinkin'.

"Suddenly a cloud moved and exposed the full moon. T'was right in the center of Jeb's web. 'Oh, what a beautiful sight!' someone said and the spiders clapped.

"But there was one mean cousin who grumbled, 'It don't look like you'll catch nothin' to eat with that fancy thing.'

"As all the spiders turned to see who said such a nasty thing, a shadow with giant wings passed over the group and nearly brushed the spiders from the tree. T'was a lunar moth, admiring the beauty of the moon and stars in Jeb's web. But the moth couldn't see the web. The huge moth floated upward, heading right into Jeb's sticky strands. The moth stuck and struggled to fly away, but couldn't.

"Whatta meal the spider group had that night in celebration of Jeb's special web. And Jeb continued his whole life making special webs and ne'er got tangled again."

Ginny stood up, "That's a good story, Daddy. You never told that one before."

Bertha frowned and picked up the last spool from the floor, placing the lid on the cardboard hatbox where she stored them. She had been quiet during the story, listening as closely as the girls. And she had a puzzled look when she said, "It's like you're rewarding her for being bad. You know, telling her stories to make her feel good."

The girls saw their father and mother looking into each other's eyes. And there was a long silence.

But Bertha straightened her back and walked into the kitchen saying, "I'm late with dinner and need to get over to make a fitting tonight. I didn't need to waste my time with all those threads and little stories."

James slipped Ellie to the floor and pulled his watch from his pocket. He didn't want to be late either, "You go ahead, Bertha. Don't bother with supper. I'll manage the girls."

Slowly Bertha reappeared with anger to face James, "You plan to go to that new tavern, don't you." She waited, but James said nothing. "No need to deny it. I know you take the girls there all the time. Ginny told me how she dances to that darn-fool music you play. I'm trying to raise decent girls and you take them huntin', fishin', swimmin', and what's worst—dancin' in a saloon whenever you can." She waited again. "Well, say somethin' cuz you're not goin' there tonight."

Not raising his voice, James answered, "I'm goin' with o' without the girls. You can start supper for them, if you want to be late, but don't tell me what I can or can't do."

Bertha started to protest, but turned with a look of hatred and huffed into the bedroom. After the bedroom door slammed, James shouted, "I guess you're dressin' to leave. Me an' the girls are going too."

Bertha shouted through the door, "Send the girls out to put the chickens in their pen for the night. And find some eggs. I need them for tomorrow."

After taking care of the chickens, James and the girls left their home, heading down the same route they always took on Tamm Avenue when going to Wally's shop. But unlike the walk in years past, Dogtown had a new bakery and there was a house turned into a hat shop before they got to the Roman Catholic Church on Wade Street. Continuing down Tamm, they passed a barbershop, a grocery store, and a pharmacy—all new.

Father Casey arrived on the sidewalk as they were passing.

"Top o' the day to ye, Mr. James and to your pretty little ones," the priest said.

"Same to you, Father."

"Why don't ye come to mass with your family? I n'er see you there."

James explained, "We's not Catholic, Sir."

Father Casey chuckled, "With a name like James August James, t'was apparent to me. But we welcome all faiths, we do." He pulled a flyer from inside his pocket and handed it to James. "See, it even states that here." At the bottom of the paper, listing the times of mass, were the words, 'Catholics or Non-Catholics Welcome.' "You keep this and join us for mass on Sunday. And please bring your Missus."

"Oh, Father, she's from strong German stock." James stammered a bit, "I, ah ..."

"I understand. But you and the girls could come." Turning away to go in a yard, the Father lifted his hat and tilted his head as a goodbye.

On the next block James smiled and said to the girls, "Just a minute, I want to say hello to Seamus," and he entered the new tobacco shop. No longer did he have to get out the horse and wagon to go to Muegge's General Store on Manchester to buy some tobacco.

When James came out, he sat a moment on a bench to fill his pipe. He and his girls were under the shade of an awning, but it was anything but cool. James dabbed perspiration from his upper lip.

He told his girls, "We gotta get over to see the Fair someday. It's the best thing to ever happen to Dogtown."

Over one thousand acres were bought by the city in anticipation of the World's Fair. Besides the prosperity that the Fair brought to Dogtown when it ended in December, the area would become a huge city park called Forest Park.

James tapped the tobacco firmly into his pipe, "We's goin' to have a park right next to us; it'll be like our own park!"

Looking across the street, Ellie watched some men who stood talking. One removed his straw hat to wipe sweat from his brow to point toward the fairgrounds. All of them held their jackets over their arms or slung over shoulders.

Elle turned her head to see why he pointed and asked, "Daddy, what's that thing up in the sky?" Something huge jutted into the skyline.

James explained, "I hear it's the biggest Ferris wheel in the world—a couple of hundred feet high with thirty or so cabins connected to it. Abouts fifty people can get inside just one cabin. So, over two thousand people can be on the Ferris wheel at a time. Ain't that somethin'?"

James stood and they proceeded to walk again.

"It's the same wheel that was at the Chicago World's Fair about ten years ago. And I heared that some people are planning their wedding in those cabins."

"No, Daddy!"

"Yep, it's the truth. And Ellie's Storm is comin' in a few days. Ellie, why, you gonna be eight years old, ain't ya? I promise to take you girls up in the Ferris wheel for Ellie's birthday. But we better not tell your ma. To go the World's Fair would be a right nice treat for Ellie's Storm, don't ya think?" James smiled his wide toothy grin and held out his hands with his little fingers sticking out.

Each girl latched on to one of his little fingers with theirs. All three promised with a simultaneous, "We promise not to tell." Then, when they pulled their fingers apart, the pact was made.

They started walking again, "You know, a promise is a serious thing. When friends or family make a promise, no one should ever, ever break it. No matter what! Sometimes someone's life might depend on you keepin' a promise."

Ginny looked ashamed, "I'm sorry, Daddy. When Mama found out about the dancing, it just slipped out. I was tryin' to show Ellie how to do a dance step and forgot Mama could hear."

"I know, I know, Ginny. It's always an accident with you. You know why?

Ginny looked up at her father, "Why?"

"Well, Ginny, it's because you are such a trusting and good person. You never think about doing any bad thing like tellin' a lie or bein' deceitful. So, you fall into the truth even though you promised not to tell." James put his arm around his growing daughter. At eleven years old, she was taller than her mother and still growing. "Just remember it's not a lie to keep quiet 'bout a secret cuz you promised not to tell."

"I do try, Daddy. How come Ellie never slips up and tells a promise? Ain't she a good and trusting girl?"

James stopped in the shade and sat on a rock wall built around an old oak tree. He put Ellie on his knee and pulled Ginny close to him, face to face. "That's a darn hard question, Ginny."

"I know, Daddy," Ginny admitted.

A bunch of flies were circling in the shade of the oak, buzzing around and around in the heat. The flies didn't land on them; they just kept flying in circles and buzzing. Ellie watched the flies as her daddy talked.

"There ain't no easy answer to it either." He stopped and thought a bit. Sweat was beading on his forehead. "Both ya girls are a lot alike," he emphasized, "But not the same!" After another moment of thought, he started up again, "Ya both are good swimmers and strong. Ginny, you can do handstands, but Ellie can't. Well, she ain't got no interest it seems. Fer sure, you're both darn good at school." Now James tried to make his point, "Ellie gits Irish dancin' lessons and is as good as you now. Have ya noticed?" Ginny nodded her head. "And she bein' three years littler than you. That's cuz she wanted it. Ellie's determined and stubborn. And you ain't, Ginny."

"But …" Ginny started to question, but James wasn't finished.

"Ellie's a lot like me. I'm stubborn and determined. I'm gonna do what I want and what I know it's good for me. Ginny you're more interested in makin' other people happy. And you do!"

Ellie was still watching the flies when he said, "Ellie's a lot like me." At that moment, she straightened her back and stared at her father's face. Her face brightened. She took a deep breath and smiled.

"We's all different, Ginny. Always be happy with yourself. And try to keep this promise about the Ferris wheel ride. Really work on it." James added, "But it's okay if it slips."

And Ginny will slip; they never will get to ride together on the Ferris wheel.

James hugged both his girls and stood. "I hear'd that Mrs. Flanagan makes ice cream to sell for a penny on Fridays. I got some pennies. Race you to her house!"

After they finished their cones, they made their way to Wally's shop.

"Wally, why, it looks like you is done with the fiddle. It's all shellacked!" James said as he peered at a shining violin. "Mr. What-his-name sure'll be happy. I'm plumb sure that every time I'd seed him he asks when it'd be done. Darn if I can remember his name."

Wally Duggan sighed and in an Irish brogue complained, "Please! Don't be callin' it a fiddle. It'll be played in the St. Louis Symphony by hands that have played there for twenty years." He shook his head, "Wish people could understand. I can't rush the makin' of a fine violin. That's your problem, James, you're too eager makin' yours. I know I promised to teach you, but you gotta put some heart into it." Wally laughed, "You put sweat in it and, since you cut yourself, a bit of blood, but not your heart."

James laughed and answered, "I know I didn't put all my heart into makin' the fiddle, but I'm interested. You know, I love to make things."

Wally continued, "And don't be tellin' him his violin is ready, because it needs more time."

"For the shellac to dry?"

"No, no, James, more'n that. It's the fine strings from Italy I ordered. They need time to sit on the violin before they're ready. And it ain't shellac."

"I heard that catgut strings are the best. Ain't that so?"

Taking a deep breath and smiling, Wally said, "James, James, catgut is just a bunch o' malarkey. E'er since we was lads here in the neighborhood, you always need to know how things work. So, here's a long answer for you. The best answer.

"In a town called Salle, Italy, where they been makin' musical strings for hundreds of years—since about 1300, I think—they discovered a secret material to make violin music more beautiful than ever before. Of course they didn't want anybody to know what it was. So they told folks it was catgut.

"They had their reasons for thinkin' this lie would work. In Italy, people have many superstitions and, if someone killed a cat, it meant bad luck for a long time. So, the violin string makers of Salle thought no one would copy their trade, if it meant slayin' cats.

"What they really used was string made from intestines of sheep. For many years their business was making saddles and they used threads from the sheep's intestines to stitch saddles. Somehow they noticed that it was good for music. So that's the story. People believed the strings were catgut for so many hundreds of years that we still hear it said today.

"Can you imagine when someone tried to play a violin with real catgut?"

Soon the men were engrossed in their own endeavors as usual. Without music, the girls practiced the steps for their Irish dancing, to be ready for their lesson later that day.

As Ellie moved in the quiet of the shop, repeating over and over each movement in perfect timing with her sister, she came to a realization. When something is repeated over and over—whether dancing steps with threes and sevens or discontent with hate and arguments—there is an inevitable final result. A chill went down her spine.

***

Later that summer on a day when even the flowers were wilting from the heat, a new family moved onto their block. As Ginny and Ellie walked down to see their new neighbors, they saw a couple of sweaty, shirtless men heave a thick wooden headboard of an oak bed onto their shoulders and carry it into the house. A boy about ten was throwing a rubber ball against the brick house while a younger girl sat moping on a dining room chair in the middle of the grass. She had one arm draped over the back with her head lolling on the arm.

Ellie went up to her,"Hi, we live at the corner. I'm Ellie and this is my sister Ginny."

Startled, the girl stood and turned to face the James sisters. She was sweet looking, with a doll-like face and soft light-brown hair that sparkled blonde when the sun caught it. Her eyes were green and sad. Despondency oozed from her words, "My name's Franny."

Ginny blurted out, "Look, I can do a handstand!" With that said, she threw up her arms raised one leg and spun upside-down onto her hands. Ellie stepped over to hold her sister's skirt from falling and exposing the bloomers. Ginny's back arched just right as she balanced for a few seconds.

Ellie released the legs, as Ginny came down, and began clapping. She turned to Franny, "I can't do that. Can you?"

Franny was amazed at these two sisters; she backed a bit from the chair and pointed to the piano the men were carrying into the house, "No, but I play the piano. Can you?"

And so, a most profound friendship began between the three girls, especially Franny and Ellie who discovered they were the same age. Within days Franny no longer was sad about moving into Dogtown. Between Franny and Ellie, the bond that formed continued into adulthood through marriage, children, and deep secrets taken to their graves.

Fall passed and winter came. Now the girls were inseparable. Franny's first outing with the James family was toward the end of the year on a crisp, sunny winter day.

Bertha and the girls heard a strange sound outside their house.

AaaOooGa, AaaOooGa!

Peering out the window, they saw James sitting in a shiny black automobile. They ran outside.

"Git your coats, hats, and scarves. Let's take a ride," James told them, "Mr. Gardner tol' me I could take my family wit me to Dyke's supply house. I need to git some parts for the automobile we're makin'."

"Can Franny come?"

James responded, "Sure, we'll stop at her house."

Bertha appeared interested and produced a small smile.

James looked pleased, "Go on now, all of you! Git your coats and bundle up; it's cold riding fast."

Automobiles were quite the rage among the wealthy in St. Louis. So much so, that the first drive-in filling station was getting ready to open between Chouteau and Market on Theresa Avenue. This made St. Louis the first city in the nation to have an automobile supply house and a filling station.

James commented as they climbed in, "Too bad we ain't got no goggles." A.L. Dyke opened the supply house in 1899 and had all kinds of mechanical parts for horseless machines and other paraphernalia for the riders, like goggles, gloves, and caps. "Guess we can't say we're 'Dyked-up' like the rich folk do."

Ellie shook her head, "That don't matter, Daddy."

While they waited for Franny to get her coat on, Bertha said in a perky voice, "Could we go the other direction and pass some of my customer's houses? Maybe they'll see me."

James obliged her whim.

The three girls sat in back and spontaneously started to sing:

When Irish eyes are shining,
And the world seems bright and gay.

James squeezed the horn. AaaOooGa, AaaOooGa! And the girls sang louder:

Too-Ra-Loo-Ra-Loo-Ral

The vehicle lurched, buckled, bounced with every hole it hit, and did anything but run smoothly. Nevertheless, the family found the trip exciting. Even Bertha was happy. She saw people she knew and exchanged waves with them.

At the end of the day, James glowed with family pride. Nevertheless, in six more years, Bertha's battering will obliterate any family unity. Actually, for James the battering will end.

Chapter 4

December 1909-April 1910
Music in Dogtown

Five more years passed, and the growth of Dogtown continued; Ellie liked the hustle and bustle. Of course, what one person considered progress could be a disappointment for another. Bertha longed for the sleepy little place it used to be. Dogtown continued to have more storefronts and places with special services. A doctor opened an office, as did a dentist, and new people kept moving in. Dogtown was no longer the once quiet country community.

James had a new story of how Dogtown got its name. It all came about because of the 1904 World's Fair. Some of the exhibits at the Fair featured exotic people from all over the globe. A group of Indonesian natives, called the Igorots, had a place at the fair near Dogtown. They built a little village and visitors had gone to watch them making clothes, cooking, caring for their children, and living just like they did in Indonesia. But officials told the Igorots that they could not cook their favorite food; they loved to eat dogs.

After the Fair had come and gone, it took about a year for the story to form. James began, "These wild natives called the Igorots were dog-eaters. Back where they came from, they ate dogs every day. Now you understand the Mayor of St. Louis and all the officials running the World's Fair disapproved of this practice. Actually, they forbade it. But those little dark-skinned people were just a step and a jump from our homes, and their mouths watered when they saw our dogs—dogs like they ne'r seen before. Bigger than they e'er imagined a dog could grow. So, at night, those Igorots would sneak from their village into Dogtown.

"Our dogs started to disappear. My neighbors started puttin' the favorite ones in their root cellars for the night. You know, their bird dogs or a fine watchdog.

"The World's Fair lasted from April 'til December. When it ended people let their dogs back out, but there weren't a stray dog to be found. Our place was called Cheltenham before this all happened, but after the Igorots went back home and the Fair was taken down, slowly people started calling our neighborhood Dogtown."

Ellie and Ginny were young ladies now. Their father still worked on automobiles and hadn't patented any of his inventions, but he and Wally had started playing at Dennis T. Coyne's Saloon on Tamm Avenue every Friday and some Saturdays since it opened. And the James girls joined them with Irish dancing.

One Friday night in December, James and Wally were playing tunes at the saloon.

"There's not room to turn around in here," shouted a patron of the tavern. "Fill me mug again, if you please."

Mr. Gittin, who owned the old grocery store on Manchester Road, commented, "I like the crowd. And, why, heaven knows I don't want to sit. I gotta have a little space to tap my feet to the music. Can't sit to these Irish tunes. Don't ya agree?"

"You hit the nail on the head. I wasn't complainin' at all. Besides, James and Wally are playing their best tonight." He turned toward the bartender to clarify, "And didn't I hear that Patrick O'Brien is acomin' right soon with his pipes?"

The bartender nodded, while mopping up the shiny oak bar.

Mr. Gittin asked, "Who's the gal with the tin whistle?"

"She's the sister of that new doctor. She plays a good tune, don't ya think?" commented the bartender. "She n'er practices with 'em. She just plays as she hears the music."

James' cap sat on the floor at the front of the little raised platform where he and Wally played their fiddles. The cap was filled with pennies, dimes, nickels and even a few shiny quarters.

While waiting for the next tune, Ellie and Ginny started talking to the waitress Sadie while she was drawing some beer from the spigot. They chattered away. Sadie had been teaching the girls to dance over the years.

"Just do a few sevens across the floor. Come on, Sadie," Ellie begged.

"Yeah," Ginny agreed, "dance with us for a little while."

Sadie placed the last mug on her tray, "Oh, go on now. You young ones are who they wants to see. And you know that my knees can hardly make it through our classes on Thursdays. Now, do me proud and show 'em what ol' Sadie teaches ya." She hefted the full tray over her head and disappeared into the crowd.

At the end of a tune, the crowd shouted, "The James Girls! The James Girls!" Ginny and Ellie wore plaid pleated skirts, ready to do their steps.

James told the crowd, "We need a break. We promise to come back with Ellie and Ginny."

The Dennis T. Coyne Saloon was not fancy, but people loved to come. The ceiling was pressed tin, the walls were made from marred bricks bought cheap from the neighborhood brick works, and electrical wires, running to bare light bulbs, looped across the ceiling. But the beer was cold, the people friendly, and the music was the best Irish music in town. No longer was it just a neighborhood place; people came from all over St. Louis when Wally and James were playing. That's where the quarters came from, some well-to-do banker or haberdasher who had come to hear the tunes.

Standing at the bar next to Ellie, Wally leaned over to James and said, "Wonder who tossed the two-bits into the hat. Oh look, Father Casey from St. James Church is here. And me thinks that's Father Erasmus with 'em. That's cuz of your girls; everybody likes ta see 'em dance."

James looked to Ellie, "I think he's right. Let's play a jig. Ellie, it's your pick."

Ellie brightened, "*Banish Misfortune* is my favorite."

So, Wally and James downed their brews and went back to the platform. They put their fiddles to their chins. James stomped his foot three times and the music began. One measure and the whistle joined in, too.

Ellie and Ginny made a simultaneous turn away from the bar and started to move like fine thoroughbred horses. The crowd cheered. They danced in unison, prancing over to the edge of the platform with knees raising and lowering, toes pointing here and there, across a knee and back down, while their sleek, dark hair bobbed like the tail of a fine stallion going through dressage. Their arms hung down at their sides, never moving. Bouncing up and down, the girls' five-feet-eight inches of height appeared weightless and graceful. White blouses, with a flounce at the wrist, rippled and billowed with their movements.

The new owner from O'Malley Bakeshop wondered to no one in particular, "Now how do they do that? They look like marble statues from the waist up, but like jumpin' grasshoppers with those legs. Now tell me, how they do it!"

And so the night went. They played a couple of reels, *The Boys of Ballysadare* and *The Bucks of Oranmore*.

When Wally and James wanted another little break, James shouted, "We just gonna whet our whistle and be right back."

And the doctor's sister held up her tin whistle and shouted back, "No, it's me who needs to unwet my whistle!" She shook the accumulated spit from her instrument. Laughter erupted.

Wally winked at James, "She's a rare woman. Not shy! And quick with the merriment. We need to get better acquainted. Oh, and if I may comment so, she adds much to the tunes. Didya hear her sweet notes on the slip jig?"

James agreed and left Wally to his own devices.

The hours passed and at midnight it was time for the music to end.

The crowd shouted, "Give us a *Shave and a Haircut*!" Like so many places across the nation, the eight-note tune put a closing to the fun:

C – G – G – A-flat – G – [rest] – B – C

And the crowd shouted, "Two-bits."

While James counted the coins in his cap, making separate piles for each player, Ellie asked, "Daddy, why does everyone shout 'two-bits' after that little tune?"

"Oh, I don't know. Guess that's what a haircut and shave used to cost when it was written. Hey, Wally, do ya know anything 'bout the *Shave and a Haircut*?"

"Me thinks a man named Hale wrote it. I first heared it 'bout ten years ago. Anyways, the name of the tune is *At a Darktown Cakewalk* but e'eryone just calls it *Shave and a Haircut*. Ain't it a perfect tiny encore?"

Bertha gave them her own encore when they arrived home. She was fit to be tied.

"Ya think I like bein' here all alone every Friday night and some Saturdays? I felt sickly all evening and here I be with nobody. What kind of family are ya?"

Ginny dropped her head, "I'm sorry Mama."

"Well, not sorry enough to stay home wit me, I bet! I shoulda had boys who'd treat their mother with more respect."

James sounded riled, "This is 'tween me and you, Bertha. Don't make the girls feel like theys done wrong. Let's go talk in private."

"Humph," Bertha continued, "All they thinks about is bein' with you."

He shouted, "Enough, Bertha!" He rubbed his forehead and told the girls to go on to bed. "Everything's okay, Ginny." As the girls walked away, he added, "Ellie, help your sister understand."

Bertha turned to get the last words in at the bedroom doorway, "Well, everything ain't okay."

James joined Bertha and closed the door a bit too forcefully. Ginny jumped.

The girl's room was on the other side of the house with the kitchen between, but they heard the raised voices—although not the words. After about twenty minutes it quieted and they fell asleep.

When Ellie and Ginny got up the next morning, their father wasn't around. "He left early for work," Bertha told them, "and I'm feelin' a little under the weather. Oh look, Ellie, you're losing a button."

Together the girls chimed in as their mother chanted, "Button's loose! Stitch it on. Before it rolls, and is gone."

Bertha grabbed a scissors and threaded needle from her pincushion, snipped off the loose button, and started sewing it back on.

As she stitched, she said, "Girls, I'm not going with you today. I have a list for you."

Every Saturday morning, the girls went with their mother to the grocery store and on other errands.

"Are you sick, Mommy?"

"No, no. I'm just a bit tired this morning."

After breakfast, when they started out, a light snow started to fall. Walking down the street, Ellie shivered as some flakes slipped into her collar. She tightened the scarf around her neck and pulled her gloves from a pocket. Quietly Ellie worked her fingers into the yellow gloves with blue rosebuds around the wrist and commented, "It looked like Mama won last night. She seemed real happy. Whatcha think?"

Ginny walked quietly, and then said, "Let's not talk about it. I get upset."

"Okay." They walked for a while before Ellie blurted, "Oh, I almost forgot, this afternoon Franny and I are going to the sweet shop. Wanna come?"

"Maybe," Ginny mumbled.

"Please, you gotta."

Ginny pursed her lips and shook her dark wavy hair while rolling her blue eyes at her little sister, "Ellie, if Mama hears you say "gotta" this and "wanna" that, she's going to punish you."

Ellie knew, "Thanks."

Ginny went on to say, "Right now, I just want a little time alone. I think I'll go to the library later."

Ellie grabbed her sister's hand, "I'll come to the library to see if you've changed your mind."

They had both grown to be striking young women. Ginny's hair was dark and shiny, almost black-brown with waves, while Ellie's hair had a golden cast to the brown natural curls. Their piercing baby-blue eyes shone from the brown frame of hair. They were full-grown and exceptionally tall for women, or men for that matter, yet they carried themselves with confidence and strength.

Later, when Ellie met Franny she explained, "Let's go the library to find Ginny."

They wandered in and out the different rooms, looking behind shelves of books and in the girls' bathrooms. As they went past a large table with many chairs occupied with people reading, Franny noticed a *National Geographic* with some native people depicted on the cover in color. In a whisper, "Ellie, look at this!"

The girls slipped into a seat and flipped through the magazine. They were enthralled with the photographs of women nude from the waist up.

Franny lamented, "Those poor ignorant women. Why don't they put some clothes on? My dad said that the Indians were savages like this until we came to teach them how to live. They're not too smart, my dad says, because they still don't know how to live like us."

"What are you talking about, Franny? These people dress like this because it's hot where they live. All the time it's hot. They don't get snow like we do here. Maybe they've never seen snow. In fact, we dress rather stupid, I think. If my mom thinks I'm going to ever wear a corset or girdle, she's wrong. I'm not going to let my mother tell me how to dress." Ellie raised her voice, "I'm not going to let anyone tell me what to wear or not wear."

Franny sat with her mouth open. "What are you talking about?"

Ellie was agitated, "Well, I got off the subject. Mom keeps trying to make me dress different." Ellie shook her head then pointed to the National Geographic, "But about these people, don't you see? They aren't stupid. On the contrary, they're probably smarter than us. They control whether they live or die … every day of their life. They have to be smart to survive. Wild animals will eat them if they aren't smart. They know everything about their land; all the plants and animals …"

Franny interrupted, "Ellie, stop. I was just telling you what my dad said. You're thinking too much."

Irritated at that comment, Ellie retorted, "You don't think enough, it seems."

"Please stop. I didn't mean anything. I never stopped to analyze what my dad thinks and I never thought about these natives. I just saw a colored picture on this magazine for the first time. Please stop."

Ellie smiled and slipped her head down onto her friend's shoulder, "Sorry. Ginny tells me I think too much, too. But I don't usually argue. I guess I am letting my mom and dad's fights get to me."

Franny put her arm around Ellie, "That's okay."

Now, Ellie brightened and sat up. She turned in the chair toward Franny and took both her hands. "We women do need to think more. We need to stick together for each other. Let's make a pact to always be there for each other."

Franny sat taller and giggled, "I like that. Let's do."

Ellie took her little finger on her right hand and looped it around Franny's little finger, "Let's swear to always be there for the other. Even if it means harm might come, we'll help the other."

"I swear," Franny pulled her little finger, making it a pact.

Ginny approached at that moment. “I heard you from the other side of the room. Look whose coming. We better get out of here.”

As a librarian came nearer, the girls rushed to the stairs and descended rapidly. They burst from the building and hustled down the street, singing:

De Camptown ladies sing dis song
Doo-dah! Doo-dah!
De Camptown racetrack five miles long
Oh! Doo-dah day!
Gwine to run all night!
Gwine to run all day!
Bet my money on a bobtail nag
Somebody bet on de bay.

***

As the weeks and months went by, Ellie couldn’t explain what it was, but her dad seemed different. He said everything was okay, but she knew he’d changed.

“Let’s see who can come up with real good words to describe Daddy,” Ellie said while walking home from school. “You don’t know him as well, Franny, but he’s quieter now or something.”

Ginny quipped, “It’s not that he is just quieter; he’s subdued.”

“Oh, I have something better,” Ellie added her two-cents, “He’s pensive now.”

Ginny stopped walking, “No. We just need a simple word. He’s sad.”

Franny wanted to know, “What would make him sad?” For the next ten minutes, they talked about their parents’ arguments.

When they arrived in front of Franny’s house, she commented, “But still, with all the problems, your family does so much. Your family is so special. My dad just works at the clay mines and my mom just cooks, takes care of me, my brother, the cow, and chickens. Oh, she cleans and cans and stuff. Gee, your parents do more important things like sewing for rich people and working on automobiles. They’re great!”

Ellie looked at Ginny and they rolled their eyes, "No, you don't know. I think something is terribly wrong. I know something bad is going to happen."

Ginny was irritated, "Ellie, you think too much. Nothing is wrong more than usual."

Franny laughed, "Yeah, you think too much, Ellie. Like I said, I think your parents are special."

Ellie hooked her arm into Ginny's arm and started to walk home, saying over her shoulder, "They behave themselves when you're around."

And Franny was around a lot of the time. James was used to doing things with the three girls. Last summer they swam or fished. They went to the Brown's baseball games and over to Forest Park. And they went down to the tavern for the Irish dancing sessions though Franny preferred to play the piano instead of dancing. The girls were always together.

One Friday night in the spring, while the three girls and James were walking home after an invigorating night of music and Irish dancing, James told them, "I'm not gonna call the Saturday dances anymore."

"Why?" Ellie wanted to know.

"Well, your ma's alone a lot. I'm going to be with her on Saturday night and you girls can go without me. You're certainly old enough."

"What about Fridays?"

James smiled, "We'll still have Fridays together for music. It's a compromise 'tween me and your ma. I think it's a good one."

Ellie's face contorted, "Daddy, no."

"It's settled, Ellie. Talking ain't goin' to change anything."

They walked Franny home and continued to their house. The redbud trees were in blossom with wild-pink-colored puffs on every limb.

James looked up at the full moon, "Sure is bright out tonight, ain't it."

Ellie wanted to talk to her dad, yet didn't know where to begin. "Daddy what's wrong?"

"Now, Ellie, there are things 'tween me and your ma—I mean your mother—that I can't tell you. We've got private things."

Ellie wasn't content with the answer, "But, Daddy, …"

James was firm, "Ellie, no more on that topic. I been wantin' to talk with both of you 'bout something else though." He sat on the front porch steps and patted the wood on each side of him as an invitation. "Now that you're both full grown, I want to talk about dreams. You know, makin' your life as full as possible.

"O'r the years, I tried ta show you girls how to follow your dreams. Life is short. Ya need to fill it with adventures of your heart. Ginny here loves to read, stand on her hands, do cartwheels, and dance. But I wonder," James hesitated and turned to his oldest, "don't you yearn for some kind of adventure that ya don't have?"

Ellie puzzled, "What kind of adventure?"

He went on, "I've been stubborn and lucky. Most my life I followed my dreams and had many adventures. I was just wonderin' do ya have dreams?"

Ginny sat down next to her dad and picked a daffodil from the edge of the house. She put it in a buttonhole on her jacket and smiled.

"Come on, Ginny. What's your dream?"

"Oh, Daddy, dreams are dreams. They can't come true if you tell someone."

"Hogwash! You know my dream to invent something that's useful. I KNOW it will happen someday even though I told ya."

Ellie looked at her dad, "I bet playing Irish music was a dream of yours. You made that happen."

"Right, Ellie. What's your dream?"

Ellie put her arm around her dad's waist and looped her thumb in his belt, "I want to write for a newspaper."

"Goodness, gracious! Ellie, you're kidding. Aren't you?" Ginny asked.

Ellie jut out her lower jaw and smiled, "Nope. That's what I'm going to do."

James said, "See Ginny. Tell us your dream. What adventure would make you happy?" He crossed his arms across his chest and waited.

Ginny relented, "Okay, just don't laugh."

"We won't."

Ginny sighed, “Oh, it’s so hard to say. You’re going to think I’m crazy. But I’ll just say it. I want to swim across the Mississippi River.”

Stunned, they looked at each other while the warm breeze rustled the leaves above their heads.

And she added, “Oh, and I want to play the fiddle like you, Daddy.”

James turned and wrapped his arms around his oldest. Ginny nestled into his shoulder. “Ginny, my Ginny. I never knew. Well, I know you’re a strong swimmer, but … to swim the Mississippi.” He squeezed her and then pushed her an arms length away. Over his bent knees, he leaned his face to hers and said, “Let’s do it!”

“Oh, Daddy, how?”

“We’ll train. My goodness, what a dream! You top me.”

Ginny seemed puzzled, “What about Ellie’s dream?”

“Remember our talk years ago? Ellie knows she can do her dream. You can do yours, but don’t know it. So, we need to work on yours; it’s a mighty big dream. Besides, I can’t help Ellie with writtin’ or saying things right. We all know that!”

They laughed.

Ginny asked, “What about playing the fiddle?”

“Oh, that’s easy, Ginny. You’ll git to learn that. I’ll ask Wally to start some lessons.”

Leaning her elbows against the upper step, Ellie commented, “Daddy, don’t you have other dreams? You know, one I don’t know about. One that’s deep in your heart and a secret?”

“Yep, I do.” He wrapped his arms across their shoulders, Ellie on his left and Ginny on his right.

“Well, tell us!”

He chuckled, “I want to own an automobile.”

Chapter 5

May-July 1910
Swimming the Mississippi

"Stand up straight, Ellie," Bertha chided. "This is the last fittin' for your birthday outfit. Ellie's Storm is coming up soon. You look lovely." Bertha turned Ellie around and fingered the buttons down the back of the straight tailored skirt, saying:

Rich Man
Poor Man
Beggar Man
Thief,

Doctor
Lawyer
Indian Chief.

"Oh, there's one more button, so I must start over with 'Rich Man' and you'll marry a rich man, it seems."

"Mama, you've been saying that silly rhyme for years. I'm not a little girl anymore. I know you made this dress and planned the buttons. As always."

Indignantly Bertha huffed, "I only want the best for my girls. You should want the best for yourself. Set your sights on a rich man. Lord knows I made a mistake. No sense in you making the same mistake."

Ellie complained, "Don't call Daddy a mistake."

"What did you say, young lady?"

"Nothing, Mama. I'll go change out of this new dress, and then I'm going to study at Franny's house."

Bertha reeled around and blurted, "Not now you're not! You and your sister have your lessons over at Lizzie O'Toole's house in … oh my, fifteen minutes. Where in tarnation is your sister? "

The back door opened with James and Ginny coming back from a swimming session. Bertha appeared livid, “Ginny, your hair’s all wet. Were you swimmin’ agin?” Not waiting for the obvious to be answered, Bertha continued her berating, “Git into your good skirt and blouse. You’re due over at Lizzie’s house for your lessons on manners.”

“I didn’t forget, Mama, I’ll get there on time.”

“Well, did you remember that your goin’ over to Mrs. Van Welton’s with me after supper? This is the last fittin’ for the bridesmaids’ dresses. I need you to help.”

“I know, Mama.” She turned to go into her bedroom, “Ellie, wait for me.” Ginny went on talking as they closed the door, “Oh, I like your birthday dress. Remember last year when Mama made us skirts so tight we could hardly walk? Didn’t they call them Hobble Skirts?”

Ellie slipped out of her new dress, “Yeah, Mommy has silly ideas sometimes. The Hobble skirt was one bad idea and these lessons from Mrs. O’Toole on how to act like proper young ladies is another. Every week she tells us how she worked for a well-to-do family of St. Louis, so she knows how to set a table properly and,” Ellie changed her voice to imitate, “which fork or spoon to use for salads or soups or a dessert.”

Ginny giggled, “How could we have gotten through life if she hadn’t taught us where to place our legs when we sit or which are acceptable topics for young ladies to discuss.”

Ellie slipped her skirt over her head, “Well, I’d rather go for the lessons than listen to them argue again. You weren’t here when Daddy told Mommy that he wanted her to teach us to cook and sew. She not only refused but also said awful things.” Ellie didn’t want to repeat it aloud, but she remembered Bertha saying that if she taught them to keep house and cook, they would just fall into a dismal life like hers.

Ginny put her hand on the bedroom door, but whispered before opening it, “At least Franny likes the lessons on good manners. She wants to marry a rich man.”

As they left their house, they saw Franny running up the street.

Franny was out of breath, “Sorry I’m late. I had to finish my piano lesson.”

Hurrying down the sidewalk, Ginny blurted, “We’ve got to remember not to clank our spoons on the soup bowl or Mrs. O’Toole will be mad again. I don't want to spend time doing things over and over. So, remember to push the spoon away from you when you eat soup or we'll have to eat spoonfuls of soup over and over again. Ugh!"

Franny laughed, "Soup! Wish there had been soup in our bowls. I ate so much water my stomach sloshed the whole walk home last week."

Ellie was curious, "Ginny, you've been going to fittings at Mrs. Van Welton's with Mama for a while. Do you hate it?"

"Not really." Ginny seemed reflective. No one said anything for a few steps.

Ellie noticed and guessed, "You like it, don't you."

"Well," Ginny hesitated, "it is interesting."

"What do you do over there? Just help Mama?

"Oh, no. Mrs. Van Welton always suggests that I go with her daughter and the bridesmaids. Mama never asks me to help her when I'm there. While we wait for Mama to call someone for a fitting, we have a refreshment or walk in the garden … or something."

Ellie sensed there was more, "Is her daughter nice to you?"

"She … well, she's okay."

"I bet she or one of the other girls is uppity with you. Why wouldn't they be?"

The three arrived at Lizzie O'Toole's and Ellie stopped with her hands on her hips, waiting for an answer.

Ginny got a twinkle in her eye, "Maybe because I walk in the garden with the son of Mrs. Van Welton. He's twenty-years-old and calls me Virginia. His name is Benjamin." She giggled and ran up the steps, leaving Ellie and Franny completely surprised.

***

Ellie was as excited as her father to make Ginny's dreams come true. They packed the summer with endeavors to help Ginny—violin lessons in Wally's shop and frequent swimming in the many rivers around St. Louis. For safety, most of the time James chose the clearer waters of the Missouri River or the Meramec to practice.

Though people swam in the muddy Mississippi, usually they only immersed themselves close to the shore for relief from the summer heat. It was a dangerous place. Along with steamboats, tugs and all sorts of watercraft, debris was a danger. Trees and pieces of boards could be seen drifting down the river all the time. It was not uncommon for farm animals to bob past after a heavy rainstorm. Who knew what lurked beneath the murky and dirty surface, hiding its terrors from view. James also told the girls that the filth of the Mississippi could cause illness.

"But today we came down to the Mississippi River to learn about how it flows. Ginny you need to look it over and pick a place to start your swim across."

After they had been watching the river for a while, Ginny chose the very place on the river, below the Eads Bridge, where Ellie's tornado had touched down fourteen years ago. Her choice was inevitable. This swim was an impending event and not to be a completely happy one.

Ellie shouted, "Hey, what's that?" A large piece of furniture rushed by.

"It looks like a wooden chifforobe. How in tarnation did someone loose that in the river?"

Though James knew she wanted this place, he made a try to change her mind, "I sure wish you'd reconsider. Ginny, you could make your dream come true in another place."

Ginny shook her head and pointed, "Look over there at the eddy by that pillar that holds up the bridge."

"Well," he said, "we ain't gonna let you near those bridge pillars. You'll swim downstream from the bridge and I'm plannin' to keep the rowboat 'tween you and any stuff floatin' down the river. It'll have to hit me and the boat first."

"Do you think I'm getting' enough practice for currents and undertows by swimming in the other rivers?"

"Yep, I do, but, you're right, those are our biggest worries."

They all stood and looked at the power of the water. They saw a place about one hundred feet away where the water was pulled down. Now James pointed, "There's something under the water over there. See how it pulls the flow down. You ain't gonna be able to see that kind of stuff cuz your eyes'll be at water level. We gotta work out some signals so you know what I see from the boat."

Again they stood silent for a while.

James mentioned, "Oh, I explained our plan to my boss Mr. Gardner cuz I figured we could use his help."

"How, Daddy?"

"I asked him if he would come with his Studebaker Runabout. That's his electric buggy. You know, just in case we need to git to the hospital in a hurry. It's only a two-seater, but there's plenty of room in the back."

Between the father and daughters, more silence followed. Of course there really was no silence. The river had a continuous roar, warning them of its supremacy.

Ellie asked, "Did Mr. Gardner agree to come?"

James nodded. Then he asked Ginny the question that bothered him many nights before he went to sleep, "Do you want to change your mind?"

Ginny turned to him and smiled, "No, Daddy." Her eyes sparkled with admiration of her father. "Just listening to how you think of all possibilities gives me confidence. I just need to swim. I know you'll make it work. I'll swim faster and stronger than I ever have."

James frowned in concentration.

Ellie gave a little shiver.

He finally made a comment. "I wouldn't let you do this if I didn't believe you to be as good a swimmer as I think. You're as strong as me! No, stronger! And you're quick and agile."

Ginny stood a little taller and took a deep breath never looking away from the water.

James had other advice, "It may be summer, but the water's real cold. So, I figured we'd put oil all over you to make you slippery in the water and to help keep you warm. You gonna look a mess."

Still Ginny gazed at her adversary, "I don't care. Just don't tell Mama." The person who always accidentally told everything was going to finally keep a secret.

When there was only a month before the real swim, James put the rowboat into the back of the wagon for every practice. They needed to work together on the water. It was hard.

One day, while Ellie sat next to her dad in the rowboat, she stood and screamed, "Look out!"

Ginny looked up just in time to see a log coming at her. She dove and surfaced on the other side of it.

James shook his head, "I was lookin' the other way. I just can't control things enough. I need another man in the boat wit' me."

Ginny grabbed the side of the boat, "Maybe Ellie?"

"Nah, I need a man. Ellie's strong but ain't as strong as you in the shoulders and chest. I'm gonna ask Wally because, if I jump in to help ya, I need a man at the oars. Yeah, I shoulda thought of this. Ain't too late though. Just need to git Wally to come practice wit us."

On the ride home, James brought up a big problem, "Ginny, I went to find the schedules of when the boats come and go, you know, the big steamboats … I learned that there's a law against swimmin' in their way. An you know they can't move fast if you do git in their way, don't ya?"

***

The girls noticed that their mother felt ill most of the time and, if it was possible, was crabbier than usual. But what worried them the most was she was eating too much and getting really fat. They knew they could not say anything to her about her weight.

Bertha stated, "All of you clear the table while I finish dustin' the floors. I was so tired yesterday, I had to stop before I was done." She went to the back porch and returned with the long-handled floor duster and started passing it over the hardwood floors around the rug in the dining room. Next she went to the girls' bedroom.

"What!" Bertha screamed. Out she stormed to the dining room with the fiddle in her fists, "What's this doin' under your bed? It ain't enough that I have to put up with James playin' his crazy music, now one of you too?"

Ginny dropped her head, "I'm sorry, Mama. It's me."

Bertha raised her arm with the fiddle intending to ram it into the back of a dining room chair. Quickly James stepped over and snatched it away with his long arms, "No you don't Bertha. That ain't right."

"What'd you know about right? I'm tryin' to make these girls into ladies so that some prosperous gentleman will marry 'em and you're makin' them into swimmers and commonplace women who dilly-dally in saloons. I ..."

"There're fine folks down at the tavern. Good wholesome people of the earth. Don't call them names," James said with furrowed brows. "Let's not argue in front of the girls."

Bertha huffed into their bedroom and flopped on the bed. "I feel bad,' she groaned.

"Girls, why don't ya go out for awhile? I want to be wit your ma ... mother."

As Ellie closed the front door, she heard her father saying, "Well, ya ain't a spring chicken any more. It's probably normal for your age. Ya need ta take it easy and have the girls help more with the cooking and cleaning."

Ellie shook her head, knowing he wasn't going to trick her mother into making her girls into housewives.

***

One Saturday morning, James decided that it was the day to do a practice swim in the Mississippi River near the Eads Bridge. They got out the horse and wagon and started over to Wally's shop where the boats were stowed. Bertha huffed, but thought it was just the usual swim they often took on a hot day.

As they started loading, Ellie walked up to James and asked, "Daddy, I want to swim a little with Ginny. You know, just to see how it is. I don't want to swim across. Just swim out a little ways. Can I?"

"Let me think on that."

Wally turned to James, "Let's put both boats in. If we need 'em, we'll have 'em." So, they lifted two rowboats into the wagon bed.

James turned to Franny, "Now don't you get any ideas about swimmin' cuz it would be too dangerous to keep track of all three of ya."

"Oh, no sir. But ..." she stammered, "can I go in one of the boats with you?"

"We'll see."

They headed down Manchester Avenue until it ended; they turned left onto Vandeventer. At Olive Street, they took a right heading straight for the Mississippi and Eads Bridge.

James shared with them, "I remember when they built Eads Bridge. T'was back before you were born. Oh, somewhere around 1874. Took 'em about ten years to build, I do think. You know, t'was the longest bridge in the world and the most fancy. Wally, am I right? I do think it's ov'r a mile long."

"James, glory be, it's o'r six thousand feet long."

On Olive Street they rode for a couple dozen blocks on down to the riverfront. The men continued to talk about Eads Bridge, taking care not to mention the fact that men died years ago during the construction.

When they got close to the water below the bridge, there sat Mr. Russell Gardner in his Studebaker Runabout. James was astounded, "Why Mr. Gardner, we just came to practice a bit. I didn't think you'd come to see us."

"Hello James, I want you to meet a reporter from *The Star* newspaper. I mentioned the swim to a friend of mine at the paper, and he decided that Timothy should come and see if a story might be written about this endeavor."

Pumping Timothy's hand, James smiled, "Mighty pleased to meet ya. Why, that's right nice of you Mr. Gardner, but this is just a practice to see what we's up against."

Timothy was a short, plump young man with ruddy cheeks and a camera resting on his shoulder—tripod and all. "You let me decide if there's a public interest story here, Mr. James. I won't be in your way. You just do what you have to do."

"Well, that's what I plan to do." James motioned toward the boats, "If you excuse me, Mr. Gardner and Timothy, I'm needin' to git busy."

James and Wally pulled the boats out of the wagon and set them in the water as the two girls started rubbing dirty oil on their legs and arms.

"Don't forget your faces, girls. Well, your necks and cheeks."

Ellie and Ginny wore knitted woolen suits with sleeves to their elbows and leggings to their knees—all in one piece and dark blue. They had put the swimming suits on at home under their clothes.

Quickly they undressed and slipped white rubber caps over their heads. With their fingertips they worked at cramming all their hair into the caps.

Franny helped apply the oil to legs, "Yuck, how you ever going to get this off?"

"Daddy works with grease and oil all day. He'll show us how to."

Wally threw blankets into the boats, ropes and oars, "We're ready to go."

It had been decided that Wally and Franny would be in one boat next to Ellie. James would devote all his attention on Ginny, "Now, Ellie, don't go far out. And stay away from the footing of the bridge. Hear me?"

"I know, Daddy. I've listened for a long time whenever you talked to Ginny. I know what I should and shouldn't do." Something caught Ellie's eye. She leaned over and picked up a smooth, flat rock. "Daddy, put this rock in your pocket for me; I want to save it." After he dropped the rock into his pocket, Ellie teased him with her oiled-up arms open wide, "Want to give me a hug before we start?"

"Ellie, be serious! You gotta be careful. Wally, don't let Ellie go far into that river. I gotta git. Ginny looks eager to start."

Ginny was standing in the water already and turned her back to the reporter who had placed the camera on the tripod. She pulled her cap down snuggly, fastened the strap, and pushed some loose hairs into it.

James told Wally, "Things look good. River's pretty calm, there's not much wind, and no boats movin' out here."

As James stepped into his boat, Ginny glanced at her dad and dove into the water.

Ellie stood a minute watching her sister and said to Franny. "She's like a torpedo and has such a smooth stroke. I can hardly see her mouth open to come up for air."

Ellie could see her father needed to get rowing; Ginny was getting away from him.

Wally watched, too. "He better not take his eyes off Ginny. Look how he puts his whole back into each pull of the oars."

Franny got into the boat and Wally pushed off with Ellie down river from him. Suddenly Wally remembered, "I got to git to the other side of Ellie and block any debris." He had to stop looking at Ellie as he started maneuvering the boat around.

The two boats weren't too far apart. Wally faced James while he turned the boat. He told Franny, "Ginny is really goin' maybe she's thirty feet from the shore."

Franny looked into the distance to see Ginny and James.

When Wally turned back around, he shouted, "Where in tarnation is Ellie?"

"She was right there!" Franny pointed with fearful eyes.

Wally stood in his boat to try to see Ellie.

At that moment, James glanced back and saw Wally standing.

Franny waved her arms hysterically at James and screamed, "Ellie's gone!"

James looked to Ginny. She had a clear path ahead, so he turned his boat and started moving toward Wally.

James hollered, "No, Wally, no! Don't you jump in! Sit down!" The distance between them lessened, "Let's change places. Git your boat over by Ginny … I gots me swim suit on and shoes off." James could hardly talk and row at the same time.

But, before he could hear all the words, Wally understood. They changed places. Wally started rowing toward Ginny, who was approaching the middle of the Mississippi.

The two rowboats passed each other and James said with gasping breath, "Git up with Ginny. I'll go for Ellie."

Suddenly, Franny jumped out of Wally's boat into the water.

"What in tarnation! Hells fire, Franny, what ya doin'?" James slipped one oar out in Franny's direction, and she grabbed it. He pulled her in. "Wally, don't look here. Git out to Ginny!" James turned around trying to look for Ellie as he pulled Franny into the boat and started rowing. "Where'd she go down, Franny?"

Pointing and shivering, Franny screamed, "No, no! More to the left. See that eddy over there? Must be something down there that got Ellie."

"Damn it, Franny, git in the middle and sit still," James yelled as he passed her the oars. The river was roaring. Waves lapped at the boat as James tore off his sweater and dived over the side. Franny grabbed tight to the oars, trying to hold it steady. James came up for air and went down again.

It's the muddy Mississippi. James couldn't see anything. But he came up again and went down again. Just then Franny saw her friend's hair, floating up and fanning out at the water's surface. Ellie was right there by the boat!

Though James was underwater, frantically she screamed, "Mr. James, here! Ellie must have pulled off her rubber cap." With haste, Franny slipped the oars into the bottom of the boat and leaned over to grab the hair. She pulled and pulled. Ellie's head came out, gasping for air. The boat bobbed and something pulled at Ellie. Down she went.

Just then James was up and saw. He went toward the boat and dived.

Franny slipped her weight down into the bottom of the boat and took her other hand over the side into Ellie's hair. With all her strength she pulled, Ellie's face came so close to the surface, but didn't break it. Franny saw the wide terrified eyes recede back into the depths of Mississippi, disappearing into a world of unknown.

"Ellie!" Franny screamed, "Come back up!"

The river was helping Franny with the pulling since the boat was being sucked downstream by the flow. Only Franny's grasp to Ellie's hair kept the rowboat from drifting away. Then Franny noticed, with some kind of ebb and flow of the river, a rhythm existed. Ellie's face broke the surface again; she managed a gulp of air, only to plunge down and disappear as fast as she had appeared.

Like some determined mother that envelopes those who enter her arms, this great river was rocking Ellie to and fro, waiting patiently for the child to fall into the depths of eternal sleep.

Meanwhile, Wally talked to himself, "I'm goin' to have a heart attack. Ginny is faster than a boat." His heart pounded in his ears like it would burst from his chest as he rowed with all his might. Of course, he was turned facing the disaster and could see James coming up and going down, over and over. "Dear God in Heaven, help him git Ellie. Please, dear God." He finally was close to Ginny. Talking aloud released fears of what he watched in the distance, "Practice! This ain't no practice. I'm gittin' further and further. Ginny is closin' in on the east side of the river."

From the shore, Mr. Gardner was trying to decide what to do. He turned to the reporter, "Should I cross the bridge to be there when Ginny reaches the other side? Or will James need me here?"

The reporter never answered. He was taking photographs as fast as he could, changing plates. Ellie was close enough to the shore for some good shots. Well, he hadn't seen Ellie yet, but he thought he got a good one of James coming up for air and Franny holding on to something. Then, Lady Luck came his way! Just as he pressed, Franny pulled Ellie out of the water again for another gulp of air—click! Timothy was so excited. He hoped it was what he thought. He was nearly jumping up and down with joy as he put in another plate.

Ellie went down as fast as she had risen. And that pull on Ellie's hair nearly tipped the boat over. In the newspaper tomorrow, the James family saw Ellie gasping and Franny grasping the tipping boat. The photograph would win a prize.

James was struggling with the opposite of joy. Under the water, he could feel that Ellie's suit was twisted around the limbs of a sunken tree. *A huge tree with lots of branches going every which way.* He couldn't get her lose. He dived again and again. He thought he saw blood.

The next time he came up Franny screamed, "STOP!"

He heard, and turned to Franny with a puzzled look.

She screamed above the water's din, "Pull off her suit! Pull it off!" Franny let go of Ellie with one hand to show him. "Here! Pull it down." She put her hand at her neckline and whipped it down, ripping her blouse off her shoulder. Quickly, she returned the second hand into the hair again and strained to pull Ellie for another breath.

James had never taken a swimsuit off a woman. He hadn't known where to start until Franny showed him. *Women wear the darnest things. How do they git into these suits?* This time, he eased himself underwater, feet first and down only far enough to get a good hold on the neckline of Ellie's suit.

Franny kept talking, not knowing if James could hear or not, "the buttons will pop off if you yank hard enough at the neck." Now she started blubbering with tears, "Please, oh please save her." Suddenly her face changed, "I felt it! I could feel the pop of a button through my fingers! At that same instant, Franny pulled again with all her might.

Ellie flew up like a cork from a champagne bottle.

Just as fast, James' head came out. Grabbing his daughter's legs, he wiggled Ellie's feet from her suit. With one of his enormous hands grasping both her feet, he pushed her to the side of the boat. Franny wrapped her arms around Ellie's armpits and held on while James swam to the other side; his stringy muscles bulged from his arms and neck as he pulled himself into the boat. It tipped and took some water, but he was in.

Ellie's back bled from a deep gash about ten inches long. Blood rolled down into the Mississippi as Franny clutched her friend. James reached for the blanket, furled it in the air and around Ellie's naked body before raising her into the boat.

Franny ripped off a hunk of her already destroyed blouse and reached under the blanket to press the soft cotton against the wound. James turned Ellie over to see if she was breathing. Wet strands of hair lay across her ashen face.

"Row, Mr. James. She needs a doctor. We can't do nothing else here."

He inserted the oars and leaned into them, "Is she breathin', Franny? Is she breathin'?" he pleaded with his mouth distorted in anguish.

"I can't tell, Mr. James. Just row! We're almost to the shore."

Mr. Gardner had to nearly topple the camera to make Timothy understand that he was needed at the water's edge when the rowboat touched land, "You and I need to lift Ellie into the car while James is getting out of the boat. Every second is important if that girl isn't breathing. I pulled the car closer and the motor's on." He yanked at the young man's arm, and they ran to the boat as it touched land.

To the relief of all, Ellie coughed as she was lifted in the blanket into the Studebaker. James got in back with Ellie, and Franny jumped in the front. Mr. Gardner leaned out the window and commanded, "Timothy, get on their wagon and go get Wally and Ginny on the other side of the river." His voice trailed off as they sped away in the silent electric car, "Take your camera and get a picture of Ginny coming out of the river."

Timothy did get that photograph.

They were at the hospital more than an hour. When the doctors let James come to his daughter, the first thing Ellie asked was, "Did Ginny swim all the way across?"

James smiled and nodded.

Ellie got fifty-two stitches. In addition, she got a tetanus shot, had her stomach pumped, and was thoroughly humiliated by having to wear a hospital gown. At least the nurses scrubbed her clean of all that oil.

Ginny, Wally and Timothy arrived at the hospital when the final stitch was being tied off. They had stayed behind to load the boats and equipment into the wagon. When the nurses saw Ginny, they decided to clean her as well.

"Oh, can I get a photograph of all of you?" Timothy beamed.

Franny, standing in her camisole without a blouse, objected, "I'll break your camera if you embarrass us. We look horrible and don't need a photograph."

Mr. Gardner took Ellie, Ginny and Franny home squeezed into the little automobile. Whenever possible James and Mr. Gardner traveled side by side; they were laughing and joking between the wagon and the electric vehicle. Night had fallen by the time they arrived at the James' house. James noticed right away that there were no lamps lit in the house.

James handed the reins to Wally and jumped down. As the girls got out of the Runabout, Wally said his goodbyes and left with the horse and wagon. "Just come to me shop tomorrow ta help git the boats out and your wagon back."

James hurried into the house.

The horrors of the day were not over.

Coming into the kitchen through the back door, Ellie screamed. Ginny dropped to the floor beside her mother. James gasped at the sight. Bertha was crumpled in a heap on the kitchen floor in a large pool of blood. She was motionless and her face looked gray.

James bent over his wife, "Ginny, run and stop Mr. Gardner from drivin' away! Ellie, don't do nothin'. You'll break your stitches!"

Carefully Ellie slipped to the floor next to her mother, "Mama, Mama, can you hear me?" Puzzled as to what was wrong with her unresponsive mother, Ellie looked to her father, but he ignored her.

James stood up and rushed to get a blanket as he heard Mr. Gardner approaching with Ginny. He spread it on the floor next to Bertha.

"Let's hurry! Ginny, take her feet and help me git her on the blanket. Careful now! Do it slow." They wrapped Bertha and James carried her to the electric vehicle for the return to the hospital.

Bertha was saved. The baby was lost.

***

At work, James kept saying to people all the following week. "Bertha done looked dead, but that electric Studebaker Runabout saved Bertha's life by gittin' her to the hospital lickety-split."

He couldn't stop thanking Mr. Gardner for being there with his little electric buggy. And, in James' mind, this just proved how important it was to have an automobile. James had gotten wind that Gardner was working on some kind of deal to build automobiles with another company called Chevrolet. This gave James hope that someday he could build his own.

Luckily, while Bertha recovered in the hospital, she never saw his excitement. James was happy about Ginny's swim, about saving Ellie and Bertha, and he was excited about the role the automobile had played.

He knew Bertha had not wanted another child, so it made no sense to him that she was depressed. The doctors said it was natural and would pass with time. For James, the whole day from the Mississippi River to the second trip to the hospital had emphasized the value of automobiles. While Bertha's pain would subside with time, James' desire to learn about automobiles would grow.

Finally Ellie understood what had been going on with their parents. It seemed unbelievable to her that anyone as old as her mother could have been pregnant. She had so many questions and no one to ask. And she had feelings cascading through her that she couldn't explain.

Sitting on the couch with her sister, Ellie complained, "Daddy won't talk about anything. I asked him when was the baby supposed to be born, and he said there's no reason to talk about things that aren't going to happen."

Ginny wondered, "Do you think they had a name picked out?"

Ellie didn't answer. They were just shooting the breeze, but Ellie wondered about many things she didn't even want to say. Her mind was full of questions. She knew where babies came from because, years ago, their dad explained why their chicken eggs didn't ever grow chicks. Right now, her mind was trying to grasp the mental image of her father mating with her mother. She just couldn't imagine that.

The situation got more complicated. While in the hospital, Bertha saw a newspaper account of Ginny's swim across the Mississippi—three pictures—Ginny going in the river, Ginny coming out on the other side, and Ellie being pulled by her hair as she gasped for life's air. Bertha was livid. She couldn't rant at the hospital, so she suppressed all her accusations and planned to make some changes.

As soon as she was well enough to get out of bed to work around the house, she started her plan. It took a whole afternoon of working and packing. Her anger grew and grew as the afternoon progressed. *How dare he let Ginny embarrass me with my clients. Surely they've all seen the newspapers. Just when Mrs. Van Welton's son was likin' Ginny too. James, you're ruinin' Ginny's chance for a good life.*

When James and the girls came home for supper, Bertha was back in bed.

They went to the bedroom to greet her.

James opened the chifforobe to hang his jacket. "Where's my clothes?" He turned and noticed that the glass dish he had won at the World's Fair and kept on the dresser to hold his pocket watch and pipe was gone. He looked at the shelf where his hats had been stored. It was empty. "What's goin' on here?"

"You can see. I knows you know. And nothin' gonna change my mind," she gushed with satisfaction.

James emphasized, "This here's my bed and bedroom."

"Not no more. You can sleep where you wants."

James put his hands on his hips, "You're my wife. I sleep wit you!"

"Not, no more," was said with a smug look.

"I'm the man of this house and you …"

Bertha couldn't hold back. It didn't matter that her innocent girls were standing at the foot of her bed, looking aghast. With hatred dripping from her voice, she blurted accusations the girls wouldn't understand until older, "I'm sick and tired of your stuff runnin' down my legs every mornin' and sometimes into the afternoon. I work hard and you always pushin' your parts on me so's I can't sleep. I ne'er liked it and now I ain't gonna put up with it, no more. You sleep where you please, but not here," she pushed a fist into his side of the bed.

"Bertha, you always hell bent on …"

But she wasn't finished, "You girls always think I's the villain. I hope you ne'er have to go through what I just did at the hospital. It was harder than havin' either of you. He don't understand and ne'er will. Men don't know what we ladies have to go through in our lives. Well, I don't need him or want him. That's for sure."

For the first time in her life, Ellie saw embarrassment in her father's face.

He flung his jacket over his shoulder and stormed out the front door.

In the dead of night James returned. He quietly picked through his few things out on the back porch where Bertha had thrown them. He stuffed traveling bags until he could carry no more. He no longer had anger, only regret for his girls. *But they're 'bout grown. I done all I can for 'em. I's got to think of myself now.*

James crept into the girls' room and knelt by their bed. Not wanting to touch them and wake them, he just looked and whispered, "Don't think of me as gone … I's in your bones and heart. Keep me there. I'll be back some day. And I have a dream that I never tol' you. I dream of having a wife that loves me for me."

Then he placed a note on their dresser that said the same.

"Daddy's gone! He's gone!" Ginny screamed in a frenzy with her hands pushing her hair taut as she rushed from room to room in search of any clue to contradict the excruciating knowledge that her father had left. Bertha emerged from her bedroom in nightclothes. With fists, Ginny beat against her mother's shoulders, "You did this! You made him leave!"

Ellie rushed to Ginny and, making a bear hug, restrained her sister. Together, they slumped to the dark oak floor on the edge of the rug fringes. Ginny dropped her head into her hands to weep. Bending over, Ellie kept one arm around her sister while fingering the fringed threads of the rug, twisting and pulling at the woolen strands. Minutes passed. Silent streams meandered down their faces. Finally Ellie released her grasp, and Ginny sat up to gaze into Ellie's eyes.

That day they lost a teacher, a coach, a confidant, and a friend. Their father was gone.

Part 2

Ellie's Single Life
1922-1927

She that was ever fair and never proud,
Had tongue at will and yet was never loud.

William Shakespeare, 1564-1616
Othello

Chapter 6

1912-1922
Ellie's Newspaper Job

In 1912 the Titanic sank; in 1914 the Panama Canal was finished and The War to End All Wars began; one of the highlights of 1917 was the appearance of Keds sneakers with rubber soles; in 1918 the Great Influenza, by far the most destructive pandemic in history, killed some 50 million to 100 million people worldwide in just 18 months.

But none of these events swept into the James' home with the same impact as their personal disaster—James A. James was gone and no one knew exactly where.

Ginny took to wearing James' trousers after he had left. One pair of serge slacks had been overlooked in the chifforobe. Of course, Bertha objected to slacks on a woman, but she relented because Ginny said she needed them to ride the horses with Benjamin Van Welton. Bertha sewed them to fit. Actually Ginny wanted to wear them for deeper reasons; she touched the strong, twilled fabric and felt a connection with her father. She told Ellie that they comforted her, "It's like I can still touch Daddy."

The courtship with Benjamin did assuage Ginny's grief.

Ellie had something else to placate the loss of her father.

After Ginny married, Benjamin bought her proper riding pants with the bulge at the top of the thighs. Soon Ginny bought Ellie a pair and they went riding in Forest Park, with or without Benjamin.

Suddenly, after a couple of years, everything was without Benjamin. He divorced Ginny. Actually, he had it annulled in the Catholic Church.

The subject of her marriage was never broached in the James household again. Ellie knew Benjamin had left Ginny when they discovered she couldn't have children, but the medical problem of why she was barren was never explained to Ellie. The James family pretended the whole affair never happened.

And the years went by.

***

May 27, 1922

Ellie opened her eyes to a sunny morning and thought, *It's Ellie's Storm*! This birthday made her twenty-six years old. The house was still quiet as she dressed and went outside, rushing down Tamm Street like she used to do with her father. She was striking in appearance, dressed like a high society woman in fashions that Bertha sewed. Ellie passed St. James Parish, heading for Wally's shop. She passed trucks unloading produce for the grocery store. The barber was opening his doors for business with the new red and white pole outside the door; it started rotating just as Ellie passed.

The red on that pole looks like blood spiraling down. She grinned to herself. *Maybe it's to warn men that the barber might cut them while shaving.*

At that moment, the barber unlocked the door, getting ready for business. "Good Morning, Ellie," he said with a smile.

Ellie nodded with a blush on her cheeks and gracefully rushed on.

Turning her thoughts back to the reason for her journey to Wally's, *Daddy never forgets, but I always worry that it won't be there.*

She pushed the back gate open and, through an open window, she saw Wally's wife at the kitchen sink. They waved, "Hello, Mrs. Duggan." She couldn't stop this morning to chat. She needed to get to Wally. He was always in the shop early.

"Hi, Wally, is it here?"

Wally bent over and pulled an envelope out of a cubbyhole. "*Dia daoibh*—Good day to you, Ellie, and a very merry birthday. How could you question that James would forget Ellie's Storm?"

Ellie took the letter and put it to her chest. "Did he write to you?"

"Yes, he most certainly did. So, I can tell you that all is fine with 'im. And, before you asks like you always do, no, I can't tell you where he is. But he tol' me he got a patent on one of his inventions. An apparatus for transmitting electrical current, it was."

"Oh, Wally, hearing about my daddy's dream coming true is the best birthday present. Remember when he wrote that he got his first car. Does your wife know that he writes?"

"Oh, no! It's a secret between me and you. And like every year, let's renew the pact." Wally held out his little pinkie, and Ellie took it with her little finger. Waves of goose pimples rippled down her body. *We always do Daddy's way to promise to keep a secret.*

"Do you know this is letter number twelve from Daddy? I read them over and over when I'm alone. I'm so happy that Daddy found a woman to love him. Now if you will excuse me, I'm going over to Daddy's stool to read. Then we can talk about what he told me and what he told you."

One would have thought James was still tinkering in the shop; all his things were in his old corner. Wally couldn't bear to throw anything away. Years ago on the very night when James left Bertha and the girls, he slept in Wally's shop. In the morning, he had told Wally he was leaving, and Wally promised to be there for him. Afterwards, James went over to his job and told Mr. Gardner who wrote a fine letter of recommendation. Russell E. Gardner may have been James' boss, but he also was a good friend.

Only a few months later, the first letter came to Wally. James always sent the letters to Wally with another envelope inside for Ellie. That way, only Wally saw the return address. James was in California, but only Wally knew what city. There was only one reason that Wally was allowed to write to James. James wanted to know when Bertha died.

So, Ellie heard from her father on her birthdays. James knew, always knew, she could keep his secret. And he knew only too well that Ginny could not, though it broke his heart, but he couldn't write to both. Ellie finished her letter and beamed. Walking back to where Wally was working on making a small table, she said with pensive eyes, "Wally, my dad could go to jail for being a bigamist … right?"

"Glory be! You better believe it! You got to understand how important it is to ne'r breathe a word about your father. And maybe you should bring all those letters down to me shop. You know, it's safer."

"I will. That's a good idea. We should've done it years ago." Ellie was quiet a moment, "I guess we can't write to him because his wife doesn't know about us. Do you think?"

"I figured the same."

Again, Ellie stammered a bit and then asked, "Do you … you know, do you think I'll ever see him again?"

"Aye! He's too curious of a man to stay away forever," Wally lied. Wally really didn't know if James would ever return. Wally never told Ellie about James' instructions to write only if Bertha died. It seemed too cruel of a fact to tell a young woman. But seeing how Ellie was turning out, Wally thought he just might tell her someday.

Ellie was strong. Ellie was determined. Opinionated. Gregarious. Political. And could argue with the best of them. She was her father's daughter. She still frequented the saloon in Dogtown—it was the place where everyone went, though there was no liquor to drink. Ellie talked with the men about world affairs, politics, the war, whatever. She had joined the St. Louis Suffrage Association years ago. She kept scrapbooks with newspaper articles of interest, so she could reread items to clarify a memory or verify a fact.

Wally and she talked about their letters from James and, as always, James never divulged many facts about his life. Wally commented, "Well, it's only fair. He don't know what's goin' on in our lives either. He don't know I got two boys or that you belong to the Women's Suffrage Movement. He don't know nothin' 'bout us."

Ellie said, "I know. He said that he hoped I was writing for a newspaper like I always wanted to do. But he knows a woman can't." Shaking her head, "It isn't fair."

"That's so true; it ain't."

"But I'll do it. Someday. I just have to figure a way. Oh, by the way, Franny, Ginny and I graduate from Duncan Business School this coming Friday. Hope you and Mrs. Duggan will come to see us get diplomas. Ginny already has a really good job as a bookkeeper for three stores. She's making good money. Mama still talks about us getting married to rich men, of course. *Humph.* Can you believe it? She's like a broken record. And even after Ginny had that horrible marriage …" Ellie stopped. No one talked about it. It just slipped out. She and Wally were so at ease with each other; Ellie could tell Wally more than she told Franny. *Franny can be so scatter-brained at times—just interested in clothes, making up her pretty face, playing the piano, and looking for a man.*

Ellie shook her head and Wally figured she was worrying about Ginny, as usual. He asked, "How's Ginny?"

"Oh, Wally, all she does is work, work, work. She seems to like her job, but she never was the same after Daddy left and her marriage ended. Well, she still goes swimming. We've made some wonderful girlfriends from our class at the business school. There's about ten of us and we go swimming most weekends. Oh, and we started a bridge club where we play a rubber on the last Tuesday evening of each month. We go to a different house each time. Oh, does Ginny like to play bridge! She's good.

"When I tell you all this, it sounds like Ginny is happy and busy. But she's not. Mainly, she spends her time alone—crocheting. She loves to crochet. She spends hours and hours crocheting the most beautiful things like doilies and whole tablecloths for wedding gifts for friends or Mama's clients. Yes, she crochets hats and different things to sew into clothes Mama makes. You know, a collar or bodice. Lots of things."

Ellie had a job. She was working at the *St. Louis Post-Dispatch*. She was only a typist. Nevertheless, she figured it was a foot in the door. She told Wally, "Hey, it may be Ellie's Storm, but I can't be late for work."

"I guess even on Saturday you must work to get a newspaper out. What about Sunday?" he asked.

"Oh, we do most of the work for the Sunday paper today. It's a busy day. But because it's an evening paper, we're busiest in the mornings. I must go."

She hurried over to the trolley stop, bought a *Globe-Democrat* newspaper from a boy in the street, and headed downtown, going toward the Mississippi River. She would have time to read most of the competition's newspaper before she got to work.

Ellie read an article about the League of Women Voters. They had been around in the east for a couple of years. They weren't accomplishing too much, but Ellie was learning about the political machinery of the nation. In St. Louis the Women's Suffrage Association had started back in 1868.

Ellie huffed to herself. *The most they accomplished was in 1885 when they got "obey" deleted from the marriage ceremonies. Well, at least that was something. But then they didn't do anything for years until the Equal Suffrage League started up in 1910.* Ellie sighed, she had joined ESL when she was fifteen—after her father had left.

The pressroom was bustling as usual on this cool day in May. After removing her hat and jacket, Ellie slipped into her chair behind a typewriter. There were several handwritten sheets from reporters that she needed to edit and type. Her fingers started to fly over the keys.

From time to time she would stand up and walk to a reporter's desk, "Morning Jimmy, hey, why don't I add a little about the President's meeting yesterday. I figured just one sentence that said …" and she usually was thanked for her suggestions. She had started working at the *Post-Dispatch* about two years ago while she went to business school classes in the evenings. Next week on Friday, she'd have her diploma. It meant a raise, nothing else; not that she wasn't happy about the additional money. She was savvy enough to know that, if she wanted to break into a man's job, she needed more than a piece of paper called a diploma. As she returned to her desk, she thought, *I just haven't stumbled on what it is I do need.* But, little by little, she was getting her words into the newspaper through the men reporters. Indirectly they were giving her experience while they benefited from her ideas and words.

However, this day on her lunch break, she would find just what she needed to accomplish her dream.

Everyone in the pressroom was working on both the Saturday and Sunday editions. The Saturday had to be done by noon in order to go to press and be on the streets before the end of the workday when people headed home.

Ellie was glad it was a cooler day. In June, July and August, the pressroom was like an oven. *It's harder on the men in their shirt and ties. Thank heavens, women's clothes keep getting shorter, looser and cooler.* Ellie's active mind worked in many directions as her fingers flew over the keys. She was typing a small article about a parade and started remembering. *Why, only six years ago, in 1916, some women still wore those corsets! When the Democratic National Convention was here in St. Louis, we women walked to demonstrate for the right to vote. I remember seeing several women in corsets as I marched. We all were in long white skirts that came to our shoe tops or ankles.*

The Women's Suffrage March of 1916 was an elegant spectacle; seven thousand women—all dressed in white with yellow sashes and parasols—marched in complete silence down the streets of St. Louis in front of the Democratic Convention. They formed a Golden Lane, a newspaper poet wrote:

Silence! My, but it did talk
Marching down the Golden Lane.
Fast the delegates did walk
Marching down the Golden Lane.
But they couldn't get away
From the Women's Vote Display, and
They'll all recall for many a day
Marching down the Golden Lane.

Missouri had worked slowly and methodically for women's suffrage, granting women presidential suffrage in the spring of 1919. Four months later the Congress of the United States passed the 19th Amendment—in the House, 304 to 89, and in the Senate, 56 to 25. In the next election, Ellie voted and learned the disappointment of not picking the winner; Warren G. Harding took office in March 1921.

Ellie jumped up from her seat, it was past lunchtime and she must finish this last article. She hurried over to a reporter's desk, "Harry, I really like your feature on Anheuser-Busch, but I think they started BEVO in 1916, not 1920." She turned to face other reporters, "Can anyone help verify this? We don't have much time to research this."

Ellie knew she was right. What she was doing with the reporters was a ploy to continue to get confidence built with them. She knew she was right because she had helped write an article for *The Missouri Women*, a magazine of the suffrage movement, back in 1917. She remembered how much she didn't like BEVO, the non-alcoholic drink that was supposed to "open the door to strength, health and a sound digestion."

I know I'm right cuz the magazine sent me over to Anheuser-Busch to hear what they were doing with prohibition coming on their heels.

Ha, they gave me a tour of the BEVO line. And on top of that, Anheuser-Busch wanted a full-page ad in the December issue as a result of my visit. And they even delivered a case of BEVO to my house.

Some of the reporters came together and a discussion started. "Well, Europe was going dry long before us. Yeah, about 1916, so Anheuser-Busch saw the writing on the wall. I think they came out with BEVO when Ellie says."

Ellie chimed in, "That makes sense. If they'd waited until prohibition started in 1920, they wouldn't have had anything to sell. They would've gone broke."

Someone else agreed, "My family has been using BEVO for more than a couple of years, so it had to be before 1920."

"Yeah, Anheuser-Busch knew Missouri was going dry long before 1920. I think almost all the counties voted for prohibition back in 1917. So, I think Ellie is right."

Ellie was hungry, "I need some food. Tell you what, let's use the date of 1916, and on my lunch hour I'll go to the library to check it out. Harry, you can blame me and say it was a typo, if I'm wrong."

He nodded and grinned, "Long as it's your job on the line, not mine."

Everyone laughed.

Ellie chuckled to herself as she waited for the elevator. Getting off the elevator and walking down the spacious hall decorated in an Egyptian motif, her heels echoed off the walls, as if she was in a gold filled tomb of a pyramid. She smiled to herself. *I just need to find the gold to complete my dream ... and not get buried alive in the process.*

She really wasn't planning to go to the library, but just in case someone was looking, she crossed 12th Street and started in the direction of the library. Reporters used the library frequently or sent Ellie over there because the newspaper didn't have any cross-referencing capabilities. At the library, volunteers in the St. Louis Historical Room went through every local newspaper—every day—and added newspaper dates onto the cards filed by subject.

As she was approaching the Jefferson Hotel on 12th and Locust, she remembered it was her birthday. *Thank goodness there are no tornados today.* She started daydreaming about the day she was born. Unknowingly, she was approaching the second encounter with one of the storm's touchdowns. Another place marked as a disaster for Ellie, just like the swim under the Ead's Bridge. But, this time, James wasn't here to save her, and she was unaware of the danger.

She went on thinking. *My dad had told me the story of that tornado so many times, and I even found a book at the library with photos and interviews of dozens of people. It was called "The Great Cyclone," published just months after the storm. What was the name of the man who put it all together? Come on, remember!*

Smack!

Ellie bumped into a heavyset man who had just stepped from a cab. She bounced off him and landed against a rack of papers before falling down on her back. Her linen hat fell to the sidewalk, her flared skirt caught on the metal rack and was lifted to mid-thigh as it tore, and the contents of her purse were strewn all around.

The man was thrown off balance and stumbling when two other men caught him by his arms just as it looked like he would tumble on top of Ellie. His felt fedora was rocking on the rim as he bent to pick it up.

Ellie was sure he looked up her skirt. She stretched out her hand, "You could help a lady up, I'm sure."

He slipped his hat into place and gave her a pull. Turning to his cronies, "Hey, youse guys help a lady get all her belongings back in her purse. Hi, I'm Al Brown. I'm from Chicago and staying here at the Jefferson."

Ellie knew this guy was lying. Working at a newspaper, she read about him, talked about him, and saw his picture all the time. He was Al Capone. But she smiled sweetly and replied, "Glad to make your acquaintance, Mr. Brown. I'm Ellie Jones." *Two can play this game.*

Capone's bodyguards were scrambling on the sidewalk, putting her coins, her powder compact, wallet, pack of gum, and other stuff back into her purse. She turned to take the purse and to make sure her identification was not seen, "Why thank you, gentlemen." She brushed off her skirt and replaced her hat that was handed to her. "That was quite a spill we took. Oh dear, I guess this skirt has seen its last days. I think I have a pin I can use to hold the tear closed. Did you gentlemen pick up a pin, you know, a safety pin? I guess I was rushing too fast to lunch."

"If you ain't got anyone special to join you for lunch, why don'tcha come on in to the hotel's restaurant and eat with me. It's the least I could do for the inconvenience I've caused ya. Maybe the hotel could sew up the skirt for ya."

Ellie decided she would accept his invitation, "Why ain't ya sweet." *Two can talk that way.* And she took his arm, letting the flap on the torn skirt expose the top of her leg and silk stockings. "Oh, don't worry about the skirt. When we're inside I'll look for that pin in my purse," she babbled.

It's not that Ellie wanted trouble, she couldn't fathom where she was going; she only figured she had bumped into the opportunity of her life. Audaciously, she nurtured this whim. *What a story I could write. My goodness, Al Capone!*

They walked to a table, of Capone's choosing, in the back of the restaurant. Ellie ordered a club sandwich and iced tea. Capone had a pot roast and coffee. They talked small talk about the weather and his family—his seven brothers and two sisters.

Ellie noticed him playing with a rabbit's foot hanging at his belt. He stroked it with both hands and flipped it back and forth between his fingers as he talked. He was talking about his little sister.

"Yeah, she's just ten and a sweetheart. A real nice kid called Mafalda. She always crawls all over me when I visit. You know what I mean?"

"That's nice that you have a little sister."

"Yeah, I had another sister who died as a baby. Little Rose." He looked down at his rabbit's foot and stroked it.

"Sorry to hear that about your other sister," Ellie said. She noticed he seemed sad. "Now you just have one … that's like me," she said brightly. When he didn't respond, Ellie asked, "Whatcha got there?"

Capone seemed to return from some deep thoughts, "This? Oh, this is my lucky rabbit's foot. Had it since I was a kid. Don't go nowhere wit'out it." He smiled and asked, "Where did you say you work?"

"Oh, maybe you noticed the cafeteria across the street. I just help puttin' out food and cleanin' up. You know, just any stuff they need done. It's great to eat lunch wit' you in this nice restaurant. You know, it's sure better than what's in the cafeteria." Ellie smiled across the table from him and asked, "And what brings you to St. Louis?"

"I'm in the furniture business and gonna talk to some guys in East St. Louis. But I don't like stayin' over there, if you know what I mean. St. Louis is more classy. But what's a fine lookin' woman like you doin' workin' in a cafeteria?"

"Oh, I go to business school and soon I'll be getting' my diploma. I plan to expand my possibilities after that. I learned to type and take shorthand. Well, I'm not real good at shorthand, but okay. Hey, do ya need a secretary while you're in town?" Ellie gave him a coy look and a smile with a come-on.

"Maybe I do. Yeah, maybe I do."

They had finished their food, and Ellie looked to the clock on the wall. She started gathering her hankie into the purse and straightened her hat as she stood. "Oh, I can't be late, so I must be goin'. Sure hope we meet again. I want ya ta tell me how you got those scars on your face. Boy, bet that's a story."

Capone stood and blurted out, "Why don't ya have dinner wit me tonight?"

"Oh, I really can't. You know, other engagements. How 'bout lunch on Monday? Would that be to your likin'?" She blushed from her neck up to her cheeks and hoped she wasn't ruining this chance. *This is Saturday and he could be leaving on Sunday.*

"Sure. See ya here on Monday. But we'll go somewhere nicer."

Ellie turned and waved, "See you Monday in the lobby at noon. Thanks for the nice lunch."

Outside she started toward the *St. Louis Post-Dispatch* building and then decided to go into the cafeteria; the buildings were side-by-side. She hoped she could go through the cafeteria and out the back. Last week in the alley when she was receiving a delivery truck with some office supplies for the *Post-Dispatch*, she had noticed the back door to the cafeteria.

As she pulled the cafeteria door open, she turned to look back across the street at the Jefferson Hotel. Sure enough, there was Capone and his two cronies. She waved and went in. Sweat gushed under her arms. *Do I know what I'm doing? He's a smart man or he wouldn't be where he is.* Looking around the bustling tables, she saw a door to the kitchen. She walked through it and to the back, sighing relief when she found the door to the alley. A boy in a soiled white jacket was dumping garbage into a can as she left. No one seemed to notice her.

Arriving home in Dogtown, Ellie plopped on the couch next to Ginny who was, of course, crocheting. Bertha was setting the table for supper; nevertheless she saw Ellie's skirt across the room.

"Goodness gracious, Ellie, whatcha do to your skirt?"

Ellie stood and slipped the safety pin off. A four-inch angle of material flapped open, "It's a rip from when I bumped into a man on the street. I fell against a sharp metal rack in front of the Jefferson Hotel."

Bertha corrected Ellie, "That's not a rip. It's a bad tear, if I ever saw one. Like I've told you girls:

"If a thread loosens or in a seam it breaks, one can sew the rip like new, but a tear one can't repair—one can only hide it to feel no rue."

Bertha was kneeling now in front of Ellie, evaluating the damage. "I can't think of a way to hide it; it's ruined."

Ginny leaned over from the couch, "Why don't I crochet a couple of patch pockets, so you can hide the tear. You know, put matching pockets on each side. No one will know, I'll find some colors that match the browns and greens in the skirt."

"Yes, yes," Bertha agreed while holding on to the arm of the couch to stand. She was still plump and her knees were giving out. Her hair had turned completely white within a month after James had left. The girls could see their mother was getting old. Bertha grunted as she straightened to a stand. She held her hand to her back and hobbled for a few steps, mumbling, "It's a triangle tear, but Ginny's got a good solution." She opened a drawer to the sewing machine while still mumbling, "If I had some of the same material left, I could've made a patch pocket with it. I must remember Ginny's idea in case one of my clients gets a tear like this."

That night after supper, Ellie changed her clothes and hurried down the street to Franny's house. She walked in after a knock on the door, "It's just me," Ellie said, greeting Franny's father who sat in the living room.

Franny was in the kitchen cleaning their dishes, "Hi, what are we doing tonight?"

Ellie took a dishtowel and started drying. "Oh, Franny," Ellie whispered, "Something exciting happened today. We've got to talk. By the way, how are you feeling? Did you get your period yet?"

Franny had what people called "female problems." Doctors couldn't tell her what was wrong, but she was very irregular with her menstrual cycle. Sometimes two months would go by with no flow.

"The cramps stopped, but I still didn't start bleeding. I feel okay. Hey, let's get out of here. I had something exciting happen today." Franny took off the apron and flipped it over the doorknob. "I'm sick of being in this house. Can I borrow your yellow dress? Hey, let's go down to hear some Irish music on Tamm Street."

As they passed through the living room, Ellie said, "Sure."

Franny's dad seemed gruff, "Don't ya be comin' here at all hours. And don't tell me youse old enough to do what you want. You're livin' here and goin' by my rules."

"Okay, okay," Franny said and opened the front door for Ellie.

Out on the street Ellie asked, "Is there anything wrong at home?"

"No, it's just the same as always. He has a hard day every day at the brick works. At least tomorrow is Sunday so he can rest. You know he's getting too old for that heavy work, but he can't do anything else. Let's not talk about my family. I gotta tell you about this man I met. He's a doctor and real nice."

"Where'd you meet him?"

"Oh, I was comin' back from an interview for a secretarial job; I went through the park because it was so pretty today. Oh, Happy Birthday. I didn't get you anything, but I made this card." Franny slipped a folded paper out of her pocket.

There was a sweet drawing of a girl's head and a poem. Ellie read it and turned to give Franny a kiss on the cheek. "Thanks, now tell me, tell me about this man!"

"Well, he was walking on the same path behind me, and I dropped my hat that I had taken off to get more sun. He picked it up and gave it to me. Our eyes met and I blushed because he was looking at me so serious. You know, I could see he liked me."

Ellie took her hand and they giggled, "Well, …"

"We walked on together and talked. He's got an accent because he came from France about eight years ago. I love listening to him talk. Oh, his eyes and hair are so dark. He asked me if I would join him for lunch tomorrow at the Chase Park Plaza. You know, that ritzy place! Oh, I have to wear something nice. That's why I want to borrow your yellow dress and maybe the matching shoes." They arrived at Ellie's house. "He told me to bring a friend if I'd feel more comfortable. Maybe you'd come with me."

"You're right, he's a complete stranger, Franny; I do think I should go."

They arrived at the James' house and talked a while with Bertha. Then Franny excused herself to use the telephone to call the doctor and let him know that Ellie was coming with her. Ellie had gotten the telephone when she started working; the newspaper wouldn't hire her unless she had one because they needed to call her to work at any hour. The telephone was in Ellie's name, E.M. James.

After the call and while lolling against pillows on Ellie's bed, Franny heard about the encounter with Al Capone as well as Ellie's plan to learn what he was up to in St. Louis.

"I hope to write an article or two under the name of E.M. James. I'll figure out a way to get the articles in the *Globe-Democrat* or *The Star.* Surely one of them will run my story. How could they not! Well, maybe the *Post-Dispatch* would run it, but they would put out my copy under the name of one of the men reporters. I know they would.

"My idea is to get it to the *The Star* or *Globe-Democrat* without them seeing me. Somehow. You know, so no one would know that E.M. James is a woman."

Franny pondered, "Isn't this dangerous? I mean, both ideas. Besides trying to get stuff in a newspaper, aren't you scared to be around Al Capone? Doesn't he kill people?"

Ellie nodded, "The rumor is that Al Capone went to live in Chicago in 1919 after committing a couple of murders in the east. Though no one could pin them on him. Also, they say he had to move because of his violence against a member of the White Hand Gang on the other side of New York. That made waves in the mob. I've read that he has a horrible temper."

Even knowing all that she did about Al Capone, Ellie had no idea how dangerous her plan was going to be.

Chapter 7

End of May 1922
Encounters with Two Men

Ellie was impressed with Franny's gentleman. They had a delightful lunch and discussion. At first Ellie was dubious because, when she first saw him, it was obvious that he was much older than Franny. They learned David Jerome Cohen was thirty-nine years old.

As he was introduced to Ellie, he explained, "I go by Jerome, my second name."

And, although Franny was oblivious to what his last name meant, immediately Ellie knew he was a Jew.

Dr. Jerome Cohen was a pediatrician with a practice located right around the corner from the most elite hotel in St. Louis, the Chase Park Plaza.

Ellie knew the area well. *Mother's clients live in that ritzy neighborhood.*

After each of them had talked about their backgrounds and immediate occupations, Ellie and Jerome dominated the conversation.

"So, you arrived here in the United States at the beginning of the war, it seems."

Jerome smiled, "Yes, I only had to take a few classes in New York and then I was ready for the medical exams. I didn't have trouble at all getting a license. I've spoken English since I was a child so that helped as well. My mother married an American who lived and worked in Paris. I have an American citizenship because of my father."

"Was your mother from Jewish roots as well as your father?"

Franny sat up and chastised, "Ellie!"

Jerome laughed and sensed Ellie's intelligence and curiosity, "That's all right, Franny. Both my mother and father are Jewish. My mother's descendents came from Rhineland, Germany many generations back."

"Oh, you're Ashkenazi. How interesting. Does that mean you are a traditional Jew? Forgive my curiosity," Ellie asked, while Franny continued to squirm though she didn't understand the questions.

"Yes, I'm Ashkenazi, but I don't practice my religion. I'm a Jew by heritage only. Even the Reform groups never interested me. I make science my religion. I'm devoted to helping children. I love children. Their innocence and spontaneity always have intrigued me."

Ellie went on, "Judaism has always interested me. And I've been reading recently about the discussions our government has been having since the end of the war about restricting immigration quotas for Jews. This seems unfair to me."

Because Jerome and Ellie were smiling, Franny started to relax. "Would someone give me a lesson on what you are talking about?"

Jerome interrupted, "Franny please, first I have a question. Ellie, how is it you know so much about Jews?" He pulled out a pack of Lucky Strikes and lit up.

"Oh, I don't. I do read a lot though, and I am very interested in current events. Remember, I work at the *Post-Dispatch*. Franny, Ashkenazi refers to Jewish people who came from Eastern Europe. That's about 80% of the world's Jews. Am I right, Jerome?"

Smoke drifted up from his head, "Please, call me Jerry. I like a nickname among friends, and I can see we are already friends. Yes, you're correct. You might be interested to learn that today's twelve million Ashkenazim descended from a small group of 1,500 people in the area of Rhineland, Germany. And," he turned to Franny, "because so many Jews immigrated here to the U.S. during and after the war, some people in the government think there needs to be restrictions. It's nothing new for the Jews. We've suffered this type of discrimination for centuries."

Ellie interjected, "Anti-Semitism is the word, Jerry."

"Ah, a severe word. Let's talk about other matters. Franny, what do you like to do for fun?" Jerry took a deep drag from his cigarette.

"Ellie and I love to dance—all kinds, but especially Irish dance. You should see us."

"Where could I see it? I would love to. I don't think I've ever seen Irish dancing."

"Shh," Franny teased, "you don't want to admit that to anyone who lives in an Irish neighborhood."

They all smiled.

Monday noon came, and Ellie traveled into the back of the cafeteria and out the front door, just in case. But, glancing around, she decided Capone and his men didn't seem to be watching. She crossed 12th Street and went into the Jefferson Hotel.

Al was arguing off in the corner with one of his cronies, "They're cuckoo here. I know the Rats knocked him off. That's why I came down this time. But I gotta git back to Chicago tonight, so you're gonna go see Egan. Got it?"

Ellie held back to hear more.

"But, Boss …"

"No buts! We know the Rats did the hundred grand heist from that bank here in St. Louis, ah … what's it called?"

"Tower Grove Bank."

"Yeah, yeah," Al continued, "use that as some leverage to find out about booze shipments."

Ellie slipped back out the door and came in again. She waved so they would see her at the door, "Hello there."

Al smiled, "Hi there, Sweetie. Right on time; see, I knew you ain't like most dames." He crooked his arm and held it out to her. They walked out into the sunlight.

"Ain't it a pretty day?" Ellie commented.

"Yeah, sure is. Here's our car," Al opened the back door for Ellie, "we's just gonna drive over to a nice place of a friend of mine. Just a few blocks away." The other two got into the front seats.

"Oh, just so it's not far. I can't be late or I'll lose my job. My mother is old and I help pay for everything."

As they settled into the back seat, Al asked who else was helping pay and Ellie mentioned her sister who worked. Al talked more about his brothers and two sisters while they drove. Al put his hand on her knee. Just her knee.

Uh oh, I better have some excuses to stop this from going further.

Down on Washington Avenue off 8th Street they stopped in front of what looked like a door to an apartment.

"Where we goin'?" Ellie asked.

"You'll see. Oh, here we are."

Al knocked and a sleazy looking man with a bulge under his jacket opened the door. Ellie's armpits started pumping moisture. There were some stairs ahead of them, but they turned right into a room with four small tables covered with red-checkered tablecloths.

"Like I told ya, my family came to the states from Italy. I love Italian food, so we gonna have some here. Nice and private here. I like that." Al held a chair for Ellie. His cronies stood at the doorway with their backs to them. "Where's your family from?"

"Oh, my mother's mother came from Germany and my daddy's relatives from England a long time ago. Plus there's some Irish in there somewhere. I guess I'm just a mix," Ellie said as she put the red napkin across her lap.

Al followed her actions and put a napkin in his lap, "That's nice. I noticed last time we had lunch you know manners. And you wear real good clothes."

He's fishing now. "For years my mother has sewn for rich people, so she copies their clothes for me. Well, she makes clothes for me and my sister. She wants us to marry some rich man. Ha!" *May as well stick to the truth as much as possible.*

"Hey, that's nice of her," he seemed to like the answer.

A man with a white apron brought two plates of steaming fettuccini in white sauce. He returned with hot bread and a bottle of Chianti with two wine glasses.

As the wine was being poured, Al talked, "Since we don't have lots of time, we's skippin' the antipasta and other courses today. Hope that's okay wit ya. I'm busy. I gotta drive across the river. Goin' south a few miles on some furniture business. But I'd like to git wit ya tonight. Now, don't tell me no. Give me a little of your time after your work." He didn't wait for an answer. He didn't seem to expect one. Al started eating like he was starving.

I think that was an order for me to meet him after work. I better do it.

Ellie took a bite, "This is delicious." She raised the wine glass, "Cheers."

He picked up his, "Cheers … ha, that's cute," and he took a big gulp. "Nice year, don't you think?"

"Oh, I don't know much about wine."

"Wouldya rather have some hard stuff?" Al started to call out to the waiter.

Ellie placed her hand on his arm, "No, this is delicious. And I gotta do a lot of walkin' in my work. Gotta walk straight and not spill anything."

Al laughed a hearty guffaw and went back to shoveling in the food. They didn't talk much. Ellie decided that eating was serious business for Al Capone.

Five minutes later, one of his cronies came over and whispered in his ear.

"Hey, are ya done? I'm sorry, but we gotta go," Al said as he stood. His plate was empty. He picked up his glass and finished off the wine.

Ellie stood, "I'm fine. I don't eat too much."

"Yeah, you're too skinny," he said and pinched her bottom.

Ellie gave out a little surprised squeal, and Al laughed as they walked to the door.

Outside a truck was behind their car. A worker had a dolly and was waiting to unload. It was obvious to Ellie what kind of place it was. *Speakeasy.*

"Ellie, can ya be at the Jefferson about six?"

She said she thought she could.

They let her out in front of the cafeteria and sped away.

Ellie stood watching the car retreat. *Hmm, he's going to be wanting more than dinner with me. How can I put him off? I have the feeling that women can't put him off. What'll I do?* She started walking. *I heard him say he had to leave for Chicago tonight. Maybe I don't need to worry. Oops!* She was starting to pass the cafeteria. *I better go through here again. Don't know who's watching.*

Back at her desk, she thought of a plan. She pulled out a clean sheet of paper and took a few minutes to type the conversation she had heard when she first went into the Jefferson Hotel. She folded it into an envelope and mailed it to herself. Then she worked hard until quitting time.

Just before six, Ellie went to the lady's room and put on a Kotex though it was not that time of the month. *Heavens, I'm living in good times; no more using rags. Glad I saw the advertisement about Kotex in* Good Housekeeping Magazine *last year.* She worked on situating the napkin properly in the belt, and then put her underpants back on. *Hope this discourages him.*

Capone wasn't in the lobby. A bellhop approached her and gave her a message on a folded paper. 'Come on up to Room 101.' He signed it with an 'A' and a loop. She walked up one flight to give herself some time to relax. The hallway was dim. Taking a deep breath at the door, she raised her hand to knock and stopped. She could hear voices. It was Al's voice.

"I know those Egan Rats knocked off Slim. I know it! Too bad that slob we grabbed today wouldn't talk. Shit, did you see all that booze goin' in where we ate for lunch? Damn, I want to git some of the business down here. Southern Illinois is callin' me. Looks like a good place to start."

When Ellie heard someone else talking and couldn't understand anything, she knocked.

Al came to the door with a cigar in his mouth and let her in. His two shadows stepped out. Al closed the door, and then seemed to think of something.

"Excuse me, I forgot somethin'. Have a seat." He opened the door. Both of his thugs were just standing there. Al started whispering to one while biting the cigar.

Ellie was going to be embarrassed with those two outside the door. *Yeah, I should have known they wouldn't go far; they're his bodyguards. Ugh, nice big bed in here. Gad, what am I going to do?*

Al came back in and opened a door to the nightstand by the bed, "How 'bout a little one beforehand." Putting his cigar in an ashtray, he pulled an unlabeled bottle out and two glasses. He poured portions to the top and handed one to Ellie.

"Thanks," was all she could think to say. She was feeling queasy. She put the glass to her lips, drank nothing, sat her glass on the nightstand on the other side of the bed, and turned to see him drain the last from his drink. Immediately, he sat on the side of the bed and started to remove his shoes. Clunk, clunk. They fell to the floor. He left his socks on and stood to loosen his belt and take off his trousers. His little rabbit's foot dangled from a belt loop. He turned as his underwear and trousers slipped down his legs.

"Watcha doin'? Git undressed!"

"I … I," she stammered. "I ain't … uh."

He kicked off his clothes and came around to her side of the bed. "You ain't no virgin, I know that no dame your age could be a virgin."

"But, I …"

He slapped his thighs, "You are. Hot damn, I got me a virgin. This'll be a first for both o' us. I ain't had a virgin." And he wrapped one of his burly, hairy arms around her waist. With the other he grabbed her head and pressed his putrid smelling lips against hers. Ellie squirmed to no avail. He laughed loudly again, "Just be calm; you'll enjoy this." With both hands, he pulled her hips against his; a steel rod dug into her belly. Though trying not to make a sound, she whimpered.

"Unbutton your blouse. You don't want me to tear … ah, don't bother." He pulled up her skirt and ripped at the special underpanties that Bertha sewed for her. They were pink satin with lace around each leg and the waistband had a pretty grosgrain ribbon running through it that was tied in a bow on the left side of her waist. The ribbon snapped under his grip and the satin slipped down her thighs, past the rolled silk stockings, and nestled at her ankles. Ellie tried to pull away from his grip.

Suddenly, there was beating on the door, "Boss, boss, the cops are comin' and Frank saw two cop cars pull up out front."

Al went like lightning. Without underwear he pulled on his trousers. He gave her a big grin, "This is why I leave my socks on. Come-on, Honey, we got to get out of here."

How can he be joking around about his socks?

He grabbed his hat and went for the door. "If you ain't comin' I gotta go. I'll leave you a message at the desk tomorrow."

The three men headed away from the elevators down the hall and clomped down some back stairs. Ellie leaned down, grabbed her panties, and stuffed them in her purse. Then she walked out and stood at the elevator, nervously straightening her skirt and hair. When the elevator arrived and swooshed open, six policemen tripped over each other, not wanting to knock her over.

"Out of the way, Lady!"

Ellie stepped into the elevator as they ran to room 101 where the door was ajar. They turned back in Ellie's direction just as the elevator doors slipped close. She could hear them beating on the elevator doors as it descended. She quickly walked from the lobby, to the outside, and into the dress shop next door. She went to the back, grabbed a dress and entered a changing room. No one seemed to notice her when she entered. She sat on a little bench in the little mirrored space, listening to all the confusion. People were hollering out front. She heard the shop door open and a man asked, "Have you seen three men or some dame in a dark dress?"

Someone answered in a soft voice, and Ellie held her breath, waiting for the police to come in. They didn't, and the voices disappeared into the distance. Sirens started up as police cars pulled away from the hotel.

A few minutes later, Ellie left the shop's dress on a hook and quickly walked away. The clerk was outside watching the commotion, some policemen were talking to the bellhop, and so Ellie walked the other way, not stopping to look back. She turned the corner and went to the library. She entered the lady's room and removed the Kotex sanitary napkin; in her fear she had peed on it. When Capone had ripped off her underwear, she had been left standing in the belt and a Kotex. *Wonder if he saw this thing. I can't always have a period. What am I going to do next time?* She tied a knot in the broken ribbon and put on her pink satin underpanties.

In the calm of the library, she waited thirty minutes in the silence among the books, thinking. *How is he going to explain to me about the cops coming for him? Will he tell me who he really is? At least I know he's leaving tonight.*

Chapter 8

June-July 1922
Summer of Research and Love

Overnight, the gravity of her situation seeped into her head. *It was just luck that he didn't do it to me.* Ellie found fear mixing with excitement when she thought of writing an article about Al Capone. She went to work earlier than usual to be able to pick up the message Capone said he would leave at the Jefferson Hotel.

As she approached the desk clerk at the hotel, she crossed her fingers, hoping that Capone really was gone. *I don't have a lucky rabbit's foot.* She squeezed her crossed fingers tighter. She didn't want to meet up with him until she had time to analyze if she should get out of this mess or not.

She asked, "Is there a note for Ellie Jones from Al Brown?"

The clerk turned and pulled an envelope out of a cubbyhole, "You know that ain't his real name, don't ya?"

"What are you saying?"

"He's Al Capone. Didn't ya know?"

Ellie was shocked that this little old balding man just blurted out the fact that he knew Al Capone was staying there under an alias. She started to be paranoid. *Is he testing me? Did Al ask this man to test me to see if I really knew?* Her face went white; she turned without a word and scurried out.

Not many people were in the pressroom when she got there. At her desk she cut the envelope open with a scissors. It was hotel stationery and had Jefferson Hotel and the address imprinted at the top in gold letters. The note was short:

Won't be back here for a while. Not for a couple of months.
I'll write the hotel on Aug. 1 and let you know.
Be seeing you.

It was signed with the 'A' and a loop.

Ellie was relieved. *He's gone from St. Louis. I must research all the facts I heard Capone talk about. The letter I sent to myself should arrive at home today. Oh, I need someone who can help me. Maybe I'll go talk to Wally.* She started her workday at the newspaper by editing a news article about a meeting in the Mayor's office. *Boring, boring,* she thought, but it took her mind off her troubles.

When she wasn't working, Al Capone dominated her thoughts; Ellie knew she needed to learn all she could about him. Also, she needed to make sense of what she heard Capone and his bodyguards saying. That weekend, she started a scrapbook to hold any articles and information she could find. And she went to Wally for help.

After telling him everything about her meetings with Al Capone, Ellie asked, "What do you make of the fact that there was no news on the radio or in the papers about the police raiding the Jefferson Hotel when I was there?"

It was obvious to Wally. "Hey, you know about corruption. With prohibition, me thinks that every politician and a lot of the police are out to make money. Nothin' else. That makes sense now, don't ya think?"

"But how do they make money going after Capone at the Jefferson Hotel?" Ellie stopped, "Never mind, I understand. The crooks in St. Louis put the police up to it—to get rid of Capone." She nodded her head, "Of course."

Wally looked worried, "Ellie, this is no game. Glory be, everyone knows Capone is a killer—no, the *Divil* himself. Maybe you should forget about this."

"Wally, the Mississippi River is a killer … but not all the time. Daddy knew this and encouraged Ginny to pursue her dream. This may be my only chance to write for a newspaper." She gave Wally a mischievous smile. "What a story this is!"

Ellie spread her letter out on a table in his shop. "These are notes on what I heard Capone and his two thugs say."

1. They're cuckoo in St. Louis.
2. I know the Rats knocked him off.
3. That's why we came to St. Louis.

4. You gotta go see Egan.
5. In April, the Rats did a heist for $100 grand at TGB.
6. Egan's Rats killed Slim.
7. Speakeasy on Washington near 8th.
8. Capone wants some of this booze money.
9. Southern Illinois is wide open.

Wally read down the list and listened as she talked about each item. After she finished, Wally looked worried, "Let me talk to my brother. He's a policeman."

"His name's Sean, isn't it? What could he do? I don't want the police giving me trouble."

Wally assured Ellie that his brother would keep this between them, but most important, "Sean is honest. Maybe the only one on the whole force, the way things are nowadays. Let me have this paper. I don't think I need to use your name. I'll talk to him."

In the coming weeks Ellie learned that Capone ran a mob called The Four Deuces in Chicago. He was the boss over prostitution and booze up there.

Wally came back to her with a lot of good information. It turned out there was a lot of corruption in St. Louis. "High up it goes. When they were atalkin' 'bout Egan's Rats, they meant William 'Jellyroll' Egan, the City Constable. He wants to keep the Italian mobsters out of St. Louis. So, when Capone sends one down, they knock 'em off. But Sean thinks Egan's Rats have been taken over by another man, a politician by the name of William P. Colbeck. They call him Dinty Colbeck. The police know what Egan's Rats are doin', but don't want to get involved. It seems state senators and representatives are cashing in on the booze. Oh, me brother don't think it's good to use Egan's or Colbeck's name in your article, just talk about Egan's Rats. It's too risky. They's as bad as Capone for killin'."

"I haven't started writing the article, but I'm not going to hold back because of fear. Ginny would have never swum the Mississippi River if she'd given in to fear." Ellie thought a minute, "You know, Franny and I go to speakeasies from time to time to dance. They're always crowded and no one seems to worry about a raid. Everyone goes back week after week to have fun." Ellie shook her head, "I just realized that we're helping the whole corrupt scene."

Wally added, "For some reason, we think of New York, Chicago, and L.A. as havin' the gangsters. Talkin' to Sean opened me eyes. Oh, by the way, Sean said that Capone calls our little mobsters in St. Louis 'The Cuckoos'. That's what he meant when you heard the word. Sean said that Capone gets respect in Chicago from the gangsters, but not here."

***

While Ellie was researching Al Capone, Franny and Jerry were falling in love. David Jerome Cohen was not a handsome man; nevertheless all of his mannerisms exuded warmth and a genuine interest in others, leaving one with the awareness that Jerry was a good man—goodhearted, good-humored, and good-natured. So, while looking into his intelligent eyes, one saw only a very good-looking man.

Franny was a beautiful young woman. Her features—mouth, nose, and green eyes—were delicately set in pearl-like skin. Of course, she wanted more color and used rouge for her lips and cheeks. Her smile with flawless teeth turned heads when she strutted by. Being shorter than the James' girls by a couple of inches still allowed her to wear their clothes. And Bertha's sewing had given her the appreciation of fine clothes.

The courtship began with fine restaurants, the St. Louis Symphony, the latest silent movies, and the theatre. They would spend time with her family, visit the James' home, or just walk in the park. Franny started volunteering time at his pediatric office. She found she could share in his work by supplying toys for children in the waiting room, filing reports, and helping to type as he dictated.

Also, Franny began cooking the evening meals at his spacious apartment. Unlike Ellie and Ginny, she had become a very capable cook under her mother's tutelage. Jerry gave her a key to be able to prepare the meal before he arrived.

"Ellie, come over to Jerry's apartment tonight for dinner with us," was a request at least once a week. "Oh, wait until you see the new china we bought together. He's a doctor and should have good dinnerware, don't you think?"

All of this Ellie could accept and was pleased to hear until one evening, over a delicious dinner of cabbage rolls and corn on the cob, Franny said, "I've decided that I would like to be called Françoise. I've always disliked the name Frances. And Jerry doesn't mind."

Ellie had a look of amazement on her face, " … but, Franny, I'll never get used to saying anything but Franny." She quickly added, "I don't think."

"Well, if you just try every once in a while to say Françoise, I won't mind if you slip sometimes. It's a French name and goes with Jerry's accent, don't you think?

Jerry was enjoying Ellie's exasperation. He covered his smile with his napkin.

Ellie looked to him and burst out laughing, "Of course, Françoise, I'll work on it. Maybe that's what I need to get my mind off the last visit with Capone." After Ellie shared all the details about the episode, she said, "I can't believe I just described that bedroom scene without blushing. Jerry, you do put me at ease; I'm so happy you and Franny … I mean, you and Françoise have found each other."

The two lovebirds leaned across the table for a quick kiss. Franny asked, "Can we tell her? Yes, I want you to know, Ellie. We plan to marry before the end of the year. I know it's only been a little over two months, but …"

Ellie jumped up to hug, first one and then the other, "Look at this, I have tears in my eyes. Oh, remember when my mother would sew a certain number of buttons on your clothes?"

Franny squealed, "Yes, oh yes. Jerry, she would always make mine come out to be a Doctor."

Jerry looked a bit puzzled, but Ellie would let Franny tell about the little girl's poem.

"Guess my mother got it right, Franny. Oops, I mean Françoise,"

"What about you Ellie?"

"You know I plan to wait for the right man. I don't care if he is rich or … not so rich. I just want to find a Mr. Perfect for me. Like you have, Françoise."

As they left the table to have a coffee in the other room, Jerry lit a cigarette and returned to the topic of Capone. "Ellie, I hope you don't plan to see him again. It's too dangerous."

"Yes," Ellie agreed, "The more I learn about good ol' Al, the more I realize that I'm wiser to just write up an article with what I have. No one seems to know that Capone comes to St. Louis. That's why it's such a story!

"Wally's brother on the police force has given me a wealth of information. When I go looking through old newspapers, I've been able to verify everything he says, but he connects events that the papers don't explain. I even have gone to some politician's offices, oh not to confront them, just to be able to write about their personalities. I pretended to be helping another reporter gather information about other things." Ellie laughed, "I asked that Egan guy what he thought about women having the vote. He replied with a 'no comment'."

Jerry remarked, "May I read your writing? I'd be glad to give you my two cents, if you'd like."

"Sure, that'd be wonderful. Unlike the other reporters, I don't have anyone to bounce my ideas off of."

"Anything I can do, you just let me know. I'm all for you women getting ahead in this man's world."

A couple of weeks later, Ellie approached Jerry for help.

She explained, "I know I have a story here; one that'll sell a lot of papers. So, I thought I'd give my boss at the *Post-Dispatch* an offer."

Jerry leaned forward in anticipation.

"Oh, I didn't show him my work yet; I just told him that I'd met Al Capone here in St. Louis and had written a story. He laughed at me. Can you believe that? He said women have no place as reporters."

Franny sputtered, "The nerve!"

Ellie agreed, "It made me want to spit. You know, like a man! Too bad you don't have a spittoon."

Jerry finished laughing then offered, "Have more wine instead. So, what's your plan?" He lit up a cigarette and reached for an ashtray.

Ellie asked Jerry if he would take the article into the *Star Times*, posing as E.M. James.

Jerry had no problem with the request, "Sure. Show me your work and let's talk about all the details so I can make this look like my work."

It was the end of July when Jerry presented Ellie's story to the *Star Times.* The editor was interested; there was just one condition. They needed a photograph to prove that Capone really comes to St. Louis. Now Ellie knew she needed to meet Capone one more time.

Chapter 9

August 1922
One More Bad Time with Al

As Ellie made her way downtown, she thought about her father and his dream to patent an invention. It was Tuesday, August 1—a workday. It was also the day when Capone's note was to arrive at the Jefferson Hotel.

Why are dreams so difficult? All my life or longer, Daddy has been working on his. Ginny's dream could have taken her life away. Humph, I've almost got my dream, but its scaring me to death. Well, let's hope I don't get killed. I don't want to be around when Capone reads my article in the newspaper. Hmm, I hope he never sees it. I don't know what he'd do.

What will I do after this? Will I be satisfied that I attained my dream? I imagine that Daddy is still working on another invention. Will I want to write other stories? Then there's Franny. Well, Françoise. Her dream to find a wonderful man didn't seem to be so difficult. Of course, she might have some kind of problem in the future. I don't think it will end like Ginny's marriage, but it can't be that easy for her to have attained her dream in just a few months.

Ellie jumped off the trolley and started walking toward the Jefferson Hotel. As often happened in the summers of St. Louis, a gypsy walked the sidewalk. Her colorful skirts (she seemed to be wearing several) fluttered as she approached. The carefree woman walked like she was dancing, swinging one leg out to the side and then the other as if a tune was in her head and she would twirl at any moment.

Instead, the gypsy stopped right in front of Ellie and their eyes met. Pointing to a loose thread on Ellie's jacket, she said, "You're lucky I see ya got a loose thread. Remember, don't pull it or all will fall apart." Without asking, the gypsy took Ellie's hand.

This startled Ellie. *What does she mean by **all** will fall apart?* There was a coin in her jacket pocket, and Ellie pulled it out. Holding the dime out to give, Ellie asked, "Do you see anything else besides loose threads?" At that instance, the voice of Bertha echoed in her memory:

If a thread loosens or in a seam it breaks, one can sew the rip like new,
But a tear one can't repair—only hide it to feel no rue.

The gypsy dropped the one hand and took Ellie's other hand to peer at the lines, "*Dio mio!* It turns like the wind in a storm!" The gypsy's face, smudged with some dirt, looked frightened. "I never see this before. The lines in your hands swirl around and around when I look." Without taking the coin, she hurried away.

Ellie cried at the departing figure, "Your coin."

While the distance grew larger between them, the gypsy repeated. "I go. Like I said. Be careful or all will fall apart. You know what I mean."

Ellie hurried on. *I was feeling sorry for her, and she doesn't even take the coin. What a racket. And what she said could mean anything.*

Capone's note was a telegram waiting at the hotel's front desk. A different desk clerk than last time handed the Western Union envelope to her. She opened it immediately.

> Be in Sunday, August 13. Call Jefferson after 12 noon to set meeting time.
> Al

Ha, I kind of miss the 'A' with a loop. But seriously, it seems foreboding— this concise message. He's not asking me anything; he's telling me. There's less than a week to plan this photograph and hope to get away alive. Looking up at the desk clerk, Ellie asked, "May I write an answer to Mr. Brown so he can have it when he arrives on August 13? I imagine that he has a reservation."

Taking a moment to check the reservations, "Is he Al Brown? Yes, we will hold the answer for him. Do you need some stationery and an envelope?"

"Yes, if you please." She wrote:

> Dear Al,
>
> Just to level with you, the clerk told me who you are. I like you a lot but to hear your real name scared me. I'm sure you remember our last meeting. I need to tell you that I'm not that kind of girl. So, I guess you won't want to see me no more.
>
> But just in case you do, I'll call after 12 noon on August 13 like you ask. Then you can tell me if you want to see me.
>
> Ellie
> p.s. I quit my job at the cafeteria and got a secretary job at a nice little office.

Across the street, at the *Post-Dispatch*, Ellie called Jerry at his pediatric office, "Hello Jerry? Yes, Al is coming on August 13th. Mark your calendar. It's a Sunday, so you won't need to get someone to take over your patients." She made a nervous laugh, "it seems funny to call small children—patients."

Jerry replied, "Okay, we'll talk tonight."

"Yes, yes, I'll come to your apartment after work. See you later."

Next Ellie performed the next step of the plan and picked up the telephone again to call Timothy, the newspaper photographer who had captured Ginny's swim across the Mississippi River.

"Hello, Timothy, this is Ellie James calling again. Yes, I would like your services as we had discussed. The date is Sunday, August 13th. Are you available?"

Timothy said, "I'm marking my calendar at this moment. What time?"

Ellie had found Timothy, the freelance photographer, by calling the *The Star*. She had found his complete name in her scrapbook where she had pasted the article about Ginny swimming across the Mississippi.

She answered, "Oh, it'll be sometime after one in the afternoon. I'll call him at noon to learn the meeting time. So, can you hold the whole afternoon open?" Ellie was being careful not to mention Al Capone's name out loud. She was at work.

Timothy gushed, "Are you kidding? To be part of a story about Capone, I'd come at any time. Oh, actually, that's something we need to discuss. It must be during good light. So, you must get him to meet before six in the evening. You know what I mean?"

"Yes, I do. In fact, I was thinking the other day; you can't use that camera on a tripod like you did at the river. It …"

He was ahead of her, "Oh, of course not. This is supposed to be photos of a bride and groom, so I'll use my Kodak. Cameras with glass plates are great for clarity and distance, but we won't have those needs for this shooting."

"Oh, please don't use that word!" Ellie laughed, "Let's hope there'll be no shooting."

The photographer chuckled, "Good joke. Good joke. Don't you worry; I'll just use my Kodak because I'll be close to my subject and, as long as there's sufficient light outside, the photographs will be good. It's a small hand held camera. I gotta be able to move fast and take pictures fast."

"That's good. Let's talk again in about a week to see if either of us think of any problem. Thanks and goodbye."

If Capone wanted to see Ellie after reading her note, the plan was for Franny and Jerry to be outside the Jefferson Hotel in bridal attire, posing as newlyweds, with a photographer. Timothy was to snap a few frames of Capone, coming out the door with Ellie. Discreetly, of course.

So far, the plan was running smoothly. *But I know all about traps, like fallen trees hiding beneath the water's surface.* She sighed. *I'll be so glad when this part is over.*

***

Sunday, August 13th was hot, in the eighties in the morning; by noon, it was a sultry ninety-two degrees. People all over St. Louis sat outside in the shade with fans and cool drinks; children looked for water in the parks or a corner fire hydrant, courtesy of the local fire department. In the darkened apartment of Jerry Cohen, Ellie and her three supporters sat in the breeze from an electric fan. The atmosphere, of closed windows and drawn shades to stay cool, made a gloom that fit the drama of the day.

"What time is it?" Ellie asked again.

Jerry and Françoise were in the kitchen making some tuna salad sandwiches for them. Françoise came to Ellie with a pitcher, "Here, have some more lemonade, Ellie, and stay calm. You have fifteen minutes before you call Capone." Françoise kissed Ellie on the forehead after pouring.

Timothy said, reaching for a sandwich off the plate that Jerry held, "It's a perfect day for photographs. We're lucky; it could've been raining. Did I tell you that the newspaper will run the Capone story today if I can get the photographs to them by four-thirty?"

Ellie nodded as she finished her lemonade, "Yep, you told us."

Françoise walked around the apartment in a pale, cream-colored chiffon wedding dress that she had borrowed from a friend who had married in June. "Boy, I'm glad I don't have to wear a suit like you Jerry. You're going to die from heat." Both her hair piece of imitation daisies with a short length of tulle and her bouquet of imitation flowers sat on a table by the door with the straw hat that Jerry would wear.

Ellie couldn't eat, "I just can't. Sorry, they look good, but my stomach is churning. Oh, Jerry did you make reservations at the Chase?"

He laughed, "Nope, remember you have to call Capone first to learn the time he wants to go eat. I did call the Chase and not many people have called in reservations. This is going to work out, Ellie."

She smiled, "I know. I'm just nervous."

Finally Jerry brought the telephone to the table next to Ellie. It had a modern design with an earpiece and mouthpiece in one apparatus that sat on a pronged cradle atop a small heavy box. It had a twenty-foot cord that he had ordered especially to accommodate his desire to talk in the living room or the bedroom or on the patio. There was a switchboard in his apartment building, so he placed the call, "Hello Millie, please give me the Jefferson Hotel, that's PRospect 4200. How are you doing down there in this heat?"

"Thanks for asking, Mr. Cohen. I have a good fan going right on me. Oh, here's your connection."

Jerry handed it to Ellie who asked for Mr. Al Brown. She took a deep breath. A few clicks passed on the line, a ring, and then Capone was saying, "Hello."

"Hello Al, long time no see," Ellie said. She turned away from her friends because she needed to concentrate and play her role."

"Hi ya, Ellie, glad you called. I got your note. What am I gonna do wit' ya? A good-looker like you has got to get it over with. You ain't gonna be a virgin all your life, are ya?"

"No, no, but it's hard …"

Capone interrupted, busting into a booming laugh, "No, it ain't hard yet."

"Oh, but …" she forced a giggle, "you know what I mean. Well, I was hopin' that you might take me to have a nice meal at the Chase Park Plaza. It's the ritziest place in town. I ain't never been there. And maybe you have some wine we could drink on the drive there and back, then it might be easier to …" She waited a moment before emphasizing, "I need to be treated like a lady, you know?"

"I know what you mean. Yeah, the Chase. Sure, I'd love to give you another first. How 'bout six o'clock?"

Ellie was afraid of this, "Oh, could we do it sooner? I'm so nervous, you know. I don't think I could wait that long. I might back out. Besides, it might be real busy at the Chase at that time. We'd for sure get a table if we go at four or something."

He was quiet.

Ellie held her breath. *I know you don't like to be told what to do, but please, please.*

"Yeah, four works for me. Where will you be?"

"Can I meet you in the lobby of the Jefferson Hotel like before?"

"Sure, see ya then," and he abruptly hung up.

Ellie turned to her friends, "I need a cold shower!"

"Go ahead," Jerry said.

"Oh, I was just talking, but now that you agree, I think I will. And maybe I'll take a nap."

At a quarter to four, they drove in Jerry's automobile toward downtown. Ellie got out before the others when they were a block away from the hotel. Jerry looked for a parking space close to the front of the hotel and found one twenty feet from the corner on 12th Street. The newlyweds walked, smiling and chattering, to the front of the hotel and Timothy arranged them as if these were photographs for a lifetime. They talked about standing here or there and Timothy was opening a small collapsible chair for Françoise when Ellie passed, ignoring them. A bellman opened the door although there was a revolving door. She smiled at him and proceeded to the desk.

"Would you let Mr. Al Brown know that Ellie Jones is here?"

"He isn't ready and wants you to come up. It's Room 101."

No, no! I don't want to do this. Ellie walked over to a chair and sat down. The desk clerk stared at her and started to say something, but she got up. *I've got to do this.*

The elevator took forever. "First floor, please." Ellie told the operator. *I'm surprised that I can talk. I'm so scared.*

When she got to the room, Al's bodyguard Frankie was standing outside, "Hi, just go on in."

Capone was arguing with a guy, "See, I have ta go. I tol' ya. No, I ain't puttin' ya off. I'll meet 'em later tonight where we said."

"Colbeck ain't gonna like this."

"Come on," Capone took Ellie's arm, but addressed the same guy, "I'm leavin' and I'll be there at eight tonight." They all left the room, and the guy headed to the elevator.

Ellie, Capone, and his two shadows proceeded to the stairs. "You don't mind walkin' the stairs, I hope. I don't like elevators. Someone could be waitin' when the doors open and there ain't nowhere to go. You know?"

Ellie smiled, "Good thinkin' I never would've thought of that." *That was dumb to say. He knows I could have thought of that. The less I say, the better.*

Frankie went out the door first into the lobby and then went back for the others. They trudged across the carpeted lobby where the doorman was holding the door for them.

Ellie pulled from Al's arm and started toward the revolving door, "Oh, I love these things! This is fun, ain't it?"

But Al wasn't smiling. He wouldn't use it either. It was like an elevator. Someone could lock you into it. Finally he smiled at her glee, but went out the door.

Click! Timothy got one.

Ellie circled again in the revolving door and squealed in delight.

Capone and his men looked nervous.

Click, click.

Timothy got more photographs. Unless someone was looking closely at him, it appeared he was photographing only the newlyweds. He had them situated so, at the last moment before he pressed the button, he did a slight turn to capture Capone in his lens.

Click again. And Ellie popped out of the revolving doors.

"Oh, you should try it. It's as good as a ride at the fair."

Frankie opened the car door. Al pushed her in, "Don't do that stuff again!"

Ellie raised her arms as he started to hit her.

But Al didn't hit her. "Are you crazy? You know who I am. I can't be just standing on the street waitin' for you to finish playin' around. Don't do nothin' like that again. Understand? Just walk wit me. I'll tell you what ta do and not ta do."

"I'm sorry. I didn't think. I'm just so excited about going to the Chase and everything. You know?"

"Yeah, yeah." Capone reached to the floor, "Ya want some wine like you asked?"

While Ellie and Capone made their way west to the Chase, so did the newlyweds. Jerry was driving while Françoise changed clothes in the back of the speeding vehicle, hoping that a change of clothing would keep them from being recognized. They too were heading for the rooftop restaurant at the Chase. Jerry had a different hat and jacket that he would don on the run.

Capone and Ellie both relaxed during their ride. He put his arm over her shoulder and pulled her head around for a couple of kisses. Ellie managed not to tense, *Wine helps with this part.*

At the Chase, one bodyguard went up to the restaurant on the roof and then came back down. He let Capone know all was clear. Capone knew he had to ride up in the elevator; it was over ten floors to the roof, but they got off one floor below and walked the last flight.

"Just as a precaution, you know? If someone's waitin' for me up there, we'll see them first."

Ellie just nodded with a look of admiration on her face.

They were seated at an elegant booth-like table against a wall covered by a huge mirror. Potted plants sat on a ledge behind them, reflecting into the mirror. As she slipped onto the white leather couch, it was obvious to Ellie why he choose to sit there—he wanted to have no one behind him. The bodyguards took a table in front of them.

A few minutes later, Jerry and Franny came in. It seemed that everything was going smoothly. Ellie had asked them to come for her protection and, though they didn't know what they could do, she felt safer. Also, Timothy didn't come with them, so that meant he had gotten good pictures of Capone at the Jefferson Hotel. Ellie smiled inside, knowing that Timothy was at the *The Star* this very moment.

Jerry asked for a table on the other side of the bodyguards, which was on Ellie's side of the booth.

"So, you like your new job?" Capone asked.

"Yeah, sure. It's just a typin' job at this little office where they do bookkeeping. I just do letters and stuff. It's easy, but it pays a lot more than a cafeteria. You know?"

"I want to ask ya a personal question," Capone said and she gave a nod, "You know Ellie, how is it that a good-lookin' dame like you ain't never been laid? It don't make no sense."

Ellie was caught off guard. "Oh, I don't know. It just never happened." *Oh, that wasn't a good answer.*

Capone leaned closer, so no one could hear him, "Well, I was thinkin' that maybe you just do blowjobs with your men friends." And he raised his eyebrows and gave a little smile. "That'd suit me just fine."

Ellie had no clue what a blowjob was. Sitting with a blank expression and not knowing what to say, she saw irritation spread across Al's face; then his expression changed to anger.

Whack! He smacked her with the back of his hand. "What's wit ya?"

A waiter saw the slap and went over to the maitre d' with his concern.

Capone continued, "I been puttin' up wit ya, but somethin' ain't right. You don't want to do nothin' wit me and I'm tired of your attitude." He smacked her harder, "Let's git outta here and you're gonna give me whatever I want." Blood was trickling down from the corner of her mouth and her eye started to swell.

Capone got a grip on her upper arm and started pulling her across the white leather couch to get out of the booth. Ellie tried to free herself from him and pushed against his chest with her free hand. As they stood, he gave her a shake; her hand went down, making contact with his lucky rabbit's foot. She clutched it just as he pulled his other arm back and socked her with his fist. She went flying backward, hitting her head on Jerry and Franny's table as her arm caught on an empty chair and snapped. She knew it was broken. She had heard the snap! Unknown to Capone, Ellie clutched the rabbit's foot that had ripped from his belt loop. She slumped to the floor.

The bodyguards got up with guns out and stood a few paces from Capone. The patrons were aghast, but no one moved. Capone was getting ready to kick Ellie. The maitre d' was phoning the police.

Françoise was beside herself and, pulling at Jerry's arm, she whispered, "Jerry, help her!"

Capone's kick landed in Ellie's ribs just as Jerry arrived next to Capone and said, "I'm a doctor. Quick, hand me a spoon."

Capone hesitated with a look of disgust before he flung the back of his arm at Jerry who slipped under it and, in a smooth movement, grabbed a spoon from the table. Jerry continued to talk, as he knelt next to Ellie, looking at Capone, "Like I said, I'm a doctor and saw that she was starting an epileptic seizure. So, I came to help you."

"Are you crazy? I don't need your help. Git outta here," Capone said as his thugs started toward Jerry.

Jerry remained calm while talking, "See I'm going to wedge this spoon into her mouth so she won't bite off her tongue. Did you know the jaw has a force like a vice grip? Why, if my finger was in her mouth when the seizure starts ..." Jerry saw Capone and his thugs finally were listening. He had to keep talking, so he said whatever came to mind, "she could bite off my finger. Bone and all! See, I could tell she's an epileptic because of the arch in her back. Usually a trauma initiates a seizure. She's going to start shaking any second," Jerry gave Ellie a little nudge, hoping she understood what she needed to do. "See her arm and hand, they're turning back away from her body."

And Ellie turned her good arm backwards and arched her back. *Thank you, thank you, Jerry.*

Jerry went on talking and emphasized, “Look, she’s clamping on the spoon now! I couldn’t remove it even with powerful tools. Can you imagine my finger in her mouth? Why, she’d just take if off. Like I said, bone and all!” And Jerry snapped his fingers.

Capone’s eyes widened.

Ellie started shaking everywhere. The pain of her broken arm was excruciating yet she shivered and shimmied like she’d never done on a dance floor.

Capone was backing away, “An epileptic seizure? Her mouth’s a vice. Shit!” He turned and strode out of the restaurant without looking back.

Jerry picked Ellie up in his arms as Françoise arrived at his side, “Let’s find a back way out of here.” The waiter heard and escorted them through the kitchen and into the employee elevator. Ellie still clutched the rabbit’s foot.

In the hospital with her broken arm set in a cast, Ellie read the front-page spread of the *The Star* about Al Capone, by E. M. James. In the photograph, Capone walked out a door being held by a doorman with “Jefferson Hotel” on his shirt. The caption across the whole page, in letters one-inch tall, was CAPONE PUTS HIS FOOT INTO ST. LOUIS.

“Franny, I did it. My dream! And I couldn’t have done it without you and Jerry. You’re always there at my most horrible moments to help me. Remember when we made that pact at the library? When is it my turn to help you?” Ellie couldn’t stop babbling and smiling.

Later that evening Capone stormed into the *The Star* offices. “I’m lookin’ for E.M. James!” he shouted. Timothy, who had rushed the photos and initiated the press run, was still there and slid under a desk.

The editor explained, “E.M. James doesn’t even work here. I have no idea where he is. He walked in here off the street with the story. I’ll show you a list of my employees,” he said as he motioned to a girl to hand him the record book. It didn’t list freelance reporters or photographers, but no one admitted to that.

Capone looked down the list of employees on the August 1922 page. Not finding the name, he threw the book at the editor. He was disgusted that he took the time to look; he knew it wouldn’t be there.

Grabbing the editor by his lapels, "Now find the name in the telephone book or you'll be fuckin' sorry," Capone growled.

Since Ellie ordered the telephone and paid the bills, E.M. James was there. Al ripped the whole page out, but he was still pissed and signaled his bodyguards. They pulled machine guns out from under their coats, aimed at the walls, and fired. The sound was deafening for thirty seconds. Stepping over debris, Capone left with his thugs.

When Capone had disappeared down the stairs, the editor shouted, "Is anyone hurt?" Everyone stood up and looked around. No one was hurt, so he continued, "Let's make a special morning edition for tomorrow. Timothy, on the double, take a good front-page photograph of this room riddled with bullet holes. And get some of the reporters in it. The rest of you get to the typewriters, and I'll run with the best of the lot."

But Timothy knew he needed to warn Ellie first. He called her home and Bertha said she was in the hospital with a broken arm. He warned Mrs. James, "Some gangsters might be coming to your house. You best go over to a neighbors for the evening."

"Humph, thank you, young man," she replied and decided she could handle any ruffians.

Then Timothy called the hospital to tell Ellie what had happened at the *The Star*, "But I gotta go. We're going to do a special edition on the mess he made here."

As Ellie hung up and walked back to her hospital room, she remembered that there was a photo of her and Ginny on the living room table at home. She turned around and went back to the telephone to call Wally for help.

Walking out of the Jefferson Hotel, Al stopped talking mid-sentence as the bellman opened the door for him. Suddenly his thoughts scattered like yellow jackets brushed from a picnic table. New ideas started to circle in his head as he remembered the photographer taking the wedding couple's picture when he was coming out this very door. *That's who took the newspaper photo of me! How'd he know I was here?* Slowly everything flew together with the image of Ellie circling in the revolving door. Now he knew she had stung him.

But he roared in laughter, knowing that she outsmarted Al Capone. As he reached to stroke his lucky rabbit's foot, his jovial face turned to anger. In his mind he remembered a little yank on his belt when he was beating her. "Damn It! She took my lucky rabbit's foot. Let's go over to that cafeteria 'fore we head over to the house of E.M. James. I wants to see if we can find that dame." He could laugh about the newspaper article now that he knew where E.M. James lived, but his lucky rabbit's foot was something else.

Capone stormed across the street and didn't wait for his men to open the door for him. He banged the door open and motioned for Frankie to fire a shot into the ceiling. Women screamed, glasses overturned and food fell as people jumped up and looked for somewhere to run. Fear rippled through the room as it quieted. *The Star* had sold out after only an hour on the street. There was no doubt that everyone in the cafeteria knew who was standing with their lives in his hands. People cringed and knelt under the tables.

Capone's face was red and distorted as he screamed, "I want Ellie Jones. Someone tell me where I can find her."

No one moved. The silence was as scary as the gunshot had been.

Al walked along the food line looking at faces to see if someone knew something. He stopped at one young girl who served mashed potatoes, "Do you know Ellie Jones?"

She shook her head.

Capone crashed his hand down on the glass covering the food—it shattered, "Where's the manager?"

The girl pointed to a tall man standing in the kitchen doorway. Capone strode over to him and grabbed him by the collar. "Tell me where Ellie Jones lives. She used to work here."

"There … there isn't anyone here by that name and … and never has been. I don't know anyone by that name."

Capone jerked him and banged the man against the doorframe, "How do I know you ain't lyin'?"

Capone let go and the man crumpled to the floor. "I have employee records I can show you. I don't even remember an Ellie or Eleanor or anything like that name."

Capone growled, "No, I don't want to see no more records."

Turning to his men, other facts were falling into place, Al realized that Ellie not only got the photographer, but also she must have told the story to that reporter E.M. James.

"Let's get out of here." Absentmindedly, he reached down again for his lucky rabbit's foot. He cursed. They headed over to the James' house.

Beating on the door with his fists, Capone shouted, "Open up!"

Bertha opened the door, complaining, "What reason does anyone have for beating on a door. Why, I …"

"Lady, I'm lookin' for a man named James. You know, E.M. James," Capone made a motion with his head, and the two bodyguards pushed past Bertha to enter the house.

Bertha was indignant, "No, he ain't here. James left me. He ain't here. You don't need to be so pushy and rude." She talked on and on about her husband who had left her with two young girls to raise. She told them she was glad he was gone.

Some things didn't make sense to Capone, but he didn't put any stock in what an old woman was saying. "Will you shut-up, woman?" He shouted as he walked past her into the house, bumping the table where the photo of Ellie and Ginny sat. It slipped down silently on one of Ginny's crocheted doilies, landing face down.

Frankie, the bodyguard, returned to Capone, "We searched the whole house and there's only women's stuff. No men's clothes or shoes, no shaving cup or razor, or anything. The pisser's clean; no man pissed in it today. I guess James went on the lam like she said."

As they piled into their car, Wally was rushing up the street. He saw them drive away.

Over a cup of tea, he learned from Bertha's ramblings that it was a sure thing that Capone never learned E.M. James was a woman. Wally propped the photo up as he left.

***

Ellie attained her dream. However, her boss considered it an effrontery. As soon as he saw her name and initials on the article, he knew. After all, she had offered the story to him. Many of the reporters in her office gave her the cold shoulder for quite a while; others thought she had pulled off a good one and let her know.

Nevertheless, the Tuesday evening bridge club did celebrate. Franny and Ginny had bought extra copies of the *The Star* to share with the girlfriends. They squealed and raved to Ellie how wonderful it was.

One said, "The headline should have said 'Ellie M. James Put Her Foot in the Door in St. Louis'."

"You're paving a path for women. We have the vote, and soon we'll have equal status in the workplace," another exaggerated.

But Ellie enjoyed the spotlight as they made a toast with their iced tea, "To Ellie!"

Al Capone seemed to disappear from St. Louis after that. For years Ellie lived in fear of running into him. She would look out over a crowded sidewalk or open a door cautiously, glancing around for him.

Ellie kept his lucky rabbit's foot. Not for luck, she enjoyed the idea that she could keep something he wanted so much. She knew, as long as she had it, he would think of her and wonder where she was.

Over the years, her fears lessened and she derived a satisfaction, with an inner smile and gleam in her eye, knowing she had fooled Al Capone.

Chapter 10

1922 - 1927
Ellie Meets her Man

In December 1922, Dogtown had a big celebration when they learned that Sinn Fein won a victory in the elections of Southern Ireland. It meant negotiations would begin with Britain.

A 1923 bond issue brought electric streetlights to St. Louis, replacing the gas lamps, though homes of the wealthy and businesses had had electricity since 1887. Ellie watched workers take down the ornate lamplights on 12th Street, in front of the *St. Louis Post-Dispatch* and the Jefferson Hotel.

That same year, there was a heist of a mail truck at 4th and Locust. It was blamed on the Egan Rats; 2.5 million dollars in negotiable bonds were taken. Ellie went with the reporter and wrote up most of the copy. Of course, her name was not on the article when it went to press.

In September of 1923, an earthquake hit Japan and killed over 200,000 people. Tokyo and Yokohama were destroyed. Ellie wrote it up for another reporter and kept that article for one of her scrapbooks; her name still did not appear in the by-line, although the words were hers.

In 1923, the Klu Klux Klan's Grand Dragon was exposed and indicted for murder. This was a turning point for the Klan. The membership went from five million down to nine thousand.

But the big news in 1923 was the aftermath of the death of the President of the United States; Warren G. Harding died in August. The scandals, as the stories unfolded, showed the depth of the misuse of power during the Harding Administration. Ellie worked incessantly on these stories. The Teapot Dome Scandal from Teapot Dome, Wyoming involved men in high places like the Secretary of the Navy and the Secretary of the Interior; bribes of $100,000 were discovered;

oilmen were leasing property they shouldn't have had access to, and on and on.

***

As 1924 approached, Ellie could see she was not going to get a second article published in her name. She wasn't going to achieve more in the newspaper business. It was a difficult time for her.

She wished she could write to her father. *What would Daddy do? If I'm my father's daughter, I should know. Would he quit the newspaper business and try another career? I really have fulfilled my dream of writing for a newspaper. I do it every day; I just don't get the credit.*

Françoise and Jerry were now Mr. and Mrs. David Jerome Cohen. Their love grew. Ellie watched their happiness and enjoyed it, until one day when medical examinations proved that Françoise could never have children. The couple didn't explain the medical problem, and Ellie didn't ask—people didn't talk about that even to their closest friends. Jerry went to work every day to care for children; Françoise went most days with him. They were surrounded by children, but none of their own. They started traveling more and even bought a home in Florida for vacations in the winter months. Their love seemed to deepen.

However, the Cohen's were worried about Ellie. She was approaching thirty years of age and had found no man to interest her. Also, they watched her follow Al Capone's life and worry that he would return to 'get' her. When the three friends were together, Ellie would share the latest news about Capone. The Cohen's got tired of hearing about him.

Bertha still had her two daughters at home. "A couple of old-maids, that's what they are," she complained to the Cohens over a Sunday lunch.

Ellie smiled at her mother's taunting, but Ginny didn't.

Bertha didn't need to work any longer; the two daughters paid for everything with their good jobs, but Bertha liked sewing and continued creating stylish clothes for clients and her daughters. And, though hating to admit slacks were becoming the style, she sewed beautiful ones—wools, gabardine, silk and cotton—especially for Ginny who loved to wear them when she was not at work. Ginny still could stand on her hands and would always show people when the chance arose.

While Ellie kept up on all the important events happening in St. Louis, there was one in 1924 she never heard about, but it would have a lasting impact on her future. A young man by the name of John Bartlett graduated from the St. Louis School of Pharmacy. He was handsome, smart, and four years younger than Ellie. He signed his classmates' yearbooks with a quote by M.H. McKee that he had read one day in his mother's *Readers' Digest*:

Integrity is one of several paths. It distinguishes itself from the others because it is the right path, and the only one upon which you will never get lost.

John Bartlett was the son of an engineer on the Frisco Railroad and one of two boys in a family with six girls. They weren't poor, but they didn't have much money. John had paid for his own college education while helping to support his family. He was the fourth child of eight and since his older brother had moved to the state of Washington, John was the only boy at home and knew he needed to help provide, so it took John longer to get through college to become a pharmacist.

Jerry brought him home for dinner one evening.

"Honey, here's the Parke-Davis salesman that I said was coming to supper tonight. Françoise, meet John Bartlett. John, this is my adorable wife, Françoise." They shook hands.

John loved to hunt and fish. He was a swimmer and loved to dance. When Françoise met him she thought of Ellie's father, James. Not only for all the things he did like James, but also for the zest of life he exuded. He was gregarious and charming.

At one point during the meal, John talked on and on about deer hunting, turkey hunting, and, his favorite, squirrel hunting on his uncle's farm, "... just off Highway 66, south of Sullivan, you know, near Bourbon." He grinned and raised his eyebrows, "I can see by the look on your faces that you don't know Missouri too well. Sullivan is about fifty miles south of St. Louis off Route 66." He made a little joke, "You do know what Route 66 is, I hope." His smile was one of those that made you just love the man. He had a twinkle in his eye that sparkled when he was joking. "I usually take the train." He smiled really wide again, "I travel free on the train because my pa is the engineer. Do you hunt, Dr. Cohen?"

"Jerry, the name's Jerry. You're in my home not the office. Dr. Cohen at the office, but Jerry on all other occasions. A deal?"

There was that smile again, "Thank you," John said, nodding at the gesture.

Jerry continued, "To answer your question, no, I've never gone hunting. Why?" Jerry took out his Lucky Strikes and tilted the pack toward John, who declined.

"Let's go next weekend. You'll love my uncle and his farm. You should come, too, Françoise. I think you would enjoy swimming in the Meramec River. Now, don't tell me you don't know that river. Route 66 must cross over it a half a dozen times." John waited a minute to let them think before he went on enticing them, "We'll go squirrel hunting because I can cook the best meal you ever tasted with a few squirrels. I have an extra rifle you can use. One for Françoise, if she likes." Oh, that twinkle in the eye.

Later that night, when they were snuggling in bed, Françoise suggested, "Jerry, do you think he would let us invite Ellie to come along?"

Jerry sat up on his elbow and kissed his wife, "Françoise, what an idea. I hadn't thought about Ellie, but leave it to you. Those two should like each other. Isn't he bright and just full of life?"

***

Ellie agreed to go.

What a weekend! Much to the chagrin of Françoise, the other three found humor in all her discomfort. Not that they laughed that day; they would all laugh in later months when they remembered the wonderful outing and all of Françoise's complaints.

"Get it out! Get it out! Some horrible bug has jumped down the front of my shirt. Someone help me!"

Jerry came to her rescue and pulled the blouse out of her slacks. A grasshopper jumped out and hurried away. "That little guy was probably more scared than you," he said as he cradled Françoise in his arms and rocked her.

"Let's go up to the big oak and do some target practice before we hunt," John suggested. The men started ahead with the rifles.

Jerry took out a cigarette, hesitated, and shoved it back in the pack, "It's too hot to smoke. Have you ever smoked, John?"

"No, I haven't."

It was not only hot, but also humid. Françoise pulled out her mirror and whispered to Ellie, "Look at my makeup, it's smeared from me wiping my sweat. Why didn't you tell me?"

"No one cares, Franny, you're so beautiful you don't need makeup. Here, let me help." Ellie took out her handkerchief and wiped the smears.

Facing each other, the friends paused and touched the other's face. "Look at you, Ellie. Your lips are deep ruby and cheeks are so rosy. You've never used makeup, have you?" Not waiting for an answer, "You don't need makeup, but I do. I'm pale. I don't have any color to my lips, eyebrows or lashes."

"Hush, Franny, we're in the country. Look at that creek and the trees. It's so lush green and … so quiet. Have you listened to the beauty of the quiet?"

Françoise turned. Her eyes saw the itchy grass, smelly cattle, cowpies, and buzzing insects. Saying nothing, Françoise walked up to the men.

Françoise was the last to shoot at the can, trying to knock it off the stump. She missed when all the others had pinged the can into the air. "Oh, look at the bruise on my shoulder from that gun. I don't want to ever do that again. Ellie, why doesn't it bruise you? Oh, Jerry, get that bug off my shoulder!"

Ellie explained how she had used a .22 rifle with her father. She knew to pull the stock snug to her shoulder. After a while, Ellie suggested, "Why don't you two men go shoot dinner for us? Franny and I are going to sit in the creek to keep cool and to be away from bugs."

“Ellie, my swimming suit is miles away where we parked the car.”

Ellie replied without hesitation, “We’ll just dip in the water with our underclothes. There’s no one to see us except the cows.”

“That’s easy for you to say, you have a loose fitting dress on and can just lift it up to sit in the shallow water. I have to take off my slacks.”

Ellie interrupted, “Why don’t you guys just go on and hunt. But I suggest that you don’t take more than an hour or two. Franny is trying, but she’s not used to this.”

After John bagged a couple squirrels, they drove to the Meramec River. Franny was happier. Like she had done in her childhood with the James family, she loved swimming in rivers, but in a swimming suit. John started a fire and swam for a while before starting to make supper. He had brought everything needed to cook, “But we all eat out of the same pan. Here’s a fork for each of you.”

As the sky darkened and the full moon came up above the trees, they loaded into Jerry’s Studebaker for the trip home. On the trip out to the farm that morning, the men had sat in front. On the trip back to St. Louis, Françoise made sure she sat in front with Jerry. He had his first cigarette in hours.

Before John and Ellie got into the back seat, Françoise whispered to Jerry, “Those two have hardly talked to each other today. Now they’ll have to.” She made an impish smile.

Neither John Bartlett nor Ellie James was a shy person. Neither John nor Ellie was ever at a loss for words. But neither of them said anything for the first five miles or so.

Jerry broke the silence, “John, I want to thank you for this marvelous day. I had the time of my life. I haven’t done anything like this since I came to the states. I hope you invite us again.” Franny gave him a little discreet shove.

Ellie joined in, “I agree. I haven’t done anything like this since my father left fourteen years ago.”

Naturally, John asked what had happened to her father and that was the topic for the ride home. Franny joined in the conversation, adding to the unfolding history of Franny and Ellie’s childhood.

After Jerry said, "I didn't know that," for the third time, Franny replied, "and I'd forgotten about a lot of this. Guess that's why I never told you."

When they were almost to Ellie's house, John commented, "What are we doing next? Anyone like tennis? Or we could go dancing. Hey, let's go see some of that Irish dancing in Dogtown. Jerry, you said that you hadn't seen these two gals dance the Irish jig."

"It's not really a jig. Well, you men will have to join in. It's easy to learn the *céilí* dances or set dances. I'm not sure Ellie and I can still do the solo dances," Franny said.

The next morning Françoise called Ellie, "I am covered with these little pink, itchy bumps. They are all around my waist and ankles. What are they? Jerry just has a couple of these pink bumps. Oh, and Jerry found this bug on my back. He called it a tick, and he had to burn it with his cigarette to get it off. He wouldn't show it to me."

"Oh, Franny, I'm sorry. I wore the loose fitted dress so I wouldn't get the chiggers.[2] That's what the little pink bumps are. It will take a couple of weeks for them to go away. Take a lot of baths to stop the itching. They get a hold on you where your clothing is tight. If you wear loose things, they can't hold on."

Franny was quiet for a while, "Did they bite me?"

Now Ellie was quiet for a while, "Oh, Franny, don't make me tell you about them." Ellie thought the chiggers went into the pores of the skin and sucked blood.

"Okay, I think. I might imagine something worse than the real thing though," Françoise lamented. "Let's talk about something else. Should Jerry and I come pick you up for tennis this afternoon?"

It was Sunday and the four had decided to play tennis. Irish music in Dogtown was scheduled for the coming Friday or Saturday.

"John is going to come pick me up. But he warned me that his Ford is really old."

At Ellie's home when Bertha opened the door a handsome, young man dressed in white greeted her. White slacks, white knit shirt, white socks, and white Keds tennis shoes. And the white teeth in his smile sparkled as much as his blue eyes and slicked down dark hair. Bertha noticed the one navy blue stripe around the neckline of the knit shirt, and thought he looked just like the wealthy people who go play tennis.

Ellie came to the door quickly and made introductions to her mother and Ginny. "Sorry, Mama, we must hurry. We booked a court and are running late."

John's Ford turned out to be an old truck, rusting here and there, with just room for two in the cab. John had folded and tucked a wool army blanket over the seat to cover the dirt and holes. The door made a loud creak when he opened it for Ellie, and it gave off puffs of dust when slammed. Looking out the window, Bertha was horrified.

The foursome played tennis that Sunday and had dinner at the Cohen's apartment. On Friday, the four went Irish dancing in Dogtown. Ellie had to work late on Saturday, so they decided to meet at Ellie's house on Sunday to teach John how to play bridge. Ginny joined them so one of the others could sit with John and explain what to do with his cards. The next week, was an evening dancing at a Speakeasy downtown, swimming in the Missouri River, and more bridge. They had a picnic in Forest Park, went to the symphony, played more tennis and more bridge.

On the telephone with Franny, Ellie pouted, "He hasn't held my hand or even tried to kiss me. It has been more than a month since we met. This isn't normal, is it, Franny?"

"I don't know what to say, Ellie. He seems to like you. He keeps wanting to do things. Do you like him?"

"Yes, I like him, but …"

Franny interrupted, "You know, you and John are never alone except for short rides in his jalopy. Maybe that has something to do with it."

While the girls were lamenting, John was waiting in Jerry's office, thinking about the same thing.

The doctor came in, rushing as always, "Sorry for the wait, John. What do you have for me today?"

"Dr. Cohen, this isn't the time or place to talk about personal matters, but I need to talk to you. Can we meet after you're finished with your appointments?"

"Sure, come on over to our apartment about seven tonight."

John hesitated, "I hoped to just talk man to man, if possible."

"Oh," Jerry smiled, "we'll go out for a walk. Stay for supper and we'll talk before we eat. How does that sound?"

During the walk, John took off his hat and started circling it around the rim with his hands as he confessed, "Jerry, I just need some advice about women. I know I should know more for a twenty-four-year-old man, but I've never really dated. Work always came first. You know, to help my family and to earn money for college. There was just never any time. Well, maybe if I had met Ellie years ago I would have made time. I'm smitten with her. Do you know what I mean? I don't want to do anything to spoil the possibility of making her mine. She's so smart and so beautiful. I keep thinking of the great kids we would have." He seemed to relax now that it was all said. He turned toward his friend, "Jerry, I want her for my wife. What do I do next?"

Jerry slapped him on the back and put his arm across John's shoulders, "Well, let me think about this." They walked twenty paces. "You're not wanting to marry her tomorrow, I hope."

"Oh, no. I need to work and save more money. I need a decent car and to be able to rent a place. You know, I'm talking to you because I don't want her to get away."

"Do you love her, John?"

John stopped in his tracks and turned face-to-face, "Gosh, I don't know. How does one know what love is? All I know is that I feel so good with her. I like the way she thinks and talks. When I'm close to her, I want to be with her for all my life." He smiled, "It sounds crazy, but I can talk myself out of what I just said … until I am near her again. It keeps happening again and again. Is that love?"

Jerry put his arm back over John's shoulder and they started walking again, "I think that's as good a way of defining love as any." They walked quietly again for a few minutes before Jerry was ready to give some advice. "You and Ellie need to spend time alone—just the two of you. You can still do things with us and other friends, but go places like parks and walks with just Ellie."

"I know, I thought of that, but what do I do when alone with her?"

"Well, start by just talking like you do when you're with us. I've watched you with Ellie. My most important piece of advice is to touch her. Women like to be touched. Start by taking her hand. If some of her hair blows in her face, you brush it away for her. If a cool breeze comes up, button her coat for her. And if …"

And on and on Jerry talked about simple things.

Jerry had observed, in the month they had been becoming friends, that John was a kind man, but not an emotional man. That John was smart and quick, but not at all aware of women's needs. Jerry had said to Françoise, "John has six sisters; how could he not know what a woman needs?"

Later that night, again when Jerry and Françoise were cuddling in bed, Jerry told her about the conversation during the walk. When he finished, Françoise told Jerry about her talk with Ellie on the phone.

"Oh, I'm so happy to hear that Ellie feels the same. I hesitated saying anything to John for fear that Ellie wasn't interested." Jerry was pensive for a moment before saying with a grin, "Françoise, he asked me if I had a piece of paper. He wanted to take notes!"

They laughed until tears came to their eyes. Yes, they agreed, he was in love with Ellie.

In the next few months, it was apparent that Jerry's advice was working. Ellie found she loved this man more than she thought was possible. She bubbled with happiness when talking to Franny, "Why, even Mama, likes him. I think Mama succumbed to John's charm the first time they met. She told me he couldn't be too poor because he dressed in the most fashionable clothing. Mama claims that he'll be a rich man someday because he's so smart. That's her way of accepting him. You know how stubborn my mother is. But how could anyone not like him?" Ellie didn't stop talking for Franny to answer because she thought of something else.

"Oh, you know one of the things I love about him?" Again Ellie didn't wait for an answer. She couldn't talk about anything except John. "He knows so many things. He just reads and reads. He likes facts and learning as much as I do. But we complement each other. I'm interested in current events, history, politics, and the like. He knows about biology, chemistry, and scientific things. And he is so good at tennis and swimming. Oh, and you know what? John can swim faster than Ginny. We went to a lake and had such a good time with Ginny."

Every night before going to bed, Jerry and Françoise found themselves talking about their friends' flourishing love. As Françoise fluffed her pillow before slipping in next to Jerry, she said, "Have you seen how they look into each other's eyes? They talk with their eyes. And they can finish each other's sentences. I wouldn't doubt that they think each other's thoughts. That's why they always win in bridge, I think.

"Oh, and isn't it amazing for a couple who didn't touch for over a month, he and she are like magnets. Ellie says she loves the way he kisses. Oh, I shouldn't tell you that. You won't tell John that I know, will you?"

Jerry slipped his arm around Françoise and pulled her close. "How are my kisses?" That ended the discussion.

***

Under the advice of his mentor, Dr. Cohen, John waited six months before proposing marriage. In fact, John returned to Jerry over and over to get advice. Jerry stopped telling Françoise all the details because it was something just between the men now.

Ellie talked endlessly with Franny. Though the wedding wouldn't happen until they saved money, Ellie was so happy about the pending marriage. But she confided her worst fear to her best friend, "Maybe I can't have children. You know, Ginny can't and you can't. Maybe it was something in the water or what we ate. We did the same things." Though she worried, she knew deep down they would have lots of children. She just knew.

One evening when the four of them were playing bridge at the Cohen's, Jerry complained as they finished, "It's as if you knew what Ellie had in her hand every play. Do you have signals?"

John, with frivolity, retorted, "I was a poker player before bridge. We don't tell our secrets. But are you accusing me of cheating?" He stood as if pulling a pistol from his hip.

Ellie got up and grabbed him by his waist, "Oh spare my friends."

As John collapsed onto the couch amid the laughter, he retorted, "However, I have observed that Jerry lifts his elbow during bidding to indicate hearts. Deny it or not?"

This time Françoise was after her man. She sat on his lap and punched him. "I told you that they'd see it."

Never to be told were all the signals that John had worked out with Ellie. John could move so many parts of his head. A wiggle to his right ear was spades, a ripple to the hair was diamonds, no movement was hearts, and a flare of his left nostril was clubs. Also, a lift to the right eyebrow meant he held more than five of a kind. Ellie couldn't move anything unusual on her face. So, John would question her by his movement when it was her turn. He never looked at her, just moved the appropriate facial muscle. No one ever noticed.

It was through their plans for playing bridge together that Ellie learned one more characteristic about John that was like her father. *John is as good at keeping secrets as I am.* She had always thought of this characteristic as an asset, although she will change her opinion after learning what he kept from her. But, during this night at the Cohen's, life was fun.

In the coming weeks, John was at the James' home most evenings. Ellie was so grateful that her mother and Ginny liked him. *But who couldn't like him?* He told funny stories, helped repair things around the house, loved to eat Bertha's cooking, and tried to learn the fiddle.

Ginny was a good teacher and they would go down to the tavern on Friday nights when other fiddlers were playing together. Ginny and Ellie always did some Irish dancing like in the old days with their father. Prohibition was still in effect, so over a BEVO, soda, or lemonade, everyone had fun and John got better at playing tunes on his fiddle.

But Wally was the best teacher, so Ellie and John would go to the shop and spend time there. John liked to go to James' corner to mull over the unfinished inventions.

"Wally, wish you could remember what he was trying to make with this. From time to time I get an idea, but I don't take the time to make it. Maybe when I retire."

Ellie laughed, "John, you're planning your life forty years from now?"

"Yep, I've lots of plans. We haven't had enough time together for me to begin telling you about them. But I'll tell you some day."

"Well, just tell me one. My Dad used to call them dreams. Are they your dreams, John?"

"Nope, these are plans."

Ellie smiled. *I love this man.* "Okay, tell me one plan. Oh, by the way, do I get any say in these plans?"

"Oh, you'll like 'em all. I plan to own my own pharmacy one day."

Ellie was floored. "John, we're saving for a car and a place to live so we can get married, and you're thinking of buying a pharmacy?"

"Well, it's a long ways off. It's after we have at least three kids. No, right after we have three kids."

Wally hooted, "Ellie, me lass, ye've found your match. I do say. Why this girl from a wee one has planned the most difficult things. But she does 'em. Yes, your marriage will be a good one."

Ellie was glad Wally approved. His words were as close to having a father's blessing as she could have.

***

During their engagement, they saved and saved. No more expensive evenings at the St. Louis Symphony or restaurants like the Chase Park Plaza. Just about every penny went into the bank. John started working part time on weekends at the Walgreens Drugstores to earn more money. John considered his job at Walgreens to be training for when he'd own his own pharmacy. Ellie still worked at the newspaper.

"Ellie, we've scrimped enough. Let's treat ourselves this weekend. Since St. Louis is called America's Best Baseball Town, surely we can afford to go to a baseball game."

"Oh, I used to go with my dad. That'd be wonderful. I still follow the games. This is exciting," Ellie no sooner said those words than she realized she didn't know which team John wanted to see. "My goodness, there's still so much we don't know about each other. Do you like the Browns or the Cardinals?"

"Nobody goes to the Cardinal games. The Browns have been the St. Louis team playing in Sportsman's Park for about fifty years."

Ellie started to sing, "Take me out to the ball game …"

The weekend turned into a typical humid summer day in St. Louis. The sun was relentless as the temperature rose into the nineties. Ellie wore a yellow cotton dress with a V-neck and an ample pleat in the front of the skirt; it was loose fitting and cool. She had a snug fitting hat of the same yellow material with a turned-up cuff that framed her face. John had bought her a nosegay of little rosebuds that was pinned to the shoulder of the dress.

John wore a short-sleeved white shirt, beige slacks, and topped his clothes with a stylish Panama hat.

At the stadium, they moved slowly through the crowd to their seats. Sportsman's Park had a seating capacity of 18,000 and was sold out. The Browns were playing the Yankees.

Vendors were hawking hot dogs and boxes of Cracker Jacks. Small booths sold souvenirs and cold drinks. John bought a couple of beers and hot dogs.

As they settled into their seats, John reminisced, "Remember a couple of years ago when the Browns nearly beat the Yankees? It was the year they lost the pennant by one measly game."

Ellie was chewing a bite of her hot dog and answered with her mouth full. "Yeah, I remember. That's the year George Sisler got that eye injury. It was bad for the Browns. It's good to see him back in the game."

"Yeah," John took out his handkerchief and wiped his forehead. "He missed all of last season. He had a .420 batting average, too."

"I think he had a .448 one season. Didn't he break Cobb's record? But I get a kick out of him stealing bases. Hope he steals some today. He just takes off like lightning."

The game was in the second inning with no runs and the Browns up to bat. Ken Williams came to the plate. He slugged a homer and the crowd was on their feet, screaming.

Ellie jumped up and down. "I love to watch Williams hit those left-handed homers!"

"I don't know how he can throw with his right and hit with his left. I went to a lot of games a couple of years ago; he had about forty home runs and 150 RBIs, I think." John had taken off his hat and rolled the cold beer bottle over his forehead as he sat back down.

But Ellie didn't sit down right away. She fanned her skirt to get some air on her legs, "Why did I wear these stockings?"

When everyone had sat back down, she became a bright yellow object in the stands. And the fluttering skirt made her more visible.

In the fourth inning, Ellie went to the ladies room and took off her stockings. She splashed her face and arms with water. As she started down the stairs to her seat, she glanced around the stands to locate John and got the shock of her life.

Al Capone stood one aisle over, glaring into the area where she had been sitting. Ellie was just fifty seats away from him and two rows above.

He's looking for me! Somehow he saw me and knows I'm here. What do I do?

Just then the Yankees hit a homer and the crowd got to their feet. Capone disappeared from her view. More importantly, the crowd blocked the sight of her from Capone. She took the opportunity to rush to John who was three seats in, but standing like everyone else. She reached across two people and grabbed his hand.

Pulling on him, she shouted above the crowd, "John, help me. Come quick."

Clamoring up the steps, she said in gasping breath, "I never told you about Al Capone and me. He almost beat me to death and ..." She pointed to her right, "and he's here."

"What?"

Ellie let go of John's hand as the crowd started to sit back down. She moved faster. She saw John looking to the right as Al Capone appeared in the next aisle. There was recognition in John's face.

"John, just do as I say." As she reached the top step, she glanced toward Capone and their eyes met.

Capone grinned and turned.

Although Ellie couldn't hear Capone's words, she saw two of his goons rush to follow their boss up the aisle.

John saw and realized that Ellie was not exaggerating. Capone was coming for her.

"John, I've got an idea! Quick, come with me." She weaved between people, glancing back to make sure John was following. Now she was on the landing and pushing people away.

John was out of sight. *I need John!* She retraced a couple of steps and he appeared. She grabbed his arm, "I'm going into the ladies room with you. Don't balk."

"Why?"

As she pushed the door to enter, she blurted, "We gotta change clothes with each other. We're about the same size." Out of the corner of her eye, she saw Capone come around the corner. *He's as close as a run between home and first base.*

Women began to scream in the ladies room and some rushed out. With one movement, Ellie lifted her dress over her head. "John, give me your slacks." She bent to slip off her shoes and pushed them in John's direction.

Now more women screamed and left.

He pulled his shoelaces open, pried his shoes off, and dropped his beige trousers. Ellie snatched them, slipped into them, buttoning only the top button, and put her feet into his shoes as John fumbled with his shirt buttons.

"Here I'll help." When his last button was free, Ellie grabbed her hat and dress from the floor. "Put your arms straight up." She furled the dress up and over his head. *Thank heavens! It fits.* Now she pushed her hat on him while pulling some of his hair out onto his forehead.

While he forced his feet into her shoes, Ellie buttoned enough buttons to keep the shirt on, opened the slacks to tuck the shirt, and grabbed his hat. So she could hide her hair, she bent over quickly, making her hair fly out, and put on the hat while still upside-down. "I'm getting out of here. I'll meet you where we parked."

"Your shoes are too short!"

"Cram the backs down!"

Cautiously, Ellie cracked the door. *Why isn't Capone in here? He had enough time.* Outside the door she could see three policemen had stopped Capone as he tried to go in. Women were around shouting about another man in the bathroom. Ellie slipped out away from the crowd. She could hear women repeating that another man was in there. *Oh, John, please act like a lady.*

When Ellie was about thirty feet away, she moved to the edge of a booth selling souvenirs. There was a wooden pillar that she stood behind so she could see what was happening back there. She finished buttoning the shirt. The police had put cuffs on Capone, but she saw his bodyguards standing with their backs to her.

Just then John came out, clutching her purse to his chest. *He looks like me!*

Unknowingly, John was coming toward Ellie. And the two bodyguards followed. Those two were closing in on John. One of their suit jackets flew open to expose a shoulder strap.

She stiffened. *Of course, they've got guns.*

Suddenly, John turned into a crowd of people and disappeared. As the two goons got to the place where John had disappeared, Ellie bent down to tie the shoelaces. *They're too close to me. I recognize them, so they'd know me if they looked at my face. Please move on, you guys.*

A groups of people passed Ellie and she joined them, heading for the exit to Grand Avenue. *Luckily, Panama hats are popular. I'm sure they saw John with me and they might want to nab him, too.* Glancing over her shoulder, she saw the two crooks split up and go different directions.

Not knowing where John was, Ellie proceeded with the plan and headed toward the parking lot. It was a block down Grand Avenue. There weren't too many people on the street so she felt conspicuous. She decided to go into a café and survey the street through the plate glass window.

There's John across the street, hobbling along.

Craning her neck to see further down the sidewalk on her side, she saw one of Capone's men. He stepped into the street, getting ready to cross over to John. *What am I going to do?*

As Ellie began to panic, the sound in the café caught her attention. Fans hummed above, plates clanked in the distant kitchen and a conversation between two policemen, sitting at the counter having a bite, became apparent. She hurried over to them and hoped they couldn't see she was a woman in men's clothing.

Lowering her voice to the deepest bass possible, she pointed, "Officers, that man crossing the street has a gun under his coat."

They stood simultaneous to look.

Ellie continued, "He seems to be rushing toward that woman. I saw the gun clearly from the window when he stepped into the street. His coat flew open."

They walked to the window just as Capone's man, grabbed John by the arm. Without hesitation, the two policemen ran to the door and out. They held up their hands to stop traffic while rushing across the street.

John pulled his arm out of the goon's grasp and doubled his fist. Pow! John packed a wallop into the jaw of Capone's bodyguard who fell against a building and slipped to the sidewalk. John kicked off Ellie's shoes and ran.

At that moment, the officers arrived. They pulled the culprit up and opened his coat quickly removing the gun. Handcuffs went on as Ellie found the back door out of the cafe.

No sense in getting involved in this.

When she arrived at the parking lot, John was waiting with the engine running. She slipped into the passenger seat, "The police got the guy, no need to worry about racing away." She started giggling and took off his hat. She scooted closer and put her head into his chest."

"How can you laugh?"

She sat up still laughing, "John, you make a great gal."

"Come on, Ellie. We could have been killed. That guy had a gun."

"I know." She sobered up and said, "Until I met you, I feared meeting up with Capone most days in these last two years. The adventure of my love with you made me forget. Let's go over to the Cohen's and get a drink. I'll tell you the whole Capone story over there."

"And any other stories that I need to know!"

Driving away, Ellie snuggled and cautiously asked, "Can I get a photo of you in this dress?" *After I call the Post-Dispatch about Capone being picked up by the police at the Browns game.*

***

The year 1925 came and went with no wedding, as did 1926 when the Cardinals won their first World Series and replaced the Browns as the favorite team in St. Louis. But Ellie and John didn't mind about their delayed wedding or the derailed baseball team. As long as they were together, they found life fulfilling.

However, at the end of 1927, they didn't need to wait any longer. Ellie was sure they had saved enough to start out with a modest apartment. One of the deciding factors was Henry Ford; in 1926, he built a Model T on an assembly line. An automobile, that had cost about $900 when John was born, now could be bought for $300.

They took the $300 from the bank for the Model T. They had $2,500 that remained in the bank to grow with interest. They planned to keep adding savings even after they were married because Ellie would continue to work.

John said, "Those funds are for the purchase of our pharmacy when the time comes. Well, it's for paying special bills, like having a baby or an unforeseen illness." He always referred to that money as their security. "Let's get married with a modest wedding. You know, just family. Of course, Jerry and Françoise as best man and maid of honor." They set the date for the spring of 1928.

One evening as the four friends sat on the floor of the Cohen's apartment, talking about the impending wedding, Ellie thought of her father. "My daddy has been gone more years than I lived with him. How I wish he could be at my wedding."

No one said anything. They understood her sadness.

John broke the silence, "It must be so hard not knowing where he is, how he is, or if he's even alive." Ellie had not told John about the birthday letter that came each year. She kept her secret.

Françoise joined in, "Yes, when my parents died, I realized what you must have felt when your father left. It must be harder when you just don't know if he's alive or not."

Jerry asked, "How old is he? We should think of him as alive until there is reason to believe otherwise."

"Oh, let me see. He's fifty-seven years old this December."

Jerry brightened, "He's young. You must think positively about him returning to see his grandchildren."

Ellie smiled, "I like that idea. I never think of him as dead. I refuse to grieve until I know there's a reason. I worry about Mama because she is aging so quickly; she's slowing down. But she's alive!"

Jerry started to talk, "I ... ah, I would like to share a death with you, my good, good friends. It is a death I have grieved for many years. Will you listen?"

Françoise scooted closer to Jerry and put her head on his knees. He was leaning against the dining room wall and pulled her up onto his chest to hold her.

"Françoise has not heard this story either. I want to take you all to Paris when I was a boy of twelve. We lived in a walkup type of brick building, renting three floors with three bedrooms and a basement. We weren't poor or rich. Just people living as most did.

"I had a younger sister named Rose who was ten years old. Two years younger than I was. She worshiped me, her older brother, the scientist. You see, I've always liked science. My father and mother always encouraged me to learn. My father worked at a book binding company and would get permission to bring a book home overnight if he thought I might like to read it. I read and read. There was a library I frequented for books. One year I was interested in biology, then geology, and so on. When I was twelve, my concentration was on chemistry.

"The chemist in the neighborhood knew me and liked me. I would go to visit him and talk science. We talked about atoms, molecules, and such. From time to time, he gave me small amounts of powders or potions and tell me to mix this with that and show my sister and parents. I had many an enjoyable evening entertaining my family with puffs of smoke, or liquids that changed colors before their eyes.

"Then one day I found a book in the library describing bigger reactions and large explosions."

Jerry swallowed, found that his throat was dry, and reached for his coffee that was on a chair. It was cold, but it was wet. He drained his cup.

"One Saturday afternoon, when my parents had walked to the market just two blocks away. I was in the basement at my chemistry lab. I had beakers and pipettes, even a Bunsen burner. I had used my pennies and saved to buy equipment like that. And my parents gave me some things on my birthday. Anyway, there was this experiment in the book that I wanted to try. My sister came down to watch.

"I told her that I needed to concentrate, reading the experiment and measuring the chemicals carefully, so she needed to remain quiet. She did.

"She leaned against the wooden bench where all my equipment sat. She had her blonde curls draped on the wood with her head on her crossed arms. Her sweet blue eyes watched my every move as I worked. She smiled from time to time for what reason I don't know. I thought about asking her, when I was done. I was going to tell her that it was distracting, and she shouldn't do that again.

"Again never happened. The explosion I created threw me across the basement. It blew off her precious face and set her on fire. Rose only cried out in agony for seconds, I think, but seconds can be a measurement of eternity. I still hear her, and it is over thirty years that she has been screaming in agony."

Jerry pulled Françoise's cheek to his face, and he wept. She wrapped her arms about his waist as their tears mixed on their cheeks.

Momentarily, he coughed and wiped his nose with his handkerchief, "Forgive me. I loved her so. I rolled her on the floor to put out the flames. I don't know what killed her, but my parents entered soon after and found us heaped together. The house was full of smoke; they knew something horrible had happened. They thought we were both dead when the opened windows cleared the basement enough to see. I think I fainted. Or it may have been smoke inhalation. I don't know. I … I killed Rose. My sweet little sister was gone. Forgive me."

John stood up. Jerry's plea for forgiveness was not just about the sobs that halted his story. John knelt next to him and enveloped—the doctor, the scientist, the brother, and the friend—into his arms and hugged. Ellie came and put her forehead on Jerry's shoulder. And so the four sat for minutes that lasted their lifetimes.

After John and Ellie said goodnight to their friends and were walking toward the Model T, they had an idea. John said it first, but Ellie was thinking the same. He said, "Let's name our first child for Jerry, if he's a boy, and for Rose, if she's a girl."

They promised each other to do that.

Though, in a few years, not only will they have a son named after Jerry, but also they will give Jerry back his Rose.

Ellie, Franny, John, and Jerry

Ellie at farm

Ellie (tallest) with girlfriends

Ellie (tallest) with girlfriends and ?? Al Capone ??

Ellie with first two children

Bertha and Ellie

Bertha with her first three grandchildren

John (rt) in Ellie's clothes with unknown friend

John with mules at farm

John and Ellie in wedding photo

James and Ginny with his dream car.

Part 3

Ellie's Married Life
1928-1950

One who learns must suffer.
And even in our sleep pain that cannot forget
falls drop by drop upon the heart,
and in our own despair,
against our will,
comes wisdom to us by the awful grace of God.

Aeschylus, 525-456 B.C.
Agamemnon, l. 177

Chapter 11

1928-1929
Mr. and Mrs. John Bartlett

The wedding was to be in the James' living room although there was barely enough room for the nine people—John's parents, Bertha and Ginny, Jerry with Françoise, the bride and groom, and the Justice of the Peace.

It was a simple wedding with few preparations. Ginny had taken care of getting flowers for the house and for the bride. An assortment of fragrances wafted here and there from vases on tables, to floating roses in bowls, to the bouquet of white roses that sat in the icebox chilling to be fresh for Ellie.

Bertha had cleaned the whole week before and had prepared a luncheon for everyone, to be eaten following the ceremony. Crisply starched and ironed linens covered coffee tables, the buffet, backs of chairs, and the dining room table. Spiders worked frantically to find the webs that Bertha destroyed, finally starting new ones in the corners of the porch and under the dining room table.

Jerry and Françoise did anything asked of them; mostly they were there for support. They called to have the wedding listed in all three newspapers; they tied tin cans on the back of the Model T; and on the day of the ceremony, they planned to drive across town to pick up John's parents and then to help dress their nervous friends, tying a black bow tie and clasping a pearl necklace.

John and Ellie had made the arrangements to spend a week at Niagara Falls for their honeymoon. Other than that, they trusted everyone else to make it happen.

The wedding's most anticipated item had been seen only by Bertha. She had insisted on sewing the bride's dress in secret. She had taken weeks choosing the material and designing it. She planned only one fitting on the evening before the wedding.

On that evening, Ellie, Ginny, and Françoise arrived together from work. They came into the house chattering with excitement to see the wedding dress.

"Mama, we're here. Bring out the dress," called Ellie upon closing the front door.

Bertha came out with the dress draped across both arms and wrapped in a white sheet, "Sit down girls. All of you on the couch, and I'll show you. I like how it came out," Bertha said as she turned her back and let the white sheet drop to the floor. Grasping the shoulders of the dress she turned for them to see.

The shock was on each of the young women's faces, but in that moment of silence Bertha walked toward Ellie as if she hadn't noticed. "Ain't this the most lovely crepe you've ever seen? Touch it, Ellie, it's so soft."

Ellie stood. She towered a head taller than her mother. Veins in her neck bulged and her voice quivered, "Mama, blue? What are you saying to me? How dare you do this!"

"Why, Ellie, this dusty blue is beautiful. This isn't a formal wedding, and I thought we could take care of the 'something blue' with the dress."

"Mama, you don't fool me. You're giving me a message that you think I'm no longer pure enough to wear white." Ellie stormed out the front door.

Up jumped Ginny and Françoise to follow. "Ellie, Ellie," they called and rushed to catch up to her swiftly striding legs.

Ellie turned to wait for them, "I don't know what to say. This is so embarrassing. Can you imagine my mother doing this to me? I just can't believe it."

The three of them walked slowly now. Françoise put her arm around Ellie's waist, "Now don't get mad at me. And just remember that I'm not being critical because," she put her mouth to Ellie's ear and whispered, "Jerry and I did it before our wedding."

Stopping to face Françoise, Ellie put her hands on her hips and started to defend her honor, "We've been engaged for three to four years and it's not …" and then said, "I just don't think …" and finally she just laughed and shook her head, letting her dark hair fly against her cheeks.

Ginny came over and wrapped her arms around Ellie, "It is the most beautiful dress. Did you see how she cut it on the diagonal? It will cling to you in just the right places. And, Ellie, you never were one to go along with all those rules and old-fashion conventions. I didn't know about the blue dress, but I would think you'd wear it with pride. You always liked to show people that you're fearless and outspoken."

Ellie sputtered a little, "Well, ah …" and said nothing. She looked to Françoise then Ginny, before throwing her head back and chuckling, "Thanks, you know me well. I should have known Mama was up to something when she wanted to surprise me. Oh, leave it to my mother."

Françoise suggested, "Just wear it. Are you worried about John's parents or the Justice of the Peace thinking badly of you? The rest of us love you just the way you are."

Ellie thought a moment, "No, I'm not worried about the others."

"Well, let's go back in, so you can try it on. I want to see it on you. Ginny's right, it's the kind of dress that looks smashing when you put it on. I just know it will."

That night, Ellie peered out the window at the crescent moon and stars before she was ready to fall asleep. She liked to open the window in springtime. A breeze blew across her bed and rippled the curtains. She was aware it was her last night to sleep in Dogtown in the house where she grew up. Her mind wandered to the excuse her mother had used for sewing a blue dress. She went over the items from the old saying:

Something old,
Something new,
Something borrowed,
Something blue.

Something old is Bertha's sweet wedding ring from James, with a small diamond in a raised gold setting that looks like a crown. Something new is the strand of pearls from Jerry and Françoise. Something borrowed is the pair of gloves that John's mother wore for her wedding many years ago. And something blue is The Scarlet Letter

I'll wear for all to see. But she smiled. *How did Mama know? John and I were so careful.* She hugged herself and goose pimples ripped down her arms as she recalled some of their encounters:

- At the picnic in the woods when they went to the farm
- In the back seat of their new Model T when it was parked in his parents' garage
- In the middle of the Meramec River when John thought no one was around, and *he couldn't put on that rubber thing in the water.*
- In Jerry and Françoise's apartment

When she thought about the many times in Jerry and Françoise's apartment, she became filled with longing for John and wished she were with him. *Tomorrow, I'll be Mrs. John Bartlett.* Other love-making scenes came to her, and she fell asleep with the repeated thought, *Tomorrow, I'll be Mrs. John Bartlett.*

John and Ellie committed to each other from the depth of their souls, with words that were not only words, but also vows from the depths of their souls.

"Now, each in turn, repeat after me," the Justice of the Peace said.

I, John, do solemnly swear to take
Elizabeth Mary James
As my lawfully wedded wife
For better or worse
In sickness or health
'Til death do us part.

I, Elizabeth, do solemnly swear to take
John Winfield Bartlett
As my lawfully wedded husband
For better or worse
In sickness or health
'Til death do us part.

***

Passion! Mr. and Mrs. John Bartlett's passion grew and grew. They couldn't get enough of each other. They made love a few times most nights and in the morning before work. On days with no work, they didn't want to get out of bed. Their small, one-bedroom flat on Parker Avenue was cozy and located one block off the main street called Kingshighway.

Relaxing in bed one Sunday, Ellie tried to express her euphoria, "It must be because you don't use those rubbers anymore. Before we were married it was never this good. Oh, it was wonderful before, but it's more. I can't tell you how it feels. I have no words. I love you, love you, love you!" She rolled into his arms.

John was not as verbal about such things, yet she knew he loved her through small gestures like when he carefully ran his finger across her forehead to catch some hair that had blown into her eyes or when he held her hand longer than need be to remove a splinter. She knew he wanted her. She knew he loved making love to her and touching her at any time, even when she was standing washing dishes. He would tell her that he couldn't get enough of her body and made the habit of whispering, when out among friends, "The sight of you excites me." But one annual event, that Jerry Cohen had taught him, moved Ellie's heart the most.

Jerry had emphasized to John that he must always remember to send a card for each birthday and anniversary. Jerry explained. "It's a small thing, but for some reason women just love it. No, I should say that women more than love it; they seem to need that card. Of course, you can send flowers from time to time, but a card, with some of your words at the bottom, is what means the most to them."

John sent a card every year. He would take a lot of time at Walgreens, reading over the cards. He would start a month before their anniversary and Ellie's Storm until, for each event, he found one he liked.

And Ellie saved each card in a drawer where she kept her underclothing. When she received the second card, she tucked it back into the envelope and tied a blue ribbon around the two. She kept them stacked in order. That was easy to do because John wrote, "To Ellie, Happy Birthday - 1928" and "To Ellie, Happy Anniversary – 1929" on the envelopes.

Over the coming years, John would never forget; John had learned this lesson well. Maybe too well.

This was a time for lessons. Ellie knew nothing about cooking, "Franny, what will I do? I don't know how to make a boiled egg." Her friend gave her a good cookbook, helped her set up the kitchen, and offered lessons, but Ellie was still working and didn't have much time.

John worked late some evenings. At those times, Ellie went to the Cohen's after her work, and the friends cooked together making double portions. Ellie took home the extra.

Also, Bertha insisted they come every Sunday to the James' house. The food was delicious, but Ellie never could get her mother to teach her anything.

"Mama, why don't we come over early next Sunday? You could show me how to make the fried chicken while John reads the Sunday paper," Ellie asked.

But Bertha didn't know how to teach. On Saturday night without Ellie, Bertha prepared the batter for dipping the chicken, "I had to do it early, because it needs to be in the refrigerator overnight."

So, Ellie didn't learn cooking easily.

She did learn about making a good breakfast as long as John didn't want a soft-boiled egg. No matter how she tried, soft-boiled would be like a hard-boiled one, every time. Stews were done easily, but her steaks were too tough to chew. She never made a loaf of bread that was not hard. She thanked her lucky stars when sliced bread machines appeared soon after they were married. She bought sliced bread and used a lot of Campbell's soups.

Her first attempt at baking a cake became her last. The Cohen's were coming for dinner to the Bartlett's flat. Ellie planned to make a meatloaf, serve some canned corn, prepare mashed potatoes, and bake a cake from the cookbook. It was called a Lady Cake.

John had given Ellie a Universal electric mixer for her birthday. Ellie loved how it made such good mashed potatoes, and she hoped it would make a good cake. She followed the directions carefully and slipped the tube pan with the batter into the oven just as the Cohens came in the door. In forty-five minutes they would have a cake. Ellie had a can of peaches to use with the cake; a half peach went onto the top of each slice.

Dinner went well. Ellie was proud of her first meal for invited guests. The smell of a baking cake added to the ambiance of the evening.

At the end of the meal, "Excuse me, it's time to take out the cake," Ellie said as she stood to go to the kitchen. Françoise followed.

Upon opening the oven door, both their mouths fell. The cake had not risen. It was still just half way up the side of the pain. Françoise took it out and pressed a toothpick into it. It seemed strange in some way. "Are you sure you put the baking powder in?"

On the kitchen table, they saw the teaspoon next to the baking powder tin and there were grains on the spoon. Ellie was sure it went in. There were two eggshells, so the eggs were in it. Françoise turned the pan over on a plate and the cake slipped out.

Françoise suggested, "We shouldn't remove the pan for a few minutes, sometimes the cake will crack and fall apart. Let's clear the dishes from the table. It'll be cool enough by then."

Although it was a flat cake, they sliced it and placed pieces on dessert plates and topped each with a peach half. John was the first to take a bite. He excused himself and went to the bathroom.

When Françoise took a bite, she understood what John had done. He had gone to spit out the stuff in his mouth. She too went to the bathroom. They called, "Don't eat it!" as they were coming back. It was the saltiest concoction any of them had ever put into their mouths.

Ellie lamented, "Oh no, you mean I used salt instead of sugar?"

The men were standing and bent in laughter.

Françoise hugged her friend and laughed. "We need to label your canisters."

Jerry chuckled, "What are friends for? It could've been worse. What if you had invited John's parents for dinner?"

Ellie saw the humor in her mistake.

What she considered more important than cooking was making a family and being a good mother. But after she had been married a year Ellie started to worry that she really was like Ginny and Françoise.

Barren!

She hesitated to share her fears with Françoise; it was a painful subject to the Cohens. Yet, Franny was her best friend, so they talked.

"No, Jerry and I will never adopt. We talked about it, but it's not for us. We've learned to live with the idea that there will be no children. We love each other, enjoy being together, and have good times. I feel fortunate. You know?" Françoise raised her eyebrows and looked directly into Ellie's eyes to make her point, "My life could be like Ginny's. But you, Ellie, need to go to a doctor for an exam. Stop worrying without any information. You're just afraid of what you might hear, right?"

Ellie talked in confidence to Jerry and got the name of a gynecologist. The physical exam was done without John's knowledge. *I don't want to worry him. We've talked about having children so many times, so I know it's important to him. He hasn't said anything. He has more patience than I do.*

Actually, John was so busy between working at different drugstores and going to the farm to learn how to be a farmer that he really didn't have time to worry why Ellie wasn't pregnant. Learning about the farm had been on his list of plans, just like owning a pharmacy was one of those plans.

His Uncle Will was teaching him how to manage the mules.

Uncle Will introduced John to the two mules. "Mules are smart, John. Don't you e'er doubt that. Horses are a dime a dozen, but good mules like Bell and Dine are worth their weight in gold."

John was listening and respectful to his uncle, but he doubted most of what Uncle Will was saying. John wanted to buy a tractor as soon as he could afford one. For now, John knew he needed to learn what Uncle Will could teach him.

Uncle Will handed John the reins, "Now you done seen me plow half the field; it's time for you to git on and finish it up."

John took the two leather straps and started to sit on the plow. "So, do I just need to say 'Gee' to go and 'Haw' to stop?"

No sooner had John rested his backside on the plow seat then he toppled off. Dine and Bell had started moving. John struggled up from the soil while Uncle Will crowed with laughter.

"Didn't you see me? When I's ready to plow, I sit and the mules start to move 'fore you can drop a hat. Then when you git off the seat, they stop."

"Oh, I see." John wondered why his uncle hadn't said that to begin with. "Well, when do you use 'Gee' and 'Haw' for them to start and stop. I saw you do that the other day."

"Well, not now! Go on now. Let's git this field plowed. Some other day I's goin' to teach you that."

That other day came months later when it was time to bring the hay into the barn. John had been working from sunup with his Uncle and two neighbors, cutting the hay with a scythe. The temperature was in the nineties with a cloudless sky, and the cicadas had been buzzing all day. The men let hay dry in the sun while they ate lunch. John's back ached like never before.

"Okay now, it's time to hitch up Bell and Dine to the wagon. Do ya remember how that's done, John?"

John wiped his dripping face with a red bandana. "I think so, but what I don't know is how to stop Bell from squeezing me against the sides of the stall when I go to get her."

The three farmers laughed.

Uncle Will took off his straw hat and passed the sleeve of his shirt over his sweaty face. After replacing his hat, he put his big hand on John's shoulder, "Bell just knows how green ya are. Like I said, these mules are smart. Come on now, I's goin' to help ya."

Once the mules were hitched up and all the men climbed on the wagon bed with a pitchfork, Uncle Will pulled himself up onto the bench and hollered "Gee" and the mules started moving. When they got the wagon down into the field, Uncle Will gave out a "Haw" and they stopped. Three men pitched hay into the wagon with one man standing on the bed to stack the hay.

After a while, Uncle Will pointed with his fork, "Look here, John. Right about here is as high as you can fill the wagon. The mules won't pull more. Remember that." They worked on and on, making trips up to the barn to unload and then back to the field for more. The sun was starting to rest on the horizon when the two neighbors said they needed to get home after the next load. The heat remained in the nineties though the sun was going down.

"John, I think there's only one more load down in the field. Do ya think you can bring it up alone while I put this last load into the barn? No sense in the others comin' back up wit ya."

"Sure," John nodded. "I've taken the wagon down and up a few times by myself today. And I don't think there's too much hay left down there."

So the three men worked filling the last wagon. John was on top in the bed stacking when the first man excused himself.

"I's got to go. My cows are needin' to be milked 'fore dinner."

After a bit, the second farmer left. John jumped down and started finishing off the field alone. He pitched hay up into the bed, climbed up to stack it, and then went for the reins and called "Gee" to move down the field for more. A full moon was rising and lit the field, but he was almost done. To make the toiling easier, he kept thinking about the delicious dinner his Aunt Laura always had waiting for them. Over and over, he tossed, stacked, gave a "Gee" and "Haw" to move on until he came to the last hay. As he stood up from the bench, he noticed the hay was stacked up to the point his uncle said was the full mark. *But there's only a little more in the field and it ain't worth another trip.*

So John topped off the load and pulled himself up onto the bench. "Gee," he called. But the mules wouldn't move. "Gee!" Still they stood. John climbed down and went around to the front of the mules. *Guess they're as tired as me. I'll just grab Bell by her harness and give a little tug.*

Bell and Dine started bawling and screeching, kicking and wiggling, and creating such a commotion that Uncle Will came running.

"Well, tarnation, John. There's too much weight for 'em to move." Uncle Will took a pitchfork and tossed some back onto the field before climbing onto the bench. With one "Gee" Bell and Dine started up to the barn.

John ran along side.

"Youse lucky they didn't hurt you. They know you're just learnin' but next time they won't be so polite."

John didn't say much, but he knew he wanted a tractor.

***

So, John was busy worrying about other things than babies.

The fall of 1928 turned to the winter of 1929, and Ellie was going to worry about other things as well. In St. Louis, February can be the hardest and coldest month; this year February would shock the nation with the hardest and coldest incident ever seen.

February fourteenth began with John giving Ellie a heart-shaped box of chocolates before they left for work. She took them to the office to share with others. For a festive touch, some people had pasted red hearts on the walls of the pressroom at the *Post-Dispatch*, but it wasn't a recognized holiday; it was work as usual ... until later in the morning.

Ellie noticed the telephones started ringing more than most mornings. She kept typing; she had a lot of copy to complete. Finally one of her colleagues came over to her desk a little before noon.

"Something big has happened in Chicago, Ellie. The word is that Al Capone is responsible."

Her heart jumped, "What happened?"

"Nothing's confirmed yet, but it seems that at half-past ten today, six members of Bugs Moran's gang were gunned down."

"Was Bugs with them?"

"We don't know."

Ellie felt sick. She knew the power Capone had. She knew how violent he could be.

By afternoon, the whole story was known. The six men, without their boss Bugs Moran, were waiting in a garage for the arrival of some illegal booze. A Cadillac arrived with three men dressed as policemen and two men in civilian clothes. The policemen went into the garage and told Bugs Moran's men to line up on the wall with their hands up. As they were standing there, the two men not in uniform entered with sub-machine guns and mowed them down.

Bloody, morbid photographs of the six murdered men made the evening paper with the story.

The public was horrified. Until this incident, people looked at Al Capone as more of a Robin Hood than just a hood. The whole nation was up in arms, and some leaders in the Mafia put a price on Capone.

With each day that passed after the St. Valentine Day Massacre, more news about the fighting mobs came into Ellie's work. She couldn't sleep at nights. She worried he would come to St. Louis to get away from the price on his head. Each day she went to work, she looked over her shoulder for Al. Every day it wasn't the weather chilling her to the bone; it was fear.

Finally Capone was arrested for carrying a concealed weapon and sentenced to ten months in the Eastern State Penitentiary. The scuttlebutt was that he arranged to have himself jailed to get away from being hunted and shot down.

Interestingly, the St. Valentine Day Massacre case was never solved. But Ellie relaxed, knowing Al Capone was in jail for the time being.

Finally spring came. A week after Ellie placed her 1929-anniversary card with last year's birthday card and tied both together with a blue ribbon, she missed her period. Immediately she called the doctor who informed her to wait two months before having an exam to verify if she was pregnant. She held her tongue and told no one while biding her time.

She kept busy at work. The newspapers were full of information of how the economy was bustling. Ellie remembered how the Dow Jones Industrial Average had been at 63.9 in 1921 when she started working and had extra money. Back then, as she watched the Dow climb, she started to invest in stocks and her stocks had increased six times. Now in 1929, the Dow was approximately 600.

However, John had talked her into cashing in on her investments when they became engaged. That had been their first disagreement. John was more conservative and cautious with money.

John explained, "I know it's your money, but we're going to be a family, and we need to agree on how we save. Look, this is what I figure. The stock market is like gambling."

Ellie interrupted to disagree, "You can't compare it to gambling."

John continued, "Please just hear me out. Yes, stocks are doing well, but I would never take all my money to a poker game. That would be foolish. I tell myself, I can afford to loose five percent of my money. So that's what I put in my pocket before I leave to play poker. I think you need to realize that it's better to have most of your money in a safer place. Like a bank."

John would change his mind about banks before the year was out. Nevertheless, for the moment, Ellie agreed and took most of her money out of the stock market, putting it into their joint savings account at the bank. That's one reason they had over $2,500.

When the day arrived for the doctor's visit, she had just tucked away the second birthday card from John—for Ellie's 1929 Storm. She had missed another period. She was so happy and positive she was pregnant.

Ellie said, "Franny, I feel different. I know I'm pregnant. My breasts tingle every so often, and, from time to time, I get an uncanny ripple in my body that I've never had before. And you know what? I think I know when it happened. One night when we made love, it just felt different. I wanted a baby so much. My whole body wanted to have a baby."

Françoise was so interested, "Really!"

"And did you know that the test the doctor does is horrible. They inject a rabbit with my urine and if the poor animal dies then I'm pregnant."

"No!"

"Yes! I will know in two weeks and then I'll tell John. Oh, this is so exciting. I feel better than ever. I seem to have more energy. The doctor asked me if I was sick in the mornings, but I'm not. I just feel like … like I have the energy of two lives now."

In July, when they were at his Uncle Will's farm where they first had met, Ellie told John about her pregnancy. It being July in Missouri, they were sitting in the creek trying to stay cool. A steady drone of crickets accompanied their discussion and excitement. John learned that the baby was due in December of that year, 1929. He hugged Ellie, splashed Ellie, kissed Ellie, and thanked Ellie.

"We'll have children to be proud of. We're healthy and intelligent. Oh, Ellie, I can't wait to hold our child." John stood up and screamed, "Yahoo," in the biggest voice he had. The crickets went quiet for a while.

Soon the evening darkened and three planets sparkled in the western sky as they walked to the farmhouse for supper with John's Uncle Will and Aunt Laura.

Uncle Will stood with an Abe Lincoln stature—tall, lanky, and long-armed. His gaunt face displayed an impressively large, hooked nose that produced a nasal twang to his speech, and he always smiled when he spoke, "What was that whooping I heared out there? Did a copperhead scare ya?" He had been working in a small garden next to the house and was rubbing dirt from his hands as they walked to the farmhouse.

Once inside, John explained he had shouted in excitement about the coming child.

Uncle Will turned to Ellie, "I'm happy fer ya both. You know, John's been coming here to our farm all his life. He may be my nephew, but he's like our own. John takes to this farm like a duck to water." Then Uncle Will turned to John, "Sorry to say I'm losin' the farm. The bank's gonna take it cuz I can't pay the taxes."

"What!" John was beside himself. Even the thrill of learning of a pending child did not diminish the pain he was feeling. "It can't be. I didn't know you were behind in your taxes."

"Yep, that's so. I's years behind. Heavens to Betsy, it's all of a sudden that the bank won't give us no more time."

Aunt Laura lamented, "Our grown children ain't no help cuz just like us they's strapped with debt. Farming's hard. Ya work from sunup to sundown and can't make ends meet."

Uncle Will plunged his craggy hands into a wooden bucket of water, "It's not the best farm though. That there's one of my problems." He reached for a hunk of homemade soap and started scrubbing while they talked.

John asked, "What do you owe in taxes?"

Aunt Laura told John, "Oh, almost two thousand dollars. Not quite, but close enough. Don't matter none; we couldn't raise half that kind of money even sellin' e'rything."

John looked to Ellie. Her heart sunk at what she saw in his eyes. *But I married this man for better or worse, and I knew he was generous and kind.* She nodded to John, and it was settled.

After the meal, they came to an agreement that John would pay the taxes and become the owner. Uncle Will and Aunt Laura would live on the farm for no rent, but there was a condition—John wanted to learn how to be a farmer. Uncle Will agreed to teach him and care for the farm.

"Looks like I'm going to be both a farmer and a pharmacist."

Of course, John figured that his uncle must be doing something wrong to not make enough to pay taxes. John decided he would study and learn all he could to make the land pay for itself and more.

In August 1929, John and Ellie became the owners of 200 acres of rolling hills between the towns of Bourbon and Sullivan, Missouri. In the first weeks of September, John used the rest of their money to buy some Hereford cattle with official papers.

Ellie was appalled at John's decision to use their money. She had just quit her job. They had a baby coming in five months.

"John, that money was both of ours. In fact, most of it was mine before we married. I agreed on buying the farm for the price of taxes, but you didn't consult with me about the cows."

"Don't call them cows. I bought some cattle for beef. I'm sorry, I would have talked with you, but you weren't with me. It was an auction and the price was cheap. I couldn't let it pass."

The anger Ellie had toward John lasted only a week. All her ire dissipated on September 24th when the rest of the world lost so much of their money in the infamous Stock Market Crash of 1929. Runs on the banks followed. The economy of the world seemed to collapse.

Ellie was flabbergasted, "Did you know something in advance, John? How did we escape with only losing those few stocks that I kept? John, I can't believe how you did it. You took our two thousand five hundred dollars and we still have it in assets when most people in the world lost everything."

"It was just luck, Ellie. I never thought the banks could lose." That day John thanked Lady Luck. However, over the years, he learned that owning land was the best way to invest his money, and Ellie believed in his decisions. John Bartlett would have assets worth over a million dollars, most of it in land, when he would die at the age of ninety-nine.

***

At the end of 1929, Ellie gave birth to a healthy boy. To the amazement and pleasure of Dr. and Mrs. David Jerome Cohen, they named him David Jerome Bartlett. In this way, they honored their friends and thanked them for twice saving Ellie's life, for bringing Ellie and John together, and for being friends who were always there.

Chapter 12

1930-1931
Motherhood and Fatherhood

Little David went everywhere with his parents. The entire family doted on him. He was Bertha's first grandchild and also the first boy child for her to enjoy. David was the first child to give Virginia James the title of Aunt Ginny. And Françoise and Jerry became Aunt Franny and Uncle Jerry before David ever learned a word.

Ellie said, "Uncle Jerry, would you change his diaper? Franny and I are right in the middle of getting the food into the oven."

"Sure, I'd love to clean this little guy up." Jerry was glad that John hadn't arrived, so he could have personal time with David.

David never lacked for love and attention.

After the meal, Franny and Ellie cleaned off the table and washed the dishes while the men played in the living room. All three were on the floor.

"Look at this, he holds so tight I can pull him to his feet." John remarked to Uncle Jerry. Little David clasped his pudgy hands around his father's index fingers. David was about nine months old, and John was amazed at each new accomplishment.

Ellie called from the kitchen, "John, I was at your sister Louise's house today—with her and the two little ones. David loves being with other children." John's sisters were becoming a part of their lives. "If the weather's good on Wednesday, we're going to have a picnic in the park. That way, we can put our feet in the wading pool and stay cool while we sit and hold the babies."

They lived very close to Tower Grove Park at Arsenal and Kingshighway. The park was only a few blocks east of the St. Louis Insane Asylum on Arsenal and had been right in the path of Ellie's tornado. The tornado had touched down many times in this neighborhood. It appeared that John and Ellie had chosen a place to live … as destiny had planned.

Removing aprons and draping them over dining room chairs, Françoise and Ellie joined the men and sat on the couch. Françoise picked up her purse and took out her compact to tidy her hair and reapply lipstick.

"You should see your lips, Ellie," Françoise commented while turning the mirror to Ellie. "Look at the color! I think it's that bright blue blouse you're wearing that makes them more colorful. Oh, how I wish I had all your natural color."

Ellie's lips changed to deep magenta when she wore clothes of blue or lavender. She glanced into the mirror as a courtesy to her friend. Ellie still wore no makeup and couldn't be bothered with discussing it either.

Besides, Ellie had something important to say, "Hey, I have some news." She smiled as each one turned to look at her. "I'm pregnant again." It was September of 1930.

Of course, John had already been told. He got up and pulled Ellie close for a kiss. They looked into each other's eyes. Their love needed no words.

The Depression was pulling everyone down as the populace dug deeper into their pockets to make ends meet. People learned to make do with less and not to waste a thing. Françoise showed Ellie how to make delicious soup without meat, just from bones and vegetables. The Cohens could afford to buy the meat, if it were available, but there were fewer items in the butcher's case, on the grocer's shelves, and in people's cupboards. People tightened their belts. In John's case, he saved everything—broken toasters, bent pieces of metal, nails that could be straightened and reused, a crooked picture frame without glass—and took them to be stored in his sheds at the farm, planning to repair them or give them to people who could. People shared.

Bertha always had some panhandlers sitting on her back steps eating something. "T'was nothin' but a bit o' beans and barley I had in the pantry for years. They's so old I had to cook them for an extra hour. But I couldn't waste 'em. I knew some poor person would come needin' to fill their empty stomach."

Ginny volunteered her free time helping at the Salvation Army kitchen, "Ellie, I'm finally learning to cook. Now, if I ever find a man, I'll be able to cook. Of course, I only know how to make portions big enough for an army."

Ellie had her hands full with little David and her growing belly, "I was never this big the first time. The doctor told me that every pregnancy is different. I believe him. And I'm so tired all the time. I take a nap every time David does." She laughed at the truth of her next statement. "I'm embarrassed to admit it, but when John comes home, I even take a nap before bedtime. Then, after we put David down for the night, I can have some time with my hubby. But I feel great in every other way."

Dr. Cohen and Françoise volunteered time at a clinic to help those who were too poor to pay. The hospital had started a clinic for this purpose. During hard times there was less of everything except illness. After months of burning the candle at both ends, Jerry and Françoise decided they needed to get away or they wouldn't be any help to anyone.

"We're going down to our house in Florida for a couple of months. Besides needing a rest, the St. Louis weather's so cold. We plan to return in the spring," Françoise told Ellie. "Oh, don't worry, we plan to be back before June when your baby comes. We wouldn't miss that!" But they almost did.

During her pregnancy, Ellie still worked at her scrapbooks, cutting and pasting current events of interest. Ellie had a bookshelf of scrapbooks, all properly labeled on the binding edge with a series of years, or a topic. For example, there was one, 1930-31, and others labeled, "Capone" or "Political Scandals."

This particular morning, she pulled the Capone scrapbook off the shelf. John was getting ready to leave for work.

"John, did you see the *Post-Dispatch* last night—that article about a reporter from the *Chicago Tribune* on Capone's payroll?" She was agitated and stood to point it out to him. "Do you realize the implications of this?" Not waiting for an answer, "Hoods and politicians are buying off the press."

John furrowed his brow, "I can't stop now. I'll be late, Ellie. Let's talk tonight."

But Ellie couldn't wait until evening to talk to someone. She got David ready for a trip downtown to the *Post-Dispatch*. Often, since she had left her job, she took trips to her old office to shoot the breeze with the reporters.

She got on a streetcar and away they went. It was cold for late March. St. Louis was like that, an early spring or a long winter could freeze the blossoms on magnolia trees. Ellie saw the browning buds that would never open. She turned to David to point at the dead buds and explain, "It just makes us appreciate those years more when we do have the huge, pink blossoms. Don't ever take nature for granted, David." Of course he was too young to understand, but Ellie believed one should talk to a child like an adult. *You never know the moment when one's words will make an impact on little developing minds.*

They had to transfer to another streetcar, but the whole trip only took twenty minutes. When they stopped at 12th Street, Ellie hefted David into her arms, even with her huge belly, and started toward the steps. A gentleman jumped up and took David from her as he offered his elbow.

"Thank you kindly," she smiled when he placed David on the sidewalk. As she took David's hand, they walked at his pace toward the *Post-Dispatch* offices. David was fifteen months old. "That coat and leggings that your Grandma made you sure keep you warm, don't they?

"Yes, Mama," he said. They were in the elevator when he asked, "Choc'late 'gain?"

"I don't know. We will have to see. But, you can't ask for it; that would not be polite."

The two of them entered the pressroom and were immediately welcomed. "Hey, David, how you've grown!"

Ellie slipped off his coat and hat.

"You're getting strong," one of the reporters said as he picked up David and went toward the candy drawer. David looked back to his mother and smiled. He knew where he was going.

After all the questions about her pregnancy, how John was, and jokes about a married life of leisure, Ellie got to the heart of her visit. "Is John Rogers here?"

Someone across the room shouted, "I told you that Ellie would be here soon. I knew she would want to hear the scoop about this."

Someone else said, "If the *Post* runs anything about Capone, you can bet Ellie will be here the next day. Ain't that right? We always check the candy drawer when we have news on Capone. There's a direct relationship between Capone and candy in this office." People laughed and said their hellos to Ellie.

The editor came out of his office to greet Ellie. They all appreciated her dedication to news and the press; no one doubted her ability either. Often it had been said, "Too bad she's a woman. She would have made a hell of a reporter."

Ellie and the editor shook hands, and she was invited into his office, "Rogers isn't here, come on in and I'll give you the scoop, Ellie."

Before they sat, Ellie started asking her questions, "I understand that the *Post* ran this information before the *Chicago Tribune.* How did that happen? Was McCormack mad? I …"

"Hold on, Ellie. Let me tell you the story. It'll answer all your questions. I won't be able to name all the names, but you'll get the gist of it all. You worked with Rogers and know he has connections all over the country. Someone called him with a scoop. This is what happened.

"Rogers gets a call from a 'friend' with the information that Alfred Lingle, the crime expert reporter for the *Chicago Tribune*, …"

Ellie interrupted, "I know who he is. Who doesn't?"

The editor continued, "So, Rogers is told that Lingle is on Capone's payroll. Up until that moment, Lingle was a respected and highly praised reporter. Like you said, we all knew his work. So Rogers had to be careful not to step on anybody's toes. His source gave him connections to verify the lead. They all checked out. That's when Rogers comes to me. We talked for over an hour. No one had ever suspected Lingle. I told Rogers that I needed to verify his details. And we both knew we couldn't print the story without talking to The Colonel." The editor took a deep breath.

Ellie interjected, "I know who The Colonel is. Robert McCormack who runs the *Tribune.*"

"Yeah, I figured you did. Well, we called McCormack. He's furious at us for accusing his crime expert. But slowly, we convince him that we've done our homework. Then he relents and lets us know, he had already heard and they too were getting ready to run the story.

His anger had been because we finished first. And get this! McCormack tells us we can go with it. So, as you saw, we did."

"Lingle being on the payroll of Capone really mars the integrity of our profession."

The editor smiled at her use of the word 'our.' As they finished talking, he paid Ellie what he thought was a compliment, "The job gets into one's blood, doesn't it. You're good at this, Ellie. Too bad you weren't a man."

She got up to leave.

"Don't forget to give us the story if your friend Capone pays you a visit."

She was seething on the streetcar ride home. *Wait until I tell John about all this.*

***

Late one evening in May, Ellie and David were alone in the flat when a thunderstorm came up. John was staying overnight at the farm. Ellie attempted to nonchalantly ignore the storm by curling up on the couch with a good book. Ignoring it was not possible.

Ellie gave up trying to read and stood at the window watching the wind bend trees to the breaking point and blow over the neighbor's outdoor table. With the lightning so close, suddenly the thunder sounded like a crack splitting the building. David started to scream with terror in his eyes. Ellie hurried to his bed and picked him up. A searing pain shot through her abdomen like a bolt of lightning had entered the house without the thunder. *This can't be labor! It's too early. I have a month to go.*

Cuddling David in her arms with soothing coos, she started to sit on a dining room chair. A contraction came again as strong as before. *Oh, my goodness!* At that same moment, the lights went out. She walked to the telephone. It was dead. *A tree must have taken out the lines. I must get some help.*

She struggled to her feet by placing David onto the table before standing. Then she picked him up again. *I'll go upstairs to the neighbors. I don't even have a way to get to the hospital since John's got the Model T at the farm.* She opened the back door out of the kitchen and proceeded to climb the stairs up to the neighbors' flat. Each step was difficult. *I can't put David down. I'll stop and rest at the landing and call out.* But with the howl of wind, rattling of windows, and bashing sounds from branches against the building, her voice was unheard. *After all those stairs, they're not home!*

Ellie turned and started down. A flood of water poured out of her. *My water broke! Oh, no!* She took one hand to hold tightly onto the banister, so as not to slip in her own fluids. *I can't go out in the storm, especially with a baby in my arms. Aghhh!* Another contraction started. Wrapped in pain, Ellie sat on the stairs and decided to scoot down the steps on her bottom.

Downstairs at her back door, she released David into the flat, "You're going to have to go on your own the rest of the way, Big Boy. I can't hold you anymore." She smiled to relax him, but he looked into her face and knew something terrible was happening. David started a hysterical cry. Ellie wanted to cry. She lifted her skirt and untied her underwear, letting the wet garment fall to the floor. Another contraction started.

Then amid all the noise of the storm, she thought she heard someone pounding against the front door. She hurried as best she could and opened the door to two soaking friends. A cigarette glowed in the dark as Jerry took a deep drag. For an instant, Jerry and Françoise talked at once, telling how they just drove in from Florida and decided to stop in this storm to see how the Bartletts were doing. They stood outside the door, shaking off the water and laughing at their dripping condition, until Ellie doubled in pain.

"I'm in labor," she gasped.

Without closing the door, Jerry responded, "Let's get you to the hospital." He flipped his cigarette into the bushes and bent down to Ellie, "Where's a coat to put over you? Françoise pick up little David to calm him."

But Ellie's pain brought her to her knees and she rolled onto her side on the floor. Jerry took the moment to look between her legs.

"Françoise, close the door. The baby's coming!" Trying to brighten the moment, Jerry said, "Ellie, how do you have babies so easily?" He turned Ellie onto her back on the wooden floor and whipped off his coat. He slipped it under her legs and raised her skirt higher.

"Françoise, it's okay." He saw his wife standing in disbelief and fear, "Stay calm, Sweetie, this will be easy." The lightening flashing afforded enough illumination to see a couple of candlesticks on the dining room table. Jerry pointed, " Get those; I'll light them, but I need you to go boil some water. Put a scissors or a sharp knife into the water. Then rip up a clean kitchen towel into strips and put them into the water. Go, go!"

Jerry went to the bathroom to wash his hands.

Françoise found more candles on the mantel and lit them in the kitchen, "Jerry, I can't find any clean towels!"

Standing in the bathroom, he pulled at his shirt without unbuttoning it. Buttons popped off and flew helter-skelter. He ripped up his shirt. "Here, use these strips of cloth." He washed his hands again and turned toward Ellie while talking to Françoise, "Go find a clean sheet to put the baby into when he's out. And get a pillowcase. Quickly, Françoise."

As Jerry knelt onto the wood floor, the baby's head slipped out. He cradled the head with matted hair in his hands and grinned, "Ellie, timed perfectly! A second earlier and I would have missed catching the little head. Now, at the next contraction, give a really hard push. We're going to have a baby in your arms before you know it."

The little girl slipped out like toothpaste from a tube just as Françoise came with the sheets. The baby started to scream when Jerry put his finger into her mouth to check for a clear passage, "She's a girl! Françoise, leave the sheet doubled and spread it out next to Ellie."

Jerry placed the baby right by Ellie's side though the cord still ran back into the mother's body. "Has the water boiled?"

Ellie turned her head and managed a smile. Poor little David had been crying in his crib, ignored by all. But when the little girl gave out her shriek, he stopped.

Françoise went to the kitchen, "Yes, it's got a good boil going."

"Put the pillow case into the sink and pour the water and everything onto it. Carefully pick it up by the dry corners and bring it to me." When she arrived to his side, "Put it here," pointed Jerry. He opened the steaming pillowcase and carefully picked up one strip of his shirt to tie around the umbilical cord. He took another and tied about four inches from the baby's belly. "Hope the scissors are cool enough," he said as he picked them up. "Yep, okay."

He cut the cord between the two ties. Pulling the sheet with the baby back toward him, he explained "Let me look her over first, Ellie, then she's yours. But, don't you move, the afterbirth hasn't released yet."

Just as Jerry finished his inspection and was swaddling the newborn in the sheet, he got the surprise of his life, "Françoise come look, there's another baby coming out!"

Ellie tensed in pain, creating a guttural scream.

Jerry tensed, "Françoise, take this baby from me, quick!"

Out popped another head into his hands, one more piercing scream from Ellie, and he held another little girl. "What a miracle. Ellie, do you have any more in there?"

They all laughed hysterically at the wonder of it all. Little David heard the laughter and started babbling as if he knew it was over. Françoise peeked into the bedroom with the new baby in her arms and talked with him, "Look what we have here. You have a couple of little sisters now. Oh, are you in trouble." Her smiles made him bounce in delight on the side of his crib where he stood. He didn't have any idea what she was holding because his little sister had quieted.

"David's standing in his crib. He won't climb over will he?" she asked Ellie.

Ellie was too tired to answer. She whispered to David, "Tell her to come in here."

Jerry finished cutting, inspecting, and swaddling the second little girl and started to hand her to Ellie while Françoise cooed at the first.

"No, Jerry, that one's yours. Françoise, give me mine." Ellie stopped talking for a moment to rest. "The only condition I make on that baby is her name. She is Rose Cohen. Mine will be Elizabeth Rose Bartlett. You can pick whatever middle name you want."

"Is she delirious, Jerry?" Françoise inquired as she handed the first baby to Ellie.

"No, I'm not. Both of you hold out your little fingers so we can make a promise to never tell." The Cohens hesitated. Well, Jerry didn't understand the finger-pulling promise technique, "Come on, Franny, explain to your husband what I want."

Françoise sputtered, "But Ellie …"

"Franny, you just returned from Florida where you went to have your baby. You didn't tell anyone because there was the chance it would be stillborn. You will make your baby's birthday a week ago. No one can tell a one-week difference in newborns. My baby is a month early. No one will guess what has happened," Ellie grinned at them, "because who would believe what I'm doing? You can hardly believe it. Right?"

Jerry went to Françoise's side and together they stared at the baby, "Rose Cohen," he whispered, pulling the bundle to his chest. Tears came to his eyes.

Ellie could see that the name had hooked Jerry, but she continued with her ideas, "Jerry as the attending doctor who delivered his own baby can request a birth certificate. Aren't I right that you can mail the information to the State of Florida to get the birth recorded as a home birth?" Ellie hesitated for it all to sink in. "The state will mail you a birth certificate. She's your daughter Rose Cohen. Jerry's little sister will live again through this child. You will watch her grow. You will have a daughter and sister, all in one." Ellie stopped for a moment, "Do I sound delirious to either of you? Could a delirious person outline such a plan at the drop of a hat?"

Jerry spoke up now, "Don't you think John should make this decision with you?"

Ellie was firm, "I'm holding my daughter, little Elizabeth Rose Bartlett. I plan to have more babies. So, this is not for John to decide. No one knew I was having twins, not John or my doctor." Looking at her friends, "It's our secret."

Françoise took the bundle from Jerry, "Ellie, how can you do this? They're twins and should be together."

"Franny, you aren't going to move to Florida, are you? These two little girls will see each other a lot. I want the two of you to understand that without you and Jerry I wouldn't be here. I could have died in the Mississippi River or under the kicks of Capone. And look what you did tonight!

"I'm giving you a life and returning the gift of life you gave me." Ellie waited for that argument to sink in. "Don't you realize, without the two of you, I would not have met John? How much more do I need to say? You would do the same for me if the situation were reversed. And look, Jerry just gave me the shirt off his back."

Hesitating in her discourse, because she saved the best for last, she put her baby's head against her lips for a kiss, "Besides, this is the Depression, haven't you heard that everyone needs to share?"

Chapter 13

1932
The Bartlett Family

David bounded into the kitchen to the smells of cooking bacon. A boy going-on-three likes to bound here and there. His father sat reading last night's paper; he had worked late at Walgreens.

"Mommy, I want a silly-side-up egg," David informed her.

John looked up at Ellie, "What's that?"

"Oh, David wants a sunny-side-up egg," Ellie just beamed. She loved her family. "Oh, David, we're going to Tower Grove Park today with Aunt Franny and Rose. Do you remember?"

"Yeah, I do," he replied as he struggled to get up on the big chair. They called the chair Mount Everest. David had informed his parents that he wasn't a baby anymore, and the highchair was for his sister now. "Can I take the net and catch flutterbys?"

John looked up again at Ellie, "What did he say?"

"Oh, David is talking about the butterfly net you made him. He just made a better name for them. Flutterbys. Actually, he made a better name for my eggs. I usually break the yolk, so they are kind of silly looking." She turned back to her cooking and giggled. John was grumpy today.

Ellie turned around, "Oh, David, tell your dad what you almost caught in your net yesterday." Ellie spread her arms and started making a buzzing sound as she flew around the kitchen.

"Oh, Daddy, I almost had 'em. It was a rumble bee. Really big."

Ellie glanced at John and burst out laughing.

"You should be teaching him to speak correctly, Ellie. Don't encourage this."

"John, you're so grumpy this morning. David, your daddy needs a hug because he has been working too much."

David jumped down and went to his father. He wrapped his arms around him and stayed there until Ellie lifted him back into his seat,

"Your egg is ready. Whee, up you go. This time you don't need to climb, I'll fly you to Mount Everest."

Ellie sat to finish her cold breakfast. She didn't mind. John was back reading the paper and as he turned a page she said, "Look at those photographs. Have you heard of this man—Ansel Adams?"

John shook his head as he looked at the display of black and whites. "Incredible work. It looks like he has made the scenes more beautiful than they actually are. Never been to California, so I don't know these places. Such beauty."

"Let's go there some day. Yosemite Valley." Ellie pronounced it wrong, never having heard it said before. "Look at the mist among those trees. He has talent or he found heaven." *Wonder if my daddy has seen this place. Maybe he lives near it. Surely he's gone there. Looking at these pictures takes me closer to him.*

Little Elizabeth started crying.

"Baby's awake. Be right back."

When Ellie returned with Elizabeth, David was finished eating. Ellie slipped the baby into the highchair and gave her a cracker.

David had a question, "Mommy, Aunt Franny said that Rose was really glowing. What's that?"

John looked up again.

Ellie explained, "Aunt Franny meant that Rose was getting bigger because she doesn't fit her clothes anymore. You know, she's growing."

"Yeah, that's what I said; she's glowing."

John had to laugh now, "It does take some time to get the tongue to work right, doesn't it? David, drink your milk and let's go see if we can find some flutterbys out in the garden or in the vacant lot,"

Ellie remembered, "John, when will we be able to move into our house? The children are glowing, and there's no room in that closet where they sleep."

"I don't sleep in a closet!" David insisted.

John took his son's hand and started for the door, "Well, in this new house the closets are as big as this bedroom you have now. So, that's what Mommy meant. You will have your own bedroom and Elizabeth will have a different one. And they both have big closets where you can play. Won't that be great?"

"John, you didn't answer me. When?"

"Start packing. I think the workers will finish in two weeks. We can start to take boxes over whenever you have some packed. You know, things we aren't using right now."

"My own house. I'm so excited."

John had found an old house owned by a ninety-year-old woman who was going to live with her daughter. The house was horrible! It looked like it had never had paint on the gray and weathered wood. Inside it was dark, wallpaper peeling, dirty and ugly. So, of course, it was cheap. When Ellie saw it she thought it looked like an old barn. John decided to put Permastone on the outside. The company that covered the outside of the house had sold John on it by saying, "It handles like plaster but's stone-like when done." The fake stone covering made the house look like a little castle. Ellie didn't like the Permastone much, but she loved the big spacious rooms and closets. There were three bedrooms on the second floor, and John had hired men to paint and wallpaper the whole house in addition to fixing up the kitchen. It was almost ready.

As John and David got to the back door, David kicked the dog door that remained from previous renters.

"Daddy, why don't we have a dog for this door?" It went thump. David kicked it again and it thumped again.

Ellie answered her son, "David, the new house has a huge back yard. Maybe we can get a dog after we move."

When Franny and Rose arrived, John was about to leave for work. Walgreens had him working different hours every day and in three different stores. It wasn't a nine-to-five job. Yesterday, he had worked ten hours; today he would work six.

"Look at the girls," John commented. "They look like sisters."

"Most blonde-haired, blue-eyed little girls look this way, especially when they're sixteen months," Ellie smiled.

"Well, I know they're almost the same age. So, it makes sense. I remember you said the same thing when they were babies. 'All babies look alike.'"

Franny joined in, "It is wonderful for them to have a best friend just like their mommies. They love each other. They even talk together, though we can't understand them."

David was ready to go, "I got my flutterby net and my rainbrella. It might rain, you know." They smiled at him as his father picked him up and hugged him goodbye.

"I must leave, Ellie. Tell Franny about the other words David invented."

Although both Elizabeth and Rose were toddling everywhere, a walk to Tower Grove Park would have been too much for them, so they were in baby carriages. On rainy days, when Franny and Rose came, the visits weren't too enjoyable in the flat; it was too crowded for three children to run around. So, whenever possible, a lunch was packed for a picnic on a blanket. Though it was fall and leaves were starting to turn colors, the day was warm and sunny.

Ellie started laughing, "Franny, wait 'til you see what I packed in the lunch. A beer! The doctor said I'm too skinny and wants me to drink a beer a day to fatten up. Yuk, I never liked beer, but I just take it like medicine."

"I never heard of such a thing! A doctor telling you to drink a beer? What does John say?"

"Oh, he said without a doubt it'll fatten me. Oh, and he teased that he'd give it to his cattle to fatten them up, if it was cheaper."

"Ellie, you always have something going on. How's the move coming?"

"We're moving in a couple of weeks. Our new house will have a lot of room for the children. Oh, Franny, I'm so excited. We're even planning to get a dog. We won't be that far from where we are now. In fact, I will be closer to Tower Grove Park. I feel like singing. Let's do! Like we did in Dogtown." Without hesitation, Ellie started an old song:

I'd like a Paper Dolly to call my own,

Franny said, "Start over so I can sing."

As they strolled and sang, little David stopped to look at them. Suddenly David started singing:

… a paper dolly to call Malone,

On the two friends sang, laughing and walking. How close they were—united through so many memories of the past and through their vow to never speak of how Rose became a Cohen. Not even when they were alone, like now, was the subject mentioned. They acted as if that night never happened. They never passed any secret looks. There never was any sly conversation or innuendos that alluded to that night. Rose was Jerry's and Franny's daughter, and that was that.

One would think that they would slip up and casually say something like, "Isn't it wonderful how this worked out?" But they never did. The script was written that stormy night and the players continued to act accordingly. Was their life a play? Or was this pact they made real? This coming night the curtain will go up and prove if it's real or not.

The evening turned into one of those Indian summer nights. The warmth invited everyone outdoors. Much later that night, clouds would drift in and drizzle, but for now, neighbors wandered outside to sit on their porches or on the concrete steps with cushions, and some families put blankets onto the grass out in their small front yards. At this time of year, it was typical for St. Louis neighbors to share their weekend evenings outside, talking as dusk changed to darkness. The beauty of the rising moon elicited exclamations and some discussion. A full autumn moon in St. Louis was a sight much anticipated each year, and the intensity of the big, orange display never disappointed from one year to the next.

John had been out turning over his garden with the help of David, who would be three years old in December. Dad had a big spade and the son a little one. The garden was located in one of the empty lots across from their flat. People began to gather. The first neighbor came out to the sidewalk to chat while John worked, and then a few others appeared on their front stoop. It wasn't long before many families were outside, talking across porches and from one side of the street to the other.

Ellie was still inside stirring some navy beans that simmered with a small slab of bacon. She turned down the heat, put down the wooden spoon, and wiped her hands on her apron as she pulled it off, catching the straps in her short brown wavy hair, which instantly bounced back into place. She went to the door that led from the kitchen and opened it, first glancing toward the back door, which led to the outside, then peering up the steps to the second-floor neighbor's flat, and finally walking out the door to look on the landing that went down to the basement. At last she caught sight of Elizabeth, who was playing on the landing.

"Come now, Sweetie. Let's go sit out in front for a bit," she coaxed while hanging the apron behind the kitchen door. As Ellie walked through the flat, she picked up a diaper and towel. Elizabeth toddled close behind her mother's footsteps. "Let's change that diaper before we go out," Ellie said as she knelt to spread the towel on the carpet. She scooped Elizabeth into her arms with a "Gotcha" and buried her face in the child's tummy. The baby giggled. Ellie removed the diaper and tossed it toward the bathroom door. On went the new one with the expertise that comes with a second child.

Stepping through the front door, Ellie could hear John's conversation carried across the street while working with his spade. "Well, sales are fair. I can't complain. At Walgreens we have to build up a stock of items for Christmas gifts, hoping to improve the sales. You know, some toys, colognes in fancy boxes, cheap costume jewelry, and things like that. Drugstores selling simply medicines don't exist nowadays. Got to be a little creative and …"

"Hey, Ellie," someone shouted, "didn't I say that Al Capone wouldn't stay in prison long? You did see today's Post-Dispatch, didn't you? It's right on the front page. There's a picture of Scarface comin' out the prison door with his hat in his hand and the biggest smile on his face. That was the shortest ten-year sentence I ever heard of. When was it that they sent him up for tax evasion?"

"Last May," someone called out from across the street.

Someone else wanted to know, "That's not even ten months, much less ten years! How can they do that?"

No one could see the tension that Ellie felt. *If Capone's out of prison, will he come to St. Louis? Does he think of me and his lucky rabbit's foot?*

She spread the towel, sat on the bottom step, and stood Elizabeth on the ground. She heard happy cries and squeals of children coming from the other vacant lot opposite the garden.

"Capone said that he was imprisoned illegally because the statute of limitations had run out in his case. I bet some lawyer probably got a big savings account overnight from good ol' Scarface."

To Ellie's relief, the topic of conversation changed. They started to talk about all the kidnappings. It was front-page news every day. Prohibition was ending, but a depression was squeezing people's pocketbooks and kidnapping was a way to make money.

"Hogwash!" an older neighbor lady replied. "That's what I think about most of those kidnapping stories. They're hogwash—just made up kidnappings. You know, the newspapers' sensationalism. They go lookin' for stories to write when there's no other good news, now that prohibition's endin'."

"Don't say that!" Ellie insisted. "We have to believe in the truth and freedom of the press. Even before the Lindbergh baby was kidnapped, didn't our own St. Louis representative, John Cockran, introduce a bill because there's too many kidnappings happening across the country? It's real. Have you read the bill?"

When no one responded, Ellie went on talking. "The idea is, if kidnappers send a blackmail letter by U.S. mail, or if they transport a kidnapped victim across a state line, they'd be committing a felony. Our state legislators want them to get the death penalty. The papers write stories to let us know how serious kidnapping is."

"Yeah, Ellie's right. There're thousands of kidnappings. How could they all be made-up stories?"

It was getting late. John stopped working on his gardening and crossed the street to join the others, but the conversations were petering out. The neighbors started saying their good nights and going in. John sat down on the steps.

Slipping off her tiny shoes, he rubbed her little feet. Half asleep, Elizabeth murmured, "Bye, Bye, Daddy?" That was an expected question because she always wanted to go 'bye-bye' in her daddy's automobile.

John whispered into her ear, "Tomorrow, Honey, it's time for bed now. When you wake up we can go for a ride."

As John started toward the vacant lot where David had gone to play, Ellie took Elizabeth and went into the flat.

Ellie quickly bathed Elizabeth and put on her yellow nightgown with a hand-crocheted bodice. There was a row of pink rosebuds where Aunt Ginny's crocheted bodice met the cotton skirt. The child looked like a doll. Out came the book and before Ellie opened it she began speaking from memory:

Wynken, Blynken and Nod one night
Sailed off in a wooden shoe –
Sailed on a river of crystal light,
Into a sea of dew.

The poem drifted into the stillness of the room and comforted the mother as well. She put Elizabeth into her crib.

Ellie had become tense from the discussions outside. As she crawled into bed, she kept thinking. *Will I ever get Capone out of my mind?* She had the rabbit's foot and kidnapping on her mind when she finally fell asleep and began to dream.

An hour later, Ellie's dream stopped and she sat up in bed. "I heard a thump. I really heard it!" she whispered. And she was right, there had been a thump in her home, but she wouldn't know what had caused it or why she had heard it until morning. In her drowsiness she dismissed the sound. Something had thumped in her dream, but she didn't want to remember because it had been a nightmare.

Oh, why can't I forget this kidnapping and Capone?

In the morning, John and David awoke to a shrill screech from Ellie, "Nooooo! The baby's gone!" John flew out of bed. David started crying. Ellie's face had lost all its color; her eyes looked frantic.

"Did you check everywhere?"

"Yes, yes, yes, the whole flat. I went into the back stairs, down to the basement, and up to our neighbors. She is not here. The horrible thing is …" She couldn't speak as the tears came.

John pulled her into his arms, "Stay calm. We'll find her. She couldn't get outside; all the doors were locked. I remember doing that last night."

Between sobs, Ellie told him, "The horrible thing is that I heard her leave. John, she went out through that dog door. I heard it thump, but I was half asleep and didn't know what I was hearing." She wailed, "Oh my, my baby's gone."

John quickly dressed. The neighbors from upstairs came down to help. They talked to other neighbors and soon a dozen people were out in the vacant lot and fanned out to look all over the area. Someone found an open shaft about two blocks away, and it was too deep to see all the way down. They called the fire department.

After two hours, the police came and did their search, to no avail.

Soon Jerry and Franny were there. Jerry administered a sedative to Ellie. She was hysterical.

Françoise commented that she had never seen Ellie like that. "She usually handles all situations." Jerry knew Françoise was thinking about the Capone episodes. Ellie slept for twenty-four hours.

Baby Elizabeth was not found. No one had seen or heard anything unusual during the night. There were no clues. The little girl just disappeared. The police suspected a kidnapping, but no request for money ever came.

Two weeks later, Ellie told Françoise, "It's the not knowing what happened that's so hard to take. I imagine all sorts of things. I even thought that Capone was watching the house and when Elizabeth went out, he took her. Do you think he could have?" Ellie was not doing well.

John had to go to work every day. At least the time at work gave John a reprieve from the pain he felt. Ellie had no escape.

To help her, John made sure she was never alone. Ginny came, Franny came, Bertha spent time when others couldn't. Mostly, Bertha took David away for several days at a time. It wasn't good for him to see his mother so distraught.

Three weeks passed. Ellie sat staring out the front room window, unmoving. It was drizzling and rain dripped from the roof. Ginny approached Ellie and placed a hand on her sister's wavy hair. Gently stroking it, Ginny whispered, "Penny for your thoughts."

Before Ellie answered, a squirrel ran across the street into John's vegetable garden and began digging. Ellie seemed in a trance. Finally, in staccato phrases she blurted, "Is she being loved? … or is she being abused?" Ellie stopped speaking and the sound of the rain tapping on a metal lawn chair matched her heartbeats—with each metallic splat, the hurt in her chest throbbed. Ellie blinked and clinched her teeth before continuing, "Is she dead? … or hurt? I find it hard imagining that she is laughing or happy. But she could be. Maybe she's with people who are loving her. I just don't know and can hardly stand the unknown. Do you realize there's nowhere I can go to find out? All my experience and all the hours I've spent in libraries and the morgue of the newspaper …" Ellie took her handkerchief and blew her nose. "You know, I'm talking about all the time I've spent seeking answers; it's all of no use. There's nowhere to learn the truth. I can hardly bear this."

Ginny stood behind her sister and bent to hug her, "Ellie, there, there."

When the rain started hard and fast, Ellie's words poured out. "And, see, I know you want to comfort me, but there is no comfort. I only feel relief when I sleep. My mind protects me and doesn't let me feel when I sleep. I used to dream so much, but I haven't even dreamed. Maybe it's the pills that don't let me dream … or don't let me remember. I don't know. I know I'm not there for poor little David. Well, people who love him are caring for him. I don't worry about him except when he's with me. He can't understand the pain he sees in my face. And I can't explain anything because I don't know anything." Ellie began to weep, "I just want to know, so I can deal with it."

Another week passed, then it was a month. They postponed their move to the new house. Ellie refused to leave the flat, "I need to be here, if she comes back somehow."

John was frantic in his own way. The first week Elizabeth was gone, he was out for hours every day looking for her. Ringing doorbells. Asking the postman, the milkman, everyone.

He went to the newspapers and had an ad run about a missing little girl. He worded it carefully in case it was a kidnapping. The editor at the *Post* warned John, don't tell all the details in the ad so we can screen the pranksters or con men. There are a lot of people who'll claim to have her, knowing you'll pay the money, but then you'll never see her. We have to be able to ask them some questions that only a kidnapper would know. Don't say what she was wearing. If they can't tell us when they call, they're lying."

John insisted that he wanted to list a yellow nightgown, "In case someone saw her with the abductors. I won't mention the pink, crocheted rosebuds on the top, so you can ask about the rosebuds."

John went to the police station almost every day. There were so many kidnappings they were dealing with. Across the nation there were hundreds. At first they let him read information about all the incoming calls and leads. But eventually they found John to be a pest.

John went to Wally's shop to share some ideas with him. Wally got John together with his brother, the policeman, but nothing came of their talks.

John walked his neighborhood at night, trying to uncover some clue. Down deep John knew he would never know what happened. He was helpless. The situation was hopeless.

Everyone who knew the Bartletts tried to help. The neighbors brought food. At least twice a week, some dish like a roast or pasta dinner would arrive from caring people. Ellie was so grateful, but she found it impossible to worry about food. She prepared nothing and ate little.

Franny made a point to never go to the Bartlett's flat with Rose. Franny was afraid. This was the first time Franny allowed herself to talk about the secret to Jerry. She and Jerry agreed that Ellie didn't need to be seeing a little girl who looked just like Elizabeth. Finally, Franny revealed what was worrying her, "Do you think she'll want to take her back. You know, now that she has lost the other one?"

Sitting and holding hands, he insisted, "No, no, Françoise. Ellie wouldn't do that," but he wasn't sure.

They learned more about Ellie's character during this time. Ellie never mentioned anything about taking Rose back. In fact, in her mind, Rose was not hers. Besides, Ellie always kept her secrets. For example, the secret about her father, only Wally knew. Only Jerry and Franny knew about Rose. With each passing day, the Cohen gained confidence that Rose was theirs to keep.

After Elizabeth was gone a month, no one wanted to say she wasn't coming back, but there was no hope—except in Ellie's heart.

***

Saturday, the day before Christmas 1932, in the early hours before dawn, someone rang the doorbell of the Bartlett's flat. They rang, knocked, and shouted incoherent words. They rang again and banged on the door.

Sleepily John headed to the front door in his pajamas as Ellie fussed to get her robe on. Opening the door, John saw his neighbor from across the street with a huge smile stretching from cheek to cheek. In his arms he held little Elizabeth.

"Look what we found on our doorstep this morning."

John stepped out the door and, with disbelief on his face, took his little girl. Often he had had dreams that seemed to be reality, and this seemed a dream. Suddenly Ellie arrived behind John and saw her daughter. A squeal of elation came from her throat. She pushed out to the stoop and grabbed Elizabeth.

"Oh, Elizabeth, Elizabeth, Elizabeth," Ellie whispered, rocking the child. The little girl touched her mother's face and smiled. Ellie smiled back, "Oh, Elizabeth, are you okay?"

Their daughter was back. They knew nothing more. It was a miracle.

Chapter 14

1933-1939
Mysteries of Life

Life was beautiful for Ellie. "Oh, Franny, I love my new house. Finally I have the space to host an evening with three or four card tables in the living room." She was bubbling with talk as they unfolded each table and set up the chairs. "When our girl friends started moving away, I hated the idea that we couldn't get together for bridge like we have for years."

"Where do you want me to put this vase of flowers I brought?"

"On the mantle. Thanks for bringing them. Beautiful colors! Actually, now that we have husbands coming to replace the gals who are gone, these Tuesday evenings are better. Don't you think?"

"Before I forget, please practice saying my name before people arrive. Go on, say Françoise a couple of times."

"Sorry, I try to remember, Françoise."

Françoise continued, "If you think about it, one of the reasons playing bridge is better is because Prohibition ended. Having an evening with cocktails instead of lemonade and tea, is definitely more fun."

Ellie was placing the decks of cards and score sheets on each table. "It's not just the drinks; it's a different kind of evening with men. The conversations are more interesting. Don't you think?"

Françoise didn't respond, she had walked back into the kitchen to start working on the food and setting out the liquor bottles. With men present, the topics were politics, business, science, and books. Somehow these topics had rarely come up with only their girlfriends.

People started arriving and, before long, smoke curled to the high ceilings and, in between rubbers there was raucous conversation and laughter. The couples had brought their children, who played upstairs. Ginny was up there with the little ones; she didn't have a bridge partner this particular night. She loved coming, whether she played bridge or played house with children.

As the hands were being dealt, they talked about their new president, Franklin D. Roosevelt, who had won the election in the fall of 1932.

"I have so much hope in this man," one of the ladies confessed.

"Well, we need more than just hope. FDR's New Deal may work and get us out of this depression. Only time will tell."

No one visiting the Bartlett house that evening had suffered as badly as most of the population. Their comments showed skepticism about Roosevelt's new programs.

"I'm just going to wait and see, but I'm keeping an open mind," said one friend.

Another person added, "Well, FDR better get moving. People are hungry and taking matters into their own hands. The newspapers are full of riots and marches to demand food. Did you see in Chicago even the children are organizing? Five hundred marched to the Board of Education to demand free lunches. And children of all ages raided a buffet lunch being given for the Spanish War veterans. They grabbed food and ran."

Someone verified the story with a snicker, "I read that they got all the food before the police arrived."

As people picked up their cards, the room quieted and the evening of bridge continued. The noise of children drifting down the stairs was a pleasant backdrop to the quiet card game.

Table by table, as people finished their hand, Ellie walked around offering some finger food. When all were done playing, she asked, "Has anyone read this new book by Aldous Huxley? You know, *Brave New World*." A few responded that they had.

One friend commented, "Do you really think it's possible for the world to change so much? I thought it was a bit of an exaggeration."

Ellie jumped in, "Oh, I was fascinated by some of Huxley's ideas. Think about it; we're already heading to a future like he describes."

Françoise asked, "What do you mean?"

"We're letting big business tell us what we want. They're convincing us that comfort and happiness are what's most important. Like Ford making everyone think that they need the comfort of an automobile. Look how many are filling our streets."

"What's your point?" someone asked.

"It's not my point, its Huxley's point. He says we're giving up truth and beauty for our comfort and happiness."

Françoise took a drink and made an aside, "That's my best friend. She's always thinking too much. I've told her this all her life." People smiled, but invited Ellie to continue.

"Don't you see? We can't have both. These comfort things like automobiles, refrigerators, electricity, and so on, are covering up truth and natural beauty. It's the greed for wealth. We're being inundated with advertisements and people telling us that all these innovations are more important than the beauty of a fine day or the quiet of nature. Our values are being manipulated. And, if you think about it, we can't have both. It seems we will have to choose between 'progress' or 'nature'."

For twenty minutes or so, friends discussed the book. Several who hadn't read it said they would.

Soon they began the final hand.

That night, John and Ellie had intense lovemaking. Her quest for answers about life and her intelligent conversations made him love her all the more.

"I'm not sure I agree with that Huxley though," he confided. "I haven't read the book. Guess I need to."

John was a practical doer. Ellie was an idealistic thinker. Wrapped in each other's arms, Ellie felt they blended into a perfect couple. The farm was taking more of John's time and he went on his days off usually taking David. When Jerry could get some time, the three "boys" went fishing. Most of the time, the four "girls"—Ellie, Elizabeth, Françoise, and Rose—stayed in St. Louis and spend time together.

The two couples, the Cohens and Bartletts, still found time to go dancing, to the movies, and to play tennis. They had eager baby sitters with Ginny and Bertha. At the end of their evenings out on the town, sleeping children were driven home and placed in their own beds.

David, at four years old, thought such happenings were magic; he would fall asleep at Grandma's house and somehow wake up in his own bed.

***

John often said, "Water seeks its own level." He believed in the laws of nature and science. He thought that the order of the universe had rules that made things fall into place.

On the other hand, Ellie would say, "Right will out" when she looked at the troubles of the world, the wrongs of mankind, or life in general.

But Ellie was inexplicably aligned with the path of the 1896 tornado. Living in the flat near Kingshighway and moving to the Permastone home, placed her in two spots where the storm had torn into Tower Grove Park. As if some magnet were pulling her to the places where the storm had touched down, Ellie was living where disasters were to happen again.

Before the end of 1933, John and Ellie questioned all their ideals and optimism. They never understood why things happened as they did.

And the coming cruel misfortune would have rippling effects to calamities in the future, washing up on the shore of their lives wave after wave for decades.

It started simply with a common cold.

David had a runny nose.

Soon the whole Bartlett family was sniffling and blowing their noses. Adding to their condition, the weather that autumn went to their bones; it was windy, chilly and rainy.

"Ah-choo!" Ellie wiped her nose and handed a cup to John, "Here, have some tea. I've made David and Elizabeth some warm lemonade. Want that instead?"

Within a week, the adults were feeling better, however the children still had dripping, snotty noses. Little Elizabeth's nostrils were red and sore. She cried if someone came close with a handkerchief.

Within two to three weeks, David was back to his rambunctious self and free from sniffling. Elizabeth continued to be stuffed up, and she developed a cough that lasted through the nights. After sleepless nights, John brought some stronger medicine, expectorant with codeine. It didn't help.

Ellie took her little girl to the kitchen table day after day and, with a towel draped over the child's head, insisted, "Just breath deeply, Elizabeth, this steaming pot of water will make you better." But it didn't.

The three Cohens came to visit one evening and Jerry looked worried, "I'm going back to my car for my medical case. I want to listen to Elizabeth's chest."

Little Rose Cohen stood with a look of concern and watched as Elizabeth cried about the cold stethoscope on her back and chest. Jerry asked, "Has she been eating?"

"Not much. I've been giving her a lot of water and lemonade, but in the last couple of days, she's been balking."

Jerry hesitated, "She has a slight fever, and she's very congested."

Elizabeth went into a coughing fit.

"Her cough is tight. That phlegm must loosen in her lungs. I'll write a prescription. Let's drive to get it filled right now, John."

The medicine didn't help.

On a Thursday night, Elizabeth, limp with a high fever, was admitted to the hospital.

Elizabeth died from pneumonia the next day with Ellie wailing, "No, no, this isn't fair!" Ellie screamed, "Twice, she's been taken. Twice! Why was she given back to be taken again?"

That's how tornados work. They touch down and destroy things only to double back and hit again.

At the funeral, Jerry was talking to John and Ellie, "It's little comfort, but there's no medicine that could have saved her. Pneumonia easily gets the little ones because they don't have the strength." [3]

Ellie nodded. John stood silently looking into the coffin at his rosy-cheeked daughter. She looked asleep.

The day after the funeral, Ellie searched through all the family photographs. Some were in envelopes, others in scrapbooks, and a few in piles in a drawer. She dumped them all on her bed and started to sort. Those with Elizabeth in the picture were put into a cigar box. Ellie was crying, but her anger prevailed. At one point, she picked up a photograph and held it a long time in her hand. In it she was sitting with David and Elizabeth on the steps outside the door of the flat where they used to live. It was just before they had moved. They were all bundled in winter coats, looking so happy because Elizabeth had been returned to them.

Ellie noticed with surprise, *My eyes are closed.* Studying the photograph for minutes, she finally shook her head and whispered to herself, "This photograph captured the truth; I didn't see it coming. My eyes were closed."

Slowly Ellie stood and went to the sewing basket to remove her scissors. Calmly she returned to the bed and picked up the photo. She stared for a long time before furrowing her brow in pain and making one hard stab to the photo. The point of the scissors pierced the photograph near baby Elizabeth, and Ellie frantically began to cut. When the oval containing Elizabeth dropped to the floor, Ellie dropped the scissors and fell back onto the bed. Through blurred eyes, she gazed at the photograph without her little girl, "I'm so sorry, Elizabeth, I must forget you and go on. I can't be like I was when you disappeared. I must live for those who are alive."

Ellie touched her belly. She knew she was pregnant again.

After sorting all the photographs, the cigar box was brimming. She put it far back into a corner of her dresser drawer underneath her jewelry box with Niagara Falls painted on the top, behind nightgowns, the special panties Bertha still sewed for her, and scarves. Ellie closed the drawer, thus sealing the life of Elizabeth in darkness.

Ellie didn't want to talk about Elizabeth. People who came to visit the Bartletts got the point. Ellie would let them talk for a while, but only a while.

While the Cohens were visiting, Françoise asked in private, "Ellie, you seem to be taking the loss of Elizabeth so well. I thought you would be so upset and need medication like last time."

Ellie explained, "Last time, I didn't know where she was. I didn't know if she was dead or alive. I understand everything this time. But, Franny, I don't want to talk about her anymore. Okay?"

Another day Ginny hugged her sister, "Just call me if you need me to come. I know you must have some bad days."

But Ellie explained, "I'll be okay this time. Thanks, Ginny. It's not like last time when I didn't know where she was or if she was dead or alive. Please, I don't want to talk about her anymore. Please understand."

After Bertha served them their usual Sunday dinner, in the kitchen while they cleared the dishes, she whispered to her daughter, "Ellie, how are ya doin'? Let me know if I can help with anything."

This time Ellie raised her voice, "I will Mama. But if you're referring to Elizabeth, just leave it be."

Bertha looked offended.

"Sorry, Mama. But it's not like last time. Please, Mama, I don't want to talk about her anymore. Can you understand? Just don't talk about her. Let me think about those who are here."

John honored her feelings; it did seem to make life easier for them. Ellie would not mention the name of Elizabeth for a couple of decades.

***

It was in the months after Elizabeth died that John began to dig out the earth beneath their new home to make a basement. With three bedrooms upstairs and a large living room, dining room, and kitchen downstairs, they enjoyed much more room than the flat, yet John wanted a workbench and play area for children. Knowing winter was coming and the ground would freeze, John worked quickly. The physical labor, sweat, and aching muscles were a catharsis for him, purging his pain. And he was glad Ellie was pregnant. As the basement neared completion and his anguish subsided, he found he could look to the coming child as a replacement for their loss.

It was during this time that Ellie spent more and more time with John's two sisters and their children. Louise had two children—an older girl and a boy about the same age as David. The other sister, Clara, had a boy a year younger than David. Clara was pregnant, like Ellie.

Now that the Bartletts had a big house, Ellie decided that they would have everyone celebrate Christmas at their house. It would be the first year that Bertha would not have them for Christmas, and she objected.

"Mama, with Christmas dinner at our house, I can invite John's sisters and their families. John's parents can come and even Wally and his wife. Just think about it; David will have children to play with. It's best. Besides a turkey is no trouble to make. But if you'd like to make a couple of your apple pies, I'd love it."

John bought a huge tree that reached to the ceiling and he bought toys for his nephews and niece. Not just one toy, many for each. The presents piled high under the tree.

To the delight of all, the Christmas at the Bartletts was a success. The children ran around the house, up the stairs and down, filling the house with squeals.

Christmas at the Bartletts became a tradition, but not with the Cohens, who usually went to their Florida home for the winter holidays. Nevertheless, they always exchanged gifts. Françoise liked to give books, and this year David received "Tales of Peter Rabbit."

As spring approached in 1934, every week Ellie got together with John's sisters, Louise and Clara.

Ellie asked, "Franny, please join us for a trip to the zoo. Rose would love it."

Françoise declined for one reason or the other, "I have my piano lessons, but you may take Rose, if you don't mind."

Another week, Françoise declined because of an appointment with the beauty parlor to have her nails done, her hair styled, or a facial. "Ellie, you should go with me sometime. It feels wonderful, and you must keep yourself looking good for John."

Ellie laughed, "Look at me! I think the baby should be coming any day. A trip to the beauty parlor isn't going to make me look like you. Franny, you're getting more beautiful with each passing year. Look at you with every hair in place and such stylish clothes." Ellie added, "You know I've never been interested in primping, and this new house takes a lot of my time."

"Oh, Ellie, your mother taught me how to dress well. After the baby, why don't we go shopping for some new clothes for you? And you should get someone to come and clean your house like I do," Françoise insisted, "John would pay for that, I know."

"Franny, John loves me like I am." Ellie was adamant, "And I'll manage my own household."

***

Every two years, Ellie gave birth to a new son. Her blue eyes sparkled with the news of each pregnancy; she loved having babies.

The only event that excited her as much as having children was receiving a letter from her father on her birthday. Ellie had learned in 1936 that James had had another of his inventions patented. This one was a transformer, and he said that it took two years and a lot of work to get the patent. *Guess he never perfected that opener for car windows, but at least he owns a car.* She smiled to herself and wondered if she would ever see her father again.

Soon she had four boys—David, Billy, Johnny and then, in 1939, James arrived with red hair. They were healthy, wild boys.

When Ellie was home from a week at the hospital, she and John talked about James' red hair. "John, everyone's teasing me about the milkman. I laugh, but it's not too funny because I really don't know how we could have had a red-headed baby."

John chuckled, "At least they all have blue eyes like we do." John leaned down to take the baby from Ellie, "When I told my dad, he said I have an Irish grandmother somewhere in my past. Maybe I'll put on an Irish brogue, and greet people with 'top-o-the-morning'."

With so many children, Ellie found no time to work on scrapbooks and only had time to skim the newspapers, with one exception: she still collected news about Al Capone who was in prison. Other than that, when at home, Ellie listened to the radio for news. The trouble was Ellie didn't spend much time at home. She didn't like to cook, iron or clean. She would take her children to the park, the zoo, the farm, or the cousins' houses. All her life, she needed to be with people and she hadn't changed. She loved being pregnant, giving birth, caring for the babies, but when they were older, Ellie found it hard to be at home all day with only her healthy, wild boys and without adult conversation.

John was the opposite; he had so much to say to the children. As soon as his boys were old enough to walk, he wanted them by his side. He had ideas and projects as well as knowledge he wanted to share with them. The basement was where they spent their time together.

One evening, John arrived home early for supper, "Who wants me to read the funnies?" Even the two-year-old knew what John meant. John plopped on the couch with the newspaper in his hand, and quickly each leg filled with a boy. David sat to the side and leaned against his father's muscular arm. Before beginning, John said, "Let's read *Li'l Abner* first. And after supper, we'll all go down to the basement to see the new butterfly that David caught. I found a good beetle at the drugstore for Billy's collection. And, Johnny, I'm going to show you a good place to find some spiders."

Ellie watched from across the room. She had made a simple supper, and it was ready. She was nursing the baby so she could eat quietly with the others. She smiled. *Yes, I married the right man. Not rich, Mama, but right for me. I just love how he is with the children.*

After supper, while Ellie cleaned up, she listened through the door that went down to the basement. Sounds of excitement flowed upstairs as often as moments of silence. Curious as to what was happening when it was quiet for too long, Ellie peered down the stairs and saw father and sons on their hands and knees looking for bugs under the workbench and washing machine.

Little Johnny whispered, "Dad, come quick! Here's one!"

John was reaching for an empty jar when Ellie turned away from the scene, smiling.

John was the same with all children. The cousins loved to be with him. It was rare that John had time to go to one of his sister's houses, but when he did, … he'd endlessly hear, "Uncle John, Uncle John, come look." John always accommodated by looking at their projects, but he usually had a plan of his own.

With the six children circling him, John raised his eyebrows to say, "I hear you boys have been spitting when your mother doesn't approve."

"Yeah, yeah," one of the girls chimed in. "He spit on me yesterday. I cried and Mama made him stand in the corner."

John started walking the path away from the house and was followed by all six. "Well, there's spitting that's not good to do and, maybe you didn't know, there's spitting that's okay." When they got to a shed, John suggested, "You boys line up along the wall of the shed."

They ran to line up.

"Now you girls, come face them. Let's see if you can spit on them."

"No, no," screamed one boy, "that ain't fair." Others rushed from the lineup protesting and gathered around their Uncle John, complaining.

John nodded. "So, you think it's not fair to be spit on? Well, I agree, but since you boys were spitting on the girls, I thought you wouldn't mind. I'm glad you don't like it. So, I expect you won't spit at the girls anymore."

Sad and shameful eyes looked at him, but nodded in agreement.

With a serious voice, John stated, "I don't want to ever hear of any of you spitting on anyone." Then he smiled, "But I think a spitting contest might be okay. We'll have one of those next time I come. So, practice to make your spit go as far as possible. Of course, you can only practice outside."

Among the cheers and happiness, John said, "Let's go," and he started walking again. He was pulling vials, small glass containers, and used, but cleaned, medicine containers out of his pockets. He handed two to every child as he walked and talked, "Speaking of spit, there's this bug that spits all day long." Now he had their attention. He turned to his niece and smoothed her hair as he asked, "Are we going in the right direction to that big vacant lot?"

"Yeah," she pointed, proud that her Uncle asked her for this important information. "It's behind the shed and outhouse. But we need to pass a real mean dog on a chain."

John could hear the dog barking already, "He sounds vicious!"

Little eyes got big. The three girls got closer. Rose Cohen, who had come with the Bartletts, took John's hand. John stopped walking and crouched down to their eye level. "Maybe I was wrong. Maybe this dog isn't mean or vicious. Let's see if we can find out." John turned to his oldest nephew who lived there, "But I would need your help with the experiment. You'd have to continue it after all of us leave today. Are you interested?"

"An experiment, yeah," the boy glowed with pride.

"Okay, here's what we're going to do." John reached into another of his many pockets and pulled out a stick of jerky that he always carried. "Today, I'm going to donate some of my jerky." He broke two pieces off. "But you and only you need to toss it to the dog. After today, every time you pass him, you toss him a small crust of bread with some grease on it. The dog doesn't need much to learn. See, if the dog is a good dog, after you feed him a couple of times, he should stop barking when he smells you. Did you know that dogs know us by our smell? Well, they do. When you see him wag his tail, you get a little closer and toss the food. Remember to be kind to him. Never yell at him or throw rocks. And don't be with anyone that does. If he never wags his tail," John shook his head and clicked his tongue, "he's mean."

Up in the empty lot among all the tall grasses, they collected spit bugs. John told them about the 'snake froth' that looks like spit. "But people just call it that; it isn't made by a snake. It's made by that little, bitty bug we collected." John explained about the beautiful red and black beetle that the spit bug was destined to become. And to entice the girls, John had them collect ladybugs and a roly-poly or two to put into their vials.

On the way back to the house, the dog got the second piece of jerky. "By next week, you'll know. I bet he starts wagging that tail in a couple of days."

Ellie had stayed back at the house with John's sister Louise. They were cooking up some eggs for the children. Louise had chickens, so fresh eggs were the most plentiful food to offer guests. Ellie smiled as John came in the back door, "Look at this delicious gravy that Louise taught me to make with the drippings from a piece of bacon and some lard. We're going to put it over some bread." Ellie was tickled pink.

That evening, when the night air began to sparkle, Uncle John and the children went out to catch fireflies. "The one who catches the most gets what I have in this shirt pocket." He smiled and winked, "Of course, after we count how many are in the jars, we let all the bugs back out into the night—except two. Understand? We're going to keep those two for the collections; all the rest go free."

Bobbing little heads, with snotty noses and grimy faces from playing in the dirt, agreed with his plan.

John had small lollypops for all of them and a larger one for the winner.

When school closed for summer vacation, the Bartletts spent more time at the farm. Rose would spend at least a couple of weeks with them and other cousins came too. Children sleeping-over at the Bartlett's house or farm was typical.

"Please, oh please, can we sleep-over at Aunt Ellie's?"

Back in the city, when cousins spent the night at the Bartlett's house, it was impossible to get them to go to sleep. At the farm, they were asleep when their heads hit the pillow. John would wear them out during the day, taking them to feed the cattle, to help carry boards to repair the barn, to gather chicken eggs, to unload supplies into the sheds, and more. John had them working hard and the oldest, David, was only eleven. It wasn't all work for the children. They frolicked in the shallow creeks while John and old Uncle Will worked in the fields, plowing with the mules or cutting hay for the winter.

At the end of the day, John gave all the children their baths in one of the spring-fed creeks. Sometimes there were eight of them to wash. They would arrive at the house in his clean, old undershirts that John had taken with him. They ate and fell into their beds.

One evening as the sun was almost down, John bathed the children. It was as hot and humid as it had been all day. John had taken off his overalls—leaving his underwear on—and stood knee-deep in the creek water with the boys. The girls were in another water hole a few yards away, around a curve and behind some bushes. The two mules munched on grass, waiting with the wagon to take the group back up to the farmhouse. As John scrubbed one little head, he remembered the four eggs in the bed of the wagon; they had gathered them from the chicken coop earlier in the morning. *Those eggs have to be going bad from all this heat today*. But he got an idea.

As little hands rubbed soap all over their bodies, John scrubbed the littlest one's hair and shared his idea, "At the drugstore the other day, we got a shipment of different kinds of shampoo. Some of it smelled like lilacs—guess they put in some lilac flowers—and other bottles had eggs mixed in with the shampoo because eggs are good for your hair. Makes it shiny and healthy. I think we should wash our hair with some eggs."

"Oh, no!" one boy said.

"Yuck," shouted another among many other protests.

John donned a towel around his waist and walked out of the creek to get the eggs. Placing them carefully on the shore, he took one, "I'll do mine first."

The girls had heard and snuck quietly over to the bushes to peek.

John reentered the water, still in his underwear, and sat in the water. He took an egg and cracked it over his head, quickly lathering before it oozed away. He rubbed with his fingertips until it was frothy. He was smiling and humming. The boys were quiet at first then started getting rowdy.

John claimed, "My hair will be really shiny later. You wait and see." Then he dunked his head to rinse, took the soap, lathered, and washed everything out into the creek. "Who's brave enough to be next?"

After John cracked one over each boy's head and started the lather before the egg slithered away, little fingers worked with the sticky raw eggs. It didn't take long for one boy to smear his slimy hands on the body of another. Soon they all began splashing water on the others while sending peals of laughter, yelps, and shouts into the night. The girls watched it all, giggling.

Later that night when Ellie and John snuggled in their farmhouse bed, their lovemaking took on the same vigor as other activities in the fresh country air. "I love you, John Bartlett," Ellie sighed. He hugged her tightly, and she snuggled into his shoulder. John fell asleep quickly; he was as tired as the children. Ellie watched him sleep in the moonlight.

Just before Ellie fell asleep, she made a decision. She had been thinking about Capone. While keeping track of him over the years, she had watched his prison term pass. She had worried about his release, but recently she learned that Capone was ill in Alcatraz. So, lying next to John at the farm, she thought about her wonderful life with John. And as she thought about the enjoyment she had received from her children, relatives, and friends; Ellie took pity on Al Capone. Her animosity toward him just disappeared.

The next morning, after the family returned home from the farm, Ellie opened her dresser drawer where she had her underclothes, the photographs of Elizabeth in a cigar box, and her jewelry box. Removing the jewelry box, she put it to her face and smelled the rich wood before she rummaged around in it, laughing at the rock she had saved from the swim in the Mississippi River; finally she held the lucky rabbit's foot. *I'll send it back to Capone.* Sitting on the side of her bed with baby James sleeping on her shoulder, she shook her head. *No, I can't!*

Later that day, she went to a Dimestore and bought another rabbit's foot. She brought it home and went to the backyard. Squatting by some dry dirt, where her boys played with their toy cars, Ellie rubbed the new rabbit's foot in the powdery soil. She spit on it and rolled it in the dirt again. Then dusted it off. Finally, she removed the real one from her pocket to compare. After a few more rolls, they looked about the same.

With a mischievous smile on her face and a satisfaction that Capone would finally be able to put two and two together, she mailed the new rabbit's foot to Alcatraz—by certified mail and with a card inside that said, "From Ellie Jones, aka E.M. James."

Chapter 15

1940-1945
Life Evolves

In 1940, John worked at three different Walgreens—the West end store, one at Grand and Olive, and another at Grand and Arsenal, which was closest to their house—when he quit. He hadn't planned to quit that year; it wasn't the time to make major financial changes with World War II raging in Europe. The U.S. wasn't yet in the war, but they were preparing for it and contributing to it. FDR transferred fifty old destroyers to Great Britain, and Congress built up the budgets for the Navy and Army.

Yet, John found an opportunity to buy his own drugstore, and it was too good of a price to pass up. Though he'd been saving to buy one for years, he still needed a bit more money. The bank didn't want to make any loans because of the war. But with John's good work record, his personality, and the integrity he demonstrated to everyone, a door opened for him; his boss at Walgreens said he would lend him the money.

John and Ellie talked for weeks before agreeing to take the loan from his boss. They had no idea how it would change their lives financially; in fact, they worried that they would have less cash to work with or wouldn't be able to make ends meet. But they knew, in the long run, it would help send their four boys to college in a few years.

When the deal was finalized in 1940, John owned a drugstore at Park and Compton in a wonderful middle-class neighborhood. All of his pharmacy friends agreed that he had made a fabulous deal. He bought it with the existing stock on its shelves, all the display cases, and beautifully made wooden furniture—a desk, a chest of drawers with a marble counter top for mixing drugs, and floor-to-ceiling cabinets in the back room for all the medicines. From one day to the next, he walked out of Walgreens and into his own drugstore.

Ellie was so excited, "Let's call Jerry and Françoise. You can give them a tour of the drugstore tonight. Then maybe they'd be interested in celebrating with us this weekend on that new boat down on the Mississippi. The one called The Admiral. Remember? We read about it in the Sunday newspaper. We haven't gone dancing in ages with Jerry and Françoise."

But there was something else besides no longer dancing.

The Cohens still came to the Bartlett's house for bridge once a month, but they had fewer and fewer activities together. They no longer were close. They were living busy and different lifestyles.

Jerry and nine year old Rose liked to do things together. Father and daughter would frequently go to Forest Park to visit the zoo or to go on long walks. Jerry called them "Our Walking Talks." He insisted that Rose go to the symphony with Françoise and him even though she would fall asleep on her father's lap during the last half. He loved to have her snuggling in his arms. When Rose came home from school crying because some children had said they wouldn't play with the "ugly Jew," she went to her father's office for comfort and an explanation. Jerry was the parent who read books to her, answered her questions, and pointed out a beautiful sunset.

Françoise, on the other hand, organized Rose's life with classes and activities—ballet, piano, and voice. Françoise wanted her daughter to be deprived of no opportunity. Although Françoise had taken Rose to Ellie's house when she was younger, with the children growing older it was different. Once she had ripped her stockings on the Erector Set, another time Billy had ruined an expensive silk blouse when he tripped and spilled his glass of milk. The Bartlett boys were boys: made of snips and snails and puppy-dog tails. They were always dirty; Françoise cringed when they rubbed against her. She preferred to rub shoulders with the upper class of St. Louis. Besides, Rose was not interested in being around the wild Bartlett boys anymore.

With the Bartlett family growing, Ellie stopped asking Bertha to babysit the children. The boys were too much for their grandmother to manage and, to tell the truth, the children didn't feel comfortable with her. Bertha found the boys to be impolite and disobedient, and Ellie thought her mother was too strict. So, they had a babysitter.

However, Ellie didn't hesitate to ask Bertha to sew an evening dress for the night on The Admiral.

"Mama, sew a dress that will swirl when I'm dancing. And would you make me a few new underpanties?"

Ellie was a bit larger in the waist after all her children. She was still quite attractive, just a bit heavier. "I have the figure of a mature woman, that's all," she told Ginny. "How can I expect anything else? Actually, as much as I run around with those boys, you'd think I'd be skin and bones."

Ginny looked like she had looked when she swam the Mississippi River. She still could stand on her hands. Françoise and Ellie couldn't understand why Ginny hadn't found a husband, because she looked like a movie star; except Ginny didn't seem to be looking for a man.

"Ginny, come dancing with us. You need to see this boat. It's all metal—shiny silver—with five decks. It's huge. A few thousand people can be on it at a time. Please come. One deck is completely devoted to dancing with a band and tables for cocktails on what they call the Moonlight Cruise. We can go to the top level to see the stars in the night sky. Please come."

Ginny agreed to go; the Cohens asked another couple; the party of seven arrived at the crowded riverfront under a crescent moon. Feeling carefree and eager to dance on this huge, gleaming metal boat—it was a block long and five decks high—the group chattered and laughed as they stood in line to board.

Ellie shared, "In the newspaper they said it was modernistic, but I think it looks like an overturned silver gravy boat; of course one made for a giant. I always wondered why it was called a 'boat'.

"I like the comparison," one of the ladies agreed, "and that's why the Mississippi looks so muddy with all the brown gravy spilled into it."

John stepped up to the cashier's booth, "This is on me. Remember, we're celebrating my drugstore."

They were all good dancers. Even John, the farmer and pharmacist, loved to dance. He insisted it was great exercise. John and Françoise were as smooth on the dance floor as John was with Ellie. They had been dancing together for years. The band played the typical dances—foxtrot, Charleston, rumba, and waltzes.

Jerry held his hand out to his wife, "Remember when you taught me to do that dance called 'The Bear'? All we did was hug each other and shuffle around the dance floor."

Years ago, when Jerry had started to dance with them, he could really cut a rug. Now being thirteen years older than Françoise showed. Frequently Jerry claimed he needed a break to have a cigarette, "I can't smoke and dance at the same time."

Photographs were taken up on the top deck when the band took a break, "Where's Ginny?" Ellie asked. "I want her in the pictures."

Françoise confided, "Haven't you seen her with that soldier? He asked her to dance early on, and they haven't been apart."

"Really?" Ellie gleamed. "How could I have missed that? You know I'm a one-drink woman. I still have the same drink I started with, so I can't blame it on the booze, but I didn't see Ginny with anyone. Oh, I want to meet him."

When the evening ended, Ginny returned to the group without him. On the drive home, she didn't say much about him, and it would be a few weeks before Ellie would meet him.

Ellie planned another trip on The Admiral. She wanted to take the children on a daytime trip—all the cousins, her boys, and Rose Cohen. Ginny wanted to come again and showed up with her soldier. His name was Jack.

The children loved Jack. He was one of those men who was a kid at heart. He had lots of stories to tell that interested kids and adults alike.

"Once, I was riding this bull called Killer in the rodeo, and he was the meanest one I'd ever been on. He had the devil in his eye. While we were in the pen before they opened the gate to let us out, that bull turned his head and looked me straight in the eye and snorted. I looked deep in his eyes and saw down to hell. He was mean. That bull was getting antsy to git out to git me off his back, so he started wiggling about. He squashed one of my legs against one side of the pen and then the other. And he kept snorting.

"When the gate opened, he was determined to kill me. You could see he was full of hate. Actually, he just loved to hate and …"

Jack took his story and made it longer and longer. The children sat in rapt attention, loving every word he told. The adults didn't like the choice of some his curse words and never knew if what he said was true or not, but they found it difficult to not listen.

"We'd been out of the gate what seemed like forever and I was doing pretty good when I noticed that the end of strap I had wrapped around my hand, was caught on my belt buckle. I got scared. How would I git off? That strap was hooked to my buckle and would hold me to that darn bull. I'd be dragged and killed by him."

John hadn't gone on the day excursion to the riverboat; he wasn't able to go many places since he had a drugstore to manage.

Ellie told him all about Ginny's beau. "Then this Jack described how the rodeo clowns came to his rescue and nearly got killed themselves. I really didn't understand exactly how everything happened at the end of his story, but the children seemed to understand. All afternoon, they kept asking questions about the rodeo. He helped the little ones onto the children's rides—merry-go-rounds, bumper cars, and little airplanes that flew in circles—down on the first deck. And he took them for ice cream or treats. I got to relax and talk with your sisters all afternoon while Ginny and Jack had all the kids." Ellie stopped talking and looked into John's face. "You'll like him. I do." She nodded, "You've got to like someone who likes your wild boys. And, even more importantly, someone who your kids seem to love already."

Whenever they could, Ginny and Jack went to the farm with John. Now the children had two men willing to spend time with them. Jack had different ways than John though. As the group marched down the dirt road with fishing poles propped on shoulders, Jack sang army marching songs and taught the children.

"Sound off!" Jack shouted.

"One-two," they answered.

"Sound off!"

"Three-four."

And Jack had little ditties that John hadn't heard before and wouldn't have taught the children, even if he'd known them. But they were songs made for boys:

Pepsi Cola hits the spot,
'Specially when you're on the pot,
Push the button,
Pull the chain,
Out comes the brown little choo-choo train.

It wasn't long before John knew the depth of Jack's love for children. When they were at the stream fishing, Rose and the little eight-year-old girl cousin needed help. Those worms were not their favorite thing, and picking them up involved pained facial expressions. Jack helped put the worms on hooks and stayed closer to the two little girls. The stream wasn't too deep, and the children had waded out into it. It wasn't like the creeks on John's farm; this was a little river they were fishing.

The boys had caught several fish. "Do ya think Aunt Laura will cook 'em for us?" David asked.

John assured all the children that their fish were going to be a part of the evening meal, "Aunt Laura will appreciate you helping to put food on the table. Uncle Will and Aunt Laura aren't rich, and we eat a lot."

Just then, Rose's bobber sunk down a couple of times. Jack was right there, "Look, Rose has a bite! Now, don't pull up on your pole yet." He just talked her through the whole procedure, and she brought in her first fish. Rose was so proud. As she turned to walk her fish over to show Uncle John, she left the water and saw some black things on her legs. Leeches!

Rose screamed, "Get them off me! Get them off! Oh, please help me!"

Jack was right there and picked Rose up into his arms, fish and all. He started talking, "Oh, they sure are ugly little guys, but they ain't going to hurt you. I'll git 'em off lickety-split." He sat her down on a fallen tree and squatted in front of her. Rose was crying and could hardly stand it. "Now, look away and it'll just be a minute."

Instead, she glanced down at the leeches and became hysterical.

"Rose, listen to me. Look at my eyes and listen."

Jack lit a cigarette, "Keep lookin' in my eyes. No, don't look down," he took a hard draw to get it hot and gently took her by the chin, "Rose, get your mind off of them. I'll have them off in one, two, three. Let's sing while you look at your brothers. Don't look anywhere else and sing with me."

Jack started with the first little song he could think of:

The itsy-bitsy spider went up the waterspout,
Down came …

John and all the children gathered around Rose to sing. She started to look down where Jack was carefully burning the leeches from her legs, and David took her head, turning it back to look at him. By the time they finished the song, Jack had removed all six leeches.

"Got 'em all!" Jack announced.

Rose looked at Jack. All of Jack's interactions with the children didn't automatically make Rose comfortable with him like she was with her Uncle John. The boys quickly liked Jack because he was such a roughneck. That was not what Rose needed at this moment. She looked down to her legs, and then up to her Uncle John. She didn't know why, but she started weeping. John picked her up.

John comforted her, "It's all over." He rocked her for a bit in his arms, and then said, "Look at the fish you caught. It's bigger than any of the boys' fish."

***

A year passed and everything changed.

It was 1941, and David's birthday was in December. Early that morning, John and Ellie presented him with a collie puppy. He named her Peggy. Also, wanting this to be a special birthday for David, Ellie planned a Sunday party for December 7th with some school friends, his cousins, and Rose Cohen.

But no one came, except Rose.

The bombing of Pearl Harbor preempted all events. Across the nation, everyone sat by the radio as the hours passed. People were numbed by the details. It seemed like the end of the world. Jerry and Rose arrived, not for David's birthday party, but to sit and listen to the news with the Bartletts.

Jerry sat on the sofa and said, "The streets are empty. I only saw a couple of people driving and no one out walking. Guess everyone is listening to the radio like we are."

Rose snuggled on her father's lap, listening to the adults. She was afraid because she had heard how the Nazi's didn't like Jews. Jerry had tried to calm her fears on the drive to the Bartlett house, but she found it confusing.

Suddenly, David came up from the basement, ran across the living room, and up the stairs with his puppy at his heels. Rose jumped up and ran off with her cousin and his new dog, letting fears disappear for the moment.

The three adults smiled and got back to discussing the bombing. They just could not grasp how the bombing could have happened.

As the deaths and destruction were described throughout the days and weeks and months that followed, people progressed from disbelief, to anger, to determination. The nation coalesced into one resolve to fight and rid the world of the evil 'Axis' powers—the Japs and Nazis.

Day-by-day more changes came. Men disappeared from cities as they shipped out to fight the war. St. Louis had troops in Jefferson Barracks and at Scott Field. Laws were enacted to regulate wages, rents and food prices across the country. Soon there were ration coupons for meat, sugar and gasoline. Defense plants had been starting up before Pearl Harbor, but now there were more, and women began to work in them.

But the bombing of Pearl Harbor meant something different from one family to the next. John Bartlett was exempt from draft; he would not go to war. Neither would Jerry Cohen have to go. But Ginny knew that the man she had waited so long to meet would definitely be going to war. He was a soldier. Ginny knew that this man she loved more than anything in the world might never come home to her. The two of them disappeared for a couple of days and returned married.

By the end of 1942, Japanese, German, and Italian immigrants became enemy aliens—not only immigrants, but also the children of these immigrants, even if they had been born in America. But in St. Louis most were spared. Only nineteen Germans and one Italian were considered dangerous and jailed; thirty-three Japanese residents of the city were interrogated, but none were jailed or put into camps, although their property was seized. Daily life continued with the milkman delivering milk, the postman bringing the mail, and children going to school, but every day people feared the news from abroad. Life changed.

At this time, Rose started asking more questions about the war and, in turn, religion. When bit-by-bit Jerry started to hear rumors about the Jews in Europe, though not the whole truth, he thought Rose old enough to understand. She was upset to hear how Jews were made to sew the Star of David onto their clothing so everyone could see they were Jews.

"How can they force people from their homes to live in ghettos? And why, Daddy?"

"Rose, the Jews have been persecuted for centuries without justification. I've told you some of the stories. People like the Egyptians picked the Jews as slaves and now Hitler has picked them."

"But there must be a reason."

"Oh, there are reasons like jealousy of success and envy of devotion to their faith, but no reason that makes real sense."

Rose wanted to go to a synagogue to understand. At eleven years old she thought she would learn why Jews were hated by seeing what they did. Jerry had never gone to the temple in St. Louis, but he started taking her to *Shabbat* services on Friday evenings. She was fascinated by the services, the reading of the Torah, and all of the tradition. Soon, Rose made friends with Jewish children of her age and went several times a week, walking to the synagogue without her father to be with her friends.

While Rose was learning the realities of war and religion, David too was maturing. He was no longer interested in the antics of little boys like his brothers. Instead, like Rose, he spent much time questioning the war. John decided to take David to the drugstore so he could have more time to talk with his son.

John told Ellie, "Besides, he's twelve, a good age to learn the business."

Ellie agreed.

On the weekends David went with his father for a few hours and returned home on the bus. David learned about ordering stock, pricing procedures, handling money and, most importantly, interacting with customers. John found time to talk to David about more than the war. John realized with his son at his side that he had important ideas to share, like integrity and the importance of truth. John also realized how much he enjoyed teaching and sharing.

After a few months, John made a family rule. "Ellie, I think I'll take each of the children to the drugstore to learn when they're about twelve."

Until they came of age to go work in the drugstore, David's younger brothers spent their time playing cowboys and Indians, building forts in the basement, playing war games, and mostly discussing their favorite topic: Farts.

One night after John arrived home at his usual time, a little after ten, they undressed for bed. As Ellie slipped her nightgown over her head, she explained that she couldn't understand her boys' never-ending fascination with the passing of gas, "John, can you help me stop them? They love to pass gas and have contests for the loudest. All of their games center around ..." She whispered that horrible word, "farts."

John just smiled and headed for the bathroom, "I know. I know," he said. "Talking about farts is part of being a boy that I can't explain." Ellie went in to brush her teeth, but John wrapped his arms around her waist and with a grin he said, "Sorry you have to put up with it, but it will pass."

"John! *Et tu, Brutus*?"

He smiled and held her tightly against his body. They kissed.

People on the home front volunteered to do their part. After Ellie became a Cub Scout leader, she learned how central fart talk was in a growing boy's life with a dozen boys in the house, talking about farts and doing their best to smell up a room. She learned, if she could keep them interested in a scout project, they momentarily forgot farts.

Ginny signed up for the Women's Army Corp and became a WAC. She volunteered for this first organized army of women to do her part for winning the war, "Besides I'm wasting my time pining away for Jack, and I want to be useful." She disappeared into the chasms of the war machine, telling her family that she would not be allowed to write home, "And I can't talk about it either. So, don't ask." Bertha was left living alone for the first time in her sixty-three years.

By the end of 1942, the Bartletts started looking for a different house. They had two people in every bedroom; there was no room for another bed anywhere, and Ellie was pregnant again.

Françoise was surprised, "Ellie, at your age, pregnant again?"

Ellie had telephoned Françoise to confide, "I think subconsciously I wanted to get pregnant, so we'd have to move. This move may be the only way I'll ever clean up this house." She looked around to verify her comment and saw the ironing board in the living room with two wicker baskets of clothes to be ironed; off in the corner by the fireplace were structures Johnny and James had made with the Erector Set; a mountain of dirty clothes were piled at the bottom of the stairs to be taken down to the basement to be washed; there were comic books scattered everywhere; toy cars were parked on the rug; baseball caps were here and there on the floor; a few dirty socks lay by the rocking chair; a sling-shot hung over the arm of an overstuffed chair; one boot with mud on the soles was on the same overstuffed chair; and some crumbled candy bar wrappers poked out from under the couch. "It's getting messier and messier. These boys make it impossible to keep this place clean."

Sitting in her own immaculate apartment across town, making braids in Rose's hair, Françoise thought that wasn't the real truth of the matter. In her opinion, Ellie didn't know how to keep a neat house. After she hung up the phone Françoise commented, "Ellie confuses me sometimes."

"What do you mean, Mama?"

"Over the years, I've tried to convince Ellie to get someone to help her clean that house. She's so stubborn. I just don't understand why she doesn't want help, but I can't stand to be in that house. It's a mess. Thank heavens your father and I no longer have to go there for bridge parties."

The two friends mostly talked by telephone now. With the war, Ellie had decided the bridge parties should stop. But Françoise decided that ending the bridge was just another excuse; with no bridge party, Ellie had another reason not to clean her house. But Françoise didn't share this opinion with her daughter.

Rarely are difficulties caused by only one problem. The truth of the matter was that Françoise was unaware of much of Ellie's life. They lived so differently. With the war, Ellie had been doing the bookkeeping for the drugstore. The man who used to do it was fighting at the front. So Ellie had to take her time to do the books, besides Cub Scouts, washing clothes, cooking, helping with homework, and caring for children. But Ellie was happy. She was always the happiest when she was pregnant or raising a baby.

John was exempt from serving in the armed forces, but he worked doubly hard during the war. He had long hours, coming home after eleven at night when Ellie was sound asleep, and sometimes working seven days a week because his help often quit. When he lost someone, he did the work himself. He also hired women to help, but sometimes the lifting of boxes was too much for them, and he couldn't find any women pharmacists. On the rare day when John could take a day off, he went to the farm. Ellie couldn't go if it was during the school year. So, she looked forward to doing the books at the drugstore because she could be with John. They didn't see each other much anymore.

In 1943 Ellie and John had a baby girl they named Rebecca.

The following year, while Ginny was still overseas, Jack came home injured. Jack was living over at Grandma Bertha's house. It was a perfect arrangement. Bertha cooked and cared for him while he healed, and he claimed he was protecting a woman living alone. With his disability check, he would never have to work again, and he helped Bertha with the household expenses.

After a few weeks, when he was almost back to normal, he came to visit the Bartletts in their new home in the well-to-do neighborhood of Compton Heights. Large expensive houses lined the curving streets of Hawthorne and Longfellow. Their house was spacious, with chandeliers hanging in the foyer and dining room; the foyer was as large as the living room in their previous house. Although there was a basement, a special room upstairs was used for all the hobbies.

Jack hobbled on crutches, slowly coming up the front walk, when the Bartlett children first saw him. They gasped, not about the crutches—Jack had lost an eye. Long, deep scars crisscrossed his eye socket and had left him with a disfigured face. And he had a glass eye!

Jack plopped down on a dining room chair and propped his crutches against the table. The four boys spread out around the table and stared.

"I'll take the glass eye out, if you want to hold it," Jack gloated.

Ellie jumped in, "No! Jack, don't you dare. You keep your glass eye in that socket."

"Aw, Mom, please," eight-year-old Johnny complained.

"That's my final word," Ellie insisted as she turned and walked away.

Unknown to Ellie, Jack started unbuttoning his shirt. To appease the Bartlett boys' disappointment of not seeing his eyeball, he had an idea, "Well, if I can't show you my eye, I'll let you see my tattoo." And before Ellie could turn around again to protest, Jack had exposed an American Eagle with wings spreading across his chest, among his hairs, from one armpit to the other.

"Wow, look at that!"

"Don't it hurt to get tattooed?"

"Does Ginny know you did it?"

Ellie was back among her boys. "Jack, please button up."

"Oh, I didn't think that'd offend ya. Maybe I could just tell the boys the story of how I lost my eye?"

As she turned to walk back to the kitchen, Ellie agreed, though she would regret it in a few minutes.

"It was in a battle with the Krauts," Jack looked at little, redheaded James who was only five. "A Kraut's a Nazi." He thought he better clarify more, "You know, a damn German."

Ellie's head shot around the kitchen doorframe.

"Sorry. Excuse me kids. I been in hell in this war and my language ain't the best. Anyway, my unit was comin' into this small town in Germany. It was all rubble from the bombing and fighting that happened before we arrived. We thought those damn Krauts were all gone ..."

Ellie realized that she would not be able to keep his bad language under control and just hoped it wouldn't get worse as she continued to prepare some lunch. She noticed that Jack was elaborating on the story and dragging it out to entice the children. *It's working. My boys are eating up every word Jack gives them.* She sighed.

As she brought in the soup and sandwiches, Jack was finishing his tale.

He leaned into the table and whispered, "As I walked toward that stairwell where the shots had been fired that killed my buddy, the Kraut jumped on me from the right side. He had this knife that looked like it belonged to Captain Hook. It sparkled in the sun just before he slashed my face, and cut right through my eyeball. I saw the blood squirtin' right off my face and …"

Ellie interrupted, "Lunch is ready! Jack, sorry to interrupt, but I think my boys have heard enough. I'm so sorry that you lost your eye, but I don't think I could eat if I heard the rest of that story." She made a feigned laugh, "We woman don't enjoy all the gore of this war. Start eating, boys." Ellie poured milk into glasses, "Jack, would you like some coffee? It's not coffee like before the war, but it works."

The Cohens came to see the new house. Rose had grown taller than Françoise; overnight she seemed to become a lady. She had seen the house before and excused herself to go find little Rebecca. Rose loved the baby.

Françoise was impressed, "Ellie, the house is wonderful. And it's so neat and clean!"

Ellie responded, "Glad you think so. I thought you'd be happy to know I have people to help me clean." Ellie stopped dramatically for a moment, waiting to hook Françoise into the punch line. "Yes, John told all the boys they needed to take responsibility for cleaning their rooms, and they each have additional tasks throughout the house. As you can see, it's working!"

They started up the stairs. John was leading the tour, "Come see what I use as leverage." They left the master bedroom and entered a room across from the sitting room at the top of the stairs. "This is the hobby room. I told the boys they're not allowed in here unless they've done all their chores."

Upon seeing the hobby room, Françoise and Jerry were amazed. Bookcases not yet filled with books lined one wall from the floor to the ceiling. There was a wooden ladder, flush against the shelves, that slid along the top. The adjacent wall had a mounted ten point deer head that John had shot last year. Turning again, they saw glass cabinets with displays of insects: bugs and butterflies.

"We're starting a coin collection," John said. "Having the drugstore gives us quite an opportunity to find old coins and collect new stamps. I told each of the boys they'd be coming to work with me in the drugstore when they reached the age of twelve. Only David is old enough right now, but I bring sacks of coins home for the others to sort through.

"Oh, look at this." John pulled out a cigar box from a lower shelf and showed them arrowheads and other Indian artifacts. "We find these at the farm. Look at this tomahawk head. Uncle Will and I have the boys looking in the fields after we plow."

"You have boys to be proud of," Jerry commented.

In 1945, just before Ellie's Storm, Ginny came home from the war. Germany had surrendered, ending the fighting in Europe. But Ginny had no stories to tell. Ellie was amazed; her sister who could keep no secrets, had war secrets. And Ginny will take those secrets to her grave when she died at a very old age.

Oh, how proud Daddy would be of Ginny. Ellie was getting excited about her approaching birthday. The trip to Wally's always was on her mind for days or weeks before Ellie's Storm. She had a shoebox full of the annual letters from James. However, with each passing year, she doubted that James would ever return. He had left thirty-five years ago. *My children will never know their grandfather. Oh, how I want him to see them. Oh, I shouldn't be selfish. What's more important is that the Germans surrendered last week, and my sister came home. What a birthday gift.*

***

After the war, John bought a second farm in Illinois. It was one hundred twenty acres of rich soil along the Mississippi River. Flat, with no trees.

Uncle Will's Missouri farm was over three hundred acres of rolling hills filled with mature woods of oak and hickory trees, several creeks and springs that twisted and curved through the land, as well as all kinds of animals—squirrels, rabbit, deer, and turkey to hunt—along with several barns and many places for children to play.

The family went to Illinois to see the new farm by crossing the most southern bridge in the St. Louis area. As they approached the farm, the boys were disappointed; they could see nothing to enjoy.

"What are we supposed to do here?" one boy asked.

"It's nothing but this black mud," said a younger boy.

Ellie tried to be positive, "Boys, we haven't even gotten out of the car. Let your father show you our new farm before you judge it." But privately she agreed with her boys because she feared John would be away from her even more with another farm. All his free days were spent at the farm.

John took them up on the levy that protected the land from the Mississippi River to get the complete view. He strolled along the ridge, "When I bought Uncle Will's farm in Missouri, I knew nothing about farming. Uncle Will taught me all he knew, and I read a lot to learn more. I have other cousins and friends who are farmers, and I learned from them as well. I bought a tractor when I learned the mules were not efficient, a baler to improve the feed for the cattle for winter, and made a lot of improvements in the fences and barns. I love our Missouri farm, but I still don't make any money from it. In fact, I lose money every year.

"This little farm," John stretched his arm out across the land they could see, "will make more money than the drugstore and then some. It's not pretty like the Missouri farm, but it will be profitable."

Ellie put her arm around John's waist and continued to walk with him. She asked, "So, this is an investment and not for vacations. Right?"

"That's the idea, Ellie. Boys, you need to understand that when you are all in college at the same time, I'll need more money than I have now. One must always plan ahead. David starts college in a little over a year. He wants to be a doctor, so he'll be in medical school when Johnny starts college." John stopped for a minute to let the boys digest that. "Why, if David wants to specialize, he might still be in medical school when Rebecca goes to college."

David asked, "What will you grow here to make so much money?"

"This land is good for corn, wheat, and soybeans. My cousin Dale will run it for me. I won't have to do anything. We'll take the profits and divide them in thirds. One-third for me, another for Dale, and the last is for the land. Every year we'll put some of the money back into the land to buy seed, fertilizer, other supplies, and equipment."

"You aren't going to sell the Missouri farm, are you?" the ten year old asked.

"No, Uncle Will and Aunt Laura can live there until they die. And we'll go and enjoy it until we die. How does that sound?"

The boys smiled in agreement as anxiety left their faces.

John looked pensive and shared his thoughts, "We all need money, but sometimes you need to consider the value of things beyond money. I don't get much exercise in the drugstore; I may stand all day, but that's not exercise. My Missouri farm keeps me fit and strong. I dig fence post holes, patch and run barbed wire, help cows with their calving, throw bales, and so much more. All that work on the farm is hard work. I feel healthy because of my farm. I want to remain strong all my life. Do you children understand?"

They all nodded their heads though it would be years before they truly understood the meaning of their father's words. One day, when they are middle-aged and gathered for a family get-together, they will notice their expanding bellies. Billy will mention what their dad had said. But, for now, the children let the deep lesson pass and turned to their mother.

Ellie asked, "Why didn't you buy land with a house, so we could come here?" She pointed to a house that seemed next to their land.

"Well, I didn't think we'd need one. When I come here, I'll stay with Dale and his family. As you see, there wouldn't be much for the family to do. I don't plan to have to come too much. Someone else bought that land over there with the house." John had walked back to the car. "Let's go over to Dale's."

John knew who owned the land with the house; he had his reasons for not saying who it was.

Chapter 16

1947-1950
Heading into the Storm

The 1896 storm was getting ready to touch down in Ellie's life again. That's the thing with tornados; they're so sporadic. The original storm that marked Ellie's birth did extensive damage in the area of St. Louis called Compton Heights. The tornado had been like a mad dog in that elite neighborhood, wreaking havoc here and there with no pattern to the madness. Jumping up and down, it had sucked homes into oblivion, and then backtracked to grab one it had passed before. Fifty years ago when the storm finally had ended, most homes had been completely demolished and rebuilt, which explained why the neighborhood looked new.

The Bartlett's home was there, in Compton Heights.

Yet, how could one explain the disasters happening in Ellie's life where the tornado hit a half-century ago? Who would believe such a phenomenon? But unexplained questions exist in the universe; this was one of many. How do salmon return to their exact spawning grounds to lay eggs? How do birds fly four thousand miles back to the breeding grounds where they were born? Mankind has asked puzzling questions for centuries.

Nevertheless, Ellie was not even aware of her relationship to the storm, so she never asked how it was possible. The random gypsy, looking into her hand, had seen a swirling motion in each palm, but it had meant nothing to Ellie at that time.

One day, Rose Cohen will see the relationship of that storm with Ellie's life.

Like the tornado so long ago, coming events will create chaos here and there in Ellie's life, jumping all around, destroying more and more. Destruction had happened in seconds in Compton Heights in 1896; the reenactment of the storm in Ellie's life will occur over several years, leaving turmoil and confusion.

***

The drugstore, the Illinois farm, and the beautiful home in Compton Heights, reflected the Bartlett's prosperity, but their relatives were having hard times.

Ginny and Jack were living with Bertha. Ginny had found a job soon after she returned from her duty, but the pay wasn't what she had been making before the war. Because of his loss of an eye, Jack had a disability check each month, but they had no savings to buy a house of their own. Even so, they were happy just to be together, and they understood that Bertha shouldn't live alone; she was frail and no longer could sew to earn a living.

Since the end of the war, John's sisters and their families were struggling more. Louise's husband worked painting homes—inside and out—and couldn't find enough painting jobs to pay all their bills. The other brother-in-law returned from the Navy and when he couldn't find work, John offered him a job at the drugstore. John wanted a manager so he could have a couple of days off each week to go to his farms.

After the war, changes were inevitable. But the years between 1947 through 1950 caught Ellie in a whirlwind of extremes. She would just regain her balance to find herself trying to cope with the next surprise. Unhappiness was followed by joy, which frequently turned back into sadness.

When school started in September 1947, Ellie was without children in the house because little Rebecca started kindergarten. Driving over to Dogtown, she marveled at how quickly life changed. *It's the first time in years I've had freedom to go places every day without children. And what happens? Mama gets sick. It couldn't have come at a better time.*

With Ginny working, Ellie helped Jack care for Bertha who couldn't get out of bed anymore. Two strong people were needed to move her about. Except for his vision, Jack was hale and hearty.

Ellie turned onto her childhood street and parked in front of the house. Slipping the key from the ignition, she swallowed, trying to relieve the lump in her throat. Then she took a deep breath, put a smile on, and left the car to go to her mother. Bertha was very ill; Ellie had been making this trip every day for a few weeks.

Bertha had a growth in her lower abdomen, and it seemed to grow bigger each day. Knowing she needed comfort, neighbors and friends came to visit. Ellie walked in and found Wally talking softly with Jack. Her mother was napping.

Wally sat on the couch amid crocheted armrests and doilies draped over the back.

Ellie greeted them and took a seat next to the photo of Ellie and Ginny when they were young.

Wally's eyes fell on the framed picture, "Goodness me, this photograph is still where it was years ago. Nothin' has changed in this house. Everything looks just like it did when James lived here and when Al Capone stopped by to pay your fine mother a visit."

"Oh, Wally, that's so long ago, but you're right. Mama doesn't want to rearrange anything."

Jack was puzzled, "What's this about Al Capone?"

Ellie laughed and summed it up, "When I worked at the *Post Dispatch* there was an article about Al Capone, and he didn't like it. He came here trying to find who wrote it. Bertha put him in his place."

"There's a wee more to the story, but you git the idea. Maybe Ginny will fill in more details for ye."

Jack protested, "You can't say stuff like that and not explain. After all, it's not every day a man hears about Al Capone knocking on his mother-in-law's door, and I won't see Ginny for hours."

Ellie's eyes teased. "Mom doesn't need to worry about Capone knocking on her door again; he died this year. In January. Did you know? *Humph, it's me who doesn't have to worry about him showing up anymore. I'm really free! All my children are in school, and Al has gone to face his maker.*

Then Ellie told the story to Jack.

When that story ended, Wally perked up and asked Jack, "Did Ginny ever tell ya James' renditions about the namin' of Dogtown?" Wally proceeded to tell the tales.

Bertha woke with the laughing, and they took the stories into the bedroom. Bertha seemed to enjoy the reminiscing.

"Now you men need to let me give my mother her bath. I'm going to wash your hair today, Mama."

"If you must, Ellie, but I'm very tired."

Ellie took extra care to be gentle with the washing. When finished, Ellie combed her mother's hair and fluffed the pillows behind Bertha's back.

"Please let me nap a bit more."

Ellie closed the bedroom door and returned to chat with the men.

Within the hour, Ellie looked at the clock on the mantle, "School will be letting out soon. I need to go home. I'll just quietly see if Mama's awake." Ellie peeked into the bedroom and decided to kiss her sleeping mother goodbye.

Bertha wasn't asleep.

While Jack, Ellie, and Wally had been reliving the sagas of the past, Bertha had ended the story of her life. She died on September 25, 1947.

The very next day, unknown to Ginny and Ellie, their father James was on a plane from California to Missouri. Bertha had died. He walked into the house that evening with Wally.

By the casket in the living room, Ginny was whispering with some visitors when she looked up and, upon seeing her father, put the back of her hand to her mouth and keeled over. Jack rushed to her side. Luckily Jerry Cohen was there and saw Ginny faint.

Although Ginny and Ellie had not spoken about their father for years, deep down each had hoped they would see him again. For Ellie, the letters from her father renewed her hope every year. For Ginny, thirty-six years was a long time to hold on to hope.

Ellie knew that her sister's hopes had slipped away slowly and been replaced with sadness on some days and anger on others. But what had never slipped away or been forgiven was that James had left her.

Jerry grabbed his black bag and pulled out the smelling salts. Jerry's sixty-four years were apparent as he eased himself down with difficulty, balancing on a knee to work on Ginny. He passed the opened bottle below Ginny's nose. She reacted instantly and shoved his hand away. Blinking her eyes, one could see the working of her mind as she looked at her father and grasped that James was there because Bertha had died. Slowly she stood with Jack's help.

Ellie glowed as she hugged James, "Daddy, you look the same. Well, you have some gray hair around your temples, but you're the same. Oh my, I can't wait for you to see my children. Did you know I have five?" Barely taking a breath and not waiting for his answer, Ellie continued to babble, "My husband, John, should be here any minute with the children. Oh my goodness, you're going to meet my children."

Ginny smoothed out her dress and watched Ellie across the room with their father. A frown furrowed in her brow, and she jerked Jack's hands from her arm, unaware of anyone in the room except James and Ellie. She took a step toward James, stopped and stared, and then took another.

Ellie and James became aware of her approach.

James smiled his wide, toothy grin and walked to Ginny. "Why, Ginny, you are a sight for sore eyes. You're quite …"

Now Ginny closed the gap between them by rushing to him with clenched fists. She pounded on his chest and arms, "You left me. Why? How could you? You never wrote me or called or anything. For years, I've been wondering, worrying, and angry." She continued to hit James until Jack arrived and, from behind, surrounded her with his arms.

James didn't move from where he was, "I deserve your anger, Ginny. I know I deserve it. But you know why I left. That ain't nothin' I need to tell ya. I just want ya to know I missed ya more than any man e'er missed a daughter."

Jack still held Ginny from behind with his arms circling her middle. Listening to James talk, Ginny started to relax. Jack let go.

James continued, "I love you, Ginny. That ne'er changed. There weren't many days I didn't think 'bout ya."

Ginny leaned into her father's chest and wrapped her arms around him. She whispered, "I missed you. And I thought about you almost every day, … until Jack came into my life." Ginny reached out and pulled Jack to her side, "Daddy, this is my husband, Jack. He's the most wonderful man."

There were several friends and neighbors present who had come to pay their respects to Bertha. All of them watched. Some had known

James, all of them knew about his disappearance. But they seemed embarrassed at not knowing what to say to him. That didn't matter. They smiled as they watched the reunion of father and daughters.

At that moment, Françoise and Rose were heading to the James house. Jerry had gone earlier. As Françoise drove she complained, "It was bad enough that you had to go to the synagogue and make us late, but now I'm hitting every red light."

"Mommy, I can't help that Grandma Bertha died on the Sabbath. Besides, I can't see what difference it will make. All we do at a funeral is stand around for hours." Rose was sixteen; she liked her friends at the synagogue, so she went every week.

"Don't be disrespectful, young lady. You know Bertha meant a lot to me. I haven't had a chance to tell you that your father called to tell me that Bertha's husband James arrived. I am so excited to see him. Why, I think it has been at least thirty years since I last saw him. He had just disappeared from one day to the next. We didn't know where he was."

Françoise's excitement about seeing James puzzled Rose, "Aren't we supposed to be sad about Grandma Bertha. You seem to be so happy about seeing him."

"Don't you remember all the stories that Ellie and I would tell you about her father? He was the one who got Ginny to swim the Mississippi. Surely you remember that."

Rose nodded.

"And that little story about *Jeb the Spider* that you loved so much, he made it up."

Rose started to remember all the tales she had heard. As they parked the car, Rose was smiling with memories about this man she had always wanted to meet.

James hugged Françoise, "Franny, oh Franny. My third daughter! That's who she is. Now don't 'spect me to call you by that fancy name. Yep, I heard 'bout it." He held Françoise at arms length and then pulled her in for another hug, "Franny, course you're all grown up, but I look at your girl Rose and I see you. She's got your blue eyes and blonde hair."

Bertha was buried amid the delight of James' return. Near the grave, not even the trees could be somber; a huge oak of at least fifty years stretched its limbs, shamelessly exhibiting cheerful red fall colors. Grandchildren thought little about death and the loss of Bertha. Instead they stared in wonderment at this mysterious tall, lanky grandfather that had appeared from California. Nevertheless, there were tears at the graveside, as James stood flanked by daughters. What a bittersweet day for Ginny and Ellie, losing a mother and gaining a father.

Grandpa James, as everyone now called him, slept at his old home in Dogtown with Ginny and Jack, allowing a couple of grandchildren to sleep over most evenings.

During breakfast the next day, Grandpa James asked, "Remind me agin just how old the two of ya are."

Johnny told his Grandfather he was ten, but little James was too shy to answer, "He's eight and I guess we gonna hafta call him Red since he's got your name."

"Is that all right with you, Red?"

All they got was a jerky nod.

"Well now, have ya e'er been to Wally's shop?" James asked his two grandsons. They shook their heads from across the breakfast table. "Let's take the dishes to the sink and git o'er there. I told Wally I'd come by."

They headed out of the house just as James used to do years ago. "I'd take your Aunt Ginny and your mother on my back and shoulders when they's small. You two are too big for that, but we'll walk the same streets." They started ambling down Tamm Street. "My oh my, how it's changed here in Dogtown. Let's turn here by the church." The boys were walking a brisk pace because James' legs were so long. "Do ya know how Dogtown got its name?"

Much to James' surprise they didn't.

"Your ma never tol' ya? Why, I'm goin' to haf ta have a word with Ellie." James favorite was about the Ignorot Indians at the World's Fair. He figured the boys would enjoy that version where these foreign people ate dogs for dinner. James finished the story as they approached the wooden fence of Wally's house.

In the shop, James and Wally laughed and laughed at his crude inventions collecting dust. Johnny and James explored everything with "what's this" and "how does that work" and "I didn't know you knew how to fiddle" comments.

"Wally, do they still play Irish fiddle tunes somewhere in the evenings?"

"Aye, James. I was figurin' we'd go on Friday."

James answered with his wide, toothy grin, "Why that'd suit me jus' fine. Let's practice a couple fer the boys."

James was to be in St. Louis for two weeks and the whole family filled the time with Irish tunes and dancing, swimming in the rivers with Ginny and Jack, working in the hobby room at the Bartlett house, and going to the Missouri farm. In all the years Bertha was with the grandchildren, they never warmed to her. Within a couple of days, the grandchildren loved James and complained about his pending departure. The Bartlett children ranged from four to eighteen years old and all of them enjoyed James and his stories, even *Jeb the Spider*.

Rose appeared intrigued with Grandpa James. She often went on the outings with the Bartletts, especially when David and his girlfriend, Suzanne, were there.

Rose said to Suzanne, "Look at David talk with his grandfather. I think he's trying to make up for all the years he didn't know him."

David, at eighteen, formed a special connection to his grandfather; they both liked to hunt and fish. James told David that he had an antique muzzle-loader back in California, "You come visit and I'll teach ya all 'bout it."

But James would not discuss his life in California with anyone, not even his daughters. Ellie and Ginny were mystified.

James admitted that he had hurt them by leaving, "I hoped you'd understand why it happened. I think you remember how hard Bertha was on me. I yearned for a woman to love me for me. Now I have one."

Ginny hugged James, "I know, Daddy. We understood, but …"

James interrupted, "I hear that you can keep secrets now, Ginny. You can't talk 'bout anything we say here. I jus' can't ruin another family. My family in California would hurt, and I figure why cause pain for another family. If ya come ta visit, we'll get together away from my family. You gotta understand. Please."

Ginny seemed shocked, "You have another wife in California? Daddy!"

"Yep, you see why you can't say nothin'. Don't even tell Jack or John. I'd go to prison for bigamy and everyone would suffer."

Ellie didn't say much. *Another secret. My daddy sure has his secrets.*

James closed the discussion with a request, "Can we go over to the St. Peter's Cemetery? My ma and pa are buried there. I'd sure like to pay my respects. Besides, I want ta buy a plot for me. My wife in California knows that when the time comes, I want to lay with my ma and pa for eternity."

At the end of his stay, everyone went to the airport to see James leave. James promised his grandchildren, "I'll be back for Christmas."

***

Snow came to St. Louis in mid-December. When James arrived again in St. Louis, much to his delight, he was greeted by a familiar crisp, cold day. He no longer owned an overcoat and needed to borrow one from John, but initially he enjoyed feeling the cold.

For the first time in years, Françoise and Jerry postponed going to Florida until January because Françoise wanted to be with everyone for the holidays.

"Ellie, I want to have your father, you, and Ginny for lunch one day. Will you talk with them and let me know when would be best? Oh, this is so exciting to be with your father again. The four of us have so many memories to share."

The Cohen's apartment was spacious, covering the whole fifth floor of the apartment building. The living room had a baby grand piano and many delicate pieces of artwork. The sitting room overlooked Forest Park from three large picture windows. There were three bedrooms, a study for Jerry, and a small sewing room. A maid came every day to do the housekeeping and some cooking.

While Françoise showed James around the apartment, Ginny and Ellie talked.

"Being with Daddy is almost like he never went away."

Ellie agreed that this second reunion erased years of agony. "I don't even notice the wrinkles covering his face anymore. In my head, I still see Daddy as the man he was years ago."

Their elation warmed them like the hot toddies they sipped.

Ginny sat, gazing around the apartment, "I should have gone with Daddy and Françoise. It's been years since I was here in the Cohen's apartment. It's more like a museum now. I can see why you don't bring the children here."

Ellie laughed, "Yes, that's obvious. One minute in here and the boys would surely break something. Rose once brought Rebecca here for an afternoon. Even though Rose is twelve years older, they talk together like a couple of old hens."

Ginny pointed to Ellie's dress, "Look, you've got a button ready to fall off."

"Oh, thanks." Ellie grasped her button and, with a slight tug, it slipped into her hand. Looking up, she saw Ginny watching. Ellie raised her index finger and shook it at Ginny, "Don't you dare say any of Mama's little rhymes."

Ginny smiled, "I was trying to remember one. You caught me in time."

James and Françoise returned from the tour.

"I ain't never seen such a gorgeous home, Franny." He had a twinkle in his eye, "I imagine Bertha was right proud of you."

Ellie walked over to them and laughed, "Oh, yes, Mama loved to come here. She preached to Ginny and me for days afterwards, saying our husbands are wonderful men, but look at what we could have had. She talked on and on. Mama never could change."

James touched the black, shiny piano, "This is right nice. I brought my fiddle; lets play some tunes before we eat."

Holding out her button, Ellie touched Françoise's arm, "I need to sew this back on." Ellie's dress gapped at her bosom.

"You know where the sewing room is. The box of threads and a pincushion with needles are in the second drawer down. Help yourself while I play," Françoise turned and sat on the piano bench.

While splendid Irish tunes filled the apartment and Ginny did some dancing, Ellie was in the sewing room. As the second tune ended and another began, no one noticed she had been gone for a long time. Ellie not only was sewing on a button but also was ruminating over some *tangled threads* she found. She pensively sat in the sewing room concentrating on the mess.

On December twenty-fifth, more snow fell on the Christmas celebration at the Bartlett home. There was a hustle and bustle throughout the house with people scurrying around the twelve-foot tree in the foyer. Françoise, Jerry, and Rose arrived with five books wrapped in colorful paper for the Bartlett children; they were tucked under the tree. Everyone was helping with preparations for the three o'clock meal. Ellie and Louise were in the kitchen making the gravy and putting food into bowls.

During a lull in their small talk, Louise mentioned, "We heard there's a boom in house construction in California, so we decided to move there. We finalized our decision this morning."

Ellie turned and knocked over a glass of water, "No! You don't mean this!"

Louise grabbed a dishtowel and started mopping up the floor, while explaining, "My hubby hasn't worked for over a month. We had nothing to give the children this Christmas. I can't thank you and John enough for having gifts for my children. Ellie, we didn't even put up a tree. We had to choose between a Christmas tree or food for some meals."

After Ellie wiped up the counter, she sat on a kitchen stool and ran her fingers through her hair. *Louise is such a part of my life. Almost every week I'm over there.*

Louise continued, "Here in Missouri, there's so little work in the winter, but in California builders work all year round."

Ellie went numb. She barely remembered the rest of the day. She ate little, picking at the food on her plate. When all the relatives had gone home, she cried on John's shoulder. It appeared she was letting Louise's plans, overshadow the delight of having her father for Christmas.

"Ellie, what's come over you?" chastised John. "This sounds like a wonderful opportunity for them. Now, if you were crying because it might not work out, I would understand. But they deserve a better life and won't get one unless they try."

Ellie wiped her eyes, "Oh, I know. I'll just miss them so much and so will the children. At least Clara will be here for us to visit. Since Jerry and Françoise have grown so distant, your sisters have been a great part of our lives. The cousins all play together so well. On the other hand, now we'll have two reasons to go visit California—my father and your sister."

At the end of James' second visit, he told the grandchildren, "I'll come again, but I ain't sure when. You gotta talk your ma and pa into comin' to California to visit me. Bet you ain't never been swimmin' in an ocean!"

By spring, Louise and her family left St. Louis for California.

Throughout the summer, letters came from Louise. They had rented a house. There was a lot of work for her husband and even for their eighteen-year-old son who was working in construction. The money was better than they ever had dreamed possible. Ellie realized that it had been the best decision for them.

When Ellie's Storm arrived, there was no secret card from her father, only one from John. In all the years of their marriage, John never forgot to have a birthday card. This year, a delivery truck brought flowers as well as the card. Little Rebecca and James rushed to see who rang the doorbell. After Ellie closed the door and placed the vase on the table by the telephone, she sat on the stairs to open the card and read it aloud to her children.

When finished with the verse, she leaned her elbows on her knees with the card in both hands and stared at it. Her face was pensive.

"What's wrong, Mom?"

Ellie turned to her son, smiled, and gave his hair a tousle, "I've saved all the cards your father ever sent to me. Want to see?" Ellie took their hands in hers and went up the stairs. In her bedroom she opened the middle drawer of the dresser.

When she lifted the stack of cards tied with the blue ribbon, Rebecca exclaimed, "Can we see them all?"

"Only if you're careful to put them back into the same envelope they come out of." Then Ellie had second thoughts, "Here, we'll look at a few together and come another day for others."

After three cards, James acted bored and grimaced, "It's all love stuff. Mom, can I look in this?" He pointed to her wooden jewelry box with the painting of Niagara Falls on the lid.

"Yes, James, you can look at it, but only now. Don't ever go into my things without me."

He lifted out the box and Rebecca's attention shifted from the greeting cards.

"What's the picture on it, Mommy?"

"Oh, your father and I went to Niagara Falls for our honeymoon. So I bought this jewelry box as a souvenir. Doesn't the wood smell good?"

The children sniffed and nodded with smiles.

"And I bought that wooden frame," she pointed to the wedding photo that always sat on top of her dresser.

Both children passed their fingers over the painting on the jewelry box—it was smooth to the touch—before James opened the lid. There were earrings that Ellie never wore anymore; Rebecca was allowed to take one that no longer had a mate. The pearl strand that Françoise and Jerry had given to Ellie for her wedding day lay nestled at the bottom corner. Ellie picked it up and some pearls dropped.

James asked, "What's that, Mom?"

"Oh, this is a pearl necklace Aunt Franny and Uncle Jerry gave me when I married your father. The string that held them together is broken." Most pearls were still threaded, and Ellie took a handkerchief and dropped them into it. "Help me find the loose pearls."

James and Rebecca dropped pearls into the handkerchief, one by one. Rebecca picked up the flat rock from the Mississippi River, and Ellie told a brief story of Aunt Ginny's swim across it. Then James found the lucky rabbit's foot.

"Mom, can I have this? Becky got an earring." The brothers had given Rebecca that nickname and, though their parents didn't approve, there was no stopping the boys.

Ellie reached over with a smile, "Oh no, James, this was Al Capone's rabbit's foot." As she held it, memories flashed through her head and her smile broadened. She said nothing else to the children about it. "Here, James, you can have this nice key ring. Now, let's put it all away."

James slipped the jewelry box back in among his mother's underwear and nightgowns. Ellie put the cards back in order by year and retied the stack.

She thought about getting the pearls repaired but then decided not to. *That thread is broken; it'll never be whole again.*

By the end of summer, Ellie was caught up in her next problem; Clara and her family decided to follow Louise to California for the same reason—to have a better life. Soon they too were gone.

Ellie had difficulty accepting this loss. *How many more upheavals will there be?*

***

One Saturday afternoon when Ellie needed to do some bookkeeping in the drugstore, she took the four youngest children over to Jack's; Ginny was working. They were still living in Dogtown in Bertha's old home.

The older Bartlett boys could have stayed at home alone, but they liked to be with Jack. Often he'd take them to the river to swim or even to the amusement park. This particular day was different.

As soon as Ellie drove away, Jack called them, "Hey, I want all of you to sit in the living room. Go ahead, some on the couch and others in the overstuffed chairs. If there's not enough seats, sit on the floor and lean against the couch."

Jack sounded serious; he wasn't joking around like usual.

"What we goin' to do, Uncle Jack?" one asked.

"Patience, patience," Jack said while picking up his pack of Camels off the table. "Here, I want each of you to take one of these." Jack gave the pack a tap on the bottom and a few cigarettes popped out the top opening.

"Why?" Johnny asked.

"Our parents don't want us to touch cigarettes," Billy told Jack.

Jack acted angry, "Take one, Billy." Reluctantly the boy did.

Rebecca started to cry.

"Don't you cry!" Jack stood over her and took a cigarette out to give her. She was the last one. "Open your mouth and put it on your lips like this." He demonstrated with another cigarette.

Rebecca looked to her brothers. Now Red looked like he would cry, but he held back his tears.

Jack pulled his lighter from a pocket. "All of you are going to smoke a cigarette. I don't care what your parents say. You can cry, if you want to be a baby, but you are going to smoke."

The room was suddenly filling with the smoke from Jack's cigarette. He stood puffing and puffing. "See, you put the cigarette on your lips and suck in." He took a big drag. Then he did it again and blew the smoke at Billy. "Billy, you first. Have you ever tried one?"

Billy muttered something, and then looked angry, "I always thought it was dumb and I still do. You can't make me do this."

Jack flipped the lighter open and spun the wheel. A flame went bright in front of Billy's face. Jack was somber, "Put it in you mouth and draw on it. NOW!"

Billy went white, but did as he was told.

Next Jack went to Johnny who admitted to smoking with his friends. He lit up without any complaints.

Red was about ten and Rebecca was only six, but Jack was adamant, "Put them in your lips and suck in. Now!" But Jack had to light the cigarettes in his own mouth for Red and Rebecca, who was really crying now.

"Everyone keep on puffing. Don't stop, Billy. That's it. Put it back in and puff. Rebecca, suck in, like this. Jack took a deep breath and inhaled deeply, exhaling into her face. "Hey, Johnny, don't stop. You told me you knew how to smoke. I want you to smoke that whole cigarette."

The room was smoky and quiet, except for Rebecca crying, and whimpers from Red. Johnny was almost to the end of his cigarette when Jack took the ashtray over to him. "Do ya know how to stub it out?"

Johnny dropped the butt into the ashtray and jumped up, running for the bathroom. Everyone could hear him throwing-up. Just listening to his brother vomiting, Billy started to gag and went for the bathroom. Jack took the half-used butt from Billy's hand as he rushed by. Then Jack went to the couch and sat between James and Rebecca. He took away their cigarettes and stubbed them out in the ashtray. Neither of them had known how to even take a puff, but the smoke was making them cough.

"Billy, bring some glasses of water in here." Jack called. "Johnny, come back here. I want to talk to all of you."

Jack pulled his clean handkerchief out and wiped Rebecca's teary face. "Blow your nose. Go ahead. I'm sorry, if I scared ya, but I had a reason.

"All of ya listen. I started smoking when I was ten and I've never stopped. I expect to die from these horrible cigarettes because they're addicting. Know what that means? It means I can never stop even though I want to. So, if you start to smoke, ya never can stop. I stink, don't I? You know, I always smell like a stale cigarette. I don't know how Ginny wants to be around me. But I brush my teeth a lot and change my clothes, because I love her and don't want her to suffer. Do ya feel sick?"

They all nodded their heads with sad eyes. Understanding appeared on their faces.

"Cigarettes are filthy and expensive. They stink and make people cough. Like I said, if I could stop smoking I would. I've tried many times. The nicotine gets into your blood or something and your body wants more. I hate them!"

Billy's lower lip was trembling, "Why do this to us then?"

"Can't you see how horrible they are now that you tried them? Now you can honestly tell your friends that you tried them and don't want to smoke. I seen men cough themselves to death. I don't want any of you to EVER, EVER smoke. Do you understand? Kids start smoking to look big or because your friends say you're chicken. Now you can say you smoked and it's dumb. Just like Billy said."

Jack looked like he was about to cry. He reached down and gathered up little Rebecca. "I'm sorry if I scared ya, but you got to promise me you'll never smoke when you're a big lady."

With a whimper, she promised.

"Now each of you boys, promise me." They mumbled and Jack insisted, "Say it louder, like you mean it!"

"I promise," they all screamed.

Jack added, “One last thing, if I ever learn ya started to smoke, I’ll be so ashamed of ya. Be strong and better than any kids that try to tempt ya. Okay?”

Jack opened the front door to let the smoke out. “Let’s go see that new movie.”

The Bartlett children would remember the cigarette event as the last time they were in their Grandmother’s house, because later that year, Jack and Ginny left Bertha’s house forever and moved to the Bartletts’ Missouri farm. Uncle Will had died and Aunt Laura went to live with one of her daughters in a small town.

John didn’t like having the farm without someone to look after it. “Oh, John, we’d be so delighted to have a place in the country,” He offered to sell them one square acre of his farm. Ginny retired from working in St. Louis, looking forward to a peaceful life in the country.

“We’re only fifty miles away from you,” Ginny told Ellie. “We’ll run in for visits all the time and you can come out.”

But it didn’t work out like that. Once they were living at the farm and busy getting their place built, planting a garden, and making a life with new neighbors and friends, their trips back to St. Louis became infrequent.

With their move, Ellie lost her last family in St. Louis.

***

John agreed that a vacation in California would be good for the family. They owned a Ford station wagon with three rows of seats, so traveling would be comfortable. John wanted to take side trips to see some sights like the Grand Canyon. Ellie wanted to get there quickly, so they decided that Ellie would fly with Rebecca.

David wanted to take his girlfriend.

John said, “Fine. Bring Suzanne, and let’s see if Rose wants to come.”

They had the trip of a lifetime. Great herds of antelope crossed the road in front of them. They found an injured falcon, set his wing, and continued the trip with the bird in the car. They stayed in cabins at the Grand Canyon and took a horse trip all the way down to the river at the bottom. The changing landscapes imbedded into their memories—endless cornfields, mountains, deserts, and then southern California with so many new plants, strange flowers, and the ocean.

When they got to Louise's house in southern California, Ellie's father came to be with them every day. Ellie was disappointed not to be able to see Yosemite Park, but she had had no idea how big California was until she was there. It was too far to go.

One evening she told John, "I love California. Do you think we could move here?"

John looked surprised. "It seems unlike you to make such a snap decision about something so important." John reminded her, "Our home is in Missouri with the farms, the drugstore, and our beautiful house that you wanted so much. You can't be serious, Ellie."

Ellie didn't say more.

John offered a compromise, "Just plan to come visit again. I know you want to see more of your father because he's getting older."

Ellie did go again; Jack and Ginny went with her in the winter while the children were in school. The three of them went for a couple of weeks.

Ellie said the children could take care of themselves, "David's going to Washington University with his girlfriend, Suzanne. That puts them just twenty minutes from the house, and they can help with meals. The boys know how to wash clothes; it's one of their duties."

Ginny mentioned to Jack, "Rebecca is so young, only going on eight, and it seems selfish for Ellie to leave her children. I can't put my finger on anything in particular, but something's wrong. Ellie's different."

After Ellie was home only a week from California, word came that Grandpa James had died in his sleep. He was seventy-three. This time James arrived in Missouri by train and in a casket. As he had requested, he was buried next to his parents. Ellie was inconsolable.

Ginny cried and cried, but somehow found happiness in knowing she had spent time with her father in his last years. Yet, she couldn't convince Ellie, "You've told me before that you can accept anything that's logical, Ellie. Daddy just died peacefully in his sleep. That's what happens when folks get old."

But Ellie stopped eating regularly and began to look gaunt. She was different.

Much to the surprise of everyone, Ellie was moved to a sanitarium for the treatment of tuberculosis.

"No visitors! What do you mean? John, I want to see my sister." But no one could visit at first. Those were the rules.

John hired a woman to help with the house cleaning and to cook the evening meal for the children. After Ellie had been away for four months, Ginny was allowed to visit. But Ellie didn't want to socialize. She talked little.

Ginny was confused, "Ellie seemed to not want to see me, Jack. She was so withdrawn. The doctors wouldn't tell me anything. They said I would have to talk to John. I don't understand."

A couple of months later, Ellie came home. She arrived just in time for the next catastrophe. David discovered by accident that he had had a baby sister named Elizabeth who died. He was furious with John and Ellie for keeping this secret.

In a raised voice he complained, going on and on, "Mom, I found a box full of photos of me and my sister that you hid in your dresser drawer. I don't remember her at all. How could you not talk about her? There was this newspaper article that said she was kidnapped and …"

Ellie was in a stupor and trying to comprehend his anger. She had arrived home from the sanitarium only a few days ago, expecting everything to be calm, and now David was ranting at her while they rode toward the hospital. Ellie tried to understand why they were heading over to the hospital. *David said something about going to visit Suzanne. I believe that I drank only one glass of wine, why can't I think?* Nothing made sense to her. *Why is David so angry about a sister that died so many years ago? And why is Suzanne in the hospital?*

Hours later, David's girlfriend Suzanne died at the St. Louis City Hospital from an illegal abortion.

Suzanne was laid out at Kreighauser's Funeral Home in a room overflowing with flowers and strangers. Unlike the death of an older person, Suzanne's funeral was anomalous. For those who loved her, it was a time to mourn the loss of a vibrant, young life, but for others, it was an attraction like a circus event for the curious and critical. Whispers filled the room. Glancing about the room, one could surmise the whispered words in the critical facial expressions. It wasn't every day that a girl got pregnant out of wedlock and died. And like vultures circling the misfortunate, here they gazed upon the person with an innocent, beautiful face who had died from her sins.

Ginny leaned over to Jack, "I wish they could have admitted people by *invitation only*. How did people find out about David and Suzanne?"

Jack patted her hands, "Yeah, don't worry. Just let 'em look. Guess they ain't got nothin' better to do."

Becky walked up to Ginny and Jack to ask, "Have you seen Rose?"

Ginny seemed surprised, "That's right, I haven't seen the Cohens. Let's go check the guest book at the door." After looking at the registry and not finding them listed, Becky wandered off, weaving between people, and Ginny walked over to Ellie.

Slipping into a chair beside her sister, Ginny said, "This is the second day of the funeral, tomorrow is the burial, and I haven't seen Jerry and Françoise. Do you know when they're coming to pay their respects?"

When Ellie said nothing, Ginny asked, "Didn't I see Rose here yesterday without her parents? She was with some of her friends from the synagogue, I think."

Again Ellie didn't answer. In fact, Ellie sat in the funeral parlor with a drooping head, staring into her lap. She appeared almost motionless, swaying slightly. Ginny leaned over closer and, with a look of surprise, jumped back upright. Ellie was reeking. Ellie was drunk.

Part 4

'Til Death Do Us Part
1951-2000

As he brews, so shall he drink.

Ben Jonson, c. 1573-1637
Every Man in His Humour

Chapter 17

1951-1957
Living in Hell on Earth

Anyone who has lived with a drunk knows how ugly life becomes. Especially in the 1950s, a time when few people—whether the general public or doctors—understood that alcoholism was a disease. The situation always caught families off guard, and they didn't know what to do. Shame enveloped their lives, flinging them into an abyss. The Bartletts were experiencing all these difficulties.

At some point, when John realized that Ellie was going to be drunk every day, he didn't know where to turn. Embarrassed, he said nothing to friends or family, but in confidence he questioned several physicians he knew.[4] They used words like "hopeless," "incurable," and "expensive" to describe Ellie's situation. Still, he was determined to do everything he could.

The first doctor had suggested sending her to a sanatorium to dry out over a period of months, "It's a discreet place where she will be admitted as a tuberculosis patient, but put into a special ward. No one will know she's been drinking."

When the cure at the sanatorium didn't work, John was angry and went to another doctor.

While in the office of this second doctor, John was asked how long she had been drinking. "I have no idea. I know that sounds unbelievable, but none of the children know either. In fact, she may have been drinking for quite a while before I noticed."

He told the doctor that one night he had come home from the drugstore, at his usual time of eleven or twelve at night, to find Ellie passed out on the kitchen floor.

"I took her up to bed and had a talk with her in the morning when she seemed sober.

"I asked her, 'What are you doing, Ellie?' And she said that she didn't realize that she had been drinking so much. She told me that she just served herself a glass of wine and that was all she remembered. I made the mistake of believing her."

John emphasized to the doctor, "In all the years I've known her, she never drank much. Even when we had guests or went out to friends' homes or ate at restaurants, she usually had one glass and sometimes didn't even finish it." He told the doctor that he worked long hours and often came home when she was in bed asleep, "I guess she could have been drinking then, but I wouldn't have known. Also, I go out to work my farm a couple of days every week. Maybe she was drinking then. But I didn't notice." John shook his head, "She's very smart and may have tried to stay sober when she knew I would be with her. Oh, I just don't know when it started."

John told the doctor that his son David had arrived home early one afternoon and found her passed out on the front steps. David helped his mother into the house. Ellie wasn't belligerent, as some drunks could be, nor was she argumentative. She apologized to her son and stumbled up the stairs to her bed.

"My son was very upset and called me at the drugstore saying, 'Dad, I just found Mom and she's drunk! I hope nobody saw her.' I didn't know what to say to my son, but at that moment it was apparent that she had lied to me when I found her on the kitchen floor. I asked my son to look for bottles and empty them out. I went home an hour later and David had found thirty bottles hidden all over the house. That was when I knew Ellie had been hiding her drinking for quite a while."

The doctor was taking notes and glanced up to ask, "Has she been seen by any other doctor?"

"Yes, under the guise of tuberculosis, Ellie went for a recovery program that basically dried her out. They sent her to some psychiatric sessions and gave her time to fight her obsession. The doctors told me that she must have had a problem that triggered the drinking. They figured the emotional upset with her parents' deaths and with loved ones moving away might have started the problem.

"I met with a group of doctors at the sanatorium. They were sure she would be fine, because they had helped her face all her problems that she had had to endure in the last few years. They explained that, in addition to the deaths of her parents, she was probably going through the Change of Life at her age."

This second doctor put Ellie into the hospital for two months and dried her out. Again she had psychiatric sessions and the doctor prescribed medicine that would make her nauseous if she drank.

When Ellie returned home, it was just a matter of time before she was drinking again. Now people were seeing her condition. She no longer tried to hide it.

John stopped giving Ellie money, but she still found ways to drink. When an itemized bill came, John learned that she had gone to a corner market and had gotten a line of credit. In shame, John went to pay the bill. He asked the owner not to sell her any more alcohol.

The market owner apologized, “She claimed that she was having a dinner party and needed a dozen bottles of wine. I’m so sorry, but I had no way of knowing. She seemed like such a nice lady.” They had even delivered it right to the Bartlett home.

Within the next few months, John found there was an endless supply of little corner markets that had wine. As soon as he went to one and stopped the line of credit, she found another.

When Ginny had seen that her sister was drunk at the funeral of David’s girlfriend, she drove Ellie home and put her to bed. Then she went to the drugstore to accost John, “How could you let Ellie go to a funeral parlor in that condition? John, what’s going on?”

They were sitting at John’s desk in the back of the drugstore. High cabinets with multiple drawers containing herbs and medicines surrounded them. Piles of literature from drug companies and other papers about medicines were stacked on his desk and the floor. His life hemmed him in from all directions.

John nervously rubbed his hands against his trousers, “Ginny, I don’t know what to say or do. David was helping me keep an eye on her, but she’s too clever. She finds ways to get more wine. And now David is going away to medical school. I’m going to try another sanatorium to dry her out.” This was how Ginny learned that Ellie never had tuberculosis.

“You lied to me? No tuberculosis! Why didn’t you ask for my help? How could you keep this a secret from me? Her sister! John, what’s going on?”

“Ginny, what could you have done?”

"I don't know, but I would have tried to help."

So, Ginny and Jack decided to stay with Ellie for a week or two. They came back to St. Louis from the farm and stayed at the Bartlett house. Ellie kept sober the whole time. They talked with her, showed her love, and tried to make her tell them why she was drinking.

Ellie never explained.

Ginny knew her sister was the queen of secrets, but was satisfied that they accomplished something. They got Ellie to promise to stop drinking.

A few months later, Rose Cohen went to talk to John at the drugstore, "I stopped by your house and found Aunt Ellie lying in the curb outside your house. Uncle John, she was so drunk that I could hardly get her into the house. She was filthy. I even smelled urine, so I put her in the bathtub before putting her to bed."

John was so tired, "I'm so sorry you saw Ellie like that, Rose."

"My Mother told me, but I didn't believe her. She said that this has been going on for years. Is that right?"

John nodded solemnly.

"I hadn't really noticed, but Mother said that's why she no longer wanted anything to do with the Bartletts. She told me it was disgraceful. Uncle John, I cried."

John wrapped his arms around Rose. She was taller than he by an inch and would be graduating from college soon. His heart hurt.

"Uncle John, what happened?"

Not offering Rose any explanation, he promised to get help. The next day he took Ellie to another place to dry out. This one was less expensive. They chained her to a bed and locked her in a room with bars on the windows. That night, after John closed the drugstore, he went home and cried.

Johnny got up to use the bathroom across the hall and heard his father's deep, sorrowful sobs. Johnny was scared. He didn't think his father could cry like that. Johnny knew his dad was crying about his mom, but to hear it made life seem hopeless.

***

This time Ellie came home and didn't start drinking right away. But she was smoking. The doctor had prescribed cigarettes to help her curb the desire to drink.

John's sister Louise came back from California to help, "John, why didn't you call and tell me? I heard from one of our cousins who came to visit. They said she started drinking right after I moved to California. Why, that was years ago! She and I were so close, but in a million years I'd never have guessed Ellie an alcoholic. We had such a good relationship, and then I just left her."

"Louise, you didn't cause this. Besides, none of us can remember exactly when Ellie started to drink. Maybe it was before you left. She hid it so well."

"Well, I know I didn't personally cause it, but think about it. After I left, Clara moved to California, and then Ginny moved to the farm. Ellie's mother died and then her father. She lost everyone. You know, you didn't help by always working such long hours in the drugstore and spending your days off at one of your farms. Except for the children, she was alone."

John agreed. Louise was right that he was always away from Ellie, but he was working for their children to go to college. "I can't thank you enough for coming. It has been wonderful since you arrived. I guess you've noticed how Ellie has aged and gained too much weight, but she's sober. I do thank you for helping with that. She does love you so much."

Louise asked, "And Franny just abandoned her? I thought she was her best friend. I couldn't believe that."

John shook his head, "Louise, you weren't around Ellie when she was always drunk. It was horrible. Please don't blame anyone. Even Ginny came from her home on the farm and could only get Ellie to stop drinking for a couple of weeks."

Louise stayed in David's bedroom. She and Ellie talked like the old days, laughing about everything. One sunny day, they decided to wash all the bed sheets. As they went around the house pulling sheets off the beds to wash, they chattered away.

Louise asked, "Do you remember what people used to whisper about the Change of Life. I was so scared to have it happen; I thought I would go insane or something. Then my periods stopped and I felt free. No more monthly messes. Even my mind seemed clearer. I've never had too many hot flashes, did you?"

Ellie laughed, "Oh, I'm still having them. The doctor told me they could go on for the rest of my life. But, you know, in St. Louis in the winter I love them."

"Don't even tell me how they are in the summer. I don't want to hear."

Just then, Ellie pulled off the sheets from Johnny's bed and a magazine fell to the floor. She picked it up. "Louise, look at this!"

They flipped through the pages of a *Playboy* magazine and were aghast.

"What are you going to do to Johnny?"

Ellie slipped to the floor and leaned against the bed, "Wait until I finish looking at this thing." She giggled, "I need to evaluate it first before I decide."

Louise joined her on the floor to look. "How can those beautiful girls take their clothes off and let people take their pictures for the whole world to see? Their reputations are ruined."

Ellie smiled, "I wasn't wondering about that. I was wondering what they get paid."

"Oh, Ellie, you were not!"

"Yes, I was." Ellie reached into the pocket of her housecoat and pulled out a pack of cigarettes. She lit one and continued looking through the whole *Playboy*. "Okay, I've decided what to do about Johnny and this magazine. You wait here."

Turning to lean against the mattresses, Ellie struggled to her feet, left the room, and returned with a pencil and pad. Slipping down next to Louise again, Ellie started writing. When finished she ripped out the paper, folded it, and slipped it into the magazine next to an article.

Louise grabbed the book, "Let me see what you wrote."

On the sheet it said:

> Johnny,
> Don't lose my place! I haven't finished reading this.
> From Mom

"Ellie, that's perfect! I never would've thought of doing that. You're such a wonderful mother." Louise stopped for a minute and continued, "But I really have to ask you. Why did you start drinking?"

Ellie struggled to her feet again and gathered the bed sheets in her arms, "You can't weave back a thread that's pulled." Ellie started down the stairs, "Come on Louise, let's go get these sheets washed and hang them in the sun. Then we'll find something else that's fun to do."

While Louise was in St. Louis, the Bartlett house was put back into order. The two of them had cleaning projects every day, but a couple of times a week, they planned fun places to go. Just the two of them. They visited some of Louise's old friends, went to restaurants where they'd never been, saw movies, walked through Dogtown and reminisced, and even had a picnic at the zoo.

Too soon the month passed and Louise returned to California.

Then, just like before, John and the children didn't notice when Ellie started drinking again. And her drinking was worse than before.

One day, Becky came home from grade school and saw smoke seeping out of open windows. She opened the door and was blasted with plumes of dense smoke, coming from the living room. At ten years old she knew not to enter. She ran to the neighbor's house.

Ellie was taken to the hospital with smoke inhalation. The firemen doused the couch where Ellie's cigarette had started the fabric smoldering. There was a six-inch hole in the couch. Ellie was fine.

The children no longer brought friends to their home, and the boys stayed away as much as possible.

Soon there were cigarette burns on the arms of the recliner, windowsills, on bedside tables, on the bathroom floor, on the kitchen table, and dining room table. Again, the doctor gave Ellie medication to make her sick if she drank. The children came home to find vomit on the carpet, on their bed, or on the middle of the table. They'd find pee anywhere and everywhere. They cleaned it up. Ellie soon devised ways to avoid the pills. The children were glad when the medicating stopped—because the vomiting stopped.

Then Ellie started disappearing for days at a time, and John would drive the neighborhood to no avail. In her absence, the whole family experienced a sense of relief that was never mentioned and a sense of guilt upon her return. More often than not, when she came home she sported unexplained cuts and bruises. One laceration that should have had stitches healed with a hideous scar across her nose. They began to realize that Ellie never explained what had happened or where she had been because she really didn't remember.

John put her into recovery homes again and again. After fighting Ellie's alcohol abuse for more than five years, his savings were gone. If she didn't stay sober, the next time he will have to start selling his farms.

***

There was only one place where the Bartletts had some reprieve from the pain of Ellie's drinking—working at the drugstore. They were too busy to think about personal problems while they waited on customers and did the many tasks that kept the drugstore running. But soon after Becky turned twelve and started working at the drugstore, the Bartletts would have an additional burden to bear.

It began one night when John, Billy, and Becky were at the drugstore. John was in the back filling prescriptions, Billy was straightening up the greeting cards, and Becky was behind the main counter filling the candy case when she noticed a customer in a felt hat, suit coat, and a loosened tie. He was neat and clean.

She smiled and asked what she could get for him. He raised his arm and slapped her with such a force that Becky's head jerked, creating a burning sensation in her neck. She whimpered from the blow and took a step back at the same moment that he pulled out a gun.

Billy reacted to Becky's whimper and turned toward her.

"No," she cried out as the robber reached across the counter with his free hand and grabbed her arm.

Obviously, Billy was unaware of the gun hidden from his view, when he dropped all the cards and came up behind the guy, "What's the problem, Becky?" he said as he reached out and placed his hand on the robber's shoulder.

The holdup guy pulled his shoulder from Billy's grasp, turned and shot.

It happened so quickly—all in one swift blur to Becky.

Bang!

The noise of the gun filled the store and seemed to go on forever.

Billy crumpled and blood began flowing out across the black and white tiled floor. Becky shrieked on and on, until she was slapped again.

"Shut up and empty the cash register," the robber seethed.

With her scream, Becky noticed two other robbers appearing from nowhere.

As John rushed toward her, one of them slipped behind the counter to block him, "Not so fast," the robber said with a grimace. "Let's go into the back room to see what we can find." John had been in several holdups before and knew to do what the robbers asked. But a gun had never been fired in any other holdup; he didn't know if anyone was hurt.

Becky emptied the front cash register and sobbed. She kept glancing at Billy, hoping to see movement, but he was motionless. She grabbed all the bills, checks, and coins, dumping them into a bag. As she pushed the loot across the counter, she noticed that her face was burning from the slap and her eye was swelling shut.

"Now the back cash register. I'm going to walk right behind you. Raise your arms above your head and wait for me to come around the counter with you. Don't try to push an alarm and don't do anything foolish."

Now Becky was bawling.

Suddenly, the other holdup guy came from the back, pushing John ahead of him, "Let's get out of here."

John saw Billy on the floor!

"You two lay down, right here. Come on!" one hollered and pushed John to the floor. Becky went down by herself, while the robbers headed for the front of the store.

Then it happened.

So much noise blasted the air as five gunshots exploded. John and Becky were on the floor and couldn't see where the shots went. They looked at each other, fearing for Billy.

One of the robbers started screaming at the shooter, cussing and shouting, "Why the fuck did you do that?" It sounded like they were scuffling with each other. They continued to curse until their voices disappeared with the close of the front door.

John looked over the counter, "For Gods sake, Billy's bleeding!" John reached below the counter and pushed the alarm. It started blaring.

Becky rushed over to Billy while John picked up the telephone to call an ambulance and then the police.

In moments, sirens could be heard. Becky couldn't stop crying as she knelt by Billy.

John felt a pulse in Billy's neck and took off his flannel shirt to cover his son, "Don't move him, Becky." Then John went to the door as men entered with a stretcher. Soon the drugstore was swarming with policemen. They took Billy away within minutes.

John pulled Becky into his arms, "We have to stay and tell the police what happened." Becky started to protest, "Calm down, Becky! Billy's in good hands now. I'm going to call home to see if anyone's there to go be with Billy."

While John called, a detective started talking with Becky. He told her that a special squad cruiser was coming to start dusting for fingerprints.

John walked up to hear the comment and asked, "Why is that?"

"When we might have a homicide, we need to cover all the bases. Now, let's get your statements."

John put his arm around Becky, "Your mother and Johnny are on the way to the hospital. Ellie sounded good tonight."

Becky understood—her mother was more or less sober.

When they finished with the police and went to the hospital, Billy was still in the operating room. The operation took five hours. The doctors took out four of the bullets. One from Billy's thigh, one in the arm, and two that had gone into his belly, but the fifth had to stay. That fifth bullet was lodged next to his spine. It went through his abdomen and stopped next to his spinal column. It couldn't be removed without the possibility of causing more damage. Billy was alive, but his life was still considered in critical condition. The bullets into the belly really messed up his insides. Tore up the intestines and colon. The doctors couldn't promise anything, in fact, they couldn't tell the family how Billy would be. They didn't think he would be paralyzed from the bullet in his spinal column, but they weren't sure. They knew he would be in the hospital for a long time with these wounds, but they didn't know how long. And they couldn't tell the Bartletts what kind of life he could have afterwards.

He was in a coma.

In fact, Billy will be in a coma for months. Ellie went every day to sit at his bedside. As long as Billy needed Ellie, she was sober.

John found the situation too ironic; he had his wife while the life of his son was in question. In his heart, he hoped it wasn't true, but he feared that when Billy was well, Ellie would revert to drinking.

Billy came out of his coma one day and was on his way to recovering. Each day for six months, Billy got a little better, and each day Ellie drank a little more until gradually she was back to being drunk every day.

***

Ginny was having a difficult time accepting Ellie's condition; worse than that, Ginny could not accept that there was no cure. How could it be that her sister, as she used to be, was gone forever? As a solace, she and Jack invited the Bartlett children to come for Thanksgiving. The children were growing up in spite of their mother's lack of mothering, and Ginny took joy in their company.

Staring out their picture window to the view of the upper-forty pasture where most of the Bartletts' cattle were grazing, Ginny said, "Let's ask Rose to come with the others. I'll ask the Cohens as well, but I know they'll decline. Franny always hated to come to the farm." Ginny hesitated, but couldn't stop herself from saying, "Every time I think of how Franny deserted her friend in need I …"

Ginny left the sentence hanging like clothes on a line; the subject had become dry—a burden she needed to fold and put away.

She turned, sheepishly placing a smile on her face; she had promised not to broach the subject of Franny. "I'll drive to town and call them. The kids love the farm. I know they'll come. Then I'll go over to the Farmers' Exchange and ask where to buy the best turkey."

"Aren't you goin' to ask John to come? I know your sis is in the hospital again, but you should ask John."

Ginny turned back to gaze out the window, "Oh, of course I will, but he'll be working at the drugstore on Thanksgiving. He's told me often enough that he makes more money on a holiday than the whole month."

Jack heard bitterness.

Ginny repeated what she had said to Jack many a time. "I can't get over being mad at him. I know John could have helped Ellie if he'd noticed the drinking sooner." Then Ginny mumbled, "We can send some leftovers home with the children for him."

Just looking at her back, Jack saw Ginny's upset. He got out of his rocker, "You can't really call them children any more." David, Billy, and Rose were in their twenties.

Jack slipped his arm over her shoulder. He knew she liked him to do that. "How do ya know they'll even be in St. Louis for Thanksgiving?" David rarely came home from medical school, even for holidays; he took summer courses and spent vacations studying medicine as an excuse to avoid seeing his mother. Billy had left home for college, and it took only one Christmas back from college for him to decide that going to a friend's house for holidays was better. Only Johnny, James and Becky were left living at home.

Ginny snuggled into Jack's shoulder. "I know because Becky sent me a card and mentioned they'd all be home for Thanksgiving."

Once the carload of six young people arrived at the farm and greeted Jack and Ginny, they disappeared across fields, into the woods, and along the creeks.

When all the fixings were ready except for the cooking turkey, Rose saw Ginny coming to join her and Becky along the creek. For a while, bluebirds flitting from tree to tree seemed to follow the trio until they trudged out into the dried grasses in a field. They talked trivia—the weather, school, life on a farm and such—jumping from topic to topic like a skipping stone across the water, not wanting to stop and sink into the depths of a dark topic—Ellie. They laughed and enjoyed the freedom of the farm, the beauty of nature and life, and, subconsciously, the relief of being with healthy, sane people.

Even Rose, who didn't live in the Bartlett house, felt helpless like the rest when thinking about Ellie. After years and years of Ellie's drinking, hopes had sunk like the skipping stone must do when it loses momentum. But today even while laughing, Rose decided she must talk to the others. *This might be my only opportunity to have all the Bartletts together. I have so many questions; I need to know what goes through their heads. How do they live with it?*

When the sun rested on the roof of the red barn, getting ready to slip down the edge of the corrugated tin and let darkness roll in, Jack rang the dinner bell. The clanging came across the creek and through drying oak leaves, calling everyone to the feast. The bell started a neighbor's hound howling, and the bobwhite seemed to take the cue to begin her evening song.

The meadowlarks had been singing all day with a slurred whistle – *seee-oooaa seeeadoo.* But now only a sharp electric buzz – *dziit* – could be heard as one by one the Bartletts came, letting the screen door slam over and over.

Jack admonished, "Hey, don't bang the door! The turkey's out of the oven so we can eat, but ya gotta go to the bathroom before we start. As you see, our little home is crowded. So, once you're in your seat, there's no getting up 'til the end of the meal. You boys go water a tree." Jack and Ginny's table, when opened for guests in their tiny cottage, spread from one wall to the other.

Jack went on and on, "If you don't relieve yourself now, you're goin' to feel like I did on the bull's back at the rodeo, waitin' in the pen to git out."

The Thanksgiving dinner was devoured. Jack removed the bony carcass from the table and returned from the kitchen with a pie in each hand, "We have apple or pumpkin. You did leave room for this, I hope."

Cheshire grins appeared around the room. "Always room for pie," Johnny attested.

Ginny reminded, "Jack, get the whipped cream from the fridge."

Red grinned. "Oh boy, even whipped cream."

The two pies disappeared in minutes, and without thinking Ginny said, "You must eat your parents out of house and home."

Ginny blushed and a quiet moment followed.

Billy changed the subject, “That was the best Thanksgiving dinner I ever had.” And quickly everyone joined in with compliments, heaping on whipped cream words, trying to sweeten the bitterness of the thoughts of their mother.

Ginny went over to Billy and put her arms around him, “I’m just glad you’re here and alive. We were so worried about you after the shooting.”

Rose stood, “You cooked, so we’re going to clear the table and clean up.”

“Oh no you ain’t,” Jack insisted. “We invited you as guests and it’s my job to clean up. Get outta here and enjoy the evenin’. By the time you walk over to your farmhouse, it’ll be dark. Oh, you’ll see that Ginny put clean sheets on all the beds, so you ain’t got no work to do.”

No sooner were they on the road, walking the mile to their farmhouse, than Rose began to talk. She had decided to be blunt, “My parents don’t ever want to talk to me about your mother, but I need to talk. I just don’t understand. Do you know what’s wrong with her?”

Billy blurted out, “What do you mean? It’s simple. She drinks!”

“But why?”

David answered, “She’s an alcoholic, that’s why!”

Rose was insistent, “What does that mean?”

Billy said, “That means that she needs a drink all the time and can’t stop.”

Rose sputtered, “No, but … David, what does it mean medically?”

“Billy said it as good as I can say it.”

Rose persisted, “Look I just don’t understand. Is this something that happens to a person all of a sudden? Like it did with your mom? Is that what they teach you in medical school?”

David’s irritation burst forth, “They haven’t taught me anything about it. I looked up some stuff about alcoholism and yeah, it can just happen all of a sudden, Rose. Let’s drop the subject, talking about it won’t help.”

“Come on, David. Don’t be like our parents. I just want some answers. This whole thing makes no sense to me.” Rose took a deep breath and changed her tone. “Look, I read that they think people are born alcoholics. They think that once they start drinking, they become the alcoholic. Maybe Johnny and Red don’t remember your mom, and

I know Becky doesn't remember her like we do David. She used to have one drink with friends and sometimes never finish it. When our parents had those bridge parties, she hardly drank at all. Then she turned fifty years old and all of a sudden started drinking. Why?"

David protested, "How am I supposed to know?"

Rose stayed calm, "But tell me, you've thought the same questions. Right?"

Johnny spoke up, "I have. I talked to Aunt Louise when she was here and she just said that a lot of things started happening to Mom around that time. You know, Aunt Louise moving, Mom's dad and mom dying, more family moving away, and that kind of stuff."

Rose was adamant, "But that makes no sense either. Listen, I talked a lot with my mom and dad about your parents keeping the death of your sister Elizabeth a secret. They probably know your mother better than anyone, and they told me how Aunt Ellie was weak when she didn't know who had kidnapped the baby. She had to have medications and was upset every day. But when Elizabeth died of an illness, Aunt Ellie accepted it and was strong. She just put the baby's death aside and went on living for the rest of her family.

"So, my point is that she would have accepted the deaths of her parents, who were old. She would have accepted that people move away for better jobs because they are tired of being poor. Now, that's the personality I remember about your mom until this happened. She was logical and happy. In fact, I would have called her happy-go-lucky. She loved having fun."

Having been reminded of his little sister who died, David spat out the word, "Secrets! They have no right to keep secrets from us when it's important."

Rose agreed, "Well, that's how I feel. We need to talk and not keep any secrets."

Red said to Billy, "Yeah, tell her about what the last doctor said. We're just like them, keeping secrets, if we don't talk," Red touched his brother's arm. "Come on, tell 'em."

Billy seemed reluctant, "Maybe we're not supposed to know. It was just an accident that I picked up the upstairs telephone when Dad was downstairs talking to the doctor. I don't know if I …"

David jumped in, "Tell us what you're talking about?"

Billy confessed, "Listen, I don't know if we're supposed to know."

David stopped walking and placed his hands on his hips. He turned to Billy, “Know what? I’m an adult and if you know something about my mom, I mean our mom, tell me. You’re over twenty-one, the whole world considers you an adult now. Besides, we’re all old enough to know anything about our mother.”

“Yeah, yeah, okay,” Billy frowned and blurted it out. “The doctor told Dad that she was schizophrenic. He wanted Dad to go to his office to sign papers to give her shock treatments.”

Now the group circled around Billy and David.

In the innocence of his youth, Red asked, looking to David, “What does that mean? They’re going to electrocute Mom like they did to Frankenstein?”

“Back off. I’m just a medical student. You know, studying to be a doctor. I don’t know everything; especially stuff about psychiatric procedures. You can go to the university library and look it up just like I’d have to do.”

Rose agreed, “Okay, let’s research that. All of you should be trying to learn more. I read that excessive drinking destroys the liver. Why isn’t Aunt Ellie really sick?” Rose raised her hands in defense as David looked like he was going to scream. Rose explained, “That wasn’t a question that I wanted answered. I was just pointing out that there’s a lot more to learn.

“Now, I want to say just one more thing. It’s something you may not have thought about and it seems important. Johnny mentioned Aunt Louise being here. Didn’t all of you notice that Aunt Ellie didn’t drink for that whole month? Right? How is it that she can turn it off and on? That’s not an alcoholic.” Rose hesitated for her questions to sink in, “And I don’t think someone with a disorder like schizophrenia can turn it off and on either.”

David was skeptical, “Rose, my mom was on medicine to not drink when Aunt Louise was here.”

“But she was medicated many times before and always started drinking again even with medicine. Let me finish my thought. Remember last year when Billy was in the hospital for months and months after being shot?”

They all nodded their heads.

"Well, remember that your mom went to the hospital every day. Was she sober? Every time I went and she was there, she seemed sober."

They all just stood there with their minds trying to absorb this new point.

Rose asked, "Don't you see? There are things that just don't seem to make sense to me. Something's missing. Can any of you help make sense of all this?"

They started walking again under all the overhanging oak trees and were approaching the curve in the road where the creek passed below a small bridge. A dog was barking far away and another dog answered. Rippling water sounds filled the night, and they walked with only their thoughts among the sounds of water in the creek and the wind lightly rustling the leaves.

Becky broke in, "I know I'm the youngest and don't remember too much about how Mom was, but everything Rose said makes sense to me. You know, we're acting a lot like Mom and Dad. We don't talk together. Well, Johnny and I talk a lot, but that's just two of us. I think it was important that we talked tonight. I'm glad Billy listened to Dad's conversation on the phone."

Red replied, "Yeah, we should talk more."

Becky continued, "I just wanted to say something. I'm so ashamed to say it, but I must."

They walked in silence, waiting for Becky to finish.

"I've wished Mom was gone so many times. You know, just gone. Maybe even dead. When I come home from school and she's not there, I hope she never comes back." Becky started to cry, "I just needed to tell someone, and you guys are the only people I can say that to."

Rose hugged Becky.

Johnny admitted, "Me too Becky. I feel the same way. Gosh, I didn't think I would ever tell anyone."

Billy started to talk and had to clear his throat, "It feels so good to be away from her. I'm glad I live at college. I just have wiped her out of my mind. And I'm sorry, but I don't even want to think about her. What good would it do? I can't make her better, and I certainly can't erase all she's done to us."

Exhausted, bewildered, and relieved by the discussion, they sank into their farm beds and let sleep take them away to their dreams. They will not have another discussion as profound until the next big secret of their parents was revealed to them; Rose will discover she's their sister.

***

While all of the Bartletts worked to complete their goals—David was finishing his medical school and scheduled to intern on the east coast, Billy was halfway through his major in mathematics, Johnny had started going to the St. Louis School of Pharmacy, while Red and Becky were getting through high school—Ellie was reaching the end. It was as if she was driven to destroy herself. Like the cyclone in 1896 that brought her into St. Louis, she seemed intent on total ruin. She had gone beyond the in-the-gutter drunk. No longer did Ginny want to help her sister; it was hopeless. No longer did Louise think her move to California was the cause; it was apparent that Ellie was driven to destroy herself.

Ellie was swept up in the twister's grasp, and no one can stop a tornado.

The winter of 1956-57 was exceptionally cold. At midnight on any given night, it was the coldest. John tapped his shoes against the doorframe, knocking the snow off, before stepping onto the enclosed back porch. He shook the snow from his coat outside the kitchen door and entered. When slipping his coat on a hook, he noticed that Becky, James, and Johnny were home. All their coats hung from hooks lining the wall. He saw no coat for Ellie. Though the kitchen was dark, light streamed in from the other rooms.

Becky sat alone in the dining room and called out, "Is that you, Dad?"

"Yep, it is."

"Come have some hot chocolate that I made. Grab a cup."

As John pulled out a chair, he inquired, "Still no sign of your mother?"

With hands wrapped around the steaming cup, Becky shook her head. A clock, somewhere in the house, chimed over and over, indicating it was the end of another day. A loaf of bread and jars of peanut butter and jelly sat on the table. Without words, John took a slice of bread and made himself a sandwich.

What could he say? The family had been out trying to find Ellie from time to time in the last two days. She just had disappeared. The police took his report, but gave no help. What could they do? He hoped she was somewhere warm. Nightmares of her frozen body, encrusted in ice on a sidewalk, had awoken him last night.

"I circled a five block radius, weaving back and forth, up and down each street and every alley, before I came in. Nothing."

Becky nodded, "Yeah, so did Johnny about an hour ago. Red rode his bike all over and down every alley for blocks before he and Johnny went to bed."

"Oh, Becky, how was your basketball game?"

"We won."

"Good."

Becky and he sat in silence for a few minutes. Little chewing noises were all they heard with each bite of John's sandwich. "By the way, I could use you at the drugstore on Friday. Can you work?"

"I was already planning on it with Christmas around the corner. What time?"

"Oh, about five until midnight. I plan to stay open until midnight every night until Christmas Eve."

"Okay," Becky stood and kissed her father on his forehead. "Goodnight, Dad." She squeezed his shoulder and went to bed.

While John sat alone staring into nothingness in the dining room, Ellie was just a block away. She wore her once-white canvas tennis shoes and some socks Johnny had discarded—argyles of blue and yellow. But the yellow diamonds looked brown, the blue looked black. She had no coat, only a cotton dress that zipped up the front and a slip beneath that. In the dim light of the streetlamp, she looked of another race. The filth on her face, hands, and legs was so thick it may have offered some warmth. Snow flurried with each gust of wind.

No stars or moon filled the sky; it was a typical St. Louis winter night, clouded and cold. The snow in the curbs, where snow shovels had piled it, was black from days of dirt, salt, and cinders being thrown in the streets. The leafless trees were somber black. Bushes were bare and a few dried grasses poked above the snow. When it had fallen a few days ago, the snow turned everything into a winter wonderland, sticking to all the trees and bushes, making a smooth, sparkling clean sheet across the sidewalks and streets. Now with mars of footprints, tire tracks, and filth, it was ugly.

The man with Ellie wore a wool coat, stocking hat, and army boots. He was better dressed for the weather, but he was just as inebriated as Ellie. They swayed like the shadows from the branches moving in the wind.

Ellie's tongue was thick and her words slurred as she stood in front of the neighborhood liquor store and said, "Chust do it!"

Her companion let a crowbar slip from his sleeve into his hands. Wobbling—a big guy with a barrel gut—he slammed the crowbar and himself, as he lost his balance, into the storefront's window. Glass cracked in slow motion and long foot-wide pieces slipped to the right and left of the impact. The man had crumpled through the window frame across a display of a cardboard photo with three people in a rowboat, each holding a bottle of beer. The sun in a clear, blue sky was shining in the top of the poster, but blood was flowing across the bottom. Ellie saw the blood and stepped toward him just as a four-foot long piece of the plate glass teetered out and crashed across her shoulder. She fell from the blow and noticed that an alarm was blaring from inside the liquor store.

She struggled to her knees and reached for the brick wall to steady her attempt to stand. Her knees wouldn't hold her. She tried again and on the third maneuver she found herself upright and leaning against the bricks. Blood streamed down from her wound. Half her dress was covered in glistening red. She stumbled into the street and headed for the alley that led to her house. Three steps forward, one to the side and sometimes one back, but she progressed. She leaned against fences, garages, gates, and whatever was there. When she grabbed for the dry hollyhocks, she fell to the ground and noted not to do that again. At one point, careening to the left, she bumped into trashcans and started a half a dozen dogs barking. But she kept going.

Now she heard sirens. *I'm only six houses from home*, she thought, and continued to put one foot in front the other.

Some people claim that a shocking situation can sober someone instantly, no matter how drunk they are. It was hard to tell with Ellie; she could have been unstable just from the loss of blood. But when she arrived at her house, no one was there to evaluate her condition. The door to the enclosed back porch was unlocked as always; she opened it and fell across the step, losing consciousness.

Thirty minutes later, the Bartlett household woke to the doorbell and a heavy-handed beating on the front door. Lights went on in every bedroom, and they stumbled out from their bedroom doors. John shuffled with one slipper down the staircase to the front door to face a policeman.

"We have an emergency here. An ambulance is coming, but I need to ask you to identify a body in the back of your house."

John's heart exploded in his chest when he heard. He was speechless, awestruck, and wide-eyed when Johnny came from behind, asking, "Where's the body?"

"She's at your back door, if we could go through the house, it would be quicker."

John found his voice, "Come in, officer."

As the three traipsed across the foyer, dining room, and into the kitchen, another policeman could be seen through the glass window of the back door. John hurried to grab the knob and open it, just as the sound of the ambulance's siren screamed through the house from the open front door to the back. Johnny flipped the back porch light switch. Ellie was heaped over the back step. Without seeing her face, John knew it was Ellie. However, he kneeled and carefully moved hair from her face anyway.

A policeman was pressing a rag against her shoulder, "We didn't move her. Thought it best to wait for the medical people to come."

Red and Becky were in the kitchen doorway now as their father slumped to the concrete floor of the porch. There was so much blood covering Ellie. John reached for her wrist and was surprised to feel a pulse.

He whispered in amazement, "She's alive."

"Do you know her?"

John looked up into the policeman's eyes and stifled a sob, "She's my wife."

Red had stepped closer and blurted, "Is that all her blood?"

"Yes, it is, son." The policeman looked sadly at the Bartletts. "In fact, there's lots more down the alley. She left a trail for us to follow from the liquor store to here. I didn't think anyone had that much blood either."

Becky started to cry.

"James, take your sister into the house and direct the ambulance people to come back here. Quickly, son."

They carried Ellie into the ambulance and drove away dodging neighbors who stood in the street as well as out on their lawns and on the sidewalks.

One of the policemen came from the house shouting, "All right, all right. Everyone go back to bed." When no one moved, he became angry, "I said get outta here and back to your homes, or I'll arrest you for loitering." Now people scrambled away.

When he returned to the house and closed the front door, John was standing waiting, "Shouldn't I dress and go to the hospital?"

"I'll want you to dress, for a trip to the police station." Realizing that may have been too abrupt for a man who just witnessed his wife almost dead, he spoke with more compassion, "She's in good hands. Let's sit down while I get some information about her."

John turned to his three children, "Why don't you go back to bed?"

"Dad, are you kidding? Who could sleep? I want to go with you,' Johnny said. He turned to the policeman, "Can I?"

"If you like, son."

John started to protest, but Becky and Red spoke up.

Together they said, "Can I go?"

The policeman shook his head, "Two people will be enough at the station. If you want to be useful, get dressed and drive to the St. Louis City Hospital. They need to know her name and other information." Becky and Red hurried up the stairs.

Johnny sat down with his dad to listen.

"What happened officer?"

"Off the record, it seems your wife and a man were attempting to break into the liquor store down the street."

John gasped and paled. Johnny gritted his teeth.

"The man used a crowbar to bash in the window. He fell against the jagged glass and killed himself. It looks like a heavy piece fell on your wife, and she walked home.

The uniformed man changed the subject, "Now, it's my turn to ask some questions. You'll hear more about the incident later at the station."

The gravity of what Ellie had done was reflected in the faces of John and Johnny.

With a pad and pen in front of him, the policeman took down some vital information about Ellie. "Okay, that's enough. You two go dress and ride with me to the station. I'll have someone drop you back here when we're done. Okay?"

John stood, but didn't leave, "But Ellie has committed a crime. Will she be under arrest? You know, after the hospital, I mean."

"Go get dressed, Mr. Bartlett. We'll talk during the ride downtown."

Walking up the stairs, John met Becky and Red coming down, "The car keys are on the buffet. Drive extra carefully, James. We've all been through a lot and your judgment may not be the best. Do you understand?"

"Yes, sir."

Basically, John knew the routine at the police station because of his experience after robberies and holdups at the drugstore. John was familiar with picking people out of line-ups, trying to identify a robber with mug shots, and cleaning up the mess at the store. Nevertheless, knowing that a family member was the criminal, made the situation unnerving and new. John's hand shook while buttoning his shirt. He fumbled, trying to tie his shoes. He opened a drawer and tucked two clean handkerchiefs into his pockets; his nose was running from the tears.

Johnny was waiting with the policeman when John came down the stairs. They piled into the police car and headed for the main headquarters. They didn't speak about Ellie's situation. The policeman asked questions about the family, John's work, and the children.

"It sounds like you have a nice life and family here."

Johnny found that to be a strange statement, but said nothing.

John offered, "My wife wasn't always like this."

"It happens in the best of families. We see it a lot."

Johnny exclaimed, "What are you talking about? How can you call our family a nice family after tonight?"

"Johnny!"

The policeman jumped in, "That's all right. Son, drinking can ruin a person. But no one should judge a whole family by just one person."

Johnny accepted the answer, though he sat there frowning.

Ten minutes later, they were in the police station. Johnny looked around at the hustle and bustle and said, "Wow, it sure is busy in here for the middle of the night."

"It's our busiest time."

Johnny pursed his lips and nodded, "Oh, yeah."

They walked up a hall and the policeman pointed toward some chairs, "Please sit here and wait. Someone will come in a moment."

Some empty oak chairs were lined up against a wall next to seated people with stoic faces.

Suddenly, a voice called from down the hall, "John, is that you?" A tall blonde-haired man with a huge smile arrived in front of them. "John, it's been a while. Come on back to my office." He clasped John around the shoulders and squeezed like a grizzly.

"Frank! Why, it's good to see you." John said with a look of bewilderment in his eyes. "What are you doing here?"

A robust and loud laugh filled the room, "John, I work here. I'm sure you meant to ask why am I inviting you back to my office."

John nodded as Captain Frank Wharton continued talking as they walked. "I saw Elizabeth Bartlett on a report that just came over my desk. So, I knew you'd be around somewhere. I got the lowdown from the two policemen who went to your house and from another who filled me in on other details. Then I came looking for you."

They had arrived at a doorway to a windowed office. Frank ambled in and went behind the desk. As he turned, he extended his hand in the direction of a couple of wooden chairs.

John changed the course of the conversation and asked, "How's life as a married man going for you?"

Frank figured John was stalling for time before he heard the worst about Ellie. "Oh John, I don't think there's another woman in the world for me. How she puts up with my slovenly habits and unpredictable hours, I'll never understand. I'm just so happy I found her."

Johnny could see that Captain Wharton wasn't too tidy as he looked around the office at the piles of used coffee cups on a side table; stacks of papers on every surface including all chairs except the two they sat in; a coat rack with garments on every hook, over the top, and on the floor where they seemed to have fallen; and dust that looked months undisturbed. But Frank beamed with affability.

"So, which son am I addressing? John, your kids are growing up too fast. They make me feel old."

"I'm Johnny, number-three son."

"Well, gentlemen, I must get down to business. And it ain't going to be easy for you to hear what I have to say." Frank leaned forward onto his elbows. His bushy, blonde eyebrows tilted and the blue eyes saddened. "It's not easy for me to tell you, either." He leaned back, passed both hands over his receding hairline, and took a deep breath.

"First, let's talk about Ellie's condition. I called the hospital before finding you." Quickly he clarified, "She's going to be all right. Her collarbone is broken, she lost a tremendous amount of blood—you might go donate some at the hospital tomorrow—and it took fifty stitches to close the wound in her shoulder. Luckily she caught the weight of the plate glass over her back and shoulder. If it had hit her chest, she'd be dead. The doctors told me that she must be a strong woman to have taken such a blow. They're looking into the condition of her organs from the drinking, but her vitals—you know, the pulse, blood pressure, temperature—are good, especially considering her drinking history."

John's head perked up. He was relieved to hear that Ellie was okay, but puzzled that Frank knew she drank.

"Yes, I know a lot about Ellie's drinking. Maybe more than you, John. There's no way for me to make this easy for you. I know, you want me to lay it on the line, and Johnny here looks old enough to handle the truth about his mother. I'm going to read some reports and tell you what my men have told me.

"Months ago we brought a woman in and she gave the name of E. Mary Bee nothing more. We hadn't seen her before this first report. She was booked for prostitution …"

John interrupted with a gasp, "No, that's not possible."

"John, please, just listen. It says she was 'observed by officers at Chouteau and Grattan about 1:35 a.m. approaching a stopped car at a stop sign and offering sex for ten dollars. The patrol car turned on the flashers and blocked the car. The man in the car said she had offered herself to him.' So, they brought her in. She was very drunk and put in the holdover cell with all the other women. Late the next day, since she had no priors, we let her go."

John whispered, "I can't believe this."

Captain Wharton wanted to finish, "Then she became a regular. We'd always pick her up around the same place and learned that she was sleeping under the viaduct at Chouteau and Jefferson. We brought her in for …" Frank shuffled through the papers, "loitering, indecent exposure, soliciting money, and prostituting." Frank looked at John, "We'd keep her for a couple of days sometimes, but she wasn't doing anything that was worth booking her. None of the johns would press charges. She was basically just wasting our time." Frank sucked in air and sighed, "She was usually drunk. Her description didn't fit any missing person report. The name E. Mary Bee didn't come up on any list. She had no wedding rings. The funny thing was that she'd disappear for periods of time, and then we'd pick her up in cleaner clothes. So, we knew she had a home somewhere."

John sat stunned.

Johnny said to Frank, "Wonder where her wedding rings are. She had two, a gold band and a small diamond ring."

"She probably hocked them. One cold night we asked her where her coat was. She had sold it for a dollar."

Johnny said, "She didn't lie about her name. She is Elizabeth Mary Bartlett, but she just gave you the initials for the first and last name. She's clever."

Gravely Frank retorted, "Not too clever tonight. This is a robbery, a felony."

Johnny blurted, "But she didn't steal anything, did she? A window was broken; maybe that guy fell against it accidentally."

John looked to his son, "Johnny. What are you talking about? You weren't there. You don't know about the law or police work."

Captain Wharton tilted his head and gave a little chuckle at Johnny's comments, "Actually John, Johnny makes a good point. In fact, my superior and I were talking a bit. It would only waste the taxpayer's money to book Ellie. What we need to do is get her off the streets. I guess you've been trying; I've heard that you put her in hospitals over the years. When we first started bringing her in I didn't know she was Ellie or I would've stopped this sooner. She didn't look like Ellie to me."

John leaned over and his head fell to his hands on the desk. He started to sob. Frank came around his desk and lowered the blinds on the windows facing into the office. Johnny handed his father a handkerchief, and no one said anything for a couple of minutes.

Finally, Frank spoke in a soft voice, "We decided to write up the report just about how Johnny described it. After all, the man with Ellie is dead and can't be booked. Like I said, there's nothing to gain by booking Ellie. I think the liquor store owner would just like someone to pay for his window."

John blew his nose, wiped it, and said, "Of course, I'll pay for that. But, Frank, she'll just do it again. I've tried to talk to her and help her. Nothing works. She's not even Ellie anymore." John face contorted in anguish as he tried not to cry again.

"I know. I know, John. Just cry it out. You have so many reasons to cry. But I hear you have children to be proud of. We need to make this situation better for your family."

Johnny frowned, "It's impossible. My dad has tried everything. It might be better to put her in jail where she can't drink."

Frank walked over to the young man and placed his large hand on Johnny's shoulder, "Well, we're not going to arrest her, but we aren't going to let her go either. Whatever happens to your mother is really out of your hands; under the circumstances, she's at the mercy of the state. I think it will be less severe than jail, Johnny, but at this moment I don't know exactly what they will do with her. I'll try to get it worked out for the best."

The family learned soon enough what the state planned for Ellie.

***

For a couple of months, Ellie was under police guard at the City Hospital while she mended and detoxified.

Ellie wasn't the only Bartlett injured; the whole family needed to heal. During those months, the Bartletts carried on with their lives though invisibly bruised. No one could go through what they had endured without wounds. At first, they were constantly reminded of the past painful years because they kept finding half-full wine bottles hidden about the house. They emptied the wine into the sink, put the bottles into the trash can, and hoped for relief. No balm or poultice could be applied to heal them. No medicine in John Bartlett's drugstore could help what ailed them. Only the medicinal magic of time.

So they worked in the drugstore together. Christmas came and went with the four Bartletts putting in long hours.

But, on the last days of 1956, the whole Bartlett family decided to go down to the farm and avoid the New Year's Eve celebrations. The four of them mended fences with the cold and sun giving them pleasure, and then they did some target practicing before it got dark, talking about how it was a shame they missed deer season this year. They vowed to fill the freezer in 1957. As the darkness crept upon them, they went to Jack and Ginny's place for a nice dinner.

John left Jack and Ginny's cottage at the end of the meal without saying anything. And after an hour had passed, Johnny went to find his father. Out in the quiet night and under all the familiar stars, Johnny wandered around, listening. As an expert hunter, Johnny knew to listen. Whether hunting squirrels, deer, or turkey, he knew his ears would lead him. Johnny also knew that, if he moved, he was making noise himself. So, when he really wanted to find his prey, he sat. Tonight he didn't want to bring down an animal—he just wanted to find his dad—so he kept moving.

Intuitively Johnny walked quietly while listening. Suddenly, he heard the strangest sound. *Maybe that's a turkey! Sounds like it could be. Don't know what other animal could make that mournful sound.* For a long time, he and his brothers had wanted to bag a turkey on the farm and excitedly he headed toward the low drone, forgetting the quest to find his father. Cautiously he proceeded, stopping, every now and then, to look at the ground to decide where to place his feet so as not to cause a noise. Because of the hills he climbed and the eager anticipation of finding where the turkeys roost at night, he started to sweat. He and his brothers had heard the flutter of their flight sometimes, even had gotten a sighting in the distance, but never had found the turkeys' roost.

Johnny was getting closer. He knew their 350-acre farm like the back of his hand and realized he was coming up to a clearing. He didn't want to pass into the open, so he started to circle the edges. As he came around, suddenly his mind knew what he was hearing.

He froze. Looking ahead, he saw, there on a stump under a big black oak, his father. The mournful, moaning put goose pimples down Johnny's spine. As he started backing away, a deep, guttural wail escaped from his father's throat. It was the sound of nightmares. Johnny was terrified.

He knew why his father wailed. Johnny had gone with his father again to the police station when Captain Wharton explained about Ellie; John had no say, no choice, and no control. Ellie had been observed and tested by psychiatrists and found to be insane.

Johnny stood in the darkness and remembered. *She is insane, isn't she? Why would a woman with such a wonderful family do this to herself? Why didn't she stop drinking when Dad tried to help her?*

A judge made Ellie a ward of the state. Instead of going to prison, she would be sent to the state's insane asylum. Ellie wasn't going to jail, but, as far as Johnny could determine, she was going to hell.

And so, Ellie returned to her place of birth. Ellie had come full circle. On May 27th in the year 1896, the tornado had chosen where to pull her from the womb; and now the unexplainable path of the storm, that had controlled so much of her destiny, was reuniting her with the St. Louis Insane Asylum on Arsenal Street. Each night she'd curl into a fetal position in the darkness, unable to leave the barred womb of her existence.

The family saw this as her demise, but they were wrong.

Returning to the place of her birth completed the cycle of the storm; it was the end of the phenomenon of the cyclone. It was the end of Ellie's tornado controlling her fate, not the end of Ellie.

Chapter 18

1958
The Secret Daughter

The trouble with secrets is they eventually float to the surface. Even if one anchors them with a concrete block, hurls them far from the shore, and into the darkest deep, they break free with time. Secrets aren't natural. People, who don't understand the power of truth, make secrets.

Ellie had prided herself on knowing how to keep secrets; her father had taught her the honor of keeping secrets. But there is no place for honor in the ability to deceive. Many years from now, Ellie will go to her grave not understanding this. She will take secrets with her in death, but not the secret about Rose and her twin. Soon it will float to the surface.

Spring was in the air and Rose Cohen walked hand in hand with Philip as they left the synagogue. After *kiddush*—drinking some wine and passing the challah for each person to break a piece from the braided bread—they had spoken with the Rabbi about their plan to marry. The following week they were to stop by his office to choose a date for the wedding. Rose was happy; Philip was a fine Jewish man whom she had known for years.

As Philip opened the car door, he said, "Rose, my mother asked me to invite you over tomorrow to learn about the Seder preparations for Passover."

The following day was Palm Sunday; Monday was the start of Passover. Sometimes these holidays were even on the same days, or they might be a month apart. Rose was always aware of when the Christian and Jewish holidays fell on the calendar because it was a time for her mother to be complaining.

Philip dropped Rose at her home. When Rose entered the apartment and mentioned that she would be at Philip's house for Palm Sunday, Françoise whined, "I'd like to go to church on just a few holidays. It's so nice to dress up for Palm Sunday and Easter as well as Christmas. Why can't you go with me sometimes? Your father was never interested in the Jewish holidays; why are you?"

"Please, Mother, I'm not doing anything to you. I like Judaism. You know that. And now I'm marrying a Jewish man. So, please stop this. By the way, I'll be with Philip's mother tomorrow, not at church with you." Rose went down the hall to her bedroom to change.

Françoise sat at the piano and started to play.

Walking back up the hall a few minutes later, buttoning and zipping her seersucker pants, Rose smiled. *It calms all of us to hear her playing. Oh, I love Debussy.*

Softly Rose asked, "Mother, is Daddy awake?"

Françoise nodded and stopped playing, "Oh, he'd like to talk to you. Go see him now. He's feeling good today."

Though Rose hadn't mentioned her hopes to anyone, she wanted to marry while her father was alive. Jerry Cohen was very ill. With his years and years of smoking, the doctors said he was lucky to have made it to his late seventies. He spent most of the day in his special hospital bed in the guest room. A nurse came Monday, Wednesday, and Friday to administer medication, give him a massage, go through some exercises, and bathe him. Those were the only days he was out of bed, when the nurse moved him to an overstuffed chair in the living room.

"Morning, Daddy," Rose leaned over her father and encircled his chest and shoulders for a long hug. "Philip and I talked with the Rabbi today. We'll go to his office this week to set a date. I'm going over to Philip's house tomorrow to have a cooking lesson with his mother. And Mother and I are going to look at wedding dresses this week." Rose giggled, "I'm feeling like a little girl getting ready to marry her prince."

Jerry took his daughter's hand, "Well, the King has …" He began one of his coughing fits. His face reddened and the hacking wrenched his body as the whole bed shook.

Françoise went quickly to the other side of the bed and picked up a bottle. "Open up, Jerry! That's it." She sprayed his throat a couple of times, and they all waited. Jerry's face calmed as he took a deep breath from a hose that connected to an oxygen tank; his body seemed to relax.

"Come closer, Rose. I won't cough if I whisper."

Rose pulled a chair closer and sat near her father's head. She kissed his forehead and leaned on her elbows to be inches from his face.

"I was going to say that this King has a wedding present for his princess. You know, I'm terrible at wrapping gifts, besides it was too big, so Françoise has a little piece of it to hand to you."

Smiling, Françoise dangled some keys from her long, graceful finger. "Jerry, you should tell her what this unlocks."

With a puzzled look, Rose stood and slipped the keys from her mother's graceful hand. "Daddy, what is it?"

"I bought you an apartment. Years ago I thought about doing that, but didn't like the idea of you moving out of my life. Now, …" he smiled and rolled his eyes, "it looks like a prince is pulling you away no matter what."

Rose sat back down and gently placed her head on her father's chest. "Daddy, you're too good to me." He wrapped his arms around her. Then with a twinkle in her eye, she sat up and said, "You know this won't make me love you more; it's not possible."

Jerry took another deep breath from the tube, "I know. I'm happy with the love you give." He pulled her back to his chest and hugged her tighter, whispering in her ear with short phrases, "If you have time, … your mother will … take you there. Of course, … she did the looking … with a realtor. I saw only pictures … but, it's my gift." They waited while he took a long suck on the hose. "Françoise, … tell her about yours."

"Oh, I'm giving," Françoise smiled, "just little things. You know, for inside the apartment. I figured I'd furnish it."

Rose jumped up and squealed, "Oh, you two. You spoil me so much." She hugged her mother and did a little dance.

Françoise laughed, "We'll go furniture shopping together, if you like. I'm really doing this for me as much as you. With you and Philip having only teachers' salaries I figured you would only buy junk. I didn't want to come visit a junky place."

The new apartment was on Kingshighway and only three blocks from her parents' place. It was called *Monterey on the Park* because it faced Forest Park. Rose was glad; she could visit her parents, staying close to her father while he was ill, yet she and Philip would have their own wonderful life.

Philip loved the apartment, "You mean it's all paid for? We don't have rent to pay or anything?"

"Nope, only the bills for electricity, water, and stuff. I'm going shopping for a couch and bed with my mother this week. Hey, since we're on spring break let's go to the farm on Wednesday and Thursday with Uncle John. You've heard me talk about the farm, but I want you to know Uncle John better. Ginny and Jack, too. Please say you'll come."

Thinking about the strong role the Bartletts had played in her life, Rose couldn't imagine her wedding without them. Yet, it was obvious, her mother wouldn't invite them. Whenever Rose had tried to get her mother together with the Bartletts, Françoise would refuse.

No amount of logic would work either. Rose tried the another day, "Mother, please come to the Bartletts' house with me; you know that Ellie's no longer there. The excuse that you don't want to be around her doesn't work; she's at the state hospital."

Françoise huffed as if insulted.

Rose persisted, "You'd make the Bartletts so happy, if you'd come."

Françoise ignored all attempts. So Rose planned to invite the Bartletts to her wedding without telling her mother. Once the Bartletts were there, Rose knew her mother would not make a scene; Françoise was too refined to do something gauche.

At the farm later that week, while Ginny steeped tea in a teapot decorated with ivy vines creeping around its round belly, Rose's thoughts turned to Ellie again. *I wonder how Ginny feels about Ellie. She never talks about her sister. I'd like to hear what she thinks.*

The little cottage was full. Becky, Red, and Johnny had decided to join Rose and Philip at the farm. John was out in the fields, like always; they would see him when the sun went down and the dinner bell called him, unless he was busy and needed to finish something. Jack was in the shed off the house with Philip, repairing a chair they would need for dinner. The leg had a cracked.

"Boy, dinner sure smells good!"

Ginny smiled, "It's just a pot roast. It needs another hour or so to be ready. Hope you aren't starving, Johnny. This tea with cheese and crackers should hold you till then."

"I'm okay, I was just saying it smells delicious."

Rose decided to talk with Ginny right there. "Becky and I went to the state hospital to see Ellie yesterday. You know I try to go at least once a month."

Instantly, a gloom seeped into the room. Looks of discomfort appeared on most faces and Red squirmed in his seat.

They feel guilty for not visiting her. "She looked good, don't you think, Becky?"

"Yeah, better than other times."

Ginny kept her head down and straightened the napkins on the coffee table.

"Most times, Aunt Ellie doesn't want visitors. The nurses said that she refuses to come out of her room when Uncle John goes."

Johnny agreed, "When I went that one time, it was the same. Yeah, I only went once. Well, she was sitting by a window, and when she saw me she shuffled off to her room. I sat there for about five minutes while the nurse talked with her and then told me that Mom said she didn't want any visitors." He shifted his weight in the chair and frowned, "So, I never went back."

"It was the same for me," James added. "Plus, I feel weird around all those people. They smell. Why do they smell like that? It's like … being crazy means you have to smell like that. It was so hard to see all those people doing crazy things. Rocking back and forth, picking their nose, you know, stuff like that. The worst was when one of them came up and picked imaginary things off my clothes. I hate it when one of them tries to talk with me. They never make sense. I can't stand seeing Mom there with them."

"Well, Aunt Ellie has been moved to a different floor and it's better," Rose responded. "On this new floor, the patients sit and play checkers or cards. They seem almost normal. Well, compared to what you saw a year ago. Don't you think, Becky?"

"Yeah, Mom was looking at a magazine when we came in. She actually said, 'Hello girls,' to us. Sometimes, when I went before, she looked empty—like nothing was in her head. But this week, she smiled and asked how everyone was. She's never done that before."

"I talked to a nurse who said that her medications had been changed. Your dad told me that he thinks they stopped the shock treatments."

Ginny poured some tea into cups, "I haven't seen Ellie for over six months. I'm just like you boys; it hurts too much to go. But maybe it would be better now."

"Aunt Ellie asked me if I would bring her a notebook with lined paper. The nurse said I could. It would be so nice to see her writing."

Ginny wanted to know, "How does she look?"

Becky grimaced, "Mom is thin and gaunt. She's lost a lot of hair; it's so thin that I can see her scalp. And it seemed to go grey from one visit to the next. She looks old."

"Well, we are old."

Becky clarified, "But you don't look old, Aunt Ginny. You're still so beautiful. Mom looks like a she's eighty years old. I bet you can still stand on your hands." They laughed.

"Aunt Ellie wanted me to bring her jewelry box to her. It was amazing, when Becky and I went to the house and got the box out of the chest of drawers, we found her wedding rings! Remember, everyone thought she'd hocked them."

Ginny perked up, "Oh, that's wonderful. The little diamond ring was my mother's wedding ring. I thought it had been lost. Oh, I want to see it again. Maybe I'll come to St. Louis and go visit Ellie with you when you give her the jewelry box. Okay? What else was in it?"

Becky said, "There isn't much in it, just some costume jewelry, a lucky rabbit's foot, a couple of birthday cards from Dad, and her broken pearl necklace."

"Ah, the pearl necklace was a wedding gift from Franny and Jerry," Ginny explained. "Maybe we should get the pearls restrung. We should ask Ellie."

"Aunt Ginny, please don't get your hopes up too much. Ellie is better than before, but she's not back to normal. Questions like that might upset her. She always talks about sewing or threads, which is a little strange, and Becky and I were only with her for about fifteen minutes when she asked us to go. She just suddenly said, 'You can leave now.'"

With a pained expression returning to Ginny's face, Rose decided to change the subject. "I'm going to be setting the date for my wedding. I'll let all of you know so you can put the date on your calendars. I'm getting so excited."

"That's wonderful, Rose." Ginny stood and patted Rose on the shoulder, "Excuse me while I take a look to see if the pot roast needs some more water."

Johnny headed toward the door, "Hey, Red, let's go find Dad. If we help him, he'll come quicker when the dinner bell rings."

Ginny called from the kitchen, "Girls, why don't you go find some spring flowers for the table?"

Branches of soft, purple blossoms from a red bud tree and yellow jonquils were piled at the top of Ginny's front porch steps. Ladybugs and spiders scurried from them. Ginny came out with a tall vase full of water and squatted down to help break off leaves at the base of the branches before slipping them into the water. She, Rose, and Becky worked quietly for a while, enjoying the warmth of the sunlight streaming through the trees.

"Aunt Ginny, I hope I didn't upset you, talking about your sister."

"Oh, no, Sweetie. That's fine."

"Since I'm twelve years older than Becky here, I remember how Aunt Ellie was. I know who she used to be. I loved her so much, and now I feel drawn to her because something doesn't make sense. You know what I mean? It just doesn't make sense what happened to her."

Ginny was still squatting while Rose sat on the top step, looking up; Ginny's eyes were inches from Rose's. They looked deeply into each other's eyes.

Ginny spoke with a forlorn voice, "I remember her before you were born, so I know her even better than you, and I agree. There's something we don't know." Now Ginny plopped her bottom onto the wooden porch. The flower arranging was postponed.

Rose listed the possible causes she and the Bartlett children had come up with the previous year: Ellie's loss of her parents; the departure of Louise, Clara, and Ginny; the Change of Life. "Ellie was able to stay sober when Louise came and visited as well as other times. You know, like those months when Billy was in the hospital." With a raised and emphatic voice Rose said, "That isn't how an alcoholic is."

Ginny held up her hands, "Ellie was drinking before my father died. No one knew except me and John. She started soon after my father's second visit at Christmas time." Looking over to Becky, Ginny said, "Becky wasn't even in kindergarten yet."

" No!" Becky exclaimed.

"Louise hadn't moved yet. So, of course, we were all still in St. Louis. My father was alive. No, those aren't the reasons she started drinking."

Becky and Rose waited. Perhaps they were finally going to learn what happened to Ellie. But Ginny's next words dashed all hope.

"I've lost sleep trying to figure out what could've happened. I just don't know. And John claims that he doesn't know either."

Becky's shoulders drooped, "I thought you were going to tell us the reason."

"Sorry. I don't know the reason. But I know there is one. Ellie is so good at keeping secrets. Whatever the reason is, it's locked inside of Ellie."

Rose was puzzled, "How do you know Ellie started drinking before Grandpa James died and before you left St. Louis?"

"I found her drinking, over and over. I was going to the house every day to keep her sober. She didn't drink if I was with her. Louise and Clara were still in St. Louis, but they didn't notice.

"Oh my gosh!" Becky's mouth was open in surprise.

Ginny continued, "Over and over, I talked to Ellie, but she'd never tell me anything. Finally I thought she'd stopped as she'd promised she would. But she was so clever at hiding it. She learned ways to not smell drunk. John said he was trying to be with her more by giving her more work at the drugstore."

Rose said, "So you know that she stopped and started when she wanted."

Ginny nodded.

Rose perked up, "I knew I was right."

"Sure, I saw her do that. Why, listen to this; you couldn't know this, but many years ago after one of the babies was born, her doctor said she was too skinny and had Ellie drinking a beer a day to fatten her up. She gained ten pounds and stopped. There were many times when she would stop on her own. Like you said, when Billy was in the hospital she stopped."

Becky was aghast, "You mean, when I was little she was drinking sometimes, and I just didn't notice?"

Ginny started putting the flowers into the vase again. "That's right, Becky. I was so worried about your safety because she was driving places with you. Then you started kindergarten and weren't in the car as much. I think she was drinking for a year before David noticed."

"Oh my gosh!"

The vases were ready and Ginny stood. "At some point I think the drinking got out of Ellie's control. She couldn't stop at will, so she would leave the house and the neighborhood. That's when she started doing all those horrible things."

Becky turned to Rose, "Would you help me make a list of all the things that happened? Maybe if it's on paper I might see something new."

"Sure."

"Then we can come talk more with Aunt Ginny to see if she can think of anything we missed."

Ginny laughed, "You're welcome to come anytime, but I've worked on this for ten years and can't think of anything. It does feel good to have someone to talk to, but Ellie's got her secrets."

The three women were energized and hopeful, but nothing will come of Becky's list, and they learned nothing new with their talking. Locked deep inside Ellie was the reason she started drinking. And only Ellie knew why. Most of Ellie's secrets were a pact with someone else; she had sealed many a pact with the little finger pull. However, this secret was different because Ellie had promised no one that she would keep it. No one, except herself.

But, one day, she will give Rose some hints.

***

Few of us live a life without surprises. Aren't those surprises—whether happy or sad—what make life interesting? How dull life would be, if one's day-to-day happenings were always the same. There are those who think people become better when life makes them suffer a bit. The Bartlett children seemed to be an example of that. But, basically most people sigh in relief when some disturbing event happens to the neighbors instead of them.

Many people whispered about Ellie's alcoholism and inwardly thanked heaven it happened to the Bartletts and not them. Françoise had had that thought. Of course, she was of the opinion that nothing so distasteful could ever befall the Cohens. She had forgotten about the skeleton in her closet that was soon to be revealed.

The Cohens' lifestyle and wealth allowed them to rub shoulders with some of the elite of St. Louis. Those in the upper crust in St. Louis prided themselves on having open minds, not being prejudiced, and welcoming all races and religions. Jerry Cohen knew this to be only half true; all people were welcome into the city, but not into the circles of those important families. Yet he accepted invitations he received from time to time, because Françoise relished mixing with those wealthy people and getting her photograph in the Society Section of the *Post-Dispatch*. Jerry surmised he had been invited as the token Jew; he was admired as a doctor and had an elegant and socially proper wife. And even the most haughty and uppity found the Cohens to be enjoyable. So, the Cohens mixed with the elite at fundraisers as well as political and social events both public and private. Many were genuinely good people and became their friends, but as one would expect, others were not.

Now that Jerry was old and bedridden, some of those good people visited him to brighten his day and reminisce. After dinnertime one evening, a former mayor of St. Louis and his wife dropped in, "We can only stay a few minutes, just wanted to say hello to Jerry and leave these flowers."

Françoise offered coffee and a slice of pound cake, but they declined. Rose came to greet the visitors, and the group chatted as they walked into Jerry's room.

The wife mentioned, "Oh, I've been so busy helping with the plans for the VP Parade. You know, the Veiled Prophet Parade dates back to the mid 1800s. We must do things, just so, as they have for decades. The people of St. Louis love this parade."

Instantly upon reaching her father's side, Rose could see something was wrong. "Daddy, are you awake?"

Jerry's mouth was slack and his breathing erratic. He blinked as if Rose had aroused him from a stupor. He made a weak groan and spoke, "Rose, I must ... talk to you."

Though Rose responded with a smile, "I'm here, Daddy," she looked to her mother. Françoise left the room to call the retired doctor who lived downstairs.

"Rose, I must ... tell you ... something ... come closer."

The visitors had not expected this. They mumbled an apology about not knowing that Jerry was so sick, "Maybe we should leave."

But Françoise was no longer there to hear, and Rose was engrossed with her father. So, they politely stood to wait for Françoise to return.

Jerry was oblivious to the visitors' presence and coughed softly before continuing, "Rose, no man ... had a better child. You made my life …" He stopped to cough. "Rose, can't talk … I must tell you … we're not your parents … I owe you this truth." He began coughing harder.

Rose couldn't understand what her father meant. The woman behind her gasped; she had heard. She whispered to her husband, "A deathbed confession."

Françoise returned as Jerry ceased coughing to say with a gasp, "Rose, listen … Ellie and John are your parents …" Now his chest heaved as he convulsed for breath. Rose grabbed the oxygen hose to put it to his lips, but Jerry was gone.

"Daddy, no! Please breathe! Daddy!" Rose opened his mouth and put the tube in. "Breathe, Daddy!" She slipped her arm around his shoulders and raised him, thinking this might help.

The couple backed from the room wide-eyed. The man stuttered, "Françoise, we … ah, we're so sorry. We had no idea Jerry was so near the end. We apologize and will let ourselves out."

Françoise stood stunned. Seeing Jerry die, after blurting out the secret they were never to mention, unnerved her.

The distraught visitor, with a hand over her mouth, whispered, "Oh, I am so sorry," before she turned and rushed toward the front door. Opening the front door, the couple found themselves face to face with the doctor. Without hesitation, he rushed past them with his black case.

Pulling out his stethoscope, he listened to Jerry's chest and felt for a pulse in the neck. With white-knuckled hands, Rose and Françoise clenched the metal frame of the foot of the bed. The doctor looked up to them and gave a simple shake of his head before closing Jerry's eyes and covering him.

Rose already had a handkerchief in her hand and dabbed her eyes, "Oh, Mommy! No!" She slipped into an armchair and bent her head to cry. Suddenly, Rose sat up, "Did you hear what Daddy said to me?"

Françoise stood dazed and nodded. In a far-off voice she said, "He must have been dreaming before you came in. He was confused."

The doctor asked, "What had Jerry said?"

Together they started to speak; Françoise said, "Oh, nothing coherent."

And Rose blurted, "He told me my real parents were our friends, the Bartletts. He sounded perfectly determined to tell me this. My mother was out of the room for most of what he said and …"

Françoise interrupted, "Please, Rose, the doctor doesn't need to hear every word. What your father said was spoken in delirium."

"But isn't it more likely, Doctor, that he knew he was dying and wanted to tell me this?"

The doctor cleared his throat and looked up from some paperwork he was completing. "If your mother tells you it made no sense to her, you might listen. I can't determine how coherent Jerry may or may not have been. I wasn't here."

"Oh," Rose blushed. Though not wanting to let the matter drop, she did. There would be time enough to talk with her mother.

As soon as the doctor left, Rose called Philip who rushed over.

Philip mentioned that in the Jewish faith, the body is to be in the ground within twenty-four hours. "I think the first step is to call the Rabbi."

Rose nodded, "The doctor arranged for the body to be removed tonight. Before we call the Rabbi, let me help my mother to bed." Philip sat with the body while Rose went off with Françoise.

In her mother's bedroom, Rose eased her mother into an armchair and knelt to remove her shoes. Françoise waved her arms to indicate she could undress herself, and Rose left to go draw a bath while her mind weighed her father's words. *All his life he was so logical and did things at the proper time. He bought a cemetery plot years ago because he knew when things had to be done. He wanted to tell me this secret just before he died. But how could the Bartletts be my parents?* Putting aside the puzzle, Rose finished with her mother and called the Rabbi, who said he'd handle the traditional arrangements and inform the congregation.

The Cohens' beautiful apartment—with artwork on the walls and tabletops, with colors blending perfectly from one room to the next, with bookshelves filled with classics as well as all sorts of medical books, and with the shiny black grand piano sitting silently—now looked different to Rose. Without her father, a hollow emptiness hung in the air; it was like a clammy cave. She shivered. After the phone call, Rose turned out all the lights but one and sat on the thick, fluffy white carpet in front of the living room sofa. Philip joined her. Innocently, as they snuggled, Rose told Philip about Jerry's last words. She was leaning against Philip's chest and didn't see his face when he heard that the Bartletts might be her parents.

"I'll question Mother after all of the funeral events are over. There has to be a reason why Daddy said that. Don't you agree?"

Philip didn't answer. He was deep in thought.

In a small family ceremony, Jerry was buried the following afternoon. People came to the Cohen's apartment that evening to give their respects. In the Jewish tradition of *shivah*, people would come for seven days, filling the apartment with talk and food. Françoise and Rose had no time to go off into a corner and feel sorry for themselves. Photo albums came out and memories flowed, as tales were shared.

When Wally came with his family, Françoise and he played Irish tunes and told stories that Rose had never heard about growing up in Dogtown. The apartment was already full of people when Johnny, Red, and Becky arrived. Seeing Ellie's children sparked a memory in Wally's head about swimming the Mississippi River.

"O, Franny, do ye remember Ginny and Ellie covered in dirty engine oil and addin' more murkiness to the muddy Mississippi?" Wally turned to face Rose, "Your mother—she was quite the hero—a savin' Ellie's life, she did." Wally smiled and looked to others in the room and told about swimming the Mississippi. "If the electric car of

Mr. Gardner hadn't been there, Ellie might o' died. She was bleedin' badly."

Rose turned to the Bartletts, "Did you know that story about your mother?"

"No," the three chimed together.

"Mother, why hadn't you told me that story?"

Wally laughed, "O, Franny me dear, have you tol' the young ones 'bout the day you posed in a bridal gown with Jerry in a fine tux in front of the Jefferson Hotel?"

Françoise smiled, "I don't believe I have, Wally, but I think you might tell a better story about Al Capone than I could."

"O, thank ye, my dear. I'd be honored, though without a doubt, ye knows more facts first hand. Help me if I go astray in me tale."

John came in when the story was beginning. He sat in rapt attention, hearing about Ellie before they had met. He had known the story about the sisters swimming the Mississippi, yet he was hearing about an Ellie that no longer was the same person. At times sadness filled his face, only to change to laughter as Wally brought humor to the story.

While Wally talked, Rose watched John with stolen glances. *What if he really is my father? Where will that fact take me? No, no! It makes no sense. How could that be?*

Then Rose looked to Philip who sat enjoying Wally's tales. *Philip has always known that I'm not really Jewish because Mother is a Christian. But he accepted me because my father gave me Jewish roots. Now what is he feeling?*

When Wally finished the story, John extended condolences to the Cohens and then excused himself to return to the drugstore.

After seven days of compassionate visitors, more food than they could store in their refrigerator, and all the reminiscing, Françoise and Rose learned how to take death calmly—the Jewish way. Confident that Jerry had left his life in order, they faced the task of hearing the reading of the will without apprehensions. Although Françoise didn't know their financial situation firsthand, she figured she was set for a life with no money worries. Françoise also knew there was a trust fund Jerry had made years ago for Rose. After hearing Jerry's deathbed statement, one would think that Françoise would have some concerns, but she didn't. For some reason, going to hear the will only meant financial facts to Françoise.

She was to be surprised.

A few days after *shivah*, Philip accompanied them as they drove to the probate lawyer's office in downtown St. Louis on Locust Street. As they passed the Jefferson Hotel, Françoise smiled, remembering the antics of tricking Al Capone. Suddenly, with that fleeting memory, she missed Ellie.

At the law offices they went into an elegant meeting room with dark, wood doorframes and wainscoting. They sat down on one side of a huge mahogany table devoid of anything except a portfolio and Tiffany lamp. Philip took a seat next to Rose and her mother. Two lawyers faced them and a secretary sat at the far end.

After introductions, one lawyer handed an envelope to Rose. It wasn't sealed and the lawyer indicated that he had a copy. "I was instructed to give it to you before the reading of the will. There are no surprises in the will. I'm sure you will find the financial aspects to be more than acceptable. You may look at the contents of that envelope now, and I will wait, or you can read it later."

Rose pulled many folded sheets from the envelope and recognized her father's handwriting as she began to read silently:

> Dearest Rose,
>
> I've tried to begin this confession many times. There is no easy or proper way to start. Just remember, you have meant everything to me. You are the child I dreamed of having many years before I met your mother. I love you as much as any man can love his child. You have been the sister I lost, and the child I always wanted. If you are reading this, I am gone. I didn't tell you while I lived because I'm a coward. I feared you would love me less. Please do not love your mother less.
>
> I have a couple of stories to tell you: one goes back to Germany when I was a child, and the second happened here in St. Louis on a stormy night in May 1931.

The first page ended. Rose stopped and, looking up and out the window where she saw some pigeons flying, she couldn't keep her mind from soaring like the birds, in anticipation of the unknown. Leaning over, Françoise had been reading the papers in Rose's lap. Rose solemnly faced her mother; both knew what was coming. As Rose shifted in her chair, the bottom paper that was smaller than the rest, fell to the floor. Philip leaned over and picked up a Certified Certificate of Birth. Before handing it to Rose, he read that Rose Bartlett Cohen was the child of Elizabeth Mary Bartlett and John W. Bartlett. His eyes showed surprise and fear as he handed the document to Rose.

Françoise saw it. "No, that's not possible," she bellowed. The loud comment surprised her and everyone in the room. She spoke softer, though still agitated, "I mean … I have a different birth certificate and it's the real one."

One of the lawyers tried to sooth the situation, "You have seen the last page without reading the three in between. I know it's lengthy, but you need to read everything completely to understand."

Françoise was completely flustered, "No, this can't be happening."

Again the lawyer spoke, "Allow me to summarize these papers. So you can read later in private. Mr. Cohen tells the story of his little ten-year-old sister dying in Germany when his science experiment exploded; her name was Rose Cohen. He explains that he shared this story with the Bartletts one evening. His second story is about the night Elizabeth Mary Bartlett gave birth to twins."

Rose let out a gasp, but the lawyer held up his hand to quiet her and continued, "Dr. Cohen was the attending physician to that double birth. When the second child was born, a surprise to even the mother, the child was given to Dr. and Mrs. Cohen. The only conditions the mother made were that the child was to be named Rose Cohen and the gift was to be kept a secret. The mother did it as a gesture to replace the sister who had died, and also because the Cohens couldn't have a child of their own."

Now Françoise was on her feet and screamed, "No! No one has the right to hear my confidential and personal matters. Stop all this. Rose, don't listen to this. You never should have heard any of this. I …" Françoise hesitated and then turned, fleeing the room.

Rose dropped all the papers on the table and said, “I need to go to her. I’ll be back.”

Quickly Philip stood and followed Rose out of the room. Just outside the door, he grabbed her elbow and said, “Rose, I can’t go on with our …” He clenched his teeth and blurted, “I find all of this to be so …” Again his sentence was unfinished, but Rose knew he was permanently walking out of her life as he handed her the car keys.

Rose found Françoise composing herself in the ladies room, patting her reddened face with a cool wet handkerchief. They returned to the lawyer’s office and explained they only wanted to hear the Last Will and Testament. In less than thirty minutes the reading was finished. Rose knew that Françoise felt disgraced. The former mayor and his wife had heard their secret. Now this law firm and its lawyers knew.

Françoise sat straight and silent on the drive home.

At home and alone, Rose read the papers through twice. Jerry had explained:

> Just a few days after the Bartlett twins had been born, I had second thoughts. The fictitious single birth I had reported to Florida bothered me because the truth of heritage is sacred. Weeks passed while I considered what to do and in that time Françoise received the Certificate of Birth from Florida that had been requested. But without telling her, I filled out a form for Florida, saying that child had died. Then I filed Ellie’s twin births in Missouri and, in secret I had held the copy of that Certificate of Multiple Births for all these years. Now you will have your real birth certificate.

Finally, Rose read the two beautiful stories: one tragic, of how Jerry loved his sister and the other, about the depth of a friendship between two women who loved each other enough to share a child.

What happened to that love between my mother and Aunt Ellie? Oh, how confusing! Ellie is my real mother. It will be simpler to call each of my parents by their first name. I hope my mother … I mean Franny, will understand.

Sitting quietly in her bedroom in her mother's apartment, Rose shook her head and thought about Philip. In her eyes, Philip's behavior was logical and at least he had been honest with her. Though abrupt, he had been completely honest. *It would have been much worse if we continued with the wedding plans and ...* Rose looked at her engagement ring. *I must call Philip and let him know I understand. What a fiasco for him to sit through everything at the lawyers' office. I must return the ring.*

Rose packed up a few things and wrote a note to Françoise:

> I want some time alone, so much has happened.
> If you need me, I'm at my apartment. Please come by if you want to talk.
> Love, Rose

As Rose walked to her new apartment, she didn't feel sad or angry. *How can three pages change who I am? Suddenly I'm someone else. My mother is not my mother. With the death of one father, another is given to me. I lost a future marriage to a Jewish man, but have been given the opportunity to learn about my real heritage. It's amazing.*

The course of her life had spun another direction, leaving her with a multitude of baffling questions about herself and, unexpectedly, giving her an inner strength. That strength only furthered her desire to learn all there was to know about the entangled bond between the Bartletts and the Cohens.

Chapter 19

1959
Revealing Their Secrets

Newspapers came rolling off the presses day after day, and the Bartletts still had a *Post-Dispatch* pitched onto their lawn every morning, but none of those newspapers had been read by Ellie for over a decade. With each passing year, all the news that she no longer cut for her scrapbooks was stacked in the garage to wait for the annual Boy Scouts paper drive.

Did Ellie hear about the McCarthy Hearings? If she knew the reasons for the start of the Korean War, there were no bridge club friends to share her ideas. She didn't vote in the election making Eisenhower president in 1953. The Rosenbergs were executed, *Brown v. Board of Education* was decided, polio vaccine was developed, Sputnik went up in space, and the Cuban Revolution exploded without anyone caring whether Ellie had seen any of this news or not. And Ellie's family never thought about the fact that their mother no longer worked on her scrapbook collection.

But Rose will soon notice.

After Jerry's death, Rose decided to move slowly before divulging that she was a Bartlett. She will wait for the right moment. Even so, Rose continued working on Franny relentlessly.

"Franny, I want you to tell me everything about your life with Ellie. I need to understand how she could love you so much that she gave me to you to raise as your own."

Françoise balked at first. But after she started reliving her childhood and laughing at the experiences, she began to enjoy it. As she shared the stories, she realized that this time was bringing her closer to Rose. Most mornings Françoise awoke with another memory to share.

"Rose, this weekend let's go down to Dogtown and walk the streets. I think it will mean so much more if you see where we lived.

Dogtown's just on the other side of Forest Park, so close, but I haven't been there in years. I want to see if the tavern where we danced to Irish music is still there. Oh, and we can stop by Wally's house. He must be eighty or more. He has an interesting workshop where he and your Grandfather James used to work."

It was during the Dogtown trip that Rose realized how fragile Françoise was. The day was extra warm for June, but Françoise seemed exhausted after forty minutes.

"Franny, where can we go to sit and rest?" Rose inquired.

"Why, the Catholic church. See, St. James Parish is down the street. Looks like I'll finally get you into a church with me."

Laughing, Rose asked, "Did you go there as a girl?"

"Of course, I did, but Ellie didn't. They didn't go to any church. And Bertha didn't think much of Catholics."

The smell of incense lingered in the quiet air. Mother Mary holding a too mature looking Jesus peered down on them as they sat in the last pew. A few other people kneeled here and there and one woman walked along the side aisles stopping at the stations to say her rosary. The altar at the other end appeared luxurious, with laced cloth draped over tables that held gold objects gleaming in the light filtering through the stained glass windows. A few people were waiting to enter the dark wooden confessional.

Rose whispered, "Did you go to confession?"

"Of course," smiled Françoise. "It's a sin not to go."

"But you don't go now, do you?"

With hesitancy, Françoise responded, "Well, times have changed. I'm too tired to do everything I should for the church. You know I just go to mass on special holidays."

"Sorry, I didn't mean anything. It's just that I'm realizing how much I don't know about you." Rose blinked her eyes a few times as her brow crunched into a pained expression.

They sat there quietly for a few minutes. What Rose had found awkward to ask in the past, was no longer, "Are you sick?"

"Oh, we just overdid the walking, and I am quite thirsty. Let's see if we can find a place with iced tea."

At the end of the summer, Rose took her questions out to the farm and heard many of the same stories from Ginny. Unlike Françoise, Ginny at sixty-six was agile and energetic. While talking, they walked the fields and dry creek beds for over an hour.

"We never went to see Ellie together like we had planned. Remember? We talked about taking the jewelry box over to her."

Ginny nodded, "Yes, I do remember. With the passing of Jerry, I knew our plans were delayed. I figured you would ask me when you wanted. Any day is fine with me."

They were heading back to Jack and Ginny's little house, working their way up a steep hill and going toward an oak tree that looked over a hundred years old.

"I've decided not to go back to teaching this fall, so any day is fine with me. Just to let you know, I've been to visit Ellie quite a few times since I last saw you."

Ginny picked up a broken branch and put it to her nose to smell the wood. It had many little underdeveloped acorns. "Oh! How does she look?" Ginny began plucking the acorns from the branch and flipping them off to the side.

"About the same. Some days she's more withdrawn. Well, she's never talkative and outgoing. I just mean that some days she's sitting doing nothing when I arrive and doesn't want to say a word to me. But I took her about five notebooks and the nurses say she works with them a lot."

They reached the porch and sat down on the steps, "That sounds wonderful. Is she cutting out newspaper articles and pasting them in the notebooks? Did you know she always made scrapbooks with newspapers?"

Rose shook her head, "No, I didn't know that. Ellie is just putting nonsense into the notebooks. Well, she writes letters of the alphabet, but there are no words and every letter is connected to the others. The nurses say she can sit for hours writing."

They sat quietly and a bluebird flew into the nearest tree. They both looked and smiled. As the bird took to flight, the burnt-orange breast and sparkling blue of the wings flashed in front of them.

Rose was excited, "Do you see bluebirds often?"

"Yes, we do."

After that trip to the farm, Rose decided to stop by the Bartlett house more often. She wanted to see those scrapbooks and learn more about Ellie. One day she arrived at the Bartletts' house to find Becky home alone.

"Hey, I'm not teaching anymore and have had more time to visit Ellie. I want to see if I can get your mother interested in something."

Becky looked confused, "Like what?"

"Ginny said she used to make scrapbooks, so I thought I'd come by to see them. Are they still here?"

Becky's ponytail flipped onto her cheek as she turned to hang Rose's jacket in the closet by the front door. Both girls, though twelve years apart in age, looked like beboppers in their pedal-pusher pants and penny-loafers. They walked under a chandelier and past the wide staircase. Becky led the way into the living room and over to a wall of enclosed bookcases in the far corner.

"We left all of Mom's things where they always were. It doesn't seem like she'll ever come home, but all of her stuff is here. Her clothes stayed in the closets and drawers. Remember when you came to get her jewelry box? It was still in her dresser with her nightgowns. And her scrapbooks still are right here." Opening a door to the bookshelves, Becky commented, "I was little, but I remember Mom working on these things. Just look at how many there are."

Lined up and labeled on the spines were dozens of scrapbooks with titles like:

- Crash of the Twenties
- Eleanor Roosevelt
- Al Capone
- Lindberghs

Rose pulled one from the shelf, "This is amazing. May I just sit and look at them?"

Becky had been working on homework at the dining room table, "Sure, come sit with me at the table or curl up on the sofa." Then Becky remembered, "Oh, I don't think you've met Sara. Come on in the kitchen. Sara rents some rooms for her family just a few houses away. A neighbor told Dad that she's a great cook and could use some extra work. So, Sara cooks an evening meal every day for us."

Entering the kitchen, a tall Amazon of a woman turned from the sink as Becky made the introduction. "Sara, this is Rose Cohen. Her parents are my parents' friends, and I wanted you to meet her."

Sara picked up the end of her apron and wiped the dishwater from her hands. Towering over Rose, with long legs that had her reaching six foot one, Sara smiled, "I'm so pleased to meet you, Rose. Would you like something to drink?"

"Oh, no thank you, ma'm."

They shook hands and exchanged a few words.

Returning to the dining room, Becky said in a soft voice, "Sara makes the best food. She keeps the books for some businesses in the neighborhood and, on her way home, stops here to fix us a meal. Sometimes she brings her little three-year-old boy Mike. He's a great kid. I especially like Sara's sense of humor." Becky pointed at the table where her books and notebooks were scattered. "I have a test tomorrow and must study. Rose, make yourself at home."

Rose started reading on the sofa with the "1925-1930" scrapbook. After thirty minutes, she went back to the shelves, returning that scrapbook and taking "Al Capone." She moved into the dining room where the light was better and slipped off her cardigan sweater before starting to read. Glued on the pages were newspaper articles and various items like a book of matches, a napkin from the Chase Hotel, and photographs. When she saw a photograph of Capone with Ellie, Rose blurted, "Look at this. Had you seen these photographs of your mother with …"

Becky looked up, and Rose stopped herself.

"I forgot you were studying. Can I take a couple of these scrapbooks home with me? I would like to go to visit Ellie to see if she'll talk about them."

"Sure. Hey, can I go with you like we used to? I was busy with school work the last times you asked me to go." Becky grimaced, "I guess I still don't feel good going, so I make excuses. Sorry."

"That's okay, Becky." Rose nodded with understanding, "Ginny and I are planning to go. When I picked up Ellie's jewelry box, I didn't have a chance to take it to her before my dad died. So, that will be great if all three of us are there to give it to her."

***

One Sunday in October, the three women headed to the St. Louis Insane Asylum on Arsenal Street. Rose had a couple of the old scrapbooks, the jewelry box, and three new notebooks. Ginny brought some wildflowers from the farm, and Becky had baked some cookies. Luckily they arrived early in the afternoon, because this trip became the longest visit anyone had ever had with Ellie.

Ellie's face beamed when she saw them, "Hello, girls."

Ginny was shocked; this was a greeting that Ellie might have used years ago. But Ginny remained calm, "Hello, Sis. How are you today?"

"I'm fine. Oh, you have my jewelry box," Ellie said as she shuffled toward them with outstretched hands, "give it to me."

Rose took Ellie by the elbow, "Hello, Ellie. Let's sit at this table. You don't want to spill anything."

Becky pulled out a chair for her mother and then sat next to her, "Hi, Mom."

Not acknowledging Becky, Ellie sat and quickly took the box. She opened it and smiled.

Ginny made a small gasp upon seeing two cracked front teeth. "Ellie, what happened to your teeth?"

"I fell."

With thinning hair, a scar across the bridge of her nose, sunken cheeks and now broken teeth, Ellie looked like an aging character in a Dickens's novel.

Ginny was upset, "But how?"

Ellie was taking things out of the box, "Just fell."

Rose patted Ginny on the arm, "We'll ask the nurse later on." Turning to Ellie, Rose asked, "Are you looking for something special in your jewelry box?"

"No."

"Do you like seeing your things again?"

"There's a loose thread. I pulled it and everything fell apart."

Rose commented, "I don't see any thread."

"It's there," Ellie insisted.

Fifteen-foot ceilings, where fluorescent lights were mounted, made the room too large to have an intimate visit. Everything was white—walls, floors, ceiling, window frames, tables, and chairs. Even the clothes Ellie and the other women patients wore were loose fitting white shifts. Perhaps all the white is what made the black bars so apparent. The black lines of steel on the outside of the six windows were a constant reminder of the severity of Ellie's condition. There was nothing soft, pretty, or comfortable in sight; several tables with chairs filled the room and nothing except more chairs lined the walls. Becky glanced down a hallway and saw open doors leading to small bedrooms.

Rose continued, "Ellie, I brought you three new notebooks, where are your others?"

Ellie didn't seem to hear. She continued to remove objects from the box. She held an earring in her fingers, turned it over, and perused it for quite a while before setting it on the table.

As Ellie reached for the handkerchief that held the broken pearl necklace, Rose moved to get it first, "Ellie, I'll take this out carefully; it has a broken pearl necklace in it."

Nonchalantly, Ellie replied, "I know." She opened the hankie and looked at the pearls, but turned back to continue looking in the box. She pulled out some other costume jewelry, set them aside, picked up her smooth, flat rock from the swim in the Mississippi River, and then saw her wedding rings. Again Ellie smiled. The front teeth were half gone, angling from the top gums to make a gapping square in her smile. It looked horrible.

Ginny got up to find a nurse and Rose said, "Will you ask where her old notebooks are when you ask about her fall?"

But before Ginny walked away, Ellie said, "Here. Rings for Rose. Pearls for Rebecca." She pushed the hankie to Becky and put the rings in front of Rose. Ellie gazed into the almost empty box and reached into it with her fingers to touch the birthday cards at the bottom. Ellie ran her fingers over the front of the card that had a butterfly with sparkles glued to the wings. Suddenly, like a child bored with a new toy, she stood. Before shuffling off toward her room, she frowned and rubbed her hands on her dress to remove the sparkles from her fingertips.

Rose got up to follow. Ellie entered her sparsely furnished room and laid on her bed that was next to a simple, unadorned table and a chair.

Left alone in the big white room, Becky took out the greeting cards. More sparkles fell when she opened the card. The butterfly one was signed "Love from John–1945" and the second card "All my love, John–1946."

Ginny peeked into Ellie's bedroom with a nurse to tell Rose, "They keep the notebooks at the nurses' station. She can have them and a pencil at any time."

The nurse entered to speak with Ellie, "Let's go back out to the table. It's time to visit." She escorted Ellie out with no trouble. "They want to see your notebooks. I brought two, but you can have more. Just let me know."

Again the four women were seated. Becky started putting all the trinkets back into the jewelry box.

"I ripped it apart. It was ruined. Can't mend a rip."

Rose ignored Ellie's comments and opened one of her notebooks, "Oh, Ellie, what have you been writing?"

"Too many loose threads. Can't fix it."

Ginny shook her head, "Ellie, you sound like Mama." Turning to the others, she explained, "Our mother sewed for a living and was always talking about sewing. We got so tired of hearing her. She always was saying little rhymes and things like Ellie just said."

While Ginny spoke, Rose opened one of the other notebooks. It looked like the first. In Ellie's handwriting, she saw lines and lines of the alphabet running together and saying nothing. Slowly, she turned page after page, finding the same. She tried not to show her disappointment. *A manuscript of my mother's life on Arsenal—confusing and meaningless.*

Becky offered a cookie to everyone and Ellie started gobbling one after another.

Rose persisted, "What are you writing, Ellie?" After waiting a bit while Ellie rocked on her chair and chewed, Rose reached into a cloth bag where she had the old scrapbooks. "Were you making scrapbooks like these?" Rose placed them on the table. "Remember your scrapbooks?"

Abruptly, Ellie stopped taking cookies, became wide-eyed and interested. With caution she reached for a scrapbook and scooted it close. She opened the cover. Her hand caressed the first page of newspaper articles. She looked up at Rose, "Thank you. Yes, I made this."

Rose asked, "Want to tell us about it?"

Letting a moment pass, Ellie began, "This one is about ER. That means Eleanor Roosevelt. He was called FDR, so I called her ER." Ellie smiled and continued talking. She talked about the articles, about seeing ER at the airport one day, about women voting, and on and on.

At one point a couple of the nurses came over to watch and listen. They had noticed from afar that Ellie was talking. They stood and listened for quite a while. Before they left, one touched Rose on the shoulder, "We'll let the doctor know about this. She hasn't done this before."

When the three visitors left the asylum that day, they were content. They took the scrapbooks as well as the jewelry box, with them.

"The nurse said we couldn't leave them, but could bring them next time. Ellie really enjoyed them, didn't she? She talked so much."

Ginny seemed pensive.

Rose asked, "Is something wrong, Ginny?"

"I just don't think that you should have my mother's wedding ring. It wasn't right for Ellie to just give it to you. It should go to Becky and stay in the family."

Rose laughed, for more than one reason, "Don't worry. But I am going to take the ring to be cleaned and polished, and I would like to get the pearls strung. Becky, I think the pearls would suit you better if I had a small necklace made instead of the long strand that women used to wear in Ellie's day. What do you think? There'll be a lot left over; I could have a matching bracelet made."

"Okay. I like that idea. I could wear them for my high school graduation in January."

Ginny smiled and patted Rose on the arm, "Thanks for understanding. I didn't mean to be rude to you, Rose."

Through the fall of 1959, the three women visited Ellie often. Ellie seemed to be doing better. Becky was happy to have Rose and Ginny dropping by the Bartlett house frequently. Ginny went there after or before her visits to see Ellie. With friends and family coming to the house again, Becky mentioned to Sara that she'd like to have all her family together at the Bartletts' house for Thanksgiving, if Sara would help with the meal.

Becky told Sara, "Bring your little boy and husband, too." Becky hoped that Ellie would have permission to come home for the holiday, but the doctors refused.

Rose decided that Thanksgiving, with everyone present except Ellie, would be the time to reveal the secret of her birth. "Franny you must come to support me. I plan to take along Daddy's three pages and my birth certificate." Surprisingly, Franny did not complain.

The week before the big day, Wally Duggan died at the age of eighty-one. In Dogtown, they had an Irish wake like the Bartletts had never seen. Before John left, he invited Wally's widow to come to their Thanksgiving.

Becky convinced her brothers to come home for Thanksgiving. Including Sara, twelve people were invited to the Bartletts' home.

A light snow fell the night before Thanksgiving. It was a moist snowfall that stuck even to vertical surfaces like tree trunks and lampposts. Though only about two inches deep on the ground, looking out the window, everything was outlined in white. The scene was delightful.

One never knew from one year to the next if Thanksgiving in St. Louis would be a warm Indian summer day or a brisk cold one. John preferred the latter, especially since he had made some surprise plans for the day. Working with Sara, John wanted Thanksgiving to be something other than the usually sedentary holiday.

Early Thursday morning before the Bartletts awoke, Sara arrived and entered the back door to begin preparing the stuffing, turkey, and pies—pumpkin, apple, and her specialty lemon meringue. Soon John got up and, while Sara worked in the kitchen, he was outside moving large logs and pieces of firewood onto the driveway in preparation for the first of his surprise events.

Sara put boxed cereal out on the dining room table with milk, bananas, and raisins; everyone was to serve themselves breakfast. Sara made a tent sign in the center of the table:

Don't Overeat Breakfast!
Leave Space for Turkey and Pies
At 3:00 p.m.

John came in the back door in his farm clothes—leather army lace-up shoes, blue jeans with suspenders over his red flannel shirt, with a gray sweatshirt underneath peeking out at the collar. "I'm ready for the first event. Is anyone up?"

Sara shook her head, "John, this is a holiday. Why would they want to get up so early? All of them still go to school and relish sleeping in. Besides, they know the turkey won't be done cooking until late afternoon. Its not like Christmas when there are gifts waiting for them." She put two cups of coffee on the kitchen table. They sat down together for a quiet moment.

John chuckled, "When they start smelling the turkey in the oven, they'll get out of bed."

"It'll start smelling really good about noon. So that's when you should plan the first event. Which one is first?"

"The log cutting contest. Just like me, my boys are so used to a chainsaw; today they'll have to cut logs with a two-man saw and split firewood with a maul."

"Why only the boys? I bet Becky will want to join in. You just wait and see."

At noon, John explained the contest, "Over the years, I've tried to make you understand that keeping strong is one of the most important aspects of life. You've helped me work on the farm, building strong muscles, but today we're going to see who's really strong."

John started David, Billy, Johnny, Red, and Becky working on cutting or splitting wood. Becky and Johnny, on one saw, were racing Billy and David to cut through nine inches of hard oak.

Becky complained, "Johnny, my side of the saw keeps getting stuck. Daddy, what are we doing wrong? Oh my gosh! Look at David and Billy go! Daddy come help us."

Johnny shouted from his side of the log, "Becky, just shut-up and work. You're pulling too hard. You gotta have a light touch."

Rose and Françoise arrived. They went inside for coffee. Only Rose came back out to watch. She found the activities hilarious, grinning from ear to ear while she warmed her hands around a cup of coffee.

Soon John was helping Red learn how to split. In a few minutes, it would be a race to see who could split three pieces of firewood the fastest. The wedge kept falling out.

John explained, "You're missing the wedge when you swing the maul. And when you miss, it shakes the wedge out."

Ginny and Jack pulled up in their car. Immediately, Jack went to Becky to help work the two-man saw.

"Hey that's cheating," Billy called.

David said, "Doesn't matter. One more pull and we win, Billy." Their log fell into two pieces and they jumped up and down like twelve-year-olds.

Becky went to greet Rose, "I haven't seen Daddy this happy for years. Well, you know, not since Mom started drinking. Well, none of us have had this much fun together for years."

Johnny grabbed some snow and balled it up, hitting David in the chest. Soon a snowball fight progressed into the front yard. Rose sat her coffee on a windowsill and ran off with the rest of them, scoring a direct hit on Johnny's back.

Ginny laughed, "John, I'm having déjà vu. Didn't we do this with your kids about ten years ago?"

John laughed, "They sure don't look their age, do they?"

Soon they were back to continue the contest. Johnny asked about the prize, "Dad, did you say we win twenty dollars on each event?"

"That's right. David and Billy won ten dollars each. I'll pay in the house when we finish."

Johnny grabbed a maul and wedge, "I'm ready. There are five mauls. Grab yours. Dad you gotta say one-two-three-go or something."

Suddenly, everyone quieted and John chanted, "One for the money, two for the show, three to get ready and four to GO!"

Johnny finished before Becky or Red had one split.

"Hey, I won twenty dollars all by myself." Johnny shouted. "What's next?"

John explained, “I’m going to separate all of you into two teams and give you a rope. We’ll go to the front yard and all you have to do to win is pull the other team across the sidewalk that leads to the front door.”

Johnny complained, “But we’ll have to split twenty dollars between four people.”

“We’ll ruin the grass, Dad,” David cautioned.

“Don’t you worry. I’ll seed it in the spring.”

Rose had left Françoise sitting in the kitchen with Sara, who she had just met for the first time. Françoise sat erect in her elegant way with her manicured hands resting on the table and displaying a two carat diamond ring; as usual she wore expensive clothes perfectly matched, a mauve sweater with a deep purple skirt, and her blond hair, with wisps of white, was braided and pinned on top of her head in the fashion of a crown. At sixty-two, Françoise’s slight frame looked as fragile as a glass statuette, but very attractive.

Sara, twenty years younger, was a contrast of jet-black hair hanging loose around her robust shoulders; her ample bosom strained against the cotton paisley dress she wore beneath a flowery apron. Sara worked, rolling out dough for the third pie; her hands were chapped red and adorned with only a simple thin gold wedding ring. Her dark eyes sparkled with life; she laughed as she talked. They were chatting about the Bartlett family, watching the fun and games out the kitchen window. When the apple pie went into the oven, they moved to the living room to see the rope-pulling contest. Jack, David, Becky, and Red were against Ginny, Johnny, Rose, and Billy. Sara squealed at the sight, and Françoise smiled with deep sadness in her eyes.

Wally’s widow arrived just as Ginny and Rose lost their grip on the rope, slipping down to the snow and icy grass. The other team pulled Johnny and Billy over easily.

“Why’d you girls let go? You made us lose.”

“Johnny, it’s just a game!” John emphasized.

Sara came out the front door with two trays held shoulder high, like a waiter from a fancy restaurant might do. Her height made for an imposing figure of a woman, and her dark laughing eyes made you like her in an instant, but the beautiful legs that extended out from her dress—with perfect ankles and calves—caught one’s gaze as the wind lifted her skirt just enough to see firm thighs; she had legs that could win beauty contests. And Sara knew that. She called out, "All right. Are you ready for the final contest of the day?"

Cheers came from everyone.

Sara continued balancing the trays over her head. "I have six meringue pies. Only meringue. They're pies for throwing."

The shouting and laughing began.

"Quiet, quiet. Here's how you play. I give a pie to all the Bartlett kids. There's one extra; who else wants to play?"

Jack and Rose both shouted.

"John, flip a coin between those two. Here's what you do. One at a time I give a pie out. That person picks someone to throw the pie at. You stand ten feet apart. John, do you have that tape measure? You throw your pie, trying for the face. If you get a hit, even a part of the face, you win. Then I'll go to the next person who chooses whoever they want to throw a pie at. You understand?"

"Yeah, yeah. This sounds like fun."

Ginny took pity on Wally's widow, standing lost among the playful youth, and escorted her into the house to where Françoise stood watching out the window. Ginny laughed, "I guess there's a child in all of us. John and Sara made up all these games. They said it was something to do while the turkey cooked." Ginny hung Mrs. Duggan's coat in the closet and showed the aging, hunched woman to a chair. "This is Françoise. Oh, that's right, you know each other from Dogtown." Ginny looked at her watch, "Oh, it's almost two, and Sara is busy; I think I'll look at how the bird is cooking."

Françoise smiled. "Hello, Mrs. Duggan. I was so sorry to hear about Wally. It has been many years since we've talked. Do you remember me? I'm Franny."

They chatted.

Soon the group traipsed back into the house. Wet from the snow and covered in mud and meringue, they proceeded upstairs to wash and change clothes.

Sara commented to Françoise and Rose as they began putting the food on the table, "I've never had such fun on Thanksgiving. Hope you enjoyed all the antics."

Françoise smiled without comment.

Rose glowed, “I never expected a day like this. I’m so glad it snowed. That made it better. And look at all this food.” Rose noticed how quiet her mother was. *She’s nervous in anticipation of telling everyone about my birth. So am I.*

Three separate times Johnny refilled his plate, while at the same time, bragging that he won the most money. “Twenty dollars for the wood splitting and twenty more for a direct hit into Billy’s ugly face with the pie.”

The younger Bartletts bantered back and forth through the meal. Sara had wisely sat all of them at one end and the older people together at the other end. Françoise and Mrs. Duggan nibbled their food and chatted politely.

Just before the pie and ice cream were to be served, Mrs. Duggan took her knife and tapped on her half-full glass of apple cider. Everyone became quiet and turned to her.

“Oh, it worked. I hoped it would get everyone’s attention. I want to thank you for inviting me to this special Thanksgiving. I must go before the dessert. With my diabetes, I can’t eat it, and I know you wouldn’t want me to suffer.”

Everyone laughed at her little joke.

Mrs. Duggan continued, “Before I go I want to get some letters out of my purse. Oh, where did I leave my purse?”

Ginny brought it to her.

“These are letters that were in Wally’s shop, but they’re addressed to Ellie, so I thought I would return them to the family.” She pulled out a packet of letters, held together with two rubber bands. She handed them to John. “Again I want to thank you for a wonderful Thanksgiving, but I must go.”

John helped her with her coat and escorted her to her car. When he returned to the table, Ginny was looking at one of the letters. She was furious.

“Look at this! Letters from my father to Ellie! It looks like a letter arrived on her birthday every year while he was gone.” Ginny stood. “He wrote to Ellie, but not to me. And Ellie never told me. Secrets. Deceiving secrets. I am so sick of Ellie and her secrets.”

Jack came around the table to be with Ginny. John picked up the letters and looked at the postmarks. The silence in the room screamed. Finally, John said, "This happened so long ago and …"

Ginny shouted, "I don't care when it happened. I am so sick and tired of secrets. Ellie is, and always was, the Queen of Secrets. My father used to be so proud of how she could keep secrets. They made me feel …" Ginny sank into her chair crying. Jack pulled his chair next to hers.

Rose stood and addressed everyone, "All of us have secrets. Even the younger Bartletts. Rose looked directly at Johnny and Billy. Isn't that so? You've done things that you don't want to tell your father or have any of us to know. Ginny, its just human nature."

"No, I don't have secrets," Ginny spat out.

Rose held firm, "Are you sure?" Eyes widened at Rose's brusque retort to Ginny. But Rose went on accusing as she turned to point to John. "And he does and Jack does. We all do. Actually, Ginny, I found out one of your secrets. Something that happened to you before most of us were born; when you were about Johnny's age."

Ginny looked up with a somber face.

Rose went on talking, "If you don't want to admit to your secret, I'll tell one. You know Bertha's wedding ring that she gave to Ellie?" Rose swallowed, "It's not a diamond, only glass. I took it to the jeweler to be cleaned and to have the setting checked. He told me. Grandpa James gave Bertha a glass ring."

Ginny's face was aghast. "Maybe Daddy didn't know it was glass."

The room went quiet.

Suddenly, Jack spoke up, "I have a secret that Ginny doesn't even know." He sat up straighter and looked directly at Ginny. "In fact, I made up a lie to hide my secret. I gotta keep talking or I won't be able to tell it and it's been eating at my gut." Jack took a deep breath, "I never went to Europe in the war. I had a desk job here in the states."

Ginny's hand went to her mouth, "But your eye! You lost it fighting."

"No, I got drunk one night here in the states with some army buddies. I drove into the side of a bridge, smashing up the car and lost my eye. Luckily none of my buddies were hurt."

Suddenly everyone went quiet again and Rose blurted, "Françoise and I have a secret to tell."

Ginny interrupted in a loud voice, "No, I want to tell my secret." All eyes turned to her; she took a deep breath and pursed her lips before saying, "I was married before Jack and then divorced. I was so ashamed that I never wanted to tell anyone. Jack, I'm sorry I didn't tell you."

Jack and Ginny looked distraught as they hugged and whispered to each other.

Rose had draped her purse over the back of her chair before they sat to eat. She reached into her purse and removed the three pages from her father. Rose tapped on her glass to get everyone's attention, "John, these papers tell a secret. Françoise and I aren't sure if you know or not, but it has meaning to all of us." Rose turned and looked to everyone around the table. "All of these secrets we've heard tonight are pebbles thrown at us compared to this one; it's a boulder. It will knock you over."

With that said, faces around the table turned to watch Rose walk to John and hand the papers to him.

A clock could be heard ticking somewhere in the house.

Silently John read the birth certificate for a twin baby girl named Elizabeth Rose Bartlett and Rose Cohen Bartlett whose parents were John and Elizabeth Bartlett. As he looked up to Rose, his eyes had a wild look; he rubbed a hand across his forehead and insisted in disbelief "No! No, it can't be." With desperation on his face, John looked to Françoise. "Is this saying that Ellie gave one of her twin babies to you?"

Puzzled eyes appeared around the table.

Françoise nodded, "I'm sorry, but it's true, John."

Rose suggested, "Please read all the papers aloud. You need to read everything on those pages, so everyone can understand."

Dessert was postponed for hours.

Chapter 20

1960-1971
Life Goes On

Anyone at the fateful Thanksgiving dinner who had taken the time to think about all the antics and unusual incidents in Ellie's life, who had listened to her argue about politics or the misuse of power, had watched her get what she wanted from a mobster or a group of wild children, had observed her amid the search for her lost little girl and deaths of loved ones, would recognize that she had the capability to give away a child. Nevertheless, the idea had taken their breath away. In fact, each member of Ellie's family looked differently at the whole charade she had been living for twenty-nine years. The false pretenses irritated most of them for their own particular reasons. And, as the months passed, everyone came to terms with the flow of their feelings; like water that seeks its own level, each person's opinion found a different level of understanding.

David, Ellie's oldest, was disgusted with his mother. He had a scientific mind and was finishing his medical studies, specializing in radiology. Ellie had always been an enigma to him. David's life centered on seeking the truth, not hiding it. This wasn't the first time he found her actions unforgiving. "She's unscrupulous with the lives of others. I was twenty before I knew about the death of my baby sister Elizabeth. Now I'm thirty and learn that my dead baby sister was a twin. It's obvious to me why Mother is in an insane asylum. She's nuts. The only consolation to this whole discovery is that I have a new sister, someone I've loved like a sister all my life."

Ginny was bruised in her heart and soul. She had had to put up with Ellie's secrets all her life, but they never were so personal as this one. Ginny couldn't have children of her own, and Ellie knew that, yet Ellie gave a child to Franny. This cut deeply into the love Ginny had for her sister, "No, Jack," Ginny confided, "I no longer have any love for Ellie. In fact, I question if she has ever had any love for me. I can't think of anything she has done for me. She had everything and threw it away; I have had to struggle for so much. I thank the heavens I met you, Jack. You have given me such peace and love."

Billy was angry. As a mathematician, he couldn't make sense of Ellie's mind. "If she had any logic, it escapes me." As smart as she was, he could never understand how she didn't see that he had been a gentle child who needed hugs and attention. Ellie was never demonstrative with her children, but Billy was so special. John was very proud of Billy and had shown it, but Billy needed his mother's love, and he didn't get enough. She was already drinking when he was ten or twelve. His anger would not go away. As Billy saw it, she chose to savor wine instead of her children. And now, he could see how little her children meant to her. "What kind of mother can give a child away?"

Upon learning that Rose was their sister, nothing but happiness came from Becky and Red. Becky had jumped with joy, "I have a sister like I always wanted. And an older sister! I always wished that Mom would have a baby girl so I would have a sister. Never did I dream I would get an older sister."

Red couldn't hug Rose enough. "All my life I looked to you like an older sister anyway. You always went everywhere with us, so I pretended you were my big sis. It's amazing that it's true." The two of them didn't try to resolve how or why Ellie gave away a child; they simply accepted that they had a new sister.

John said nothing against Ellie; he only showed love to Rose. "You missed the opportunity of working at the drugstore like all my other children. Rose, you must come down and spend time there. It's a good experience."

"Yeah, if she can dodge the bullets from the holdup guys," Johnny jested. "She doesn't need that kind of experience, Dad. She's almost thirty and wants to find a man and start her own family." Johnny had talked with Rose and was aware that Philip had left her. Johnny's sensitivity had drawn him to Rose. They spent many hours talking and found that their minds worked similarly. They liked the same books and movies. They liked sitting outside watching nature or people. They shared their deepest thoughts, and they never had anyone with whom they could do that before.

Rose confided to Johnny, "I don't know how to talk to Ellie about giving me away. Besides, it's not the time with her in the asylum."

A few months later, as spring arrived with new budding leaves, Françoise told Rose she needed to talk, "Maybe you don't see it like this, but I've been hurt the deepest. All the others gained a daughter, sister, or niece. I had just lost your father and now I've lost my place as your mother." Françoise was pleading, "I can't imagine how difficult it was for you. But, you know, I'm your mother as much as Ellie is. In different ways, we're both your mother."

Rose took her hand, "I know. There's no erasing all our years as mother and daughter. I cherish those years."

Françoise seemed relieved to hear that, "But our life is different now. I feel so lost."

Rose hugged her, "Oh, Mommy, I'm sorry. I knew it was hard for you."

"No, Rose. I am talking about something else." Françoise hesitated and gave a little smile, "Remember, on Thanksgiving, when everyone was telling their secrets and clearing their consciences?"

Rose nodded and stroked her mother's hand.

"I wanted to shout, 'I have a secret,' but I didn't. It wasn't the right time." Françoise blew her nose before saying, "I have cancer and very little time left to live."

"No, Mommy. No!" Rose protested.

"I wish I could have died with Jerry. That would've been such good timing, wouldn't it?"

"Oh, Mommy, don't talk like that. It's not right to say that."

"I knew about the cancer, but didn't tell Jerry. What would it have accomplished, him dying and concerned about me? But it would have been so romantic to die with him." Françoise shrugged her shoulders, "I don't know what's right, but I would have avoided all this embarrassment about your birth."

Soon Françoise was gone, and Rose undertook another burial.

Everyone was gracious at the funeral, though full of clichés:

"They say older couples usually follow the other quickly."

"She lived a full and wonderful life."

Someone was gauche enough to tell Rose, "Statistics say that a woman has a life span of just about Franny's age. She timed it just right."

But to Rose, the most insulting statements were the references to the state of her finances when people said things like, "At least your parents didn't leave you with financial burdens."

Just before the hearse was to take Françoise to the cemetery, Rose walked over to Johnny Bartlett and whispered, "This can't end too soon. I'm so tired of people's condescending remarks."

"Don't be so hard on them. They mean no harm."

"Yes, I know. But I prefer a squeeze to my hand or a hug. When Dad came in with Sara, I walked over to greet them and she just wrapped her arms around me. That was such a comfort." Rose looked directly at Johnny with a new thought. "Oh, by the way, when she hugged me I noticed that she's pregnant. Did you know?"

"I thought so. She's not too big yet."

Rose asked, "Do you know her husband? When she was making dinner at your house one day, she told me he's disabled and can't work."

"I've seen him. Why?"

"Oh, just curious. But it's interesting; everyone has problems to bear."

***

A few weeks after Françoise died, Rose realized she had the right as Ellie's daughter to talk directly with her doctors. She mentioned this to Johnny and Becky, "From one visit to the next, Ellie can be so different. I wonder if her medications are causing the changes. What do they give her?" None of Ellie's children knew what the doctors were prescribing or doing with Ellie.

Probably John knows.

When Rose talked to John, he explained that the medications changed so often that he stopped asking. "Rose, there's no cure for alcoholism or schizophrenia, but the doctors are trying new methods and medications all the time."

Rose was appalled, "They're experimenting with her?"

"Ellie is a ward of the state."

Rose decided it would be best to talk with the doctors.

The next day, when Rose arrived in Ellie's wing, the nurses told her that Ellie was having a bad day and was in her room, "It's not a good day to visit her."

"I'll stay only a few minutes. I haven't seen her for three weeks and want her to know I came today." Rose still had not broached the subject that they were mother and daughter, but Rose did want Ellie to know that Franny had died.

Rose pulled up the chair next to Ellie's bed and took her hand. Ellie opened her eyes and pulled her hand away. Rose spoke quietly, "It's just me. You know, Rose Cohen. I can't stay long, but I wanted to know how you are."

Ellie made no comment, but her eyes smiled.

"I did bring you two more notebooks and gave them to the nurses."

The gapping hole appeared as Ellie smiled and pulled the covers closer to her chin.

"I haven't been here in a while because my mother, you know Franny, was very sick. I want you to know that she died last month."

Ellie raised up on her elbow. Her eyes went wide.

"She had cancer, but didn't suffer too much. We talked a little about you, but I have no message."

Ellie spoke, "That's okay." Ellie slowly slipped back down onto the bed, resting on her side, facing Rose.

"Did I upset you, telling you?"

"No."

They sat in silence for a while until Rose asked, "Can I bring you anything on my next visit? You know, one of your scrapbooks or the jewelry box?"

Ellie hesitated, then said, "I'll think." Another brief moment later, Ellie told Rose, "You can go now."

Rose left and asked one of the nurses if she could speak with Ellie's doctor after showing the nurse her birth certificate to verify she was Ellie's daughter. The nurse made a phone call and escorted Ellie down to the doctor's office on the first floor.

After introductions, Rose asked, "My mother broke her teeth recently. Are there plans to have caps put on?"

"Oh, we have no funds for cosmetic dentistry."

"If there's no possibility to do anything here, I'd be more than happy to make an appointment with my dentist to have it done. Are there any problems with me taking her out of the hospital?"

"I think not. We'd medicate her heavily on the day before the appointment."

Rose was aghast, "What? Why?"

The doctor opened a folder, "On several occasions when she went home to visit, she became very agitated. It would be best to have her manageable when you leave with her." [5]

"Actually, I was going to ask you to reduce her medications. What is she taking now?"

Scanning the chart in the folder, he said, "We have Mrs. Bartlett on two kinds of antidepressants, a blood thinner, medication called chlorpromazine for calming schizophrenia, and some liver medicine."

"Why is she on liver medication?"

He explained, "She had been drinking heavily before she came to us and her liver was near failure."

Rose inquired, "Ellie's been here for about five years. Can't her liver recover with time?"

"Hmmm, it seems there have not been any new liver tests since she came. How could that be?"

"Doctor, she is so much better than just a year ago. I'd like to see her without the antidepressant drugs. Is it possible? And, by the way, is she on any special treatments? I heard she had electric shock therapy."

"She no longer has any special treatments. The ice baths stopped a few months after she was admitted, and we tried insulin shots a while back. Now she seems stable. I'll discuss your request with our staff, but you understand that it's our decision. She used to get terribly upset when she left the hospital. I see notes that we had to medicate her more after she went home for a holiday. So we stopped letting her out for visits. This short trip to the dentist will help us see if she is better."

Rose frowned, "You didn't really say, did she have shock treatments?"

He nodded, "But that was long ago."

"Of course." Rose sat quietly for a moment, "I just want what's best for my mother, like you do. Maybe each of her medicines could be reconsidered. If she no longer needs some of them, it would be best for her to stop them and save the hospital money. Am I correct?"

"Yes, you are. Let's talk again a week from today."

Rose stood and shook his hand, "Thank you for your time and concern. In the meantime, I'll make a dental appointment and let you know about it next week."

When Rose returned to see the doctor and visit Ellie, they had already reduced the medications. Rose noticed the difference immediately.

Ellie was speaking in longer sentences, "Rose, you asked what you could bring me. Do you have a typewriter? You know, a small one I could use?"

Rose smiled, "Yes, I do. It's a little portable Remington. It's nice. I didn't know you could type."

"Oh, you just forgot. Remember I worked for the *Post-Dispatch* newspaper where I typed all day. I used to be fast."

"What're you going to write?"

This time Ellie raised her eyebrows with a twinkle in her eye, "You're going to have to wait and see."

***

The dental visits went on for months. One day, Becky asked," Why is it taking so long to fix her teeth?

Rose let her know, "I think he's almost done. Mom has caps on her front teeth now. Come with me next time. I'd like you to meet the dentist. He's really good."

After accompanying Rose and Ellie, the reason became apparent. The dentist working on Ellie turned out to be the son of Rose's regular dentist, and he had eyes for Rose. By the time Ellie's teeth were cleaned, old fillings replaced and new caps put on the broken front teeth, Rose and the dentist were seriously in love.

A person in love can exude happiness that spreads to others. Within the year, all the hard times and emotional stress that the Bartletts had borne for a dozen years were fading into the past.

Life was good.

Rose was engaged and planned to use the family wedding ring that had been Ellie's and Grandma Bertha's. Of course, Rose had the ring reset with a diamond; she dropped the old glass setting into Ellie's jewelry box with the rabbit's foot, two birthday cards, and other items from the past.

Ellie too was content. Whenever Rose went to visit, she was typing. Much to the surprise of everyone, Ellie had coded all her notebooks by just writing words backwards and running all the letters together. She had written from the right to the left, so no one would see what she had been writing. Ellie propped a notebook, written months ago, on the table in front of her as she translated all the unreadable encryption into words. When she typed:

The Civil Rights Act of 1957,

in the notebook it looked like: 7591fotcasthgirlivicehT.

She had fooled everyone into thinking she was writing nonsense. Of course, Ellie never explained why she had done it. Nevertheless, now that she was talking more and working on the typewriter, the hospital staff decided that Ellie was well enough to be moved from the State Insane Asylum to a small cottage, a halfway house.

In the cottage there were a half dozen other women and three staff members to work with them. Ellie passed her time watching television, reading the newspaper, typing, helping with the housework, and walking with a staff member to the store or park. For the most part, her only visitors were Rose and Becky. Ginny was still mad about the secret letters her father had sent to Ellie, so she and Jack didn't visit.

One afternoon while Rose sat with Ellie on a bench in the park near the cottage, Ellie said, "I don't want more visitors. I like how things are now."

Rose insisted, "Don't you want to talk to your family? You never ask about anyone. Aren't you curious about them?"

"No."

"What if the doctors said you could go home. You know, leave the cottage because you were well enough to go home. Wouldn't it be nice?"

"No."

Rose was puzzled, "Why?"

"With Sara there?"

Rose sat quietly for a moment, "How do you know about Sara?"

"She was there for one of my trips home for a holiday. It was my last trip home."

"Are you afraid that John will divorce you?"

"No."

Rose didn't understand this, but decided to change the subject. "Earlier, I invited you to my wedding. I really want you to come to my wedding. Won't you change your mind?"

"No."

Rose stood and put her hands to her hips. "Ellie, you're so stubborn. I don't understand you. In fact, at this moment, you are making me so mad."

"I am?"

"Yes, and I think you're well enough to hear me out. I want to say a couple of things to you. I want to know why you started all this drinking? What happened to you? And don't give me the 'I'm an alcoholic' excuse; you aren't one and never were."

"Are you an expert on alcoholics?"

"Don't avoid my question. Please explain to me what happened."

Now Ellie stood, "Rose, Rose, what started all this?"

Standing face-to-face, Rose thought it was time to say it, "I know you're my mother. Jerry told me before he died. He told me about the night of my birth. I know everything."

"I know you know, Rose."

Stammering, Rose was startled with Ellie's comment, "How?"

"Years ago, Jerry told me he was going to tell you someday." Ellie raised her arm in a gesture, "Besides, look at you. You have more interest in me than any of my other children. So, I knew he'd told you before he died. Did you tell the rest of the family?"

"Yes, everyone knows. If you knew I knew, why didn't you say something to me?"

Ellie turned, "Please, let's walk. I get stiff and need to walk." They strolled down the walkway, "Why would I be the first to say anything? You had to be ready to talk. Or I should say that you had to be ready to confront me."

They were approaching a pond with lily pads in bloom. As they left the path and began to circle the pond, Rose not only realized how astute Ellie was in pinning down the essence of the coming conversation, but also she realized that Ellie was mentally whole again. And Rose was ready to ask acrimonious questions, "As long as you brought it up, may I ask if you ever regretted giving me away?"

"Let's stop and appreciate the lilies for a while, and then I'll answer you." Ellie took her hand as they looked to the pond in silence. In almost a whisper, Ellie began, "I never felt ownership of my children. I gave birth to you, I named you, but I didn't own you. I knew I was not putting you into a harmful situation, quite the opposite. As a mother, I shared my life with my children, even you much of the time, but children have their own lives. I strongly believe that at birth, a child is already who he or she is going to be. Of course, I mean if there is no horrible abuse or disasters. I could see the different personalities in each of my children, long before they were grown. I knew you would be who you are today, whether raised by Franny and Jerry or by me." Ellie waited while some little children ran by with wooden boats in their hands. "You called someone else by the name of mother, but I was in your life. So, you can see that I don't feel I gave you away. You're not like a piece of land or a house that is owned. No one can change the truth of who his or her natural mother is. What happened was that you filled the life of Jerry and Franny with a joy they never would have had. You did that. Not me. Do you regret that?"

Rose shook her head and said, "No, not ever."

Ellie started walking again, "If you had been in my shoes, could you have placed one of your children into the arms of loving people, like I did?"

"Before this day, I would have said I couldn't. But now I don't know. Since my father died, I've learned so much about you and Franny's life together, so maybe I could, but I don't know if I would have been generous enough to even think to do it."

Having circled the pond, they came back to the pathway.

Ellie said, "Well, we're back where we started; we made a circle, literally and figuratively. Have we talked enough about this or do you have more questions?"

Tears rolled down Rose's face, "How can you be so nonchalant?" Rose leaned her face to Ellie in frustration and pleaded, "You're my mother. We're talking for the first time in my life as a mother and daughter. Don't you feel emotion? I do! I want to shake you; I want to bang my fists on your chest; no, I want to hug you."

"Then hug me, but carefully. I ache here and there."

And as Rose embraced her mother she realized that Ellie had cleverly avoided the question of why she had started drinking.

***

Years passed with Ellie in the cottage. Life went on. Rose had one child in the first year of her marriage, and a second child followed soon after. Her brothers and Becky married, one by one moving out of their childhood home. Sara's husband died, and she and John no longer tried to conceal that she was more than just a cook in the Bartlett home.

Soon grandchildren were old enough to go to the farm with their Grandpa John. In the summer months, Sara always went and could be seen in her shorts across the fields with her long, beautiful legs.

Yes, life went on.

One cold, winter night in the early hours of the morning, the phone rang in Rose's apartment; she lived with her husband and two children in the Cohen's spacious apartment where she grew up. She rented out her little one-bedroom apartment her father had given her. Before she lifted the receiver she knew no good news could be coming at this hour. Her husband leaned on his elbow to hear the problem.

It was John calling, "Rose, sorry to wake you, but I knew you'd want to know that Ellie was rushed to the hospital. She fell and broke her hip. She's still in surgery and will be for a couple more hours."

"Oh my! Will she be all right?"

"Oh, I think so. The doctors are putting in a hip replacement. Listen, I've been here for hours and need some sleep. Could you relieve me? I think someone from the family should be here."

"Oh, of course. I'll come as soon as I dress."

John sighed, "Thanks, I'll wait for you so we can talk for a while."

Rose explained to her husband what had happened and rushed from their apartment.

Driving over icy roads, Rose surmised that Ellie had more than likely slipped on ice.

"Yes," John confirmed her assumption, "Ellie left the cottage and slipped on the only two steps that exist there. Only two steps down and she broke her hipbone. Obviously her bones are brittle. She must have osteoporosis like older people do. Ha, look at me talk."

Rose added, "But you're fit. Ellie has done nothing for years. You exercise so much at the farm; that makes for stronger bones, doesn't it?"

"Yes, but I'm sure her years of drinking added to the problem. By the way, hope I didn't wake your whole family with my call."

"No, no, the children sleep through most noises. How is everyone at your house?"

"Oh, thanks for asking. I guess you know that Sara and her two boys live with me now. We're all fine."

Rose had known that. "Becky told me a while ago when she stopped over to visit. I think that's good for you and Sara to have each other."

"Thanks," John started putting on his coat and scarf.

Rose blurted without any previous thought, "Why don't you divorce Ellie so you can marry Sara?"

Wrath contorted John's face. John raised his voice in anger, "What are you saying? Divorce my wife? What do you take me for? Ellie's your mother. How could you even think that? I married Ellie 'til death do us part. She knows that I would never go back on a vow. Do you understand what a vow means?"

Suddenly, John was aware that a nurse peeked around the corner into the waiting room. She asked, "Is everything okay? We need to have quiet here."

John raised his hands, "Sorry. We're a bit emotional with my wife being in surgery. Please excuse me." The nurse left, and John turned to Rose.

Rose begged, "Please don't say any more. I spoke without thinking. I can see that you and Sara have a wonderful life and …"

John was calmer, but irritated, "You younger people think of divorce too quickly. People used to divorce for real reasons like physical abuse. Ellie knows and has always known that I am here for her all of her life. If I would be killed driving home, Ellie knows she has money for the rest of her life. If I divorce her, where would she be? Rose don't ever …"

"Please, please stop. I'm so sorry. Please don't be upset with me. I really understand. Like I said, it just came out. I didn't think."

John hugged her; he noticed they stood cheek to cheek. He too regretted his actions. "And please forgive me for my outburst. I can't remember ever doing that before. I think its because I need sleep. Let's forget this ever happened. Okay?" As he pulled away, John gave his daughter a kiss for the first time.

Ellie recovered. She was determined to walk again and left the hospital with a cane. The doctors were reluctant to send her back to the cottage where she might fall again. Seeing an opportunity to be closer to her mother, Rose offered her little apartment.

"The lease ended for the renters I had. It's perfect for Ellie. There's an elevator to take her to the third floor and a doorman twenty-four hours a day. He could help her in any way, like calling a cab, carrying groceries, or whatever she needs. And I live just three blocks away. I'll go to visit frequently, if not daily." And so Ellie was discharged from the care of the State of Missouri. She was considered completely sane.

Living close to Rose, Ellie slipped into her role as a grandmother quite easily; the children were full of questions about everything and she enjoyed answering them. But, whenever Rose asked that one question as to why she started drinking, Ellie ignored her.

One day, Ellie was telling the grandchildren about making their dreams come true, "Wait here while I go take some things from my jewelry box." Ellie returned with the stone from the Mississippi River and the lucky rabbit's foot. She placed them on the table.

"What are these, Gramma?"

"I keep these to remember the dreams my sister and I had when we were young." Ellie picked up the flat, skipping stone. "Your Great Aunt Ginny dreamed of swimming the powerful Mississippi River. I saw this rock on the ground just before she entered the water. It was flat, and I knew it was a perfect skipping stone; and, if thrown just right at the water, I knew it would skip and sail over that river, just like my sister could do. I dreamed that she would sail like this rock across the mighty river. That day she did it and fulfilled her dream." Ellie placed the rock in the hand of one of her grandchildren.

"And I had a dream. Mine was to write articles for a newspaper with my name on them. I wrote a story about the man who owned this lucky rabbit's foot. He was called Al Capone. My dream came true, when I saw E.M. James on my article in the newspaper." With that said, Ellie placed the rabbit's foot into the hand of the other child. "But you can't keep these. Just look at them now. When you finish looking, they go back into my jewelry box."

Rose frowned, "E.M. James. Where have I seen that name recently?"

Ellie walked across the room to retrieve a scrapbook, "Here, look in my latest scrapbook." Rose opened to see article after article of Commentaries, Rebuttals, Letters to the Editor, and Opinions from Readers that Ellie had sent to newspapers, using her maiden name of E.M. James, Elizabeth Mary James.

"These are all from the last few years. Why didn't you tell me?" Rose got excited, "Yes, I remember reading some of these. I didn't know it was you."

Ellie got serious, "Dreams are important. Your children are too young, but you should have a dream. Do you?"

Rose seemed offended. Her two children looked to her. Finally Rose responded, "Yes, I do have a dream. I want to know what happened to you, Ellie. I know I'm right that something happened to make you start to drink."

Ellie started to laugh. Not a little chortle, but a big hearty laugh. The children looked surprised, not understanding. Finally, Ellie quieted, "Rose, you must stop asking me about this. I won't say anything more than this one hint: My story is a mass of tangled threads. In the past and now, you see clues, but you don't notice them.

Look everywhere and don't leave any stone unturned. If you think of a possibility, pursue it, and you'll have your dream."

Rose's heart raced. Rose swallowed. It was the first time Ellie had acknowledged that a reason existed. Rose's eyes gleamed, "Thank you, Mother."

After hearing about their Great Aunt Ginny and her swim, Rose's children wanted to go to the farm to visit Jack and Ginny. Surprisingly, Ellie agreed to go one warm day in May. She hadn't been to the farm in more than a decade and hadn't seen Ginny for over five years.

The station wagon bumped through a muddy puddle as they turned into the dirt drive to Ginny and Jack's place. Before Rose turned off the engine, the screen door slammed and they saw Ginny hurrying down the front steps.

"Oh, it's Ellie," Ginny cried as she rushed to the car and opened the door. Not even letting Ellie get out, Ginny had her arms around her sister. Ginny stood and called, "Jack, Jack, come look who's here."

"Long time no see," Ellie said.

"If I'd known you were coming, I'd a baked a cake," Ginny sang.

Rose's children ran up to Ginny and hugged her, "But, Aunt Ginny, how can we let you know we're coming when you don't have a telephone?"

"I know, Sweetie. Jack and I came to the farm to get away from all those contraptions of city life, but at a time like this it would be good to have one. Don't you worry cuz I have lots of food. That's just a song your Grandma and I used to sing. Let's go in and have some sassafras tea. I just cut the roots and made it this morning."

All through the day, Rose watched the two sisters and wished Franny could be there to join in the laughter and memories.

"Oh, it's almost Ellie's Storm," Ginny exclaimed. She turned to Rose's children to explain. "That's what we call your Grandma's birthday. She was born during the worse tornado to ever pass St. Louis. So, my daddy decided we'd call her birthday Ellie's Storm. I'll get a candle to put on the pie, so she can make a wish."

"Ellie's Storm. No one's said that in years," Ellie said. "Ginny, do you remember that storm?"

"I was only three, but I do. So many strange things happened. I remember a magic carpet floating by," Ginny turned to the children, "without any genie in sight. A bench bobbed through the air like it was on a Ferris wheel without the wheel. But, mostly, I remember the noise and how scared I was."

Rose looked disappointed, "Wish I knew more about it."

Ellie smiled, "That's an easy wish to make come true. Ginny, what's the name of the book about the storm?"

"It's at the downtown St. Louis library. I think it's called *The Great Cyclone*."

Rose told her children, "Let's go get it and find out what happened."

Ginny got excited, "Oh, speaking of downtown. Have any of you been to see the arch that opened last year? What do they call it? Something like the Gateway to the West?"

Ellie's eyes sparkled, "Rose, would you take your children and these two old kids to that arch? Ginny and I missed going on a Ferris wheel ride so many years ago. This would be as good as that, maybe better."

Ginny looked surprised, "Ellie, how do you remember that? Daddy felt so bad that he didn't take us. Of course, it was Mama who wouldn't let him. You're right, I'd like to go up in the arch."

They planned to go. Rose joked, "Do you think they'll let two old women in their seventies get on it?"

Ellie turned to Ginny, "We can't be that old, are we?"

As the time came to leave the farm, Ginny seemed emotional. "This has been a wonderful visit. Ellie, for so many years I stayed mad at you about Daddy's secret letters. I'm sorry."

Ellie looked surprised, "I didn't know you were mad. You must tell me if you're mad at me. Since I didn't know, you sure don't need to apologize."

"Ellie, you're so frustrating. We both need to say we're sorry. You're supposed to apologize to me about keeping that secret."

Rose knew Ellie would never apologize for keeping a secret.

Ellie chose her words carefully as she said, "Ginny, I am sorry that you hurt so much. I never wanted to hurt you."

Anything Rose could learn about her mother was important to her—not only to uncover Ellie's secret, but also because Rose was fascinated by her mother's life. At the library, Rose checked out *The*

Great Cyclone and read it from cover to cover. After she had read it all, Rose picked out special parts to read at her children's bedtime, hoping they wouldn't have nightmares. Since it was full of photographs, the children enjoyed the book.

It was during the nighttime readings that Rose started noticing how the storm had occurred in areas where Ellie had lived. Rose, eager to show Ellie, got a map and marked the path of the storm.

On the day of the trip to see the arch on the banks of the Mississippi River, Rose arrived at Ellie's door early with the map. She spread it out on the table and asked her mother to take a seat. After Rose tracked the path of the storm across St. Louis, she made her point, "Look, isn't this strange that, on this ten mile swath of the tornado, I can mark most of the events of your life." She explained with examples of the Mississippi swim, Al Capone, and other events. "It's like the storm planned your future."

Ellie started laughing, "Oh, Rose, what about the farm. It's not here. I took trips to California and they aren't here. What are you trying to see?"

Ellie got up and put on her coat, "Let's go see the arch. I'm excited as a kid to go. Ginny and Jack are going to meet us down there. We can talk more about this another day."

So they left. But on the drive downtown, Ellie exclaimed, "My goodness, Rose, you showing me that map makes me remember things." She peered out the window, turning in her seat. "You're driving the same route Jerry took when we went to meet Al Capone."

Ellie explained to the children, "It was the day that your Grandmother Franny and Grandfather Jerry were dressed like a bride and groom." Ellie told the story as they drove. Suddenly she interrupted herself, "Oh, my!"

"What's the matter?"

Ellie asked Rose to pull over to the curb a minute. "This is where I got out of the car so we wouldn't be seen together. I walked the rest of the way to the hotel. I remember a gypsy stopped me and looked at my palm." Ellie hesitated.

"What happened, Grandma?"

"I just remembered what the gypsy told me. She was upset and wanted to get away from me as fast as she could. She said that she saw something that frightened her. I think I can remember her exact words. She said:

> 'It turns like the wind in a storm! I never see this before. The lines in your hands swirl round and round when I look.'

and then she scurried away."

A chill went down Rose's spine. "Does that mean the gypsy saw something to do with the tornado? Like what I was talking about this morning with the map?"

Ellie looked into Rose's eyes and nodded, "It didn't mean anything to me back then, but today …"

Rose was stunned. *What does this mean? It seems like witchcraft.*

***

In 1971, Rose and her husband promised their children a trip to California to see Disneyland. "Mother, we'll be gone for two weeks, but I talked with Becky and the others. They said they'd drop by a couple of times to see you."

"Rose, don't fuss so. I'm not that old that you need to worry. I take my walk each day across the street, but I don't do much else. You've brought me enough groceries to last the year."

Rose left phone numbers with Jimmy, the daytime doorman—John's, Billy's, and Becky's—just in case there would be a need. Rose had said to Jimmy, "My mother's right; I don't know why I'm fussing so." But Rose was worried and even gave Jimmy the phone number of her hotel in California.

After Rose and her family had been gone ten days, a small change in Ellie's routine occurred.

Every day since Ellie had come to live in Rose's one-bedroom apartment across from Forest Park, she had gone for a morning walk. The doctor who had preformed her hip replacement had emphasized the importance of walking. And Forest Park had paths around a lake, other routes among big rocks and little ponds, and the sidewalk along

Kingshighway where she could do a faster pace. Only bad winter weather had prevented her from being able to take her morning walk for thirty minutes.

But this wasn't one of those bad weather days; it was a September day and beautiful.

Ellie sat on a chair in her apartment to put on her walking shoes and pulled a small twig from the end of her shoe, not noticing it had been caught in the sole that was loose at the tip.

Then Ellie checked the pockets of her favorite coat. She talked aloud to herself now that she lived alone and was tickled pink that she could do it. No one was there to say it was a sign of insanity, "Yes, here's the rock." She looked at the skipping stone and rubbed her thumb over the smooth black rock before dropping it back into the pocket. Rose had loaned Ellie this beige, twill coat a few years back and Ellie liked it so much that she never returned it. "Rose said she didn't mind because she has so many coats." Ellie liked how the extra rich satin lining felt on her arms when she slipped it on. Ellie liked the roomy patch pockets in just the right place where her arms could stretch almost straight. *It's uncomfortable to have a crook in one's arm for thirty minutes.* She told herself, "Oh, I love these pockets; they're padded inside and keep my hands so warm." Not that it was a cold day; old thin hands were always cold.

Now she went into the other pocket and took out the lucky rabbit's foot. Every day while she walked, she moved her fingers over the smooth rock in one hand and the furry foot in the other. For some reason, she liked touching them.

Ellie was living alone for the first time in her life. "One of those doctors at the hospital would think I was crazy to carry these around. They always look for the hidden or complicated meaning of things. It's just simple. Touching them brings back memories of my dad or Ginny." Now she was buttoning up her coat. "And sometimes I laugh out loud at things Franny and I did."

It was six in the morning.

Going out into the hall, Ellie locked her door, slipping the apartment key into a pocket in her dress because she didn't like it touching her hands while she walked. Now it was time to stop talking aloud, so she thought. *I put the key in the dress pocket because the key is cold.*

She turned to get on the elevator and saw an "Out of Order Until" sign with a clock at the bottom that had hands twirled to six-thirty.

I don't want to wait. Well, the elevator should be running when I come back, so I'll just use the stairs. She knew she could not climb up three flights. *But going down shouldn't be a problem.*

Heavy fire doors enclosed the stairs. They had been installed not too long ago in order to comply with fire codes. Ellie tugged the door open and went to the concrete stairs. Holding tight to the banister, she began her descent, counting the stairs because she wondered if every flight would be the same. There were ten steps until she got to the landing and twelve more before she reached the second floor. Big, black letters were painted on the door to tell her it was the second floor.

She started counting again and, sure enough, there were ten steps to the landing and twelve more to the first floor. Again, she read big, black letters on the door indicating the first floor. She pulled it open.

"Oh," escaped her lips as she stepped out into a carpeted hall with apartment doors. *Of course! This isn't the lobby. I knew the elevator had buttons for three, two, one, and an 'L' for lobby.*

She turned around and reopened the door. Sighing, she went to the stairs and started down again. But the loose sole at her toe caught on a small ridge on the top step. It was not much of a ridge, maybe the thickness of the blade of a knife, but that ridge was as deadly for her as if she had fallen directly onto a knife.

She fell.

Down those ten steps Ellie went with the first impact being the worst as her good hip crushed against the edge of the third step from the top. When she reeled over the fifth step, ramming her knees, the back of her head hit the metal slats in the banister; by the seventh, the bones in her right hand crumbled when she reached out to try to stop her descent. On the eighth step, her shoulder hit and she rolled again bruising her chest and cheek on the last two, until she reached the landing.

She didn't move. She couldn't move. But she was alive.

When she fell, she made quite a bit of noise. But no one heard. Jimmy the doorman had gone down to the basement to be with the maintenance man working on the elevator. When Jimmy got back to the lobby, he noticed it was six-fifteen, and he hadn't seen Ellie. He figured that she was waiting to take her walk at six-thirty when the elevator would be working again.

At a couple of minutes before six-thirty, the elevator was ready. "Let me check it out," he told the workman. "I need to go up and take away all the signs anyway." Jimmy got in and pressed the button to the first floor.

In the stairwell, Ellie could hear the elevator moving; it made a lot of noise. When it stopped, she knew it was at the first floor. She cried out, "Help!" Not once, but three times.

Jimmy stepped out before the doors were all the way open. He was removing the sign just as the swish of the door went quiet. He thought he heard something. He looked up and down the hall, cocked his ear and listened again, but decided it was nothing and reentered the elevator.

When Jimmy got to the third floor, he went to Ellie's door. She didn't answer. He decided that she must have gone out walking when he was in the basement.

Although only a couple of drops of blood from a cut on Ellie's head were on the landing, internally she was bleeding profusely. Perhaps, if only her hipbone had fractured, she could have made it. But the femur cracked, splintered, and thrust upward, puncturing organs in her abdomen. She was in so much pain, she kept blacking out. Time passed.

Ellie faded in and out of consciousness. However, at one point upon waking, the excruciating pain disappeared when a profound thought surfaced from deep in her subconscious. *The wedding ring! My mother's ring that Rose told me was glass! Did Mama know it was glass? Did Mama give it to me out of spite? The same kind of cruelty she had sewing me a blue wedding dress?*

Regardless of Bertha's hardhearted nature, Ellie had always loved her mother. Even seeing the daily harassment that Bertha had given James, had never lessened Ellie's love. But this revelation that her mother might have called the ring a diamond, keeping a secret that it was glass, stung more that the pain from the fall.

For the first time in her life, Ellie saw the flaw of keeping secrets. Desperately, she wanted to know if Bertha had known the ring to be glass and if her mother had meant to hurt her. Ellie agonized.

Was she giving me a fake ring to make a point? Did she die smiling at the secret she kept from me? Oh, Mama! Or, maybe only Daddy knew it was glass. No, he was too clever to be tricked like that. Oh, I don't know. But Ellie did know it was too late to learn the answers to these questions.

At that fleeting moment, Ellie wanted to tell Rose the secret of why she had started drinking. *I must get help. I must tell Rose. Rose has been so kind to me; she above anyone has a right to know why I started drinking.*

Jimmy had gotten busy with people leaving for work, deliveries coming in, and the phone ringing. At seven-thirty he was alone in the lobby; the activity had quieted for the moment. Suddenly, he realized he was hearing a tapping sound. He went outside, but the noise wasn't there.

He went to the elevator, "There better not be a problem with this thing." But it wasn't coming from the elevator.

He walked slowly toward the sound and found himself in front of the fire door. Tap, tap, tap, he heard. Opening the door, he saw Ellie crumpled on the landing, with a rock in her hand. Somehow, she had worked the skipping stone from her pocket and used it to tap the concrete that vibrated the metal banisters, and echoed in the stairwell, making enough of a sound to alert him.

After the ambulance left, Jimmy called the phone numbers that Rose had left. The first call rang the drugstore, but John was at the farm. Becky's phone just rang and rang. Jimmy crossed his fingers and held his breath as he started dialing the third number. With relief, the call was answered; Billy hadn't left for work.

Immediately Billy called the hotel in California and woke Rose. Before Billy arrived at the hospital, Rose was on the way to the Los Angeles airport.

Hours later, Ellie rolled out of surgery and Rose's airplane rolled to the terminal in the St. Louis airport. Billy sat by his mother's bedside, knowing she didn't have long and hoping she would wake, so he could talk to her. As Rose arrived at the hospital's front doors, just an elevator ride away from her mother, Ellie opened her eyes and said two words.

Five minutes too late, Rose was standing next to Billy and Ellie. In a pained voice and tearing eyes, Billy said, "Her last words were 'Where's Rose?'"

Chapter 21

1977-2000
A Time to Die

Life holds surprises right to the end. John had thought his children would always want to have the Missouri farm in their lives. They certainly had enjoyed hunting and spending time there when they were growing up. John hoped that one of his children might want to farm it and share with the others, like he had. Unlike John, who never could imagine living anywhere except Missouri, the Bartlett children moved to Texas, Colorado, Montana, and California. Ellie was right after all; parents only give life to their children. Parents don't decide who their children are, what they become, or where they live. A little of John died when he realized that having the Missouri farm in the Bartlett family forever was only his dream, not his children's.

Ginny's time finally came after living eighty-fours years. She died one night peacefully in her sleep. During Ginny's last day, she had mentioned to Jack, like a hundred times before, that none of the Bartlett children drank at all. "See the doctors were crazy. If alcoholism runs in a family, why aren't those children alcoholics? It should've happened to one of them by now. Why, the oldest is almost fifty, I think." She had wanted so much to know why Ellie had turned to drink.

Jack was sickly and resting in a rocker, but he had to agree with Ginny.

Ginny had been spry to the end; except for not doing handstands, she carried in firewood, went on long walks most days, and cared for Jack and their home.

John Bartlett had dropped off firewood to their house in the afternoon of her last day. "She looked chipper. Jack was the ailing one." John couldn't believe she died that same night.

Within a few months, Jack died. Without Ginny, life had drained out of him.

Again, John was surprised. But it got him thinking.

Ellie had died years ago, but now John finally decided to marry Sara. He hadn't thought there was any rush. Sara was living with him, and he was in his early eighties, still feeling strong and virile. But surprises can make one think.

Becky told Rose, "I think Dad was looking around to see if he could do better than Sara. Men! They think they're god's gift to us women. He hurt Sara so much. I talked to her. She loves him. She's a great cook, a lot younger than Dad, and still good-looking. She's the one who could find someone else."

John married Sara and built a brand new house on his Missouri farm for them.

But that didn't stop the surprises from arriving.

After a few years, Sara was diagnosed with diabetes. This news brought the children to visit them at the farm more frequently.

One Christmas all the children went to celebrate at the farm. As always, Sara was still full of spunk and humor, though she couldn't stand on her feet to cook for the holidays. She teased, "I want you all to come for Christmas, but bring lots of food. It's my turn to eat and yours to cook."

During the Christmas dinner, Becky asked, "Why did you name your sons, Mike and Pat? Are you Irish?"

In an Irish brogue Sara answered, "No, me darlin' There be ne'r a drop of Irish in me." Snickers erupted around the table.

Embarrassed with his mother's antics, her son Mike spoke up, "My mother is from German parents."

Now Sara started a German accent, though she spoke no German, "Ya, I fromen Deutschland. Ser gut."

When the laughing lessened, Becky repeated her question, "So, why did you name them Michael and Patrick?"

Sara was still giggling. She took a deep breath and settled down, "Oh, Becky, can't you see, I thought it was fun to name my boys Irish names? It always amused people when they knew I was from German stock."

With a puzzled look, Becky let out a little, "Oh."

Sara had an idea, "Why don't we all go down to Dogtown on St. Patrick's Day? It's so much fun." Despite having diabetes, Sara was still full of enthusiasm.

So when March 17th of 1985 arrived, they went. Mike, Pat, Becky, and Rose got together with some of the grandchildren and went to Tamm Street in Dogtown.

Rose knew of this street. *Tamm Street is the street where Grandpa James had walked with his girls, Ginny and Ellie, almost a century before.* But the saloon where the James' girls had danced their Irish jigs was gone; another stood almost on the same spot.

Sara complained, "Where's the Jack O'Shea Tavern? It should be right here. I know this is the right place!"

Mike explained, "Mom, just this year, they opened this new place called Seamus McDaniel's. Let's go in."

Once inside, Sara exclaimed, "Oh, it is the same place. Look at that!" Sara laughed. "Look at those tin plates on the ceiling, just like it was. Listen to that music. It's the same." A group of men with fiddles and penny whistles were playing a favorite called *Rakes of Mallow*.

Green sawdust was on the floor for the occasion. They sat at a table and had beer.

Rose felt somber for a moment as she remembered Ginny and Ellie telling her about a tavern on Tamm Street where they danced. They said Franny would join them sometimes or play the piano while they danced. Rose closed her eyes and pictured the three young friends, all dead now, dancing to this same music. *Life goes on, but I never attained my dream. I never learned why Ellie started drinking. And now it's too late.*

***

Diabetes works slowly. Sara deteriorated over fifteen years. She died a couple of weeks after her first leg was amputated and before the doctors could remove the other. She departed from life in anger after discovering her leg was gone; her humor, that had always been present every day of her life, disappeared with the amputated leg.

Sara screamed and cursed, "Damn it! Why didn't you tell me before you sawed it off?"

Soon after the first leg was gone, she heard accidentally from a nurse that her other leg was to go. She willed death to come and save her the embarrassment of being wheeled around with two stubs. Life wasn't worth living without her long, beautiful legs; she died the day before the scheduled surgery.

Sara was buried in a stunning pink linen suit with matching shorts. Just like her humor in life, she went to eternal rest giving people a little laugh—though they couldn't see the pink linen shorts or the one beautiful leg—everyone knew she would meet her Maker in those shorts that lay hidden in the half-closed casket.

John withered away without Sara. Life has a way of pulling humans closer and closer to the grave as their bodies shrink and settle into a smaller and smaller state; by 1999 John, who once was eye-to-eye with Rose at five feet ten, barely reached to her shoulder. That amazed Rose.

Rose gave up calling him John. Now that only one parent was left for her, she reverted to the endearing name of Daddy. "Daddy, I dropped by to read more of that book to you. Oh, and everyone is coming for Thanksgiving. You know, all your kids. We're going to cook a meal as delicious as Sara's. So, you must eat until you burst."

John no longer wanted to eat. John no longer wanted to live.

During the Thanksgiving meal with family around the big table and others sitting on the sofa and chairs, John made a comment that seemed simple enough when he turned to Billy to say, "I'm not strong anymore." But it wasn't simple.

Even those who were talking to others stopped their conversation. Quickly the room quieted as the words passed from one to the other, "He said he's not strong anymore." Like a group of flies making a hum as they circle and circle, a murmur curled around the room repeating, "He said he's not strong anymore."

Of course, the grandchildren had no idea what their Grandpa's statement meant. But they were to learn before that Thanksgiving Day ended.

Rose recalled, "I remember the first Thanksgiving with Sara when all of us competed in log cutting contests. Daddy prided himself on staying strong all his life."

Some were taking the dishes into the kitchen, but Johnny and Rose were so moved by the comments, they had to talk. Grandchildren gathered around to hear.

Johnny whispered, "I remember other times; he was always talking about keeping fit and being strong. He gave us a lecture once when he bought his farm in Illinois, explaining how the Missouri farm kept him strong because he had to work so hard. So, you know what this means for him to admit he's not strong anymore?"

One of the grandchildren asked, "What does it mean?"

Carefully Johnny said, "His whole life, your Grandpa lived to be strong."

The children weren't satisfied, but the adults couldn't say the words they all were thinking. *Our father is ready to die.*

Just before his 100th birthday in December of the year 2000, John Bartlett died from not eating. He had no ailments; he was still healthy; he could walk and do most things a man of sixty could do, but he wasn't strong.

At the funeral parlor, the room was packed; even with people coming and going, it was always full. There were people from his life in the drugstore. Others drove fifty miles or so from where he had his Missouri farm. Even relatives never known by his children came from Illinois. Those who had gone to high school or college with John arrived.

One could feel the room filling with crowding thoughts. One could see the thoughts by looking at the array of faces.

Someone puzzled, *Does one cry for the death of a man who lived a century?*

Another person smiled to herself wondering, *How can I cry for a man who made us double over laughing doing so many funny antics like the time he socked Al Capone when he was dressed like a woman?*

Billy shook his head as he gazed into the open coffin, *How can I ever be sad about my dad who taught me so much and left me with memories of fun times, like the time he cracked raw eggs over his head to wash his hair?*

An old man from the drugstore, who was poor but always had the medicine he needed, looked at John in the casket. *Why cry for someone whose life was filled with giving and loving? We should be happy we knew him.*

So, people laughed as they told stories and honored John Bartlett.

Like their father before them, the Bartlett children didn't look old. Though seventy, David didn't think he was old. Even Becky was getting up there at fifty-seven, but she looked and moved like a woman of forty. They were happy with what their father had taught them about life; happy for the man he was.

Only Rose felt deprived. She couldn't put her finger on why, but she was going to miss him. Just knowing that there was only one more day before he was buried, bothered her. At the end of the first day in the funeral parlor, Rose put on her coat, walked up to the coffin, and bent to kiss her father's forehead. She gave a little jump when her lips touched his skin. *He's cold as ice and hard as a rock!* She took a step back and the tears came.

Johnny saw Rose and went to her. He hugged her. They said nothing. Rose smiled a thank you and turned to leave while buttoning up her blue, wool coat with three large buttons. One fell to the floor, rolling across the room. Rose hastened her steps to retrieve it, heading in the direction of a small group of people who were still seated and talking. The button stopped under a chair and, as Rose bent down to reach for the button, she overheard the conversation. The topic startled her.

Her father's cousin Dale who managed John's Illinois farm was saying that Françoise owned a farm next to John's. "Françoise was quite the lady. Beautiful, poised, and interested in learning about farming. Why, she and John would come over to see how I was doing with their farms, and we would have the best conversations. She would study the records I kept and ask so many questions. Yes, those were wonderful times with John and Françoise. Now they're both gone."

Rose interrupted Dale with an outstretched hand, "Hello, I'm Françoise's daughter Rose." The group looked up at Rose and she smiled. "I'm sorry I don't know you all by name, but thank you for coming."

They murmured some kind words and started donning their coats for the cold weather.

Rose touched Dale on the arm, "Excuse me, but I overheard you speak about Françoise owning a farm next to John's. Are you sure?"

Dale gave a big grin, "Of course I'm sure. Why she sold it to me many years ago. And John wrote into his Last Will and Testament that I could buy his farm at a nice discount."

Not wanting to embarrass herself or Dale, Rose didn't mention that she knew nothing about Françoise owning a farm. *I don't think Jerry knew either because he would have told me. I'm sure he would have.*

By the time Rose arrived at home, she was agitated. Upon entering the apartment, she went directly to her parent's file cabinet that still stood in the sewing room. *Dale said Franny sold her Illinois farm to him.* One particular thought kept screaming in her head. *How could she have had a farm I didn't know about?*

Frantically Rose flung her blue coat on a chair in the little room; the button she had lost in the funeral parlor fell from the pocket and rolled across the floor, but she didn't notice. She pulled out file folders, rummaging through them. *This is like looking for a needle in a haystack. Oh, if I only knew a date.* Then she thought of an alternative. *I should see details on tax records.*

Shoving folders back in the top drawer, she carefully lowered her sixty-nine year old body down to her knees and sat on the floor to pull open the bottom drawer. Starting with the 1958 tax return, she opened the folder across her lap. *This is the year Jerry died; maybe she sold the farm then.* Rose saw nothing. *Oh, I don't know where to look in all these papers. I don't know when she bought it either. I think I need to go back farther. Here's 1947.*

Now she found evidence. There were papers for the purchase of corn seed, a receipt for tractor repairs, and an electric bill from Illinois.

By the time Rose finished looking at the 1946, 1945, and 1944 tax returns, on her hands and knees with papers spread all over the floor, she felt clammy perspiration under her arms and down her back. Rose could see that the farm was bought in 1945. *Why did Franny keep this a secret from me? Did Daddy, I mean, did Jerry know? I remember that they had an accountant who did their taxes, so the taxes could have been prepared without Jerry knowing.*

Dale said the farm was right next to John's farm. Dale said Franny's farm had a house that she went to visit from time to time. I'm so confused. How could I not know? I was about fifteen years old when she bought it.

Still on the floor, Rose started to gather up the folders and papers. As she lifted the last folder, she saw the coat button that had fallen from her pocket. *The needle and thread is right here; I may as well sew it on. Taking the time to sew on a button might calm me.*

Using the chair, Rose placed her hands on the seat to pull herself up enough to sit down. Once on the chair, she placed all the files on top of the sewing machine and leaned over to open the drawer with all the spools of thread.

I'm exhausted.

Perhaps her mind was still in the state of confusion, after learning her mother owned a farm without her knowledge, but when she opened the thread drawer, she was puzzled. There were envelopes in the back of the thread drawer. She reached for them, instead of the blue thread. *I've never noticed these envelopes. Of course, I don't sew too often and, being tucked in the back of the drawer, these cards were out of view.*

There were ten envelopes addressed to "Franny" with a year below the name. As Rose flipped each envelope in her hand, she read the years from 1937 through 1947, noticing that two envelopes were empty. And one of the empty envelopes had been crumpled and smoothed back out, but the wrinkles were still there. Her intuition made her tense.

This is not Jerry's handwriting.

Placing the stack in her lap, she took the first envelope and slipped out the card with

Happy Birthday
To my Love

printed on the front among colorful flowers in a vase. Rose hesitated to open the card. Now perspiration formed in little droplets on her brow. She ran her fingers over the front of the card where a piece of padded silk cloth formed the vase. The air seemed heavy in the little room; she took a long, deep breath. *Open it!*

When opened, it was as if the card was empty, except for the signature of the sender, for that was all Rose saw.

"Love from John – 1937" was signed at the bottom.

Rose's hand went to her chest and she gasped. Time had no meaning as her mind raced for understanding. She opened the second and third cards. All were from John Bartlett. Finally her fingers came to the wrinkled envelope that was empty. The date read 1945.

Her head exploded with understanding.

Rose stood, spilling all the cards and envelopes across the rug, and rushed to her bedroom. She reached for Ellie's jewelry box that sat on her dresser and took a step to her bed where she dumped the contents out. Al Capone's lucky rabbit's foot tumbled out, some costume jewelry, the rock from the Mississippi, Grandma Bertha's old piece of glass from her wedding ring, and … *the two cards signed by John that have been sitting under the skipping stone.*

Remembering the hint from so many years ago, *Ellie had said not to leave any stone unturned.*

She told me!

Rose picked up the two cards and hurried back to the sewing room. Excitement rushed through her as she hesitated and gazed at Françoise's scattered cards. She went down on her knees again to retrieve the two empty envelopes, but she already knew Ellie's secret. She wiped her sleeve across her face. The two cards from Ellie's jewelry box fit perfectly into Françoise's empty envelopes, and, of course, the dates matched.

Oh, no! John and Franny what did you do?

Stunned, Rose sat on the floor as she imagined Ellie's discovery of the cards. *Probably Ellie went to the sewing drawer, just as I did, looking for some thread.*

The reference to the word thread made Rose's heart jump.

I've found Ellie's tangled threads.

Endnotes

---

[1] (Pages 4 and 71)

The book, *The Great Cyclone of May 27, 1896*, by Cyclone Publishing Company, was published just weeks after the storm and was put together by Julian Curzan, author, compiler, and editor. Dozens of photographers from Chicago and other cities flocked to St. Louis to preserve the facts through photographs and interviews with survivors of the storm. These photographs and firsthand accounts, compiled into a book, let the world see the destruction, since newspapers only printed engravings at that time and could not have the number of photographs that the book had.

A cyclone [tornado] had been predicted, unofficially, for the closing days of May. But during those times people believed that tornados did not strike large cities. The twister first touched down on Arsenal Street near the Poorhouse, crossed the street and clipped off the roof of The Female Hospital and headed for the huge stone Insane Asylum before it continued into the city. It left a ten-mile long path through St. Louis and East St. Louis, leaving more than 300 people dead and over 1000 injured in 20 minutes.

[2] (Page 113)

For the readers who want to know more about the bug called a chigger:

Harvest mites (*Trombicula alfreddugesi*) are called chiggers in the larval stage. These relatives of ticks are nearly microscopic measuring 0.4 mm and look reddish. They often live in berry patches, tall grass, and other plants on woodland edges.

The larval mite feeds on skin cells (not blood as most people think). The six-legged parasitic larva crawls onto their host (animals or humans) and injects digestive enzymes into the skin to break down the skin cells. They form a hole in the skin by chewing up tiny parts, thus causing severe irritation and swelling in the form of a red pimple-like bump that lasts for a couple of weeks. Within a few hours from the initial contact the itching occurs, but it is after the chigger has dropped from the skin.

[3] (Page 182)

Although, in the late 1800s, Pasteur had discovered what was thought to be penicillin, it wasn't until the 1920's that the antibiotic effects of penicillin were confirmed in a paper by a Belgian team of scientists. The paper received little attention. In 1929, Sir Alexander Fleming noticed a halo—the inhibition of bacterial growth—around a contaminant blue-green mould on a staphylococcus plate culture. However, the mould, which seemed to be inhibiting the bacterial growth, was not stable and could not be produced in large amounts until 1938, four years after little Elizabeth died. From 1941-1944, methods were finally developed to produce penicillin for pharmaceutical distribution.

[4] (Page 233)

In 1939 in Akron, New York, and Cleveland a fellowship published a basic textbook, *Alcoholics Anonymous*, which covered the twelve steps for recovery, along with case histories of some thirty recovered members. One of the originators of the AA process was an alcoholic and physician referred to as Dr. Bob Smith; during the formation of AA, he did not know that alcoholism was a disease.

In March 1941, *The Saturday Evening Post* featured an article about Alcoholics Anonymous. There was a great response and, by the end of that year, membership reached 6,000. The Twelve Steps of AA emerged as a practice, and by 1950, there were 100,000 recovering alcoholics worldwide. This seemed like spectacular progress, but the period 1940-1950 was nonetheless one of great uncertainty. Doctors and the general public were not yet sure if AA was effective. To many in the medical profession, alcoholism was still an unsolved problem.

Until 1951, the Fellowship was in the hands of an isolated board of trustees, but then the first worldwide meeting was held with delegates from all states and Canada. Ironically, the second international convention was held in St. Louis in 1955. Progress was slow, but steady; yet too late for Ellie Bartlett.

5 (Page 302)

In this book, *Tangled Threads*, Ellie Bartlett began drinking sometime between 1947 and 1950, when the ideas of Freud were considered important. To justify how the medical profession handled her case back then and to clarify how Ellie acted in the story, I researched several books. I would like to quote some passages from *In Search of Memory* by Eric R. Kandel, W.W. Norton & Company, Inc. New York, NY 2006.

Pages 39-40

"Freud argued further that psychological determinacy – the idea that little, if anything, in one's psychic life occurs by chance, that every psychological event is determined by an event that precedes it – is central not only to normal mental life, but also to mental illness. A neurotic symptom, no matter how strange it may seem, is not strange to the unconscious mind; it is related to the other, preceding mental processes. The connection between a slip [of] the tongue and its cause or between a symptom and the underlying cognitive process is obscured by the operation of defenses – ubiquitous, dynamic, unconscious mental processes – resulting in a constant struggle between self-revealing and self-protective mental events." From Freud's *Psychopathology of Everyday Life.*

Page 336

"In 1960s … methods for examining the brain … were too limited to detect subtle anatomical changes. As a result, only mental disorders that entailed significant loss of nerve cells and brain tissue, such as Alzheimer's disease, Huntington's disease, and chronic alcoholism, were classified as organic, or based in biology. Schizophrenia, various forms of depression, and the anxiety states … were classified as functional or not based in biology. Often, a special social stigma was attached to the so-called functional mental illnesses … because [it's] 'all in a patient's mind.' We no longer think [the above] … all mental illnesses are biological."

Page 337

"The anxiety states and various forms of depression are disorders of emotion, whereas schizophrenia is a disorder of thought."

Page 338

"Thus, there is no single gene for schizophrenia, just as there is no single gene for anxiety disorders, depression, or most other mental illnesses. Instead, the genetic components of these diseases arise from the interaction of several genes with the environment. Each gene exerts a relatively small effect, but together they create a genetic predisposition – a potential – for a disorder. Most psychiatric disorders are caused by a combination of these genetic predispositions and some additional, environmental factors."

Page 355

"[The] drug, chlorpromazine, calming schizophrenia in 1950s [was the first drug to be effective against major mental disorders].

CPSIA information can be obtained at www.ICGtesting.com
Printed in the USA
268235BV00003B/2/P

9 780977 975211